The House on Mulberry Street

Maan Meyers

Bantam Books

New York Toronto London Sydney Auckland

THE HOUSE ON MULBERRY STREET

A Bantam Book / August 1996

Book design by Ellen Cipriano

Map design by Jackie Aher

Genealogy chart by Kathryn Parise

Library of Congress Cataloging-in-Publication Data

Meyers, Maan.
The House on Mulberry Street / by Maan Meyers.
p. cm.
ISBN 0-553-09706-7
1. Police—New York (N.Y.)—Fiction. I. Title.
PS3563.E889H68 1996
813'.54—dc20 96-1289
CIP

Published simultaneously in the United States and Canada

Bantam Books are published by Bantam Books, a division of Bantam Doubleday Dell Publishing Group, Inc. Its trademark, consisting of the words "Bantam Books" and the portrayal of a rooster, is Registered in U.S. Patent and Trademark Office and in other countries. Marca Registrada. Bantam Books, 1540 Broadway, New York, New York 10036.

PRINTED IN THE UNITED STATES OF AMERICA

BVG 0 9 8 7 6 5 4 3 2 1

For our friends

in photography:

MARIANA COOK

HANS KRAUS

DENISE BETHEL

For their resources we thank Linda Ray and Cathi Rosso;
Kathy Schrier and Ken Nash of District Council 37;
Larry Gartner of Gouverneur Hospital;
Eric Holzenberg, curator, the Grolier Club;
Professor Josh Freeman, Columbia University;
and Todd Gustavson, Archivist of Equipment Collection,
George Eastman House in Rochester.

Very particular thanks to Denise Bethel,
Vice President, Photography, Sotheby's,
our Nestor to photography past;
and John Erdman and Gary Schneider.

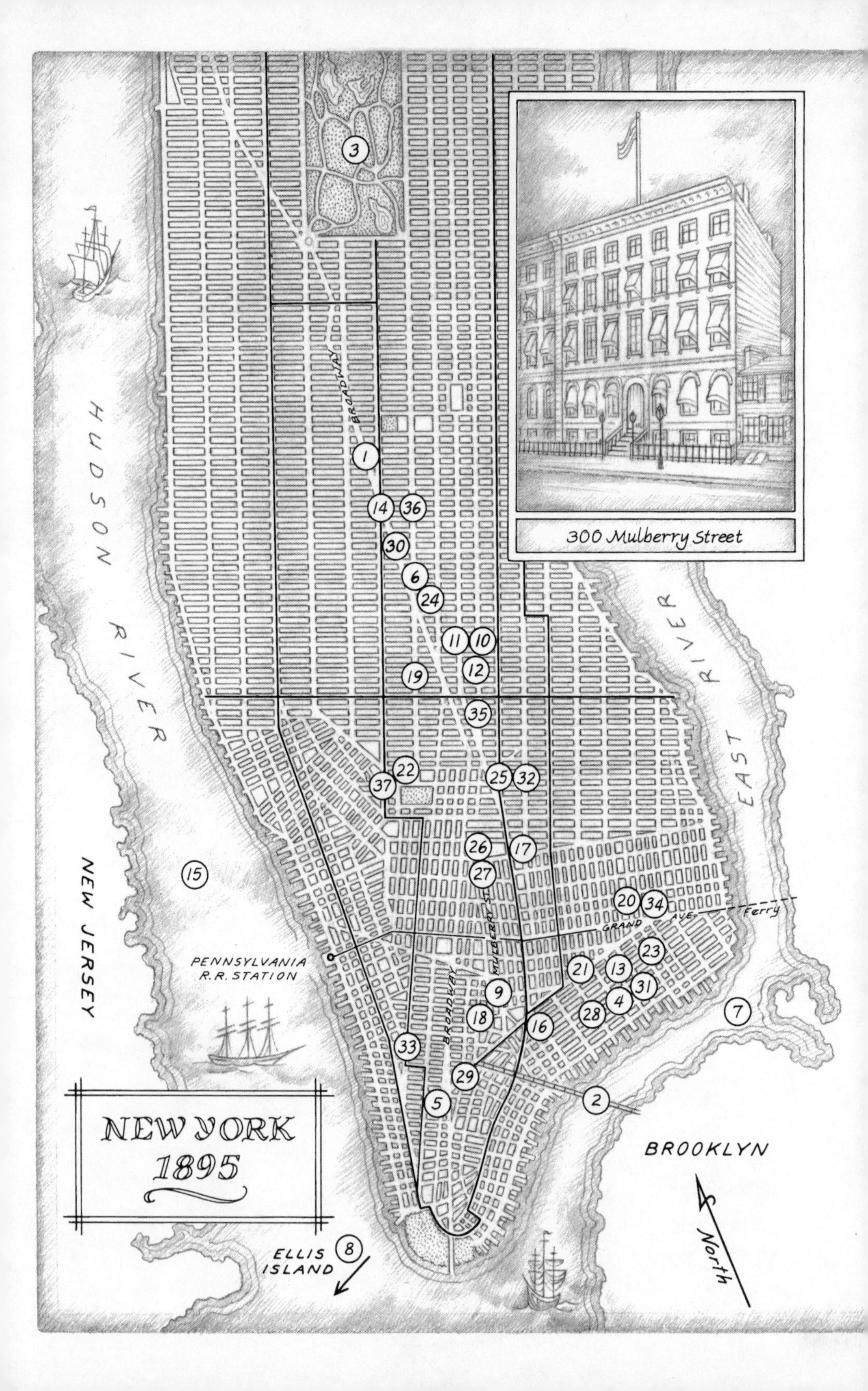
NEW YORK
1895
300 Mulberry Street
HUDSON RIVER
EAST RIVER
NEW JERSEY
BROOKLYN
PENNSYLVANIA
R.R. STATION
ELLIS
ISLAND
BROADWAY
BROADWAY
MULBERRY ST.
GRAND
AVE.
Ferry
North

1. Abbey's Theatre (38th and Broadway)
2. Brooklyn Bridge
3. Central Park
4. Cherry Street (Vander Smith's and Brevoort's Lumberyards)
5. The Dead Line (Fulton Street)
6. Delmonico's (Fifth Avenue and 26th Street)
7. East River
8. Ellis Island
9. Five Points (bottom of Mulberry Street)
10. Gramercy Park
11. No. 5 Gramercy Park West
12. Healy's Café (Irving Place and 18th Street)
13. Henry Street Settlement House (Nurses Settlement)
14. The Herald--Herald Square
15. Hudson River
16. Jewish Cemetery (St. James Place, below Chatham Square)
17. Katz's Delicatessen (bottom of Second Avenue)
18. La Belle Association (Worth Street and Chatham Square)
19. Ladies' Mile (Fifth Avenue, 14th Street to 23rd Street)
20. The Lower East Side (Jew Town)
21. No. 45 Ludlow Street
22. Macdougal Alley
23. Madison Street and Gouverneur (The Alley)
24. Madison Square
25. McSorley's Ale House (Bowery and 7th Street)
26. 300 Mulberry Street
27. 303 Mulberry Street
28. Pike Street Synagogue
29. Park Row--Printing House Square
30. The Rialto (Broadway, from 23rd to 42nd Street)
31. Sophie's House (No. 79 Clinton Street)
32. St. Mark's Place (off Second Avenue)
33. The Allen's Saloon on West Broadway
34. The Tonneman Home (Grand Street, between Sheriff and Willet)
35. Union Square
36. Waldorf Hotel (Fifth Avenue and 33rd Street)
37. No. 26 Washington Square N.

The Tonneman Family
19th Century

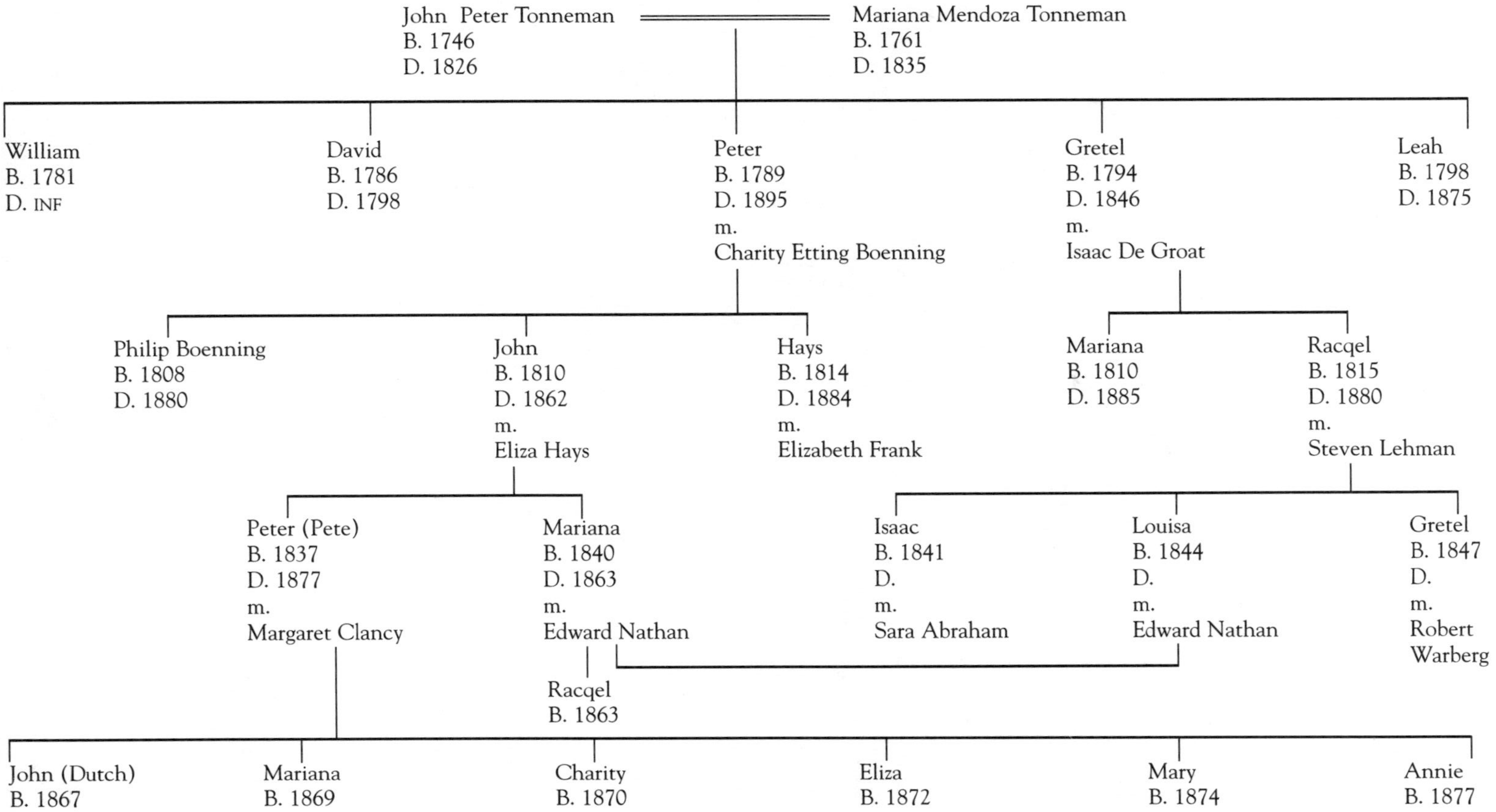

John Peter Tonneman
B. 1746
D. 1826

Mariana Mendoza Tonneman
B. 1761
D. 1835

William
B. 1781
D. INF

David
B. 1786
D. 1798

Peter
B. 1789
D. 1895
m.
Charity Etting Boenning

Gretel
B. 1794
D. 1846
m.
Isaac De Groat

Leah
B. 1798
D. 1875

Philip Boenning
B. 1808
D. 1880

John
B. 1810
D. 1862
m.
Eliza Hays

Hays
B. 1814
D. 1884
m.
Elizabeth Frank

Mariana
B. 1810
D. 1885

Racqel
B. 1815
D. 1880
m.
Steven Lehman

Peter (Pete)
B. 1837
D. 1877
m.
Margaret Clancy

Mariana
B. 1840
D. 1863
m.
Edward Nathan

Isaac
B. 1841
D.
m.
Sara Abraham

Louisa
B. 1844
D.
m.
Edward Nathan

Gretel
B. 1847
D.
m.
Robert
Warberg

Racqel
B. 1863

John (Dutch)
B. 1867

Mariana
B. 1869

Charity
B. 1870

Eliza
B. 1872

Mary
B. 1874

Annie
B. 1877

From top to bottom the New York police force was utterly demoralized by the gangrene of . . . a system where venality and blackmail went hand in hand with the basest forms of low ward politics, and where the policeman, the ward politician, the liquor seller, and the criminal alternately preyed on one another and helped one another to prey on the general public.

THEODORE ROOSEVELT
May 1895

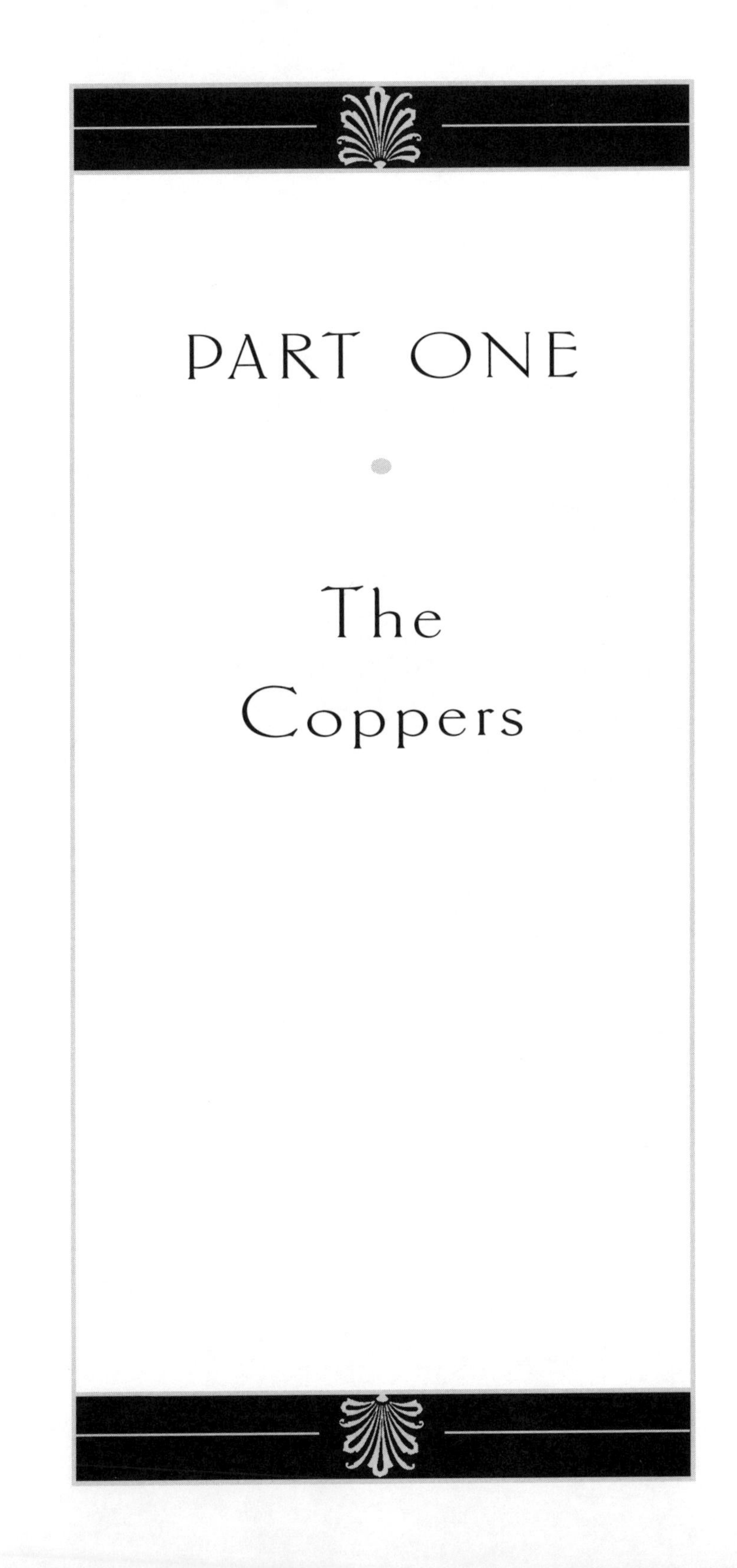

PART ONE

The Coppers

Prologue

Monday,
May 6.

Queenie Landry strolled along Mulberry Street as if she were taking her daily promenade, which it was suggested a lady should, to ease digestion and breathe fresh, clean air.

When Queenie was told that she bore a startling resemblance in face and figure to the English Queen Victoria, she lost no time in recreating herself in the old monarch's image, even swathing herself completely in black, affecting Victoria's mourning costume for Prince Albert who'd passed on way back in '61.

Mulberry Street was incredibly congested. Even at night, pushcarts lined either side of the road. During the day, low awnings shaded the displays from the sun or rain. And day or night the street gave off the raw gamey odor of death from its dark, filthy back alleys to the reeking tenements hastily erected here and in the surrounding area.

Day and night the flotsam of the City now draped itself over the stoops: men and boys in various stages of dress and undress, all looking for trouble. Drunk and slatternly women leaned out of the windows screaming at people on the street and one another.

Still, Queenie's promenade had little to do with health, unless one considered it for the health of her business. And one certainly didn't stroll for one's health along the netherworld of Mulberry Street at any hour.

Not long ago, the buildings along Mulberry had been the elegant homes of New York's oldest families, wealthy descendants of the Dutch and the English. They had now moved farther uptown, making way for the horde of immigrants pouring into the Lower East Side. The newcomers had puffed the population of the City to 1,600,000 souls. The once-magnificent interiors of these Mulberry Street dwellings had been carved into tiny warrens where ten or twelve slept in dens scarcely larger than coffins.

Day and night the flotsam of the City now draped itself over the stoops: men and boys in various stages of dress and undress, all looking for trouble. Drunk and slatternly women leaned out of the windows screaming at people on the street and one another.

Queenie lifted her dress to cross from pavement to pavement over the refuse-strewn cobble. A twitch of amusement pulled at her painted lips. It had been a long time since she'd lifted her skirts for the other reason.

Hooded eyes followed Queenie's progress on the street, watched her stop in front of one of her subjects, several to each block. Most stood head and shoulders above Queenie, but all depended on her for a place to sleep and enough to eat. They attended patiently at her approach, like soldiers ready to give their all for sovereign and country. For Queenie's realm was the street, and her subjects were streetwalkers.

She made her collections personally, often, and at no particular time, so as to discourage duplicity among her Mabs. Each coin she collected she dropped into a fat little purse, hung from a leather thong and buried in the space between her ample, wrinkled breasts.

Today, however, was also the first Monday of the month, so she carried two purses and had an additional purpose for her customary evening stroll. Everyone knew what sums Queenie carried, and any stranger bearing such sums would have been brutally murdered many times over. But no one dared touch Queenie Landry, for she was protected.

On the east side of Mulberry, between Houston and Bleecker, lit by dingy street lamps, stood No. 300. It was a grand four-story house, square and squat with a marble face, albeit a touch yellow from years of New York soot. A flagpole bearing the forty-four-star ensign of the United States rose from the roof. The house was ringed with a low iron fence that traveled up the sides of the steep front stairs leading to the majestic arched entrance.

Most of the structure's forty-five front windows were beautifully presented with fine dark blue awnings. Only the seven basement windows were bare—except for the somber bars that covered them and what lay beyond.

Patriarch of the House on Mulberry Street was one Thomas J. Byrnes, who'd risen from Irish immigrant street fighter to Union soldier to Commander of the Detective Bureau of the Metropolitan Police of the City of New York. The much-feared Byrnes and Old Hays—Jacob Hays, the City's first and only High Constable, who had died in 1850—were cut from similar cloth. But unlike the High Constable, Commander Byrnes's moral fiber was weak and his bluster barely covered his deep corruption.

Byrnes's House on Mulberry Street was Queenie's destination.

On the second floor, in the small outer chamber of the Commander's spacious office, Queenie emptied her second purse into the little tin box Clubber Williams held out to her. This weekly penance of one hundred dollars was what kept her in business. It was a small fee to pay, Queenie felt, to receive the protection of the Metropolitan Police.

"How's tricks, Clubber? What's doing at the 29?"

"Tricks is your business, not mine."

"Had your chat with the new Commissioners yet?" The minute she spoke, Queenie knew she'd misstepped.

Clubber's eyes narrowed. "Mind your own business, Queenie, you'll live longer."

His birth name was Alexander Williams and he was the boss of the 29th Precinct. Before going to the 29 he had served in the 21, which was situated in the notoriously tough and lawless Gas House district. Clubber became Clubber because he employed his wooden club to such a degree that the fear he generated enabled him to hang his watch and chain on a hitching post on Third Avenue and Thirty-fifth Street and come back two days later to find them untouched.

He was a handsome figure of a man, tall, well built, with a magnificent walrus mustache. But Queenie didn't like him. How could you like someone you were that afraid of?

The Chief's door opened. At first only the black-clad arm showed, then a big, balding, gray-haired man, built for heavy lifting and fighting, came into view. His stiff wing collar jutted out like two white knife blades, framing his immobile face. His cold crafty eyes stared at Queenie. They did not blink. The only thing that moved on his face was his mustache, which hung down loosely at both ends, covering his mouth completely.

"It will be better that we call on you," Byrnes muttered without salutation, "from here on."

Queenie left the anteroom chewing over what she'd just heard. She was halfway down the staircase leading to the outside door when she was nearly bowled over by a robust bespectacled man coming up the stairs like a wild young lad playing soldier charging up a hill.

Great white teeth broke out of his sun-red face. Lord, they looked liked they belonged to a horse. No, a moose. Queenie Landry, born in a shack in the woods in western Connecticut, and baptized Josephine Ann, indeed knew what a moose looked like. If memory served, she'd even eaten of the beast more than once.

The excited fellow politely tipped his hat, saying, "Beg pardon, ma'am." He had a rasping, haughty voice; his thick brown hair was cut short. He flashed those teeth again, broad and straight, in a perfect line, and resumed his gallop up the remainder of the stairs, wild moose that he was.

Loud yelling came from outside as Queenie finished her descent of the marble stairs. She had found herself a shadowed place around a corner before the doors burst open. As she suspected, the new arrivals were a gang of reporters.

Queenie knew half these boys. Leading the pack were Jacob Riis and the newest of the hounds, Robert Roman, a lad who liked his itch scratched.

It wouldn't do for her to be seen here today of all days. Bringing up the rear of this army were three other fellows, solemn as you please, dressed like morticians. Queenie knew one of them, too. Only too well.

From her hiding place, Queenie watched with curiosity until the entire band disappeared; her thoughts were still on the aristocratic Moose. Moose he acted, Moose he was. It was a fitting monicker.

He was a reformer just appointed, along with the morticians, to the Board of Commissioners. There'd been others before him, but the City of New York would never change. The corruption was built on poverty and riches, side by side. The evil was too ingrained.

And, other than his appearance, Moose did not impress Queenie. He was just another man with his pistol between his legs.

• I •

Wednesday,
May 29.
Evening.

"Stay, Mary."

"You're a sweet bloke, Robert, but Sophie don't like us to linger. She ain't in the charity business, she tells us." So saying, Mary Simmons gathered her skimpy peignoir about her buxom figure and left him with his thoughts.

Even with the window up, the room was close. The brick wall of another building directly behind kept the air from the room. This was not one of Sophie's best accommodations. Those she saved for the big spenders. Robert lit a Jack Rose from the lamp and leaned back into the cloying but still agreeable scent Mary had left on the red satin pillow.

Robert was a reporter. A free-lancer. So he worked for himself. And while he liked that, Robert Roman didn't pay Robert Roman every week. Jim Bennett, the editor of the *Herald*, always took Roman's stories when he came up with something special. He could always sell a piece on police corruption and criminals, for instance. That was a laugh. Jake Riis and Linc Steffens had that sort of thing tied up but good. Still, Robert thought, taking a deep drag of his cigarette, if he could come up with something new, a new slant on it . . .

An intrusive voice pierced his musings. "I'm getting tired of this sort of shit."

Robert frowned. He saw no need ever to curse at a woman. Even a whore.

"I don't care how tired you are, you're out, I'm in. We'll do it my way." A second voice, and not a woman's.

The frown became a smile. He hadn't known that Sophie went in for that sort of thing. Men and men. He sat up. In fact, he was sure she didn't.

"Don't worry about Moose or the new boss. I know just how to handle them."

That did it. Robert's feet were on the floor. Where were the voices coming from? The air shaft from the window? They were somewhere not too far away. He waited, listening.

"I'd like to break Moose's neck."

Robert's eyes burned with hope. What he was overhearing was not *amóre*, or even *sèsso*.

"This is no Tenderloin slaughter. Moose will go down. Not the way you want him to. But he will go down."

Damn. It wasn't from out the window. Robert looked around the room. The wood stove, unused in the summer.

"He'd better," the stove said, "or we'll do it my way and it won't be pretty." A door creaked. "I can't believe you're in the House on Mulberry Street and I'm not." Then a slam. The voices ceased.

"*Nóme di Dio.*" Robert reverted to his childhood tongue when English did not express enough for him. Two evil bastards had had their little talk in another room in this house, while standing next to another cold stove. Their words had passed through the metal pipes as if over the telephone.

After dressing hurriedly, Robert ran down to Sophie's parlor. He ordered two bits' worth of whiskey and, sipping, tried to guess which of the distinguishedly attired men sitting around, smoking and drinking, listening to Piano Man's music, had been the pair he'd heard. But this didn't make sense. What if they had gone out the back? He'd have to talk to Mary. Or Sophie. But what good would it do? Dozens of men came and went at Madam Sophie's.

The question was had they left yet?

He caught the eye of Sophie's colored girl who worked the front door. When she came over to see what he wanted, he asked, "Daisy, has anyone come down in the last fifteen minutes?"

"You." She smiled sweetly at him.

He gave her a dime. Now he was really broke. He'd used his last three dollars to buy the brass token from Sophie that got him Mary's honeyed charms.

"Not for thirty minutes, Mr. Robert."

"Has anyone left the house?"

"Night like this, most traffic is coming in."

He wouldn't get anything more from her, he was sure. Sophie paid her well to be discreet. Robert slipped out through the back door and looked around the alley. Either Daisy had purposely missed seeing the men, or they were still upstairs. Most likely dallying with a couple of girls after their business talk was concluded. He went back in and stood looking at the staircase leading up to the rooms.

"Need any help, Mr. Roman?" Sophie's bullyboy and bodyguard, Leo Stern, had left his solitaire game to follow Robert.

"Thought I lost something on my way down," Roman replied, fingering his fountain pen in his pocket.

"You find what you was looking for?" Leo Stern raised an ominous black eyebrow.

Roman displayed the pen.

"After you then, sir," Leo said, indicating the return route to the parlor.

Roman smiled weakly and walked. Just as well, he thought. It didn't make any sense wandering the halls, listening at doors, waiting for Leo to pounce on him. All he would have heard would have been the moans of the clients and the pretend joy of the girls.

Obviously what he'd heard had to do with the House on Mulberry Street. And if that was the case, he'd recognize the faces. Waiting outside to see who departed could be most productive.

When Roman and Leo Stern came back into the parlor, Sophie was watching. She never missed a thing.

• • •

A short time later Robert Roman stood outside Madam Sophie's on Clinton and Rivington Streets and waited. God was good. He'd found the story he needed. Now all he needed were some facts to prove it.

He didn't have to wait long. Two men came out of Sophie's establishment not twenty minutes later. They were arguing in low rumbling voices. Were they his quarry?

Ducking behind a horse trough, he followed them as they approached a carriage. Suddenly he was grabbed by the scruff of the neck and lifted into the air. "What do you want?" A very large individual stuck his brutal jowly face into Robert's.

"Nothing." Mother of God, he thought. He was dead.

The man sent him crashing to the cobblestones. "Get lost."

Robert Roman held his terror at bay. The two men were getting into the carriage. This was his big chance. His big story. All he needed to do was see one face, for just one second. He scrambled to his feet and ran to the corner, knowing all the while that he was being watched by the brute.

Luck was with him. The carriage was coming his way. He could see the two men under the lamp and moonlight, but not their faces. Not yet. He moved closer.

A rocklike fist knocked him to the ground. "I told you get lost, didn't I? Now I'm going to have to hurt you." The monster pulled his foot back to kick.

Robert rolled quickly out of the reach of the boot. All thought of the big story gone from his mind, for the moment; he ran for his life.

Thumping footsteps followed him. Robert was strong; running the half mile to Cherry Street didn't faze him. But he couldn't lose the big man.

Had he an alternative, he never would have headed for the river. But the decision was not his. The big man was close on his heels, forcing him toward South Street and the docks.

Perhaps a warehouse, a blind pig, a ship. Something. Somewhere. He was panting now, his lungs working hard; he felt a sharp pain in his side.

Uptown there would be crowds of people. People who would come to his aid. Or call for police. Down here, no people—at least none who would guarantee help.

In this part of the City everyone minded their own business. And the life or death of Robert Roman was of no importance in their business.

"Got you now, you son of a bitch." The brute was right behind him. Robert could practically feel his hot breath. Ahead was the East River.

It was Hobson's choice: no choice at all.

Robert Roman chose the East River.

2

Thursday, May 30.

*He concentrated on the task before him. There'd been word that Amo*rous Al Beatty, one of New York's meaner Moll buzzers and a Billy Noodle if there ever was one, had crossed the Fulton Street Dead Line and been seen loitering near the Bank of America Building. A look around the side streets had uncovered neither hide nor hair of Amorous Al.

It was one of those truly soft spring days in the City. The sky was a cloudless blue, what you could see of it through the tangle of overhead wires that gave New York electric light and the telephone. And the sun was just gentle enough to kiss the skin like a lass's soft and fragrant lips.

One duty done, a second duty awaited him at Grand Street.

It was hard to believe that the old man was gone. A mere strip of a lad: one hundred and six years. The young man would have laughed, but that might have brought the tears and that would have been unseemly.

This is when he saw her. Almost a block away, just shy of Wall Street. She wore a wonderful blue straw hat with a big white cabbage rose, and she was carrying a heavy wooden contraption under one arm, which nearly dragged her down on the left side. The thing she carried was all legs. With her right hand she was dragging a small cart, loaded to the brim.

She stopped. As always happened in the City, the curious began to gather out of nowhere on the hitherto fairly quiet thoroughfare, blocking his view.

He hurried his step to get closer.

The girl, for she was not more than that, had stood the contraption on its feet. From the cart she'd taken a camera and set it on the contraption.

She seemed much in command, ignoring the crowd of onlookers as she worked. Reached into her cart, she brought out a flat object. She placed it in the camera and pointed the instrument at the Bank of America Building.

So taken was he by her animation and precise movements that for the moment he almost forgot where he was headed and what he was supposed to do.

And as he turned his steps again toward Grand Street, his thoughts remained with the young woman: her slim form, the excitement in her stance, the lustrous dark hair under the stylish hat with its fine white rose.

3

Thursday, May 30. Afternoon.

Ned Clancy, *the feisty bantam of the family, and him six foot, was doing* all the talking. "So Moose says to him, he says, 'Why aren't you at your post, Officer?'

"Fat Billy Rath, he don't recognize him. Billy, he looks at the four-eyes, takes a big snotty oyster, holds it high above his head and pours it into his gob, down his gullet. Then he says to Moose, 'What the fuck is it to you?'

"Now Jim Batton, the counterman at McNulty's Oyster Saloon, puts his in. He says to Moose, 'You got a nerve, comin' in here and interferin' with an officer.'

"And Moose he says, 'I'm the Commissioner.'

"Right away Fat Billy reaches for the vinegar bottle. I got this from Jim Batton. Jim told me he didn't know if Rath was going to hit the four-eyes with the bottle or what. Anyway, Rath says real cute-like, 'Yes, that you are. You're Grover Cleveland and Mayor Strong all in a bunch, you are. Move on now, or . . .' " Ned Clancy paused to survey his audience. He saw with satisfaction that they were all rapt in his story, waiting for him to continue.

Impatient with his cousin for stopping at the good part, Dutch

Tonneman prompted him. "So what the hell happened?" Though Dutch, who was christened John, was only half Irish on his mother's side—she was a Clancy—his voice was thick with the brogue as always when he was with his cousins. And drinking.

"Don't be rushing me," Ned said, relishing the attention his grand story was getting. "Then all at once Batton figures it out. He whispers to Rath, 'Shut up, Bill, it's his nibs, sure. Don't you spot his glasses?'

"Then like the Pope himself, Moose says, 'Go to your post at once.'

"Batton told me he never saw Fat Billy Rath run so fast in his life!"

The men surrounding Ned Clancy laughed and shot back their whiskey.

Dutch Tonneman lifted his glass to Ned and was about to move on when Ned stepped close up to him. "So, as of day before yesterday, Tommy Byrnes is out, Pete Conlin is in. Byrnes goes on full pension."

Dutch tilted his head. "Conlin is only Acting Chief. Who knows when the ax will fall on him?"

"There's talk of firing everybody."

"A lot of rubbish. The sun shines, the moon glows, God's in his heaven. I got along fine yesterday, I'll get along fine tomorrow."

"That's a good one." After a moment Ned added, "I pulled another man out of the East River last night."

Dutch looked at his cousin's expectant face. "Good for you. That's great. How many does that make?"

Puffing up his chest, Ned said, "Fourth this year. He's a journalist. Robert Roman. Said he was going to put me in the newspaper." Ned examined his hands as if surprised to find them empty of a drink. "My whistle's dry as a bone." And he was off to find a remedy.

The black-clad women in the corner were singing high-pitched laments. Dutch couldn't understand the Gaelic. From time to time, however, he could make out the many wailings of "Alas, alas, alas." The emotional content of the songs was supposed to ease the grief, but Dutch much preferred the joke-telling to do that.

He squeezed past assorted cousins, ancient uncles, and old friends, out of the parlor, into the small dining room off the kitchen, where the women were congregating.

Meg Tonneman, *née* Clancy, came from the kitchen with a huge platter of sliced corned beef, while Mrs. Gallagher replenished the enormous bowl of potatoes. Meg was surrounded by neighborhood women, female cousins, and aunts, not to mention Dutch's five sisters. All were dressed in suitable black. "Ah, here's my boy," Meg exclaimed. "John, you remember Mrs. Gallagher?"

"Yes, Ma. How are you, Mrs. Gallagher?"

"Good as can be expected," Sheila Gallagher replied, wiping the edge of the potato platter with her apron. She was tall and big-boned, with no meat on her.

"I think Old Peter would have been happy with this, don't you?" A tiny frown wrinkled Meg's brow. Meg Tonneman was a small plump woman, whose green eyes, clear and inquisitive as a young girl's, belied her pure white hair.

Dutch kissed the wrinkle. "It is good, Ma. Old Peter would have blessed you for it."

"And I bless him," she said, crossing herself. "He was a good man, if ever there was one."

A thumping sound came from the parlor, and a shout from Cousin Ned. "All gone!" He was whacking at the beer barrel fair to beat the band.

"If that don't take the cake," said Meg, hands on her ample hips. "Kenny Ryan was supposed to fetch another keg." She sighed. "I'll see to it now."

"That's all right, Ma. There's plenty of whiskey to guzzle."

Meg stretched up to pat his cheek, for he was well over a foot taller than she. "Stop funning your own ma. You wouldn't go drunk to the job and you know it." Her eyes twinkled. "Besides, what would the ladies have to drink?" She moved off to the kitchen, found her straw hat among the others on the row of wooden pegs, and opened the outside door.

"Don't you try to lift a big keg all by yourself, Ma."

"And what makes you think I couldn't if I had to?"

"You're absolutely right, Ma," Dutch said, poker-faced. "I lost my head. Forgive me, Ma."

A chorus of female voices, cousins and sisters, rang out. "Forgive me, Ma!"

Dutch Tonneman grinned; his mother shook her finger at him and went out the door.

"And so do you have a nice Irish girl you're seeing yet?" Cousin Lizzie asked.

"Now, none of that," Aunt Molly scolded her daughter. Molly was his ma's sister. She cocked her head at him. "So do you?"

"I wouldn't tell you if I did," Dutch told her. "You'd all scare her off."

Saluting the ladies, Dutch returned to the parlor, directly to the back of the room where Old Peter Tonneman lay in state under the plain wood crucifix. Jesus's carved head, instead of being bent in death, seemed to be cocked at Old Peter's coffin.

The ritual of guests passing around the open coffin, the "Don't he look like himself" comments, and everyone agreeing that Old Peter was in a better place, had been completed early on. Now only the elderly clustered around the corpse, as if seeing to a grand send-off for Old Peter would somehow assure them of the same.

Dutch breathed in the scent of rosemary which emanated from the twigs lining the coffin, helping to preserve the body. Old Peter had specifically forbidden any newfangled embalming.

He laid his hands on Old Peter's, cold and white though they were and holding rosary beads the way he'd never held them in life. "I'll miss you, old man." He looked up at Jesus. "Take care of him," John Tonneman told the wooden crucifix.

With this, his last valediction to his great-grandfather, Dutch acknowledged the sad smiles of those surrounding the coffin and continued his circuit of the crowded room, his blond thatched head standing out among the rest. He wore his hair thick and somewhat longer than the style because, truth to tell, he had a vein of vanity, and he knew from Old Peter that his ruddy coloring and flaxen hair were an inheritance from his Dutch ancestor, the first Sheriff of New York.

Dutch was lured by the voice of his favorite cousin, Bo Clancy, a great storyteller. Bo, as usual, was spinning a yarn. He was surrounded by a pride of Clancys, all big lads, Bo being the biggest of the Clancys, and by Father Duff, no half-pint himself. Though the old priest's shoulders were now slightly stooped, he had a barrel chest and hands like two hams. Except for his collar, a stranger might assume that Father was one of the Clancys and did what they did.

Dutch's mother Meg liked to say, "Father Duff swears and drinks like the trooper he used to be. But there is more of the good Lord Jesus in him than any man I ever met, bless his soul."

Bo took a healthy taste of his whiskey. "So it happens one fine day Saint Joseph approaches the Pearly Gates. In tow is a disreputable sort of chap, the likes of Phil Malone, a miserable sod, still wearing the blue of a New York copper, though he's got a bullet in his nose and has just been killed in an alley not far from here, down in Africa Town.

" 'Yes, Joseph, what can I do for you?' asks Saint Peter in his lardy-dardy tones, for he is a snob, he is, and snoots everyone."

"Watch it," Father Duff cautioned, holding out his glass for the refill Ned Clancy was passing around.

"Now, Father, we all know that Saint Joseph, on the other hand, is a regular fellow and always looks out for his mates. 'I've got a friend here,' says he to Saint Peter, 'And I'd like you to let him in.'

" 'Was he a good man?' Saint Peter asks."

"Ask the coon whores in Africa Town!" Dennis Clancy, Bo's brother, roared, slapping his thigh.

Mike Clancy, who thought this was the funniest thing he'd heard since Hugh Kelsey got his nuts caught in the wash wringer, started laughing high like a banshee.

"Shut it down," Bo said. His authority as the oldest of the cousins was undeniable. Dennis and Mike went quiet.

Tonneman dragged an empty chair to a spot between Bo and Father Duff and sat. "Carry on, Bo."

"Jesus Christ—excuse me, Father—but with all this interrupting, where the hell was I?" Bo grinned at his cousin John Tonneman, then closed one eye. "Ah. 'So was he a good man?' Saint Peter asks.

" 'I wouldn't say that exactly,' says Saint Joseph.

" 'What would you say, Joseph?'

" 'I say he's a friend of mine and Saint Patrick vouches for him, too.'

"And Saint Peter says, 'But does he belong here, Joseph? The rules are the rules.'

"Saint Joseph, who has a short fuse to begin with, is getting mad, now. 'Feck you and your rules,' he tells Saint Peter. 'Does my friend get in or not?'

" 'Not,' says he.

"Now Saint Joseph is really pissed off, let me tell you. And he's not the sort to burn a lot of kindling getting his fire started. 'Is that your last word?'

"Saint Peter is carved in stone, not budging, not giving an inch. Not a stir. 'Yes,' says he.

"Meantime, Saint Joseph is having the apoplexy. 'Absolutely?'

" 'Positively,' Saint Peter says.

" 'Are you sure?' Saint Joseph asks.

"Saint Peter says, 'As sure as I am about damnation and salvation.' "

"Amen," Father Duff murmured, making the sign. Again Ned refilled his glass.

" 'That's it then,' Saint Joseph says, shoving Saint Peter aside, and poking his head inside the Pearly Gates. 'Are you *sure?*' he says, raging, but giving Saint Peter one last chance.

" 'As sure as the Resurrection,' vows Saint Peter.

" 'All right then,' Saint Joseph says. And he gives a yell, 'Hey, Mary, get the kid. We're leaving.' "

The men about Bo Clancy bellowed and brayed, holding their distended bellies. Bo laughed the loudest. "What do you think of that story, Father?" he asked.

The priest adjusted his black eye patch, which covered the hole where his left eye had been. The empty socket, though healed all these many years, still gave him the itch from time to time. Now his hand went down to his dewlapped neck and traveled from there to pick lint from the great expanse of black cloth that stretched across his ample body like a becalmed sail. Taking a deep wheezing breath, Father Duff flicked his tongue, froglike, into his large glass of whiskey.

"Hm, what?" The priest sipped his whiskey. "Pardons, boys, just having a bit of prayer for Old Peter."

"Saint Peter?" Dutch Tonneman asked.

"No," said the priest. He swatted Tonneman on the shoulder, nearly knocking him from his chair. "*Old* Peter, you sinner. Your sainted great-grandfather."

Dutch Tonneman may have favored his father's people and his Dutch lineage in height as well as fair coloring, but in disposition he was his mother's son, pure Irish, and always ready for a laugh. Now he put on the brogue thick as molasses. "You do know Old Peter frequented the Scot Church, Father, when he went to church at all?"

"Sh-h," said Father Duff, raising his whiskey glass. "Or the Lord will hear and smite you where you sit. For I have no doubt that at this moment, Peter Tonneman is standing beside the Lord Himself, handing Him advice on how to run the force of angels."

4

Thursday,
May 30.
Afternoon.

"A *toast," said Father Duff. "To Old Peter Tonneman."*

"Old Peter," everyone shouted, raising their glasses.

Dutch Tonneman drank, then took out the heavy gold watch Old Peter had left him. Precisely half past two. He and Bo had to be on the job by three.

The blast knocked the watch from his hands.

It rocked the house and shattered every window facing Grand Street, raining glass equally on the mourners and on Old Peter Tonneman himself resting for eternity in his handsome coffin.

"Listen, boys," said Father Duff, alert as any man in the room, "that sounded like a bomb." Before he'd taken the Orders, he'd fought with the 69th Light Infantry during the War; his black patch was its mark. So if he said it was a bomb it might very well be a bomb.

Dazed, Dutch slowly became aware of the screaming of the women, who rushed into the chaos, and the curses of the men, who were instantly sober. He bent to retrieve the watch from the glass-strewn carpet and noticed his hand was bleeding, a fine crimson trickle from wrist to finger. Miraculously, the glass over the watch face was intact.

"It's nothing but Ned banging outside on the beer barrel," Mike Clancy said. His countenance was nicked as if a blind man had shaved him. "Or farting."

Dutch quickly noted the time and rubbed the small amulet on the chain for luck before returning the watch to his pocket. On the same day his mother had given him a gold cross for around his neck, she had also presented him with the small gold-and-seed-pearl amulet in the shape of a shield for his fob. The charm had magic properties, she said, in its ancient symbols, that would keep him forever safe. Old Peter himself had hooked it on his great-grandson's cradle the day young John was born.

Ma! She'd gone out. She might be in the thick of it. He started for the door. "Ma!"

Meg Tonneman stood in the open entrance. "I'm fine." She was toting a keg of beer on her shoulder. In the midst of all this she'd finished what she'd set out to do, so in the midst of all this Dutch Tonneman had to smile.

The room was swarming with women, all exclaiming about the destruction and clucking over the blood and broken glass. His mother set her keg on the floor and scrutinized her only son.

"Not hurt, Ma," he assured her. "Did you see anything out there?"

"No. I was already on the stairs."

Tonneman looked about the crowded room. "What a mess. This place has been to the wars. Someone, dust off Old Peter."

"Forget it, it's thunder," Dennis Clancy said, knowing full well it wasn't, brushing the shards of glass from his blue sleeve.

Ned kicked away what was left of the pane in the front window. "Look at that sky, idiot. You see rain?"

"A joke," Dennis protested. He leaned out the window and emptied his glass of splinters, then swirled his handkerchief around the inside, opened a surviving bottle of whiskey, and poured himself a fistful. In spite of the jostling, he drank with only a trifle spill.

"Bomb maybe," said Bo, who was also no stranger to hearing such. The fact was all the men in the room knew what bombs were, what sort of mischief they could do. The new batch of greenhorns from Eastern

Europe was rife with anarchists. "Or a gas explosion. Close to the river. Can't you smell it?"

"It's got to be pretty big," Dutch said. "It's eight blocks from here to the water."

Bo Clancy wiped his mouth with the back of his hand and got to his feet. "I reckon we should go see what it's all about."

Leaving the women to clean up the mess, the men all trooped out to the street, where the entire neighborhood stood gawking toward the East River. Great clouds of black smoke billowed upward against the gray sky. Police whistles blew, and then came the clanging of the fire brigade.

The City did not need another big fire. Bo Clancy had been on the scene for the one in '89, up on Seventh Avenue. Stabbing and shooting Bo could handle, but burned people wrecked his soul. Ten people dead that time.

Eighty-nine had been a terrible year for Bo. While he was at the fire, his wife went into labor. Grace had died delivering Dennis, leaving Bo with two infant sons to raise, the newborn and Bo Jr., born the year before. If it weren't for his Ma, the two boys would be as good as orphans.

Without another thought, Dutch Tonneman and his various cousins began heading for the riverfront. It was only fitting and proper that they should.

That's what policemen did.

5

Thursday, May 30.

It was perverse of her, Mr. Cook told Esther, that she loved the smell of the chemicals. But since the first day, the acids had blunted the fetid memory of the tenement on Ludlow Street that had filled her nostrils, her very being.

She lived in the Woloshins' tiny back room, which was farthest from the warmth of the kitchen and the staircase down to the privy in the yard.

The length of the walk to the outhouse did not distance her from the privy's fragrance, as the room's only window faced the brick wall of the air shaft that led to the yard. And for this grand accommodation Esther paid dearly: seventy-five cents a week.

But here in the sanctuary of Oswald Cook's photographic darkroom on Gramercy Park, with the comforting red light casting a rosy twilight on her, and wonder of wonders, a sink with running water inside the house, Esther could let herself dream again. All the magical ingredients that made the enchanted science of photography possible surrounded her—the sinks of harsh washes, shelves stocked with all shapes and sizes of beaker and bottle, and developers for the dry plates Mr. Cook used to take his photographs.

She'd learned their magic names, letting them roll knowledgeably off her tongue, loving the sound of them. Ferrous oxalate or plain pyrogallic acid. Magnesium powder. Sodium hyposulfite. Ferricyanide. Potassium bromide.

She loved, too, the slotted wooden boxes of prepared plates that stood in a corner ready for use. Most of all she loved the cameras, every one of the fifteen that Oz Cook owned.

Merlin certainly never had finer tools in his sorcerer's tower with which to cast his spells.

Esther thanked God every day for the blessed presence on this earth of Miss Lillian Wald, who had taught Esther her English at the Nurses' Settlement. It was Miss Wald who had introduced her to Mr. Cook, one week before the end of the previous year.

"Sit down, Esther," Miss Wald had said, beaming at her. Miss Wald was a sweet-looking woman, with a straight nose, thin lips, tightly bound hair, and a great heart. So proud, so strong. And only twenty-seven years old herself, a Jewish woman in charge of her own wonderful settlement house. "This is Mr. Oswald Cook. Mr. Cook, may I present Esther Breslau, my finest student."

Esther had blushed, but she was proud to be thus described. The praise brought tears to her eyes.

Oswald Cook had taken her hand. "How do you do, Miss Breslau?"

"Very well, I'm sure," she'd said, just like a real American lady.

Miss Wald had said, "Mr. Cook is an artist, Esther. He works not with a brush and paint but with a camera. You know what a camera does?"

"Yes," she'd replied. "I have seen and admired Mr. Jacob Riis's photographs."

"She's perfect, Lillian," Mr. Cook had said, making Esther blush once more. "She doesn't even sound like a greenhorn. You are an angel. Bless you."

"I'm pleased you agree with me, Oz."

Mr. Cook had sat on the corner of Miss Wald's desk, his eyes sparkling. Esther could see his eyes now as she stood in the red shadows of the darkroom: the bluest of blue, like the clearest of skies. "I'm looking for an assistant," he'd told Esther. "An immigrant, such as yourself. I understand you speak Yiddish, German, Russian, Polish, and Italian."

"Only a little Italian."

"It will do," he said, curling a delicate hand, displaying stained brown fingertips. Mr. Cook smelled of whiskey and cigarettes, and the whites of those otherwise compelling blue eyes were shot with blood. Deep lines marked his eyes and mouth, making him appear to be a man no longer in his prime. Still, he had a boy's face which lit up with a boy's smile and a boy's enthusiasm when he talked of photography. "Miss Breslau, you will be my interpreter and guide into the life of your people. And, of course, my model."

But more important than his appearance, and as important as his words, was what he intended to pay her for her work. Two dollars and fifty cents a week.

Esther had gotten off the boat at Ellis Island in the heat of the summer in August of 1892. The examiner, a strange, stooped-over man with shiny skin, had peered at her through thick glasses, mumbling over and over, "They keep on coming, they just keep on coming."

Her English was small at the time, but he said it so often Esther finally understood him. Her clothes had been a drab immigrant dress. A kerchief covered her hair. The crowd of Jewish women struggling with bundles who disembarked with her all had their heads covered with awful orange *sheitels*. The orange wigs served to remind Esther of the fate she'd escaped. In Poland, her father had arranged for her to marry Mottel Goldberg, a fat widower twice her age, with four young boys.

If she had not run away she'd be in Zakliczyn, married to Mottel; she'd be pregnant, wearing an orange wig while she chopped the wood, fed the chickens, and cooked in a mean kitchen, preparing food for the unruly Goldberg clan, leading a predestined life of toil and sorrow, with nothing to look forward to but more children and empty dreams.

That first day in America she'd been tired and hungry but incredibly happy. Though the paper-and-string-wrapped parcel she clutched to her bosom was all she owned in the world except for the clothes on her back, she was alive, and free of the old country, free of the old ways, free of Mottel Goldberg.

In her hand she held the scrap of paper with the name of the family where she was to stay. She knew it by heart. Ezra Woloshin, 45

Ludlow Street. The Woloshins were *landsleiter* of the in-laws of her third cousin Peretz. Cousin Peretz had taken her in when she'd run from the marriage with Mottel and eventually brought her once more to kind feelings with her parents, which was a good thing, because soon after, Abraham and Sara Breslau died of smallpox within days of each other. After Esther had sold the few possessions her parents had left her, she had just enough money for passage to America.

She was to live with the Woloshins and pay for rent and food. They had even found her a job doing piecework for the Niven Brothers.

Jew Town, as the Lower East Side was called by the *goyim*, had been a shock to Esther. The extreme poverty, the reek of the outhouses, the horse droppings, both fresh and stagnant, in the street. Graffiti covered every building. The streets themselves teemed with people and were clogged with pushcarts selling everything from hot chickpeas to *sheitels*. And the noise—the noise was staggering—as if everyone was yelling at once. Which everyone was—men, women, and children, leaning out of windows, or standing on the street, shouting to neighbors or children or peddlers, the vendors crying their wares.

It was worse than the ghettos of Polish cities. Esther's people had been poor, but they had lived in the country. Her mother, in her *sheitel*, earned the family's keep with the milk, butter, cheese, and eggs she harvested from three cows and a small flock of chickens.

Her father was an ascetic man who studied and prayed all day in the *shul*.

"Greenhorn!" a little boy screamed at Esther as she arrived at the address on the paper; he pointed a grimy finger at her. And everyone laughed at her discomfort. She had heard the word on the boat. Greenhorns were those who wouldn't leave their old habits from Europe behind them. Those who would not become American. Esther Breslau vowed to become so complete an American that no one would call her *greenhorn* again.

All too soon Esther came to understand the currents of desperation she saw all around her. Was this better than *di alte heym*? It had to be, because she was never going back. In America, marriages were not arranged and young women were free to wed whom they chose.

But the Woloshins were crude people clinging to Orthodox ways, and she was not happy in the mean, murky room she let from them. Yet with her first earnings Esther did not move. Instead, she bought herself a splendid forest-green hat, with a large ecru feather, at one of the many shops on Clinton Street. The minute she put the hat on her head she felt different, no longer greenhorn. American. At least when she kept silent. When she spoke she was still Esther from Zakliczyn.

Esther learned quickly how to take the elevated steam train out of Jew Town, to Union Square, to Madison Square, to the Ladies' Mile, where beautifully dressed American women bought their clothes in the shops along Fifth Avenue. She listened to the soft, stylish chatter of the grand ladies, saying their words over and over in her head, then finally out loud in her grim little cell.

The Polish she spoke was sophisticated, for her teacher, Mr. Epstein, had been to university in Cracow, where Jews were usually not made welcome.

From Mr. Epstein, a man with a misformed foot who wore a boot with a thick sole, Esther had learned Russian and German to go with the Yiddish which was spoken in her home. She had a good ear.

This good ear she'd had as a child now made it possible for her to imitate the English she heard on her trips away from the Lower East Side. And along the way she even learned a little Italian from the girls she sewed with.

In the fall of 1893, Esther had picked up a handbill printed in Yiddish, that invited her to learn. Eagerly, she went to the house on Rivington Street mentioned in the handbill, called the Nurses' Settlement. It was there she met the first person who would completely change her life.

Lillian Wald became Esther's teacher and the model she would use to pattern her life. By the time the settlement moved to temporary quarters on Jefferson Street in '94, Esther had become Miss Wald's most promising pupil. And now through Miss Wald she had met the second person who would completely change her life. Oswald Cook.

All Esther had was the dream, and now it was coming true. She knew gold in the streets was a grandmother's tale, but she also understood the reality of it. The gold in the streets of America, she knew, was the prospect of advancement. In Europe you could never be more than what your father and mother were. Born in dirt, you died in dirt. And in Europe a girl was a commodity to be traded or sold. But in America you could better yourself. In America she would choose what her life would be.

She had agreed immediately to Mr. Cook's offer. Esther Breslau would do no more piecework in the Woloshins' horrid little room; she would sew no more sleeves for the Niven Brothers.

"Not so fast. I'll need you to come with me on the odd evening."

Esther looked at Lillian Ward, who nodded.

"That will not be a hardship for me, Mr. Cook," Esther told him.

Oswald Cook III owned a fine brick town house on the west side of Gramercy Park. No. 5. The house had been in his family for many years and had the new electric lighting and indoor plumbing. The first Oswald Cook had come from Bristol after the war in '15 to open a bank in Wall Street.

The manservant who greeted her the next day was the first yellow man Esther had ever spoken to. She was amazed that he talked just like an Englishman.

"Wong," Oz Cook said, "this is Miss Esther Breslau. Miss Breslau is going to be working for me."

The Chinaman was no taller than she. His face was hairless, as smooth as a baby's behind. His clothing was a shiny black smock over baggy black trousers, and his fine black hair, topped by a black skullcap, was tied in a long pigtail. Were there Jews in China? she wondered. Impossible. Wong bowed his head. "Welcome, Miss Esther."

Oz Cook was inordinately pleased with himself. He had hired himself the key—someone who would unlock the secrets of these strange people, these immigrants, who lived like animals packed into narrow crates. The immigrants fascinated Oz. Crude as American louts, but different. These new people aspired not only by the dint of their muscles, but also by the dint of their brains.

They would make wonderful subjects. And the photographs he would take would help build the book he and Robert Roman were writing.

That Esther was an intelligent little mouse, with her mass of dark brown and her knowing brown eyes, he had no doubt. What he hadn't expected was her immediate, inspired response to his work and to the process of making photographs. Oswald Cook was a man who had little place for women in his life, for his life was his work and women were not fond of the smells and the damage his chemicals did to carpet and furniture. And he had no intention of changing.

Esther had found Oz's library her second day in his fine house. It was an amazing place: busts of famous writers and tall glass-enclosed bookcases filled with books of every size and description, many leather-bound. Rolling stairs made even the highest up and farthest away accessible.

The man, when he came bursting in, did not see her at first because she was high on the rolling stairs reaching for a volume of poetry. The man slapped a large leather envelope on one of the library tables and proceeded to take out pencil and paper.

Esther sneezed, giving herself away, although she had not been hiding but was in plain view. At least her ankles were.

"Here, missy," the man ordered. "Come down from there."

In her embarrassment, she dropped her book. Like a baseball player, he scooped it easily from the air before it hit the Persian-carpeted floor.

"Bah!" he said scornfully when he read the spine. "A second-rate poet. If you're going to risk your neck up there, missy, read someone worth reading."

"Lord Byron is not second-rate," she cried, outraged.

He dropped the book on the table and ran his hands through his shaggy black hair. The voluminous mustache he sported was in the style of the day. It covered his entire upper lip but appeared never to have experienced comb or wax. Of stocky build he was covered in, rather than wearing, a brown suit with narrow trousers. Every part of him seemed to move and dance, as if it pained him to be still.

"Do you need a hand?" he asked her now.

"No. Thank you." She descended the ladder with as much decorum and grace as she could muster.

But he had already turned away and was scribbling on his pad of paper, as if he'd forgotten her completely. But he hadn't, not really. Esther stood for a moment watching him. She had decided he was a rude young man. "What about Mr. Whitman?" she asked at last, meaning Walt Whitman, the poet, whose work she loved.

"I am Robert Roman," the rude young man announced, ignoring

her query, and without turning to look at her. "One of Oz Cook's Catholic waifs. You must be the Hebrew one. Oz would have us remade in his likeness. A weakness of our benefactor, I'm afraid."

She didn't know how to react, so stayed silent.

"Oh, I see," the young man continued, with a dash of irony. "You thought it was due to your intelligence."

"I—" She felt her cheeks grow warm.

"Well, let's give Oz that," he said, still writing. "Oz has an instinct for the best." Finally turning to look at her, the young man said, "Now, Dante, *there's* a giant. A true poet." He offered her a book. "Have you read Dante, missy?"

6

Thursday,
May 30.

That was how it began. Oz was not her only teacher. Esther had two. Her second teacher was the decidedly uncivil Robert Roman. On occasion, Esther was not certain which of the two men was the more important.

Robert Joseph Roman, born Roberto Giuseppe Romano in Naples in 1865, came from a long line of cobblers. But young Roberto wanted to be more than a shoemaker. Even at an early age, the boy was precocious enough to want to be a cobbler of words. He loved words.

His parents had emigrated to New York not too long after the conclusion of the American Civil War. And Roberto went to public school. There he disappeared, only to be replaced by Robert.

He wanted to be an important man in America. With that goal in mind he studied and he read. He became a reporter. That was only the first step. He planned to write books, many books, and to be known as the greatest writer America ever produced.

To say the least, Robert Roman was an impatient, explosive man.

But then, he was a product of the City streets. An only son and orphaned young, he had fast learned to live by his wits. He'd worked his way up from selling newspapers to free-lance journalist, sometimes getting to events as they were happening because he knew just how to listen to the flow on the streets.

"Do you know what I am?" he had asked Esther the day they'd met.

"You're a journalist."

"Journalist! I'm better than that. Like the knights of old I am a free-lancer, a knight-errant, seeking the Holy Grail of truth."

"That sounds very grand." She was impressed. But he seemed a little silly, with all his pretensions.

"Look at me. I am a chosen man. You can understand that, being one of the Chosen People."

And thus their odd friendship began.

Robert read his treasured Dante to her in his native tongue with exquisite care, from time to time translating difficult passages, responding to her questions without the abrasive tone and manner with which he usually cloaked himself.

Together they had little Italian conversations during which he attempted to correct the deplorable New York-Sicilian dialect she had picked up and believed was Italian.

His dream, he confessed to her one late afternoon, was to write books. Like Jacob Riis. Like Riis, he intended to achieve great celebrity.

Until Oz, Esther had not allowed herself to dream. Her only goal had been to educate herself for a better life. Now, she wanted to use what Oz had taught her, to wield her camera, to give dignity to women's lives by taking their photographs as they did ordinary things. She'd said as much to Robert. He would understand, she knew this.

He looked at her a long time before saying a word.

"Nonsense," he told her curtly. "You must marry and raise intelligent children."

In the meanwhile, Esther Breslau grew to be more than Oswald Cook's interpreter and photographic model. She became his photographic apprentice. For, much to his surprise and delight, he found that she had the true eye of an artist. The mouse knew instinctively what would make a good picture. He'd seen it the first time when he photographed the Hebrew Madonna and child in their cluttered tenement room on Montgomery Street.

That day, after handing him the plate, Esther had stood behind him as he prepared to shoot. Something bothered him; something was not right.

She'd said, bold as you please, "Wait!" Cook was shocked. But with his temperament, the shock was tinged with amusement. Then she'd plucked a sad, broken straw hat from the top of a bundle of clothes and hung it on a nail on the wall behind, just above the woman's head. The crown of the battered hat made an odd and telling halo.

It was extraordinary. The girl was a pearl among the ashes.

If he'd been the marrying kind he would have taken her as his wife. Ha! And what would Mother and the Anglican Church have said to that? But both Mother and Church had been out of his life for some time. Mother's ghost notwithstanding, Oswald Cook could not deny the temptation of the prospect. Esther was comely, albeit more than twenty-five years his junior. Still, he had to do something to keep her from wasting this talent in the sort of marriage these women usually made. Marriages that wore them out with childbirth and hard work long before their time.

Get a hold of yourself, Oz, he'd mused. Why such concern over this little foreign mouse? An Israelite mouse at that.

Oz was the last of his line, and he planned to remain so, for in spite of his random thoughts about the little mouse, he had no intention of marrying.

He had heard how she lived from Lillian Wald, and had offered Esther three small rooms in the unused servants quarters on the top floor of his home. This was no inconvenience to him, for the old house had more than twenty rooms, and he hadn't been up to the fifth floor since he was a lad. Wong could have lived up there, but the Chinaman preferred his room near the kitchen on the ground floor.

When at first Esther had refused, for the sake of propriety, Oz had maintained that he would not, could not, be responsible for her welfare when she worked evenings if she did not take him up on his offer. So she had agreed.

For all that, she insisted on paying him what she'd paid for the hovel on Ludlow Street. Oz was impressed by her principles; while seventy-five cents a week meant nothing to him, it was surely a serious amount to her.

7

Thursday, May 30.

Cherry Street lay near the southern tip of Manhattan Island and was dense with loading platforms and warehouses. The fire was at a lumberyard, one of several in the area, located along the waterfront where it was easy to load barges and ships.

The loading dock in front of the yard on Cherry Street was smoldering already when a goodly force of Metropolitan Police, a mob in blue and brass, many of whom had been at Old Peter's wake, streamed toward the explosion site, half business, half festive in mood, all full of the booze that had flowed generously.

Clouds of black smoke blotted out the afternoon sun, and it was raining cinders and ash.

"What is it?"

"Looks like Vander Smith's. Nothing left but a few struts and a pile of burning timber."

But the burning was hot and treacherous. One live cinder, and the whole of lower Manhattan could go up. It had happened before. All at once they were working, rushing to help put out the blaze.

"Move aside, let them pass!" A contingent of firemen pushed

through. Most were bearded, because wet whiskers were added protection inside a burning building. Dutch Tonneman had at first considered joining the Fire Department, but beards itched and drove him mad, so he never gave that vocation a second thought. Which was good. Because his joining the police had made his great-grandfather very happy.

The firemen drove their water-and-hose wagons as close to the flames as the horses would allow before they shied. While some of the men in blue kept the curious crowd orderly, others, including the Detectives, rolled up their shirtsleeves to pump water and help with the hoses.

The fire was still burning hot, flames everywhere, eruptions from all corners, sending wheels of sparks into the air and debris onto the ground. Even as far back as the horse trough it was hot and threatening.

"Talk about luck," Ned Clancy shouted, handing Bo a bucket of water. "Having his trough right out front."

"I doubt that Vander Smith would agree with you about the luck part," said Dutch, coming up from the trough, passing another bucket to Ned.

"That's because he's not one of us . . . Dutch."

Dutch couldn't help wonder if Ned's implication was that he, too, was not Irish. His Irish cousins treated him almost as a mascot, with them but not of them. Except Bo.

John Tonneman had Dutch blood in his veins, and his father had been not a cop, but a journalist. For the Clancys, not being a policeman was almost as bad as not being an Irishman. Still, Dutch had been accepted because his mother was a Clancy and because his great-grandfather Peter Tonneman, once the illustrious Jacob Hays's right-hand man, was revered by the force.

When Dutch was a boy, Old Peter had taught him the police trade. One of the first rules was to walk the crowd and let your five senses—and the sixth and most important, common sense—guide you. "Old Hays taught me that, and I'm teaching it to you," Peter would tell his great-grandson.

Now, as he walked the crowd gaping at the fire, taking care not to step on the dead birds littering the street, Dutch wondered idly if his grandchildren would call him Old Dutch. The birds had been struck dead by the blast as they'd flown by.

Birds weren't important. But people were. How many hurt? How many dead? And how much damage? Putting how many people out of work?

The smell teased his nose. Not the smoke, something else. Dutch closed his eyes. He knew that smell. What they called Jewish butter. Goose grease. Some people used it for burns.

He opened his eyes. Damn, sticking up out of the crowd for all the world to see was the snaky frame of Down-to-the-Ground Conn Clooney, who'd been known to set a fire or two in his time. And wearing a yellow slicker, to boot. To protect him from the hose water, no doubt. This was too easy.

Conn was watching the fire with that wild look in his eyes fire setters always had. Drifting into the mob, Dutch came up behind the arsonist, who was rocking on his heels and having a heigh-ho time. The smell of goose grease was strong. And the oily glint on Conn's face showed the reason why.

"Nice fire," Dutch murmured.

Conn nodded, and without turning said, "Good bang, too. Did you hear it?"

"The whole fecking City heard it, Conn."

Conn turned. The grin on his face fell away when he saw Dutch. "Hello, Detective. I didn't do this. Pretty work, but it ain't mine. I swear." The angry burns on the cull's forehead and cheeks gave the lie to his protest.

For further proof, not that he needed it, Dutch grabbed Conn's right arm and pushed up the sleeve of his loose oilskin raincoat, exposing shiny blistered skin. "Grease for your burns? They give you that at Gouverneur Hospital after you put a bomb to this place?"

"No, sir. Burned myself last week when the stove blew up."

"More likely your little bomb blew up before you could get far enough away. Stop the blarney, Conn, it's me. What have you got to say for yourself?"

Conn's grin returned, all sheepish and meek. "I should have used less black powder and more match heads. I'll never do that again."

"You are a stupid cove, coming back, sticking around with greasy burn marks all over your dumb Mick face. Don't you know better than to hang around after the deed is done?"

"That's where you're wrong, Detective. The most fun is watching it blaze, watching everyone scramble."

"Who paid for this game?"

Conn didn't answer. He was watching the fire.

Dutch took Conn by the collar and dragged the arsonist to the water line. He showed Conn to Bo, then delivered him to Ned. "First give him a bucket and let him help undo his handiwork, then to the hoosegow, if you please."

"How'd you spot him?" Bo asked.

Dutch laughed low in his gut. "Old Peter told me where to look," he said.

8

Thursday, May 30.

A*t first she didn't hear the pounding. It was the shouting that finally shook* her from her deep concentration.

"Oz, damn it all, where the hell are you?" This exclamation was accompanied by fierce thumps on the darkroom door.

"Miss Esther!" Now it was Wong's voice.

More pounding now, along with rattling of the doorknob. "Oz!"

"Just a moment, please," she called.

"Oz, come out. We have things to do."

"He's not here." Esther removed the plate from the solution, set it under the cold running water and peeled off her stained cotton gloves. Leaving the red light burning, she opened the door and slipped from the darkroom into the small studio.

"I am sorry, Miss Esther." The occasion was unquestionably disruptive, but Wong's customary reserve did not falter.

Beside him, Robert Roman stood bristling, hands akimbo, hair in disarray, hat and collar askew. But that was of no moment; this was Robert's usual appearance. He and Oz were each other's foil in this. Where Cook was composed and well-groomed, Roman was nowhere near as fastidious. The journalist's mode of dress was catch-as-catch-can, like a wild man. In clothing and in demeanor. How he and Oz Cook managed to work together, let alone be friends, was a mystery to Esther.

Today there was a fresh tear near the lapel of his usual brown tweed coat. Removing his hat and dealing it from hand to hand, he peered agitatedly past Esther into the darkroom. "Where is he?" His eyes were frenzied, his face shiny with perspiration.

"He's not here, Robert." Esther glanced at Wong. Oswald Cook had not been home in four days. He was on one of his "outings," as Oz dubbed his own intemperate forays.

It was one of the things she'd learned to accept about her employer. The calm and immaculate Mr. Cook often disappeared for days at a time, only to reappear in a sorry state, emaciated, red-eyed, his skin ashen, leaning heavily on Wong's steady arm.

He would lie abed for a day or so while Wong carried tray after tray of steamy soup and mysterious potions mixed with rice up the stairs to his patient. Then Oz would emerge as if nothing untoward had happened. Only his eyes betrayed an unspeakable sadness.

Esther did not ask any questions, accepting that her employer was a man overly attached to hard spirits. Nor did she question that Wong always knew where to find him. And when to collect him. "Where the hell is he?" Robert Roman demanded again.

Esther said, "He had business out of the City."

Roman stared at her. "I told him I was on to something and he chose *now* for one of his sabbaticals?" The journalist wrenched his shaggy head toward the servant. "Wong, where the hell is your master?"

The Chinese man's lips seem to grow even thinner. "I'm afraid I cannot say, sir."

"Drivel," Roman exclaimed, pacing back and forth, apparently unable to compose himself. "Oz promised me this. He swore he'd be ready. I know you have your orders, but this is different. This is *important*."

Wong waited stoically. Nothing moved in his body or face.

"I have no idea where he is," Esther said.

"Wong does. I know damn well he does."

Wong waited patiently, politely, silently.

"Damn it all, Wong. This is important. You've got to tell me where he is." Roman reached out to catch the smaller man's shoulder.

Wong seemed almost not to notice, but one moment the Chinaman was standing passively, and the next Mr. Roman's arm had shot harmlessly past his narrow shoulder. And the next, Wong was standing very close to the journalist. "Are you quite all right, sir?" he inquired.

"No, damn it, by the Deity, I'm not all right." Roman's arm moved again. But this time it was to pound his frustrations out on the studio wall, causing a hairline crack to appear on the rose-patterned wallpaper. Esther, who had backed against the darkroom door to avoid his fury, bit her lip. He frightened her with his shouting and his violence. She sighed. Robert was not an evil man, merely excitable. And he was, after all, Oz Cook's friend.

"I'm sorry," Esther said timidly, stepping out from the haven of her doorway. "Is there anything I can do?"

He gaped at her, then pointed a blunt finger. "You," he said.

She looked bewildered.

"You'll have to do. Get what you need and come with me."

"I don't under—"

"I've had a tip that something is going to happen at Union Square. I need you to make pictures."

A ripple of excitement ran through Esther. She could do it. She'd taken Oz Cook through the tenements, helped him with his photographic shots. And she'd gone out herself, on her own.

Wong was watching her, as usual giving no indication of what was going on in his mind.

More quietly, with some deference, Robert Roman said to Wong, "Get the cart." To Esther, he said, "Tell me what you need."

Esther pointed to the tripod leaning against the wall. She would take the precious new camera from Kodak, scarcely used. "One moment." She reopened the door to the darkroom. She examined the plate under the water that she'd been working on. It was too soon to take it out. If she left it . . . ?

"I'll have to prepare the plates," she said.

"Do it, then," he said.

Shutting the door again, she turned off the red light. The photographic plates came individually wrapped in black paper. By feel, she removed the paper from each plate and placed it in a lighttight holder.

Robert Roman thumped on the door. "Can't you hurry this—"

Trying not to let him unsettle her more than he already had, she completed her task, switched on the red light, and returned the prepared plates to the slotted box.

"I'm ready now," she said, opening the door.

"I'll take that." Robert hefted the box of plates onto his shoulder. "Wong, you get the tripod."

"Please be careful," she cautioned him, as they made their way down the broad staircase to the front entrance. She set the camera on the hall table while she drew on her light cloak and settled her hat upon her thick hair, attaching it with a hatpin.

"Come along, come along," Robert muttered. His impatience ruled him.

Esther looked about. "The cart—"

"Outside," Wong told her, opening the door.

When they were on the street, the equipment piled into the four-wheeled cart, she thought, what am I doing? But it was only for a brief moment, for Robert was talking.

"Please tell me where we're going," Esther demanded. "And I must know what it is you want me to photograph."

"A rally . . . police . . . take as much as you can . . . Damn Oz, anyway . . ." He was racing ahead of her, jerking the cart with an angry energy in the direction of Union Square.

She clutched the precious camera tightly. "Where will I be? I need the light, and unobstructed lines of sight—"

"I have just the place," he called over his shoulder. "Can't you move faster? We must get there before the riot begins."

9

Thursday,
May 30.
Noon.

The sounds of Union Square thundered in her ears when they were a good two blocks away. Still, it was only another slice of the babel that was New York. It mixed easily with the bells of horsecars and the clatter of vehicles on the cobblestones.

The square was landscaped with lawns and trees, bordered on all sides by fine buildings, some lofty, their flags all flapping in the brisk spring breeze. Benches and asphalt walks and the music of a bubbling fountain created an illusion of country in the city. This section of town swarmed continually with New Yorkers of every stripe, but it was often the setting, too, for rallies and demonstrations. New Yorkers were vocal about their rights; quick to take offense at real or imagined slights, they were indeed a demonstrating lot.

Esther knew there were lamps among the greenery on the square that transformed the darkest night into day. No need of that now, although the sun was hazy, in and out from behind clouds. But Union Square was the perfect setting for making photographs.

And oh, the many subjects! For here, the ordinary mixed with the poor and the rich. But by far the most visible and constant in the square were the street cleaners and the nannies.

In their crisp white uniforms topped with snowy caps, nursemaids pushed perfectly garbed babes in ornate carriages or held the hands of toddlers, who stepped unsteadily on fat little legs.

Vying with the white caps of the nannies were the uniforms and caps of the ubiquitous White Wings. In January, Mayor William Strong's appointee, Colonel George E. Waring, had assumed office as Street Cleaning Commissioner in charge of a new corps of street cleaners. For the past week, one could not walk the respectable parts of the City without seeing a White Wing in his white ducks pushing his broom, filling his cart with refuse.

The White Wings were less visible in the poorer sections, more was the pity. Still, they were more evident than the blue-suited policemen, the sadder pity.

Today no huge parade of workers crowded the avenues around Union Square. A straggle of fewer than a hundred painters, plasterers, and carpenters circled the square in some formation, while many more congregated in the Park and on the streets watching the entertainment. The marching workers, however, were a vociferous lot; their voices made up for their lack of numbers.

They bore placards proclaiming:

"On to Victory!"

"We Build Good We Should Live Good!"

"Pay No Rent."

"Agitate. Educate. Organize."

"Labor Creates All Wealth."

"All Men Are Born Equal!"

"The True Remedy Is Organization & The Ballot."

"Labor Pays All Taxes."

"8 Hours Constitute A Days Work."

"Come along, come along," Robert chided.

Esther was walking as quickly as she could to keep up with him and the cart. The journalist pivoted slightly, indicating something behind him with his chin. "Keep your wits about you," he ordered. "It's about to start."

Turning, she saw a group of toughs begin to congregate. As she watched, their numbers swelled.

Robert explained, "They work for the La Belle Association, the contractors." He stopped and pointed to a slight rise in front of a shop, where someone had just tugged down its window shade. "Can you make your pictures from here?" He didn't wait for her to answer, but was already planting the tripod.

She studied the light from the spot. It was perfect. "But what shall I photograph?"

"Everything."

"But I have only ten plates."

"That will have to suffice. Here, I'll do that."

"No," she said firmly. This was something she had learned to do by herself, knowing she would not always have a male companion to help her. With concentrated effort, she lifted the folding Kodak view camera from the cart. It measured six inches by eight inches, was a foot deep, and very heavy. She set the camera on its tripod and adjusted the angle of the lens.

Robert watched her intently. He said, "My idea will revolutionize journalism. I've convinced Mr. Bennett—he's the Managing Editor at the *Herald*—that we can use halftones from your photographs to illustrate my story instead of line block illustrations. No one has done it yet in a respectable daily." Roman laughed bitterly. "It takes a Guinea to show them the way."

When she was sure the camera was steady on its legs, she inspected the bellows.

"Can't you hurry, girl?"

"I'm trying, Robert, but making a photograph is a lengthy process." What it was, was a science, she thought. A science and an art combined. But this impatient man wanted miracles. Not even Oz could shoot so fast and get proper photographs. If she rushed it, the picture would not be clear.

Roman's face was flushed with excitement. "Do you see that?" He pulled on his mustache, pointing at the crowd with his other hand. "That's Clubber Williams behind those cops. He's off the Force. Why is he here? Keep an eye out for him. I'd love to have a photograph of Clubber in the middle of something." Agitated, he turned this way and that, searching every face, examining every cluster of men. "I've hired a carriage to take me to the paper. Are you ready?"

"I am working on it." She could barely see the large man with the big mustache that Robert had pointed out, and as she watched, he disappeared from her view entirely.

"Very well. Perhaps I'd better stand on the street and point out what you must photograph," Roman called to her as he stepped into the fray, but she was already deep into her preparation; later she would remember only vaguely what he had said.

The bellows was all right, but there were so many things to see to. It was taking her too long. She was working faster than she'd ever worked before and it wasn't fast enough. A rumble of noise came from the square, a change in tempo which she grasped unconsciously.

Esther removed the first of her ten dry plates from the slotted wood box. She loaded it into the camera. She looked out at the confusion on the street. Finally, she saw Roman waving at her.

She ducked under the hood and looked through the lens. What she saw was what she was supposed to capture, but the image was upside down. This was normal. There was a smudge on the lens. She cleaned the smudge with a dry cloth and looked again. The focus was wrong.

At last, after two more adjustments, she was ready. She pulled up the holder.

A shout and then a piercing scream caught her unawares. Two brutish men lifted a man who clutched a placard and threw him into the street, then kicked him about as if he were a soccer ball. Like the Cossacks, she thought. And no one stopped them. Where were the police? Where was Robert? She should have made a photograph of the Cossacks. It would have been a good picture.

They were doing it again to another now. The sun slipped out from behind the clouds in time to confuse her light; nevertheless, she pressed the bulb, and shoved down the holder. No time to wonder if she'd been quick enough to catch the brutes on film or if her lens had been correct. Or if her exposure was right. Two seconds. Had the shutter been open long enough? She doubted it.

This was her first attempt of making photographs of people in real life. Moving. All of her work heretofore had been of buildings, or of Oz. Not Wong, for he would have nothing to do with the camera. Oz sat perfectly still in the studio where she could hold the shutter open for a count of three, or four, and be certain of getting enough light and a good exposure.

She removed the plate and inserted a fresh one.

Under the hood again, she saw through the lens a black-bearded organ grinder standing with his organ watching the fray. His beard would look wonderful in a picture. Such contrast. She made his photograph.

When she changed her plate once more and looked through the lens, she saw four boys racing through the crowd, snagging wallets from the onlookers. She made their photograph just as one stopped and looked directly at her.

The square had become a madhouse. Yelling, cries of pain, and obscenities came from all sides. The German band began to play. She took a picture of the band just as the clarinetist used his instrument to fend off a blow. He did not succeed. The instrument, however, survived. The clarinet player was a different story. His face was bruised, his ear torn and bleeding.

In spite of her sympathy, Esther found herself concerned not with the musician, but with whether her photograph would come out. She flushed at the shame of it, but was immediately distracted by more screaming.

Things were happening too fast. The band fled, all in a swarm, clutching their instruments. Changing plates again, Esther made a photograph of the band as they ran for their lives across the teaming square, away from men with clubs.

Through the lens she saw the fearful bloody face of a dark-haired lad of fifteen at the most. The boy was short of stature, wearing loose-fitting coarse brown knickers that drooped at the knees and waist. His shirt had once been white, but now was filthy. He had no collar, his sleeves were rolled up, and he wore a green vest and a black cap. The sole of his left shoe was tied in place with cord.

He was beautiful. Esther made his picture.

Blood streamed down young Jack Meyers's face. The boy dabbed at it with his bare forearm and dodged into an entranceway. He patted his face for cuts. Nothing bad. He'd taken the tough's blow square in the nose, but it wasn't broken. The only bad thing was his ears: they still rang like fire alarm bells. His heart beat fast from the fear of it. A good schnapps could cure that, but alas, he had no hope of that. On the street they were all still beating on each other. No more for him, thank you. Down the dark hallway Jack found a dry spot under the stairs. He would catch himself forty winks until the riot was over.

Howling in Yiddish, waving her hands, an old woman clutched a little boy. One of the thugs kicked the woman to her knees and picked up the boy. The boy bit the thug's hand; with a curse, the man dropped him. The lad crawled quickly to the old woman, who had fallen facedown in the gutter.

Esther made the photograph.

There were shrieks, panicky horses neighing.

Esther made a picture.

A police wagon arrived, heralded by a piercing whistle. It rode into the crowd, knocking people down, scattering others, hugger-mugger.

Esther made the photograph. She'd been counting. This was number ten, the final plate.

PART TWO

The Puzzle

10

Thursday,
May 30.
Early afternoon.

Two men, each wielding a club, were fighting barely two feet in front of her. The clubs made dreadful thudding noises as they clashed. Esther was afraid for herself, the camera, and the plates. Part of her mind was telling her what a good picture the fight would make, but she had no more plates, nor a proper way of capturing such motion. She was suddenly stifling. She tore off her cloak and dropped it on the box of plates in the cart.

Carefully, she saw to her camera, setting it back in the cart next to the box of exposed plates. She tucked the tripod in beside the camera and spread her cloak over the lot. No sense in letting would-be thieves know what she had. Seeing nary a sign of Robert, she started away.

A policeman's nightstick buzzed by her head; it whacked one of the two brawlers, who were now rolling on the cobble. The officer sped past her, retrieved his club, then wielded it again and again, not caring which man he hit.

Esther murmured a prayer for the poor souls injured this day; she felt faint, as if she were going to be sick. Jostled by others all eager to leave the scene of the riot, she lifted her skirt and tugged the cart, not looking back till she reached the Sixteenth Street corner. The cart banged along behind her. Worried that the fragile glass plates were now nothing but shards inside their holders, she dared not stop; the violence was too terrifying.

At last! She was in the clear. She slowed and took deep breaths. She was sure her face was dirty, but she desperately wanted to assure herself the plates were not damaged. So in spite of being out of danger, she couldn't dawdle. She must get back to Oz's brownstone. She had to develop her negatives.

The blow came without warning, striking her behind the knees as she approached Eighteenth Street. Esther crumpled backward on the rough walk. "No!" She grabbed for the cart, struggling to pull herself up. A powerful hand swatted her easily to the ground. She heard the cart moving away.

"Please . . . don't take his camera . . ." Esther moaned.

Jack Meyers woke to the sound of rain. He rubbed his eyes, finger-combed his thick black hair, and ventured toward the light and the front door of the building. Not rain, but the water wagon.

This was a new parade. The White Wings, pushing their brooms, followed the water wagon. The water dispenser was nothing more than a giant barrel resting on its side on a wooden bed. It sported three spigots at its back; each rained on the roads. Street arabs, urchins, ran behind, poking their bare legs under the barrel's flow for a quick wash and cool.

Jack was cautious. None of the *mamzers* who'd beat on him earlier seemed about. He ran to the back of the wagon and joined the other boys, thrusting his hand under the center tap for a palmful of water.

"And who do you think you're shoving?" The burly red-haired boy's fists were clenched and there was fire in his eyes.

"Pardon," Jack said, but he managed to get his measure of water before he withdrew. Eagerly, he sucked the water from his hand.

"Look at the sheeny bastard, sucking like a whore." It was the red-haired Irisher again.

Jack shrugged and started off.

But the Irish boy wasn't having any of that. "Hey, Yid, where the hell do you think you're going?"

"My own way."

"My own way," the boy whined, mocking Jack.

Jack Meyers turned and walked. When he heard feet smacking the cobble behind him, he ran. He could hear the boy gaining. Suddenly Jack stopped and stood with his right hand cocked. When the Irisher came in range, Jack Meyers let go. *Slam*, right into his face.

The red-haired boy took the blow, shook his head only a little, then laughed. "My name is Spike Riley, and I'll make you crawl on your belly. I'm the toughest there is in the Frog and Toe."

Oh, shit, Jack Meyers screamed inside his head. Why do all *goyim* have to be such *shtarkers*? A carriage passed him slowly, then halted beside the curb. If he could get into it and out the other side, he could outrun the Irish *mamzer*.

Spike Riley jabbed a left. Jack Meyers, who always raged at the heaven he didn't believe in about his small stature, now thanked the God he didn't believe in for his speed as he swiftly sidestepped one punch, then another.

When Jack saw his opening, he threw a right.

Spike knew how to sidestep, too. That's what he did; he hit Jack with a blow that just about crushed his chest. Jack fell to his knees, gasping for breath.

His enemy approached, both meaty hands hanging loose and feet at the ready.

But Jack's luck stayed with him. From where he was kneeling on the ground he punched. He missed the Irisher's groin but connected solidly on the thigh, sending the other boy sideways with a yelp of pain.

This was his chance. Jack bounced up and ran for the carriage, whose big black horse was drinking water from a bucket. Jack wrenched open the door. "Get, get, get," he yelled impulsively, hoping the animal would carry him to safety. The horse flicked his tail as he would for a pesky fly and did not even look up from its drink.

Scrambling across leather seats to the opposite door, Jack Meyers pushed it open, only to see Spike awaiting him on the other side. He slammed the door, held a moment, then opened it again. The Irisher hadn't been fooled. He was waiting. This time with a mouthful of spit. He spat. That was *his* mistake.

The spittle missed Jack Meyers, who had slammed the door shut again. Now the ugly gob was dripping down the stately black carriage door.

"How dare you," roared the carriage driver, a gigantic man with hair so closely cropped the skin of his head shone in the sun. He'd been watching the little bout of fisticuffs with some amusement. But he wasn't amused now.

The driver leaped down. His huge head seemed to sit directly on his keg chest. Two hundred pounds of solid muscle. Only the many small scars around his eyes betrayed the fights he'd been in. Seizing Spike Riley, the driver used him bodily as a rag, wiping the offending spittle from the door with the boy's fat ass. When he was satisfied with his char work, he flung the boy to the cobbles.

Much to his credit, Spike jumped up again, his fists ready.

The carriage man grinned. "Don't try me, boy, you're far from ready." He pointed like an actor in a melodrama. "Go! Before I forget you're only a snotty kid."

Spike backed away, so angry he sputtered at the driver. He no longer cared about the little sheeny in the carriage.

The driver opened the carriage door.

This one had his fists up, too. But this one made him laugh. The carriage man spread his hands. "Out, boy," he told Jack Meyers. "No more fisticuffs today."

"Yes, mister," Jack Meyers said, but, wary, he didn't move.

"What are you waiting for? An invitation from Victoria? Out. I've got to pick up my gent." The boy stepped to the sidewalk and the driver closed the door. "A minute," he said, eyeing the offensive smudge on his otherwise shiny black door. "There's a rag under my seat, boy. Steal some of my nag's water and buff this up for me."

The boy climbed up on the seat, found the rag, and was down on the ground straightaway. "Good afternoon, old horse," Jack mumbled to the animal, rubbing the horse's muzzle.

"His name's Sullivan," the carriage driver said, admiring the lad's manner with the horse. "You know who Sullivan was, boy?"

The boy shook his head.

"Heavyweight champion for ten years, till '92. John L., the best. The world's greatest pugilist. Get on with your work."

Jack took a handful of water, took a taste, then dribbled the rest on the cloth he'd gotten from under the driver's seat.

"What's your name, lad?" the driver asked as the boy rubbed zealously at the door.

"Jack, mister."

The driver laughed. "Don't that beat all? That's my name, too. Battling Jack West they called me, when I fought. Well, Little Jack, how'd you like to work for me? With my horses. You could do worse. I started in horses, but I'm planning on bigger things."

Little Jack grinned. "I'd like that a lot, mister."

"Climb on back while I go pick up my gentleman, and I'll think on it. Meanwhile you think on not leading with your right anymore. You could get yourself killed that way."

II

Thursday,
May 30.
Early afternoon.

A *detective, wearing the suit and derby that marked his office, stepped out* of the café. He jammed his bowler hat onto corn yellow hair that grazed his collar. "What in hell is going on here?"

The detective had stopped in at Healy's Café for a beer and a bite and a word with Healy, himself, about who Down-to-the-Ground Conn Clooney had been talking to lately. Because as much as Conn liked setting fires, he never lit a match without cash on the barrelhead. Conn liked to say that no man but a blockhead ever set fires except for money.

A woman's angry "Stop, thief!" had pulled the detective outside on the run.

He observed two things immediately: a man bent low, his rear end disappearing 'round the corner on Eighteenth Street, and a dark-haired girl, her face and clothing streaked with dirt, searching the disordered contents of her cart.

Two strides took him to her. Good God, it was the white-rose camera girl he had seen earlier in the day taking photographs of the Bank of America Building. He picked up her blue straw hat from the street. Like the girl, it was dainty, pretty, and dirt-smudged. "Did he get anything?"

When she silenced him with her right hand, the detective had the grace not to laugh at her haughty manner. "I am investigating," she said, in some sort of greenhorn accent, he didn't know which. From the look of her she was going to have a beauty of a black eye tomorrow. She probed under the cloak covering the contents of the cart, then lifted her head, and granted him a small smile. Her hand twitched nervously on the cloak-covered box. "All here," she reported.

The detective liked her pluck as much as he liked the look of her. She was like a small dark bird in her white shirtwaist and black skirt. Her waist was so narrow he could span it easily with his hands. The thought took him by surprise. "Are you all right?"

The girl braced her shoulders and said, "I'm fine, thank you." She tucked up the escaping strands of her dark hair and reached out to him.

"Oh? Yes, here." He gave her the hat. "Glad to be of help, miss. Anytime. Detective Sergeant John Tonneman, at your service."

While he spoke she was pinning her hat to her hair with a long pin.

Practically mimicking her actions, Dutch Tonneman adjusted his derby to his head and placed his fingers to its brim in salute.

Esther stole a look at the young policeman. He was tall and very fair, with ruddy skin and serious blue eyes. He looked quite impressive in his suit and derby hat. Tonneman? Esther's ears were as good as her eyes. In spite of the name she detected the lilt of Irish in his speech. He had come to her aid, and she was grateful. "Thank you, Sergeant Tonneman. I was afraid for my equipment, but everything is safe. Good day."

"Pardon me, miss. Your name? For the records." He produced a small pad and pencil from his pocket.

She seemed reluctant to answer. "Esther Breslau," she said haltingly.

"Where do you live?" He liked her soft accent.

"Gramercy Park."

"What number?"

"Five."

Was she Russian? Gramercy Park was not home for young immigrant girls unless they were housemaids. The homes around the park were still occupied by fine old families, though some had started moving uptown along Fifth Avenue, to the fifties and farther.

"May I go now?" she asked, disquiet in her dark eyes.

He didn't answer. He didn't want her to leave, but he had no reason to detain her. No, he decided, she wasn't part of the upper crust, either. Her face was exotic, with high cheekbones and feathery eyebrows. But her hands, though small, were a working girl's. They'd been stuck with needles and soaked in hot water along the way. Seamstress maybe? Maid? Perhaps a nanny not wearing her white. A Hebrew, most likely. Tiny as his ma, yet dark as Meg Tonneman was fair. "I'm John Tonneman."

"So you've already told me," the girl said curtly. "May I go, please?"

"Yes, ma'am." He tipped his hat.

She picked up the handle to the cart and, head high, marched up Park Avenue.

He watched her go smartly on her way, hauling the cart behind her. The girl showed slim ankles above short black boots which accommodated her feet quite nicely.

Dutch was disappointed that their exchange was over. But now that he knew where she lived, he intended to see her again.

"Help! Police! Somebody help me!"

The shout came from near Seventeenth Street, from the direction the would-be thief had gone. Tonneman ran. When he turned the blind corner, he had just enough time to duck before the cosh came crashing down.

Esther watched the detective race off at the cry for help. He was certainly a brave young man, but she had no time for young men, brave or otherwise. She had to get back with the plates and equipment. Optimistically, she hoped that Wong would have Oz home by now. If not, Esther knew she was competent to develop the negatives herself.

She was stunned when the blow came as before, in the back of her knees. Only this time, making it even more horrible, a bag was slipped over her head as she fell. Her scream was muffled in burlap that stank of onions.

• • •

Tonneman was quick enough to take the blow on his right shoulder. He staggered but didn't fall. Perversely, he was heartened by the pain. Had the blow struck its mark, he knew his head would have opened like a pumpkin. The hitter wore a bandanna over the lower part of his face. White spots on blue.

Moving in close, Tonneman grabbed the throat beneath the bandanna. His strong fingers tightened; the man sank to his knees.

A muffled scream floated on the balmy May air.

"I got it, Terry!" Both the scream and the shout came from behind Tonneman. The girl! This was a ruse. He must get back to the girl.

Tonneman shook his attacker and threw him to the sidewalk as if he were a rag bundle, leaving the man tearing away at his bandanna and vomiting in the gutter. Tonneman ran back to the girl. She lay on the ground, flailing, her head and shoulders hidden in a burlap bag. What the hell did this lass have that these culls wanted? The second thief was running up the street. Spying a chunk of brick in the gutter, Tonneman scooped it up and threw it at the running man's legs. The brick hit, but not true enough; the man stumbled only momentarily and kept going.

Muffled cries came from the girl. She sat up, pulling the burlap bag from her head. She was a tough one, she was. Tonneman, satisfied that she was unharmed, went on in pursuit of the second thief. This one was also masked; more important, he was toting a wood box that must have come from the girl's cart. The first thief had been big, Tonneman's size. This one was a skinny fellow. And fast. Tonneman ran harder. He ought to have been gaining on the skinny Bone, but in spite of his tote the Bone was pulling even farther away.

Behind him Tonneman heard the girl yelling through the sound of hooves and wheels. "Robert, he has the box of plates."

"Thief!" Tonneman yelled. Who the hell was Robert?

Bystanders took up his cry. "Stop, thief!"

The pound of hooves, then the clattering of wheels was on top of him. A brougham flew past, rattling over the cobble, it climbed the sidewalk. The big black stallion who pulled it all but pinned the thief to the wall of a building. The cull, still hugging the box to his chest, slid down the wall.

The thief took it all in: the black horse, slavering on him, blowing hot rancid hay breath, its huge teeth ready to devour him; the giant of a driver, wielding a long whip; and the copper approaching on the run. Delicately the thief set the box on the sidewalk under the horse's massive head and raised his hands.

The brougham driver held his black horse back, but not much. "Easy, Sullivan. Shall I give the bony bastard the whip, Mr. Roman?"

"That won't be necessary, Jack. All I want is the box."

Suddenly the thieving cull had the box in his possession again under his left arm. Barely touching the drooling animal's head with his right hand, the miscreant leap-frogged onto the animal's back. The stallion whinnied and nipped at him. With the agility of a bridge worker, the thief traversed the horse's back, ducked under Battling Jack's outstretched arms, and scrambled across the flat-topped carriage, over, and down onto the cobble before the three watching men could blink.

Battling Jack was the first to move. Up he went from his driver's seat, over the top. At that moment Little Jack Meyers lunged from his station on the carriage boot and tackled the thief. Down they both went, neither letting go of the box. Esther, watching it all, held her breath.

High atop the carriage, Battling Jack roared. The cull heard, cast one frightened look at Battling Jack, then gave up the box in favor of his life. He ran like the thief he was, leaving Little Jack Meyers in possession of the precious wooden box.

• 12 •

Thursday,
May 30.
Early afternoon.

T*onneman didn't know if he could catch the wily son of a bitch. He was* ready to give it a try when the gent in the brougham called, "Never mind, Detective. The important thing is we've got the plates." The gent opened the door and stepped out. For all the big voice, he was a stubby man. His straw hat had a dent in its brim and was set back on a thatch of shaggy brown hair. Disheveled though his appearance was, he sported an oversized yellow cravat.

Aha, Tonneman said to himself. So that's what was so important about that wooden box. Plates. What kind of plates? Gold? They had to be something special indeed to warrant two culls doubling up on the girl, giving her the one-two like that.

Dutch Tonneman was his own man and he was no rookie. Experience had taught him that one didn't ignore a man in a fine carriage. You never knew who he was connected to. And this one felt very connected; there was the smell of Tammany about him. One thing Dutch didn't need was to have the Democratic political machine down on him. "Yes, sir." Tonneman glanced at the girl, who was brushing herself off. "And no one seems to be hurt," he added.

"That, too," the gent replied, handling the box with utmost care.

The two men both began to move toward the girl, as if in silent competition for her attention.

At their approach the girl stood straight and still, indicating she needed no aid at all. She spoke to the gent. "I pray the plates are all right. I'll take them back to the darkroom and develop them for you."

Roman scratched his head under the dented boater. "I think not. I need them for my story. *I'll* take them to the *Herald*. There's a man there can do the job for me."

From the crestfallen expression on the girl's face, Tonneman saw she was upset. Photograph plates. These plates were the glass plates used in photography. End of the puzzle. All so simple.

"Of course, Robert," the girl said quietly, her animated spirit squelched.

The journalist nodded to Tonneman. "Thank you for your help, Detective . . . ?"

"Tonneman, sir."

Robert Roman brought a silver coin from his pocket and pressed it on the detective.

Tonneman flipped the two bits to the lad who'd saved the box. "Here, boy. You earned it."

The ragtag's deft hand reached out and caught the coin. He grinned. "Thanks, mister!" Finally, thought Jack Meyers, America was starting to fulfill its promise to him.

Not to be outdone, Roman pulled out another coin. "You have a fine sense of what is proper, Detective. No one can say Robert Roman doesn't value that, or is ungrateful. Please take this dollar for your trouble."

Tonneman lifted his bowler. This time he accepted the coin. Let the man have his gesture. Besides, a dollar was a dollar. "What's so important about those photograph plates?" he asked.

"The riot in Union Square," Roman replied.

"Riot? I'd better be off then, to see what's what."

"It's done with now. I've got the story. The unions against the bosses' thugs. Mayhem and blood everywhere. And if this little girl took even one picture right, I'll revolutionize the newspaper game. My reputation will be made."

"I hope I haven't failed you, Robert." Though the girl was all manners and politeness, Dutch knew by the two red spots high on her cheeks that she was more than unhappy with the turn of events.

"Detective Tonneman, if you would be good enough to see Miss Breslau home—"

"There's no need," Esther said quickly.

"I should see what's happening in the square," Tonneman protested, even though he was more than willing to take Miss Breslau home.

"Never you mind. Your comrades have no doubt cleaned it up by now. Besides, Moose is a friend of mine. I'll make it good with him."

Moose? So the man was not Tammany, after all. Nonetheless, Tonneman had heard that Moose-is-a-friend-of-mine story before. But it was true enough. Moose had friends everywhere, from Injun chiefs to fire chiefs. "I'll be glad to, sir."

"Let's go, Jack," Roman called to the huge driver. He handed the box to the boy, who stashed it on the floor of the carriage.

The big driver leaped to his seat, the boy scrambled to the carriage boot. "Ready, Mr. Roman." Battling Jack's whip cut through the air. "Let's go, Sullivan." The black horse took off along Park Avenue, and turned uptown toward the *Herald*'s new offices on Thirty-fourth Street in Herald Square.

The girl stared after the departing carriage, its shiny exterior dazzling in the afternoon sun.

"Here, miss, I'll take the cart," Tonneman said. He was trying to remember where he'd heard the name Robert Roman before, for he surely had, and recently, too.

This time Esther made no effort to stop him. He touched her elbow. How small the lass was. The skin about her bruised eye was rapidly turning blue.

"He should have let me finish the work," she murmured, as if to herself.

"What would a thief want with your picture plates?" Tonneman asked.

"I don't know." They were walking now. Gramercy was not far. "I would have thought they wanted the camera." She tilted her head toward the cart where the new Kodak camera sat untouched. "It's very valuable."

No. 5 Gramercy Park West proved to be a fine town house. To the left of the entrance, behind a painted wrought-iron fence, was a little garden. Ivy climbed the building all the way up to the roof. There were flower boxes in the windows on the lower floors. Three slate steps led down to a tiny court and the front door.

Tonneman lifted the cart down the steps and pushed it to the door. "This is where you live?"

"Yes," the girl said, following. "The house belongs to Mr. Oswald Cook, the eminent photographer. No doubt you've heard of him?" She lifted her chin higher. "I am his assistant," she declared, conscious of his touch on her elbow, the tobacco scent on his clothing.

"Ah, that's quite a job for such a young girl."

"I am eighteen, sir." She drew herself up to the fullness of her meager height. Only then did she catch the twinkle in his eye. "Oh," she whispered, blushing.

An onion skin had attached itself to her shirtwaist sleeve. He picked it off. "And are you spoken for, Miss Breslau?" He raised his hand to the brass knocker, but the door opened before he knocked. Good Lord, there stood a living, breathing Chinaman, pigtail and all. It was the first Dutch had seen this side of Pell Street.

"Miss Esther." He looked Tonneman over, identifying him immediately as a policeman. Now he looked at Esther's left eye. "Is there trouble?" Another surprise. This Chinkie talked like a Limey.

Esther's only response was to shake her head.

"She's going to have a proper black eye," Tonneman told the Chinaman. "Better see to it."

The Chinese fellow picked up the cart and placed it inside. He didn't respond to Tonneman.

"Spoken for?" Esther was frowning. "What does that mean?" Now a smile played at her lips. John Tonneman was intrigued. Who was teasing who this time?

"It means," he said, "May I call on you? . . . Miss Esther." He liked the foreign taste of her name on his tongue.

She looked at Wong, who remained, as usual, without expression. The big policeman was expecting an answer. What should she say? He wanted to call on her.

"Put a steak on that eye," Tonneman said. "It'll keep the bruising down." He pulled his watch out. "I should be getting to Mulberry Street. . . ."

Dangling from the watch on a small chain was a gold-and-seeded-pearl pendant in the shape of a shield, engraved with Hebrew letters. The word they spelled was *Shadai*. How extraordinary, Esther thought. Had she been ready to say yes to his invitation before she'd seen the name of God hanging on his watch?

"Perhaps you can tell me all about your work," he said, pocketing his gold watch.

"Perhaps I can." And perhaps he could explain how a Jewish man had come to be a policeman. "Thank you for your assistance." She smiled at him. "Good afternoon."

Tonneman waited till the fine oak door closed. In his left hand he still held the onion skin he'd plucked from her sleeve. He raised the petal of onion and breathed its sweet perfume. Only then did he turn toward Mulberry Street.

• 13 •

Thursday, May 30. Late afternoon.

Clubber Williams, *also known as Whiskers, because of his large handle*-bar mustache and a sprouting of whiskers under his lower lip, had moved doggedly up through the ranks of the Metropolitan Police Department with the determination of a bullmastiff until he reached the pinnacle of good fortune: the 29th Precinct.

The 29 was Clubber's own private little fiefdom. It included not only the juicy Rialto—the theatre district—but also the most fertile spot for vice and graft in the City: the Tenderloin.

Clubber liked to boast that he'd given the area its name when he was transferred there from the 21st, nineteen years before.

According to Williams, on his arrival at the 29 he had licked his lips at the corruption and the money-making vice going on there. Neither facts nor morality ever got in Clubber's way. He'd just as soon steal your words or your thoughts as your money. At the 29, envisioning huge bribes and every form of graft he could imagine, Clubber told a friend, "I've had nothing but chuck steak for a long time, and now I'm going to get a little of the tenderloin."

The truth about how the Tenderloin district got its name was that one night shortly after he had taken over the 29's station at West Thirtieth Street, Clubber took a little walk and dropped into Delmonico's Restaurant at Twenty-sixth and Fifth. There, he spotted Abe Hummel, the renowned lawyer of Howe & Hummel fame. Hummel, with his partner William Howe, was responsible for most of the criminals in New York City still being free to ply their trade.

Clubber, who thought he was a jokester and wasn't, rubbed his big nose and wiggled his big ears and called in his whiskey voice, "You'd better behave yourself, Mr. Hummel, or you won't be coming in here for any more of them juicy beefsteaks you're always eating."

"Speaking of that, Inspector," Hummel replied, continuing to gnaw his enormous steak, "that's a pretty juicy tenderloin they just handed you."

Clubber's collections from the vermin in the Tenderloin paid for his good life, his suite at the Broadway Central Hotel on Third Street between Broadway and Mercer, and all the fine things in his house in Cos Cob, Connecticut.

But alas, that was now in the past. Six days earlier, on Friday, May 24, Clubber had been kicked out of his office in the House on Mulberry Street. He was no longer Inspector of the 29th Precinct. Out on his ass.

Forced into retirement by the fucking four-eyed Moose.

Retirement? Maybe from the cops, but not from the Tenderloin. And certainly not from any other succulent cuts of the beef New York had to offer. With all that money still to be got, Clubber Williams was not yet ready to retire.

But he'd been one step ahead of the fecking Moose, he had. Alexander Williams, he was now, private citizen, with a nice little business going for him. And a nice little gang, augmented by the newly ex-cops from the Department.

Alexander Williams, private citizen, offered services. That's what it said on his business card in big bold letters: SERVICES.

These services included cracking skulls for various bosses. Hell, he'd even been asked to crack boss skulls for strikers and demonstrators. Clubber had no problem with that. As long as the money came in. His services also involved protection from rioters and any damage they might cause. And should a businessman or landlord want to start from scratch, thorough housecleaning services could be supplied.

Alexander Williams's company was always ready with the right men for the right job. Clubber was particularly good at finding people to burn the trash.

14

Thursday,
May 30.
Afternoon to evening.

Jack Meyers's heart sang. After dropping Mr. Roman at the Herald *on* Thirty-fourth Street, Battling Jack had told Little Jack he was a first-rate sheeny and that the job was his. The boy was to be at the stable at 26 Washington Square North at five the next morning. Without another word, Battling Jack flicked his reins and clattered away.

Little Jack had a quarter burning a hole in his pocket. It was enough to buy a frankfurter sausage, what they now called a hot dog. Hell, he had enough to buy twenty-five. With something in his belly, he would find himself a hallway to sleep in till the morning.

But the best-laid plans . . .

Little Jack wasn't on the street three minutes when, to his astonishment, he saw Mr. Roman being hustled out of the Herald Building by two mugs. One, a big bastard, had a hold of Mr. Roman's arm and looked ready to break it. The second mug was the bone-thin guy Jack had tussled with over the box. Mr. Roman, who still carried that box, didn't look too happy in their company. When the mugs pushed Mr. Roman inside that bakery wagon waiting on the corner, he looked downright miserable.

The bread wagon moved through traffic heading downtown. Little

Jack, with hopes of money to be made, instantly gave chase. He was fine till the cord on his left shoe slipped and he had to go five blocks with the sole flapping so loud he was sure the devil and those in the wagon could hear. The boy was near exhausted when the wagon finally stopped at St. Mark's Place on Second Avenue, across from a church.

The Bone, who'd been driving, jumped down off the wagon box. Jack thought to hit him with a loose cobble, if he could find one, but the only thing available on the street was steaming horse dung. Even if he brought the thief down, then what? He'd still have to deal with the bigger guy.

So Jack waited, his back against a lamppost, playing the sleeping drunk. Pretty soon a third man, even bigger than the second, came out of a gray stone building. The man had his hat pulled down low over his face, so all Jack could see was his big mustache, but hell—almost every man in New York sported one of those. Mustache was angry, cussing something about, "Can't you do a simple job?"

Mustache pounded on the back door of the bakery truck.

"For Christ sakes, open up, Terry," the bony one called. "It's the Boss."

The back swung open. Mustache climbed inside. Little Jack heard a scuffling noise and a yell, followed by a sickening thud that he knew was someone's head being hit. The Bone got back on the box but he didn't touch the reins. Instead, he waited, his head slumped between his narrow shoulders.

The wagon stayed where it was. From time to time, it trembled as if the earth were shaking under it. At first Jack heard cries of pain. Passersby gave no notice at all. When the cries stopped, Jack reckoned Mr. Roman had passed out or had been gagged. Jack wondered what was happening and why. He even considered looking for a policeman. But he hated Cossacks, no matter what they were called. The detective who'd given him the coin was a rare one. Jack didn't trust the others one whit.

So who said America was any different from Lithuania?

15

Thursday,
May 30.

Sophie Mandel was an odd beauty.

Sophie's white-blond hair, which she never covered, and blue eyes were distinctly un-Rumanian, and were the only things of value she had inherited from her Polish father. Though she never laid claim to it, some said her mother was the Rumanian "Marm," Frederika Mandelbaum, who had been an active receiver of stolen goods in New York between 1862 and 1884.

Tall, thin as a wraith, Sophie had alabaster skin and a full bosom to which she was not averse to calling attention. Her beautifully fashioned mouth promised heavenly joys on earth.

There was nothing about Sophie that looked like her supposed mother. Marm, a grossly fat woman, had had a sharply curved mouth and bulging cheeks, beady black eyes, and furry black brows. She wore her black hair tautly wound on top of her head, covered by a tiny black bonnet adorned with limp feathers.

Marm was married to a sharp trader aptly called Wolfe. No one thought Wolfe—not even the man himself—was Sophie's father, for Wolfe, if anything, was an even darker Rumanian than Marm.

Sophie's real father was a Polish actor, born Paul Skidelsky, now known as Byron Brown. The actor lived in a tiny room on Madison Street. Work was fitful in Byron Brown's trade, and it was Sophie who saw to it that he didn't starve. Sophie always took care of her own: her father and her cousin, Leo Stern.

For in spite of her delicate frame and pale skin and her genteel impoverished father, Sophie was a woman of property, and that property, coincidentally, was 79 Clinton Street, corner of Rivington. The Clinton Street address was where Marm and Wolfe had run the most famous fence in New York, if not the world, before Marm jumped bail. Then she and Wolfe had run off to Canada with a son and two daughters and their many millions.

When 79 Clinton Street was Marm's home, it had been furnished with some of the elegant prized possessions from dwellings of the uptown rich. Marm had been First Lady of the criminal elite. Invitations to her extravagant entertainments, dances, and dinners were much sought after; they were frequented by thieves, highly placed police, and politicians.

The same held true now that this was Sophie's house. Except, Sophie's taste in furniture, draperies, rugs, and accessories was a bit more flamboyant than even Marm's. And now all those fine folk *paid* to enter. Sophie's house at 79 Clinton Street was a bordello.

16

Thursday, May 30. Late afternoon— Friday, May 31. After midnight.

N*ot long after the church clock struck twelve, Wong stepped out of the* house on Gramercy Park. Nothing had changed. She had called on the telephone; he would go. It was time.

Two men in evening dress were just being dropped off by a hackney cab in front of the Players Club, on the south block. Wong did not hurry. And the cab did not move; the driver had stopped to light a cigar.

Wong rapped on the cab door as a signal to the driver, calling out, "Take me to 79 Clinton."

"No you don't, Chinkie," the driver said. "First let me see your *gelter*."

Wong, taking a purse from a hidden pocket under his blouse, showed the driver four bits and entered the cab. The ride to Clinton Street was short and uneventful.

The Chinaman drew the window curtain, leaving just a slit, enough to see and not be seen. The only traffic this time of night was wagons and carts bringing produce and meats from the markets, and cabs taking men to and from whorehouses and blind pigs.

On his arrival at Clinton Street, Wong handed the driver fifty cents and spoke to him in the coolie voice the man expected. "You wait, you make double twice." He then made his way to the entrance of the building in shuffling coolie steps.

Above the door of 79 Clinton was a red-globed incandescent lamp. To the side was a red-tasseled pull. He tugged the tasseled cord. The bell inside chimed seven notes of the "Wedding March" from Mendelssohn's *A Midsummer Night's Dream*. Though he did not smile, this always amused Wong. The door opened.

A demure little colored maid, neat and clean in her white lacy apron over her black silk dress, stood in the doorway. "Good evening, Mr. Wong." Daisy giggled. She always giggled when she spoke to Wong. If Wong was small, Daisy was tiny. Even with her lacy white cap the little maid stood hardly to his chin.

On the wall to the left of the entryway was a row of metal hooks, tonight as usual covered with gentlemen's hats. When Daisy reached for his black cap, Wong shook his head and did not remove it. She giggled again; it was a ritual between them.

Under the hooks was a mirror. Most used it for a last-minute inspection. Wong did not take the trouble; he had no interest in mirrors.

On a table, the apparatus stood, candlestick receiver and earpiece, inlaid with mother-of-pearl. When it rang, Daisy seemed to jump a full foot.

She unhooked the listening telephone and placed it close to her ear. "Good evening, Miss Sophie's residence . . . Yes, Mr. Reeves." Painstakingly, Daisy marked an X in one of the boxes on the page in the big book open next to the telephone. "We'll expect you at one." Daisy turned the crank at the base of the telephone and the bell rang sharply, signaling Central that she'd finished. She put the telephone back on its hook.

Wong, who'd been watching the colored girl perform her task, dipped his head almost imperceptibly to her, then strode into the main room. He knew his way.

Tobacco smoke clouded the all too familiar scene. Heavy crimson draperies, matching overstuffed couches, and everywhere silver and gold pillows, and a brand-new gleaming black Steinway piano, all reflected over and over in the many images of the mirrored parlor.

A white china bowl piled high with apples rested at one end of a sideboard. At the sideboard's other end sat a gramophone. Etched red-and-blue flowers decorated the hem of its large copper horn. About the room on every surface were small Venetian glass vases. Each displayed a lone red rose.

The apples did not quite match the color of the gramophone's flowers, but the roses did. At the moment the gramophone was silent, for Piano Man—the lean Negro had no other name—was banging away at the Steinway, its lid propped open to heighten its sound. The instrument Piano Man played stood at the rear of the chamber, to the left of the sideboard and just short of the door. This door opened to a hall. Wong knew that in the hall a steep staircase led up to the bedrooms.

Madame Sophie, her white-blond hair settled on her head like a crown, sat on the center, fancy couch in front of the sideboard. Each time Sophie moved, her low-cut black satin gown threatened to spill her brimming breasts from their tight bodice.

Two black velvet purses rested in her lap. The first held the brass tokens customers bought in order to go upstairs with the beauty of their choice; the second held the cash paid for the tokens. Sophie was surrounded by women of all shapes and sizes, each resting attractively against the plump pillows, each dressed in a tasteful manner.

Sophie and her ladies took delicate sips from their glasses of Dr. Brown's Cel-Ray Soda. Capped bottles of the mixture of celery seed, sugar, and seltzer were arrayed on the low table in front of the couch. When gentlemen bought drinks, the ladies switched to coffee-colored water, for which the gents were charged whiskey prices.

The always immaculate Leo Aaron Stern sat at his table to the right of Sophie. Stern played solitaire with a deck of Black Eagles, his curly hair lustrous with brilliantine, a thick cigar clamped between his gold teeth. On his upper lip, a well-waxed mustache. A brand-new black bowler hat, resplendent with a burgundy band, rested on the table. Leo spat out a bit of tobacco leaf into the brass spittoon, one of several placed about the room. He drew a handkerchief from his inside pocket, took a second to admire the Gothic lettered monogram on it, then with strangely dainty movements wiped his mouth and returned the handkerchief to its place.

The Piano Man was so tall that no matter what height he set the stool, his knees jammed under the piano and his arms arched too high above the board. He was never comfortable reaching for the keys. So most of the time he stood, dancing around, banging away, usually playing what they called ragged time. Mendelssohn to ragged time on the piano. It made no difference to Wong. Western music was all noise to him.

The Musician, in his own way, was as elegant as Leo Stern. He wore a crisp straw hat banded with a blue ribbon the same color as his vest. His yellow-striped shirt collar was fastened with a glistening ruby collar button. He wore no tie, and his sleeves were pulled back from his wrists with crimson garters. A cigarette dangled from his lips. His white teeth reflected the dim red light. The smell of cannabis flavored the smoky air.

Wong preferred opium. The poppy was more soothing than hemp.

"Let me play, I want to play," a drunken oaf was demanding of Piano Man. The Negro glanced at Sophie. She dipped her head ever so slightly. Piano Man pulled his shirt away from his armpits, which were dark with sweat. He took a deep drag from his cigarette without ever putting a hand to it. Then he stood back from the Steinway and waved the customer to the stool.

Only two other customers were in the parlor. They sat at a table near Leo Stern, talking quietly to two young ladies of the establishment. Apparently, for the moment all of the private rooms were taken. Both men, dressed like bankers, were obviously annoyed by the buffoon at the piano.

One of the men raised his voice and said, "If someone doesn't show that idiot what for, I will."

The speaker spat tobacco juice at the spittoon nearby and missed. His associate scrutinized his pocket watch, then blew his nose resoundingly into a large handkerchief. Wong shuddered at this practice of white people. The idea of carrying one's snot about on one's person horrified the Chinese man. Not even the lowest coolie on the docks of Hong Kong did that.

"Here's one from *A Milk White Flag*," the loudmouth shouted, collapsing on the stool. "I saw it last month at Hoyt's before it closed. 'Wouldn't You Like to Fondle Baby.' " Drool dribbled from his mouth. "And that's what I'm here for as soon as my divine Laura can come to me. Get it? *Come* to me. Ain't that a riot?" With this last remark the intoxicated man fell facedown on the keyboard, creating a dissonant chord equal to his behavior.

Leo knew that if the tobacco spitter said it, it would happen. Leo knew this and more, by virtue, if that was the word, of a clubbing and arrest years back in the Tenderloin by the tobacco spitter himself, former Inspector Clubber Williams. Which is why Leo decided to shut the drunk up: in order to save his life. Or at least his health.

Leo laid his cards neatly on the table, rose from his place, and started for the man. Suddenly, the drunken fool lifted his head, sat up straight on the stool, and pulled a small Colt from inside his coat. "Nobody puts their mitts on me."

Leo lifted his arms in surrender, but all the time he was moving closer.

The kick came in midstride. Leo's well-polished shoe tip caught the drunk square on the chin. The man's head snapped back and he was out.

Leo tossed the man's weapon to Daisy, who, having had lots of practice, caught it deftly. But not deftly enough. The Colt went off, shattering a lamp, but luckily not harming any of the mirrors.

All went dead still. Then Sophie roared, "I never did like that light."

Everyone laughed. Daisy said, "I'll put this gun with the others, Mr. Leo."

Leo grinned at the colored girl and lifted the sprawling man from the piano stool by the back of his trousers and coat. He dropped him in a chair across the room. Piano Man took up his position again; following a lingering arpeggio, he began tinkling some blues.

"Well done, Leo," Clubber bellowed.

"Quit those blues, Piano Man," Sophie ordered. "Too early for sad."

Piano Man immediately swung back into ragged time.

Wong studied each of the working girls from under veiled eyes.

He could not understand why American men went so wild over breasts. Chinese men did not consider breasts erotic. In China, breasts were neither concealed nor exposed with the intent of exciting men. Women sat in the sun with naked breasts thrilling no one.

It was further amazing to him how ugly Western women were. Their coarse features, their large cow udders, all that offensive hair on their bodies . . .

While they couldn't possibly excite him, the idea of being here where other men found solace made him think of little Mai Ling in Chinatown. He would have to visit her again soon.

Leo, his small chore completed, nodded a greeting to Wong. The Chinaman answered in kind. Leo walked past the piano to the back door leading to the staircase. Silently, Wong followed him up the stairs and through the long hallway.

Wong knew the route well. Leo's fingers tapped a tattoo on the last door at the end of the corridor. Without waiting for a response he pushed the door and entered. Wong followed and closed the door. The sign on the back of the door jiggled noisily in its frame. Wong didn't read the sign, but he knew what it said. *The women in this house wash their mouths with Listerine, and douche after every rendezvous. They bathe each night after the last client.*

Oz, fully dressed, was half reclined on the bed, his head thrown back on fluffy pink pillows, his topper, stick, and gloves to his side on the bed. "Hello, Leo," he said languidly. "Ah, Wong. It's too soon. I'm not ready to go back." He started to cough, a dry hacking sound that shook his emaciated body.

Wong glanced at Leo. Leo lifted the protesting man and carried him like a baby down the stairs. "So good of you to come," Oz mumbled, his head lolling, as Leo delivered him to the waiting cab.

For Wong, opium was soothing. For Oz Cook, it was mind-killing.

Instructions For N.Y. and N.J. Telephone Subscribers

Turn crank briskly, unhook the listening telephone, and place it close to your ear. Central will ask, "What number?" *Give the Central Office your number, and the number wanted.* If a local call, keep the listening telephone at the ear, until you hear the party asked for.

When through talking, hang the listening telephone on the hook and give your bell a sharp ring to notify the operator that you have finished, thus clearing the line for another call.

17

Friday,
May 31.
After two A.M.

"*It was a good night.*" *Leo whistled a bit of* "*East Side, West Side*" *through* his teeth as he set his bowler on the mantel.

Jangling her velvet pouches, Sophie dropped them on the massive bed. "Any night I make money is a good night to me."

"What an angel you are, dear Sophie." Leo picked up a dog-eared copy of the *Police Gazette* from the table beside the bed. He'd been trying to finish it for a month.

"No, I'm not, and you know it. Daisy?"

The maid appeared instantly.

Leo flipped through the pink pages of "The Leading Illustrated Sporting Journal in America" while Daisy undid the buttons on Sophie's gown, and helped her out of it. "Listen to this story here in the *Pinky* about two girls on Bushwick Avenue in Williamsburg getting into a wrangle over a guy named Dwyer."

The maid loosened Sophie's stays. Sophie murmured, "I can do the rest myself, Daisy. Prepare my bath, then you can go to bed."

"Yes, ma'am."

Leo chuckled. "A ring was set up and everything. The girls wore loose sweaters and 'went at each other savagely.' The cops came and broke it up, but the girls vowed to fight it out another time." Leo opened the night table drawer and took out a packet of Sweet Caporals, the smokes Sophie favored. He lit one, crossed to Sophie, and placed the cigarette between her lips. "Would you go at another woman savagely for me?"

"You know I would."

Leo knew she wouldn't.

Sophie stepped out of her stays. Her breasts did not sag. She knew Leo's eyes were on her. He could never get enough of her. And she liked it that way. The man should want the woman more than the woman wants the man.

She took a hearty puff of the Sweet Cap, snuffed it out in a saucer on her pink vanity, then slipped on a silk dressing gown and sat at the dressing table. Among her creams and pots of colors and powders were two painted miniatures, one of a blond man with a perfect waxed mustache, mature but still almost beautiful. The other was a fat-cheeked older woman with small black eyes, thick black brows, and a turned-down mouth. A wee black bonnet adorned with drooping feathers was settled on tightly rolled black hair, which accentuated the slope of the woman's prominent forehead.

This was Sophie's favorite time of day. Slowly, she removed her gold hairpins. Her thick white-blond hair cascaded to below her waist.

Leo, too, relished their day's end, when all the suckers were gone and he had Sophie to himself. He gathered her hair to his face and breathed deeply.

"Let me brush first."

He kissed the back of her neck, and stepped away, slipping off his coat.

They could hear the dumbwaiter making its passage upward with the hot water, then Daisy's quick footsteps on the stairs.

When she was through brushing her fifty strokes, Sophie climbed on the bed and began to empty the bags to count the money.

"That can wait," Leo told her. "The count won't be any different in the morning."

She smiled. "Marm taught me that men can always wait but money can't."

He took the velvet purses from her hand and dropped them to the floor. "Maybe *men* can wait, but I can't."

Outside the dumbwaiter creaked its slow descent.

18

Friday,
May 31.
After two A.M.

Theodore Allen, known to one and all as The Allen, kept a particularly prosperous saloon on West Broadway.

It wasn't that The Allen made so much money on liquor in his saloon, which he did. But the cream in the coffee was the wheel, the cards, and the dice a man could find upstairs.

The bar itself was what you'd expect. A length of polished mahogany for the drinks, the mirror behind. For the boozers to drool over, sepia photographs of *Police Gazette* Hall of Fame beauties in tights or corsets were tacked on the walls. And for those with baser tastes, naked women.

There was no entrance to the smoke-filled den on the second floor except through the busy saloon and up the narrow staircase where a beefy guard stood, his baseball bat at the ready to enforce his orders. No admission without The Allen's sanction.

The Allen sneered as Byron Brown went sweeping up the stairs like the fucking poof he had to be.

Tall, slender, but decidedly robust for an old man, especially a drunk, Brown's attire was from back in the days of the War, in a fashion usually seen on a stage and not in real life: coat draped nonchalantly over his shoulders, black hat tilted back so his eyes and pomaded and dyed blond hair could catch the light.

The Allen's approval for the old hamfatter was grudgingly given. The cadaverous actor, in his once-fine overcoat trimmed with ratty molting mink, the rings on his fingers sporting glass stones made to look like diamonds, was not The Allen's kind of people.

Still, the old fart lost money, and that was the drill, wasn't it? So what if he didn't have any? The Allen had no complaints. Sophie always paid up, even though she Jewed him down for less.

The good part was he got ten percent off when he went to her house. Sophie treated her girls right and kept them clean. Anyway, he had a thing for redheads, and everyone knew that most redheaded whores were sheenies.

The Allen, a big man by anyone's measure, sprawled in his high chair behind the bar, smoking his Perfecto. Every so often he tugged at the garters that held his sleeves secure and kept his cuffs off his thick wrists. How he relished the noise of happy patrons, the steady clink and rustle of cash in his cash box. Half snoozing, he listened with satisfaction to the creaking floors overhead. Restless feet, all anxious to give him their money.

A bingo-boy collided with a tray of beer and sent it crashing to the sawdust floor. "Clean up that mess!" The Allen shouted. "And make sure that drunk pays before you toss him out."

Without missing a beat he went back to snoozing and smoking and ruminating on the money he was going to make this night. His mellow mood came to a sudden and unpleasant end when an army of coppers stormed through his doors wielding nightsticks. His patrons scattered and ran.

Shit. What the hell was going on? He'd paid this month. Calculating how much more he would have to give, The Allen lumbered to his feet. He started toward the cash box behind the bar. Too late, he saw that New York's Finest were heading up the damned stairs.

"Wait a minute, *boyos*," he shouted, trying to head the cops off. "A fecking minute, if you please. I'm paid up, I swear on the Virgin Mary I am!"

"Theodore Allen?" The blue boyo sergeant laid a fat paw on The Allen's arm.

"That's my monicker, don't abuse it."

"I'll abuse *you* if you don't shut your mouth. You're under arrest."

"For what?" The Allen shook off the meaty hand, but back it came, fingers gripping while all hell broke loose upstairs. His upstairs customers were herded down, policy slips flying like snow in the wind.

Complaining bitterly, The Allen was shoved out to the street with his customers and his help. A crowd had gathered.

"For what?" The Allen shouted again. "I got a right to know. Why the pinch?"

A barrel-chested wheelman, wearing eyeglasses that twinkled in the streetlight, leaned his bicycle against a lamppost and stepped forward.

"For running an illegal gambling establishment," said the man known as Moose, showing everyone a big toothy smile.

• 19 •

Friday, May 31. After two A.M.

The jangle of the telephone sounded in the downstairs foyer.

"Damn," Sophie said. She had just settled into the hot soothing balm of her tub. From out of the rising steam she shouted, "Honey! Tell them we're closed, call tomorrow. Afternoon."

Leo groaned. He was lying under the satin sheet, almost asleep. "Daisy will get it."

"Daisy's in bed. Answer it."

He hated that imperious tone of hers. If he didn't love her so much he'd strangle her. Leo pulled on a silk robe and stumbled down the stairs, his eyes half closed. The telephone on the hall table kept ringing and ringing. He picked up the earpiece. "Yes?"

He heard shouts and curses, then a gravel voice exploded in his ear. "Where's Sophie?"

Leo recognized the dulcet tones of Desk Sergeant Francis Dulaney. "She's indisposed."

"Better get her disposed, else her old man's arse will be on its way across the East River to Blackwell's Island in the morning."

"Oh, shit," Leo said.

"He got picked up in a raid at The Allen's. I got him on ice in a cozy little cell just waiting for someone to pay for his ticket."

Of course, ticket. Leo was well aware there was no ticket. But he was also well versed in how the game was played. "Who to? How much?"

"Sophie knows." The copper hung up in his ear.

It was close to four in the morning when Leo left the house at 79 Clinton Street. The sky was a black dome with no moon, and the lighted towers of the Bridge to Brooklyn appeared as buildings on an island in the East River.

Three hansoms, horses and drivers dead asleep, were queued up in front of Noonan's blind pig, where Noonan illegally dispensed his rotgut till the cock called in the dawn.

"Hey, wake up." Leo gave the first driver a prod with his walking stick. "Take me to 300 Mulberry."

The driver woke with a snort. The chestnut mare stirred, pawed the cobblestone. "Waiting for my fare," the man mumbled.

"He's good for another hour or two. You can bet on it." Leo two-fingered a silver dollar from his waistcoat pocket. He held it so the lamplight caught on the coin.

"Get in," said the driver. He flicked his reins, bringing the horse full awake.

"I'm going to 300 Mulberry to pick up a package. We will drop the package at Madison and Gouverneur, then come back here."

"Going to Police Headquarters alone is worth two bucks," the driver said truculently.

"Okay," said Leo, getting into the carriage.

The whip cracked, and they were off.

The driver turned onto Grand and, as he approached the Black Horse Tavern, in what was still Little Dagoland, wisely skirted Five Points, the intersection of five streets that formed a star at the bottom of Mulberry.

The abomination called Five Points was a cruel place to live and a likely place to die. From the 1820's on, the area had become New York's center of depravity, the City's major cesspool of criminal activity, the domain of infamous gangs such as the Dead Rabbits, the Roach Guards, and the Plug-Uglies.

Police Headquarters was lit up like a carousel where it stood, fort-like, on Mulberry Street, surrounded by the reeking tenements. The reporters, who usually congregated in 303 across the street, milled in front of Headquarters.

"Pull around to Bleecker," Leo said. The routine was: Give the envelope with the twenty-five dollars to the doorman manning the front door, then wait around the corner on Bleecker. He climbed down. "I'll be right back."

"I'll be here." The driver tilted his battered plug hat over his eyes and leaned back.

What Leo hadn't figured on were the journalists. Moving smartly, walking stick leading his way, he attempted to sail right in, but the journalists made themselves a stone wall.

"Who are you?" one demanded.

"Who are you here for?" shouted another.

Good luck, the doorman knew him by sight. "Let the man through."

Bad luck, so did some of the reporters. "That's Sophie's boy, Leo."

"Hey, Leo. Hey, Leo." The rest picked it up and it became a chant. "Hey, Leo."

This time, instead of accepting his envelope and telling Leo to wait on Bleecker, the doorman jerked him inside and steered him to the desk. Leo was peeved. It was bad enough being manhandled by a regular officer; he didn't like taking it from a doorman rank, who was nothing more than a broom-and-mop cop in a uniform.

Florid-faced Desk Sergeant Francis Dulaney rubbed his firm beer belly and peered up the stairs where, on the second floor, Commissioner Moose was burning the midnight oil as usual. Dulaney hurried Leo downstairs to the dank cells in the basement.

At the base of the stone staircase Dulaney stuck out his hand. Leo gave him the envelope. He watched while Dulaney tore it open and counted his bribe.

"You're a trusting soul, Sergeant."

"Mrs. Dulaney didn't raise no idiot child." The sergeant stuffed the bills inside his blue coat. "Follow me."

Like caged monkeys at Barnum's, inmates chattered at them as they went by the line of cells. Their noise, their metal cups on bars, their demands to be free, their imprecations, were deafening. The stinks of vomit and urine battled each other for precedence.

Leo and Dulaney were greeted in a different fashion at the end of the first rank of cells. "Ah, Leo, my boy. The charges are false, of course," Sophie's father said good-humoredly. "They say I was gambling. Truth is I had not yet made a bet. Slander, I say. Calumny." Byron Brown was in a cell no bigger than a closet. The old man was leaning against the rear wall, under a small high window, a barred rectangle that brought in no air at all. He threw back his noble head and declaimed, " 'Virtue itself 'scapes not calumnious strokes.' "

Dulaney unlocked the cell door. "Get going."

"I most heartily agree, Sergeant, it is time. But first I must tend to my toilet. An actor is not an actor without a proper wardrobe. Especially his shoes."

"Time to go, Paulie," Leo said.

"Ssss," the old man hissed, his forefinger to his lips. "There is no Paulie here," he whispered, attempting a heroic pose. "The name on the marquee is Byron Brown," said the old actor. And fell flat on his face.

Leo shook his head over the old man and helped him up. He could never get used to Paul Skidelsky being Byron Brown. "Let's leave before they change their minds."

"You're a good boy, Leo," Skidelsky said in feeble but still stentorian tones. He smelled like a still. His coat was torn and stained, the worn fur collar matted. Though his trousers were well cut, the cut was from the long-dead past, and they were stained as well. Worse, someone had thrown up on his fine shoes. Most likely the old boozer himself.

After quick-marching up the stairs and through the hall, the sergeant pulled the bolt on the back door and shoved Leo and the old man outside.

Leo propelled him toward the hansom. "Come on. Before they put you back in that hole and me with you."

" 'Farewell, farewell, parting is such sweet sorrow, that I—' "

Seizing the actor, Leo dragged him into the cab. Out of the corner of his eye he caught sight of a reporter coming round from Mulberry Street.

Byron Brown saw him, too. He thrust his head out the window. "My public," the old actor declaimed. " 'When lilacs last in the dooryard bloom'd—' "

Leo yanked him back in.

"I'm afraid you have no soul, Leo, my boy," the old actor said, halfway through a belch and a hiccough.

"I don't care about my soul, it's my body I want to keep together. Driver, let's get the hell out of here."

Little Jack, his cap in his hand, sat in front of the churchyard, across the road from where the bakery wagon was still standing. His waiting wasn't all wasted time; he had made three cents, one from a preacher.

When the preacher had asked Jack his name, he pretended he didn't speak English. When he invited the boy in for soup, Jack was tempted, but he didn't want to lose sight of the bakery wagon. Finally, the preacher gave Jack the penny, patted him on the head, and went into his church.

Jack, restless, bold as brass, crossed the street, and took himself alongside the bakery wagon. Pretending to search his pockets for a butt, he leaned against the wagon wheel to listen.

"Who is she? You'll live a lot longer."

"I don't know who you mean." That was Mr. Roman, for sure.

The familiar sound of body as a punching bag came again, with a stifled cry. Jack winced.

"Let's kill the bastard and be done with it."

"Patience, Terry. The girl, Mr. Roman, and you walk away."

"Go to hell."

"Keep this up and you'll be there to greet me." A pause, then, "Terry, take a look outside."

Jack scooted under the wagon and held his breath.

" 'Gallop apace, you fiery-footed steeds, toward Phoebus's lodging.' " The old actor was trying to stand. When the hansom hit a pothole in the road, he fell back in his seat, and passed out.

Byron Brown, *né* Paul Skidelsky, lived in a small top-floor room on

Madison Street, only blocks from Gouverneur Hospital, which had been his home during much of the last winter; after he'd been found almost frozen to death after falling asleep in the street.

If Jack hadn't opened his eyes at just that moment, he would have been run over by the bakery wagon pulling away. It was dark as pitch. What the hell time was it?

In no mood to run blind in the dark, Little Jack jumped on the back of the wagon. The sweet-sour smell of yeast trickled out to him, making the boy briefly forget about Mr. Roman. As he held on for the bumpy ride, he considered how he could steal a loaf of bread for his supper.

"Can you walk?" Leo asked when they arrived.

" 'I am that merry wanderer of the night,' " the old man said, clambering down and sinking to his knees. " 'I jest at Oberon and make him smile.' "

"Jest at Oberon in your own bed." Leo took Skidelsky by the arm, once more guiding him.

"My money," the driver barked.

"Wait for me. One more stop. I'll be right out."

"Money in my hand."

"All right. Here's one dollar. You'll get the second when you take me back to Clinton Street. I expect you to be here. What the hell, you've done the job right—I'll give you two bucks more."

After trying to push the old man aloft along the creaky wood stairs, Leo gave it up as a bad job. He hoisted Byron to his shoulder and hauled him the five flights like a sack of potatoes, while the old man recited Hamlet in German. " *'Sein oder nicht sein. Das ist . . .'* "

When they turned at Delancey Street and the slamming and hollering within began, Jack started to think that his being there wasn't such a good idea. But he wasn't about to quit till he saw this thing through.

He'd gotten a dollar for the box; who knew how much he could get for Mr. Roman himself?

The wagon raced down to Madison Street, then turned. Jack held on for dear life. When the bony driver shouted at the nag, and the wagon shuddered to a stop in an alley just short of Gouverneur Street, Jack's resolve became dust and he jumped off quick, looking for a place to hide. Nearest was best. He darted down the first few steps of an open cellar.

Leo propped Skidelsky against the hall wall and searched the old man for his latchkey. No key. He tried the door. It was open. He took a Lucifer from his pocket and lit the match on his thumbnail. On the other side of the small room was a brick fireplace. Leo picked his way to it and found a stub of a candle on the mantel.

Leo had been here before. A bare room. No electricity or closets. The iron crane used to hang cooking pots on was rusted. A space under the one window was for keeping food cool. When there was food. The tap coming out of the floor in front of the supporting pillar carried a weak flow of rusty water and was thick with cockroaches that dispersed in an instant when he lit the candle. Skidelsky's snores and the tap's steady drip into the grated opening in the floor were the only sounds he heard. The furnishings were spare: a narrow bed and a chair, no table.

Returning to the hall, Leo found Skidelsky slumped on the floor fast asleep. Leo heard the scratching progress of rats in the walls; he hoped they weren't at his feet with the cockroaches.

"Tell my beloved daughter her father blesses her," the old man muttered grandly as Leo hefted him.

Leo dropped him onto the filthy linen of the unmade bed. The old man didn't move. He was hopeless; even Sophie despaired of him. And now Leo had had enough of being Paul Skidelsky's nanny for this night.

He ran down the stairs and out onto the street, only to discover that his hackney was gone.

Resigned, Leo took off his derby, scratched his head vigorously, then set the new black bowler back in place. Sophie had just given it to him. And whenever Sophie gave Leo a present it made him feel good, even if the present was just a derby with a wine-red band.

He began to whistle softly. It wasn't that long a walk back to Clinton Street, but maybe he could find a hack at the hospital.

As he passed the alley just beyond Skidelsky's tenement, he caught the faint glimmer of a light. The tail lamp of a wagon. He heard a horse nicker softly. What luck. He could buy himself a ride in comfort.

Terry, the big one, vaulted out of the back of the bread wagon, laughing like a lunatic, blood on his fists and clothes. "What now, boss?" Terry asked, sticking his head inside the wagon.

"First get rid of these." Unseen hands gave Terry the box. He set it on a pile of garbage.

"Not like that, idiot. Destroy them."

Terry dumped the stuff from the box, its contents crashing to the ground.

Leo heard the thud. Then he saw by the dim carriage lamp a man spilling something on the ground.

Terry picked up a photographic plate, broke it in two, and in the dim light, watched the glass splinters rain from the jagged edges of its wooden holder. Now he stomped on another plate, denting the holder, cracking the glass. He laughed. "Hey, Harry. Come on down and help me. This is fun."

The bony mug climbed down, and between them they did a mad dance on the plates and left the remnants of their destruction scattered on the ground of the alley.

"All done, boss," Terry called.

"About time. Now get rid of him and we'll be out of here."

Terry jumped into the wagon, bone Harry went on top. The next instant the body came flying out. It hit the cobble with a dull thump.

. . .

"What the hell?" Leo said, jumping out of the way.

"Why didn't you throw him down a cellar?" the muffled voice demanded.

"Sorry, sir, you want me to go back?" Terry asked.

"Cheese it, boss," Harry called from his box. "We got eyes watching." The wagon came to a halt. Harry yelled, "Terry. He saw."

Terry jumped out.

"Kill him," cried the man inside the wagon.

Leo ran. But everywhere he turned, Terry was in front of him.

And now the wagon was coming after him.

A metal ladder hung perhaps six feet off the ground from the outside of a building. Leo leaped for it and pulled it down. He started climbing, Terry right behind him. Terry seized Leo's right foot, while Leo kicked at his pursuer with the left. Now the man had both of Leo's feet. Not content with this, and so eager was he to get his hands on Leo's throat, Terry started climbing Leo's body. Leo did the only thing he could. He let go of the ladder.

Both men crashed atop the bakery wagon.

"I got him," Terry yelled triumphantly.

Leo kneed him in the groin.

"What the hell is going on down there?" a woman screamed from above.

"Shut up, you old hag," Harry yelled to the woman leaning out the tenement window.

"I've got the telephone. I'm calling the police."

"Yeah, sure," said Harry.

"Harry," the man inside the wagon called in his peevish tones. "Skedaddle."

"Yes, boss." The bakery wagon hurtled along the cobble, Leo pummeling Terry in the ribs while the other man was doing his best to strangle him.

"Terry," Harry warned. "People coming."

"Tell *him* that," Terry grunted.

The wagon rattled toward the river. Leo was giving as good as he got when the wagon careened into an empty lot near Cherry Street and hit a deep rut. He had just broken Terry's hold on his throat and had reared back to swat the other man a good one in the face, when he went flying off.

Jack Meyers bided his time before daring to poke his head out of the cellar again. He counted to ten. And again. And eight more times. Only then did he crawl out. On hands and knees in the darkness, he listened and waited. When he was sure there was no one about, he came out all the way. Shit. Something bit him. He slapped at his right wrist and prayed it wasn't a rat. The ground crackled with broken glass. No rat, he'd been cut. He stood and dusted arms, hands, and knees with his cap. That's when he noticed a large lump in the dirt in front of him.

He lit one of his precious few matches. A torn and bloody piece of yellow silk caught the light. "God in heaven." There would be no reward this time.

Jack could tell by the bloodstained yellow cravat. The lump was Mr. Roman.

20

Friday,
May 31.
After three A.M.

A*t the House on Mulberry Street, Desk Sergeant Francis Dulaney stared* at Down-to-the-Ground Clooney in his cell. "You're a good torch, Conn, but you're a lousy criminal."

Clooney gave his greased skin a delicate touch and sighed. "Tell me about it, Francis."

It was late, and there was none of the usual prisoner yammer; only the noise of laborious snoring came from one of the other cells. Everyone but Clooney was sound asleep. Sergeant Dulaney wanted to keep it that way. "Time to go, Conn," he said.

Clooney was up on his feet at once. No need to tell him twice that the train was leaving.

Dulaney held up a quieting hand as they stood at the bottom of the stone staircase and squinted at the stairs leading up to the street level. Satisfied the coast was clear, he nodded to Clooney. "Follow me."

They went up the stairs and down the empty hall. At its end, Dulaney released the bolt and eased open the back door.

"I don't know how to thank you, Francis."

"It's been taken care of, Conn. Get going. The Boss says be more careful next time. And keep your mouth shut."

"You know me, quiet as a mouse."

"Better be. Else you'll end up a dead rat."

Clooney wanted to smile but he just didn't have it. "Good night, Francis."

"See you in church."

"I know that man, Bo," Dutch Tonneman said to his cousin. "I met him just yesterday. He's a journalist. Robert Roman." And then he remembered where he'd heard the name before. At the wake. "He's the one Ned fished out of the East River a couple of days ago."

"Well, this time it looks like they got him."

The detectives hunkered down again, examining the body in the piercing light of two galvanic battery-powered bull's-eye lanterns.

Off to the side, waiting permission to place the corpse in the wagon, stood a pair of patrol officers. Each held the two poles of a stretcher. They were all in the alley off Madison Street waiting on the medical examiner.

Detective Sergeant Bo Clancy and his cousin Detective Sergeant John "Dutch" Tonneman were here because Moose and the other three commissioners—dubbed Peacock, Badger, and Fox—were in the process of tearing down the Metropolitan Police Force and rebuilding it, so that instead of answering to crooked Precinct Police Commanders, the detectives would answer to Police Headquarters.

"What did they say when you telephoned the station, Sam?" Bo Clancy asked Sam Ryan, one of the officers. Bo patted his coat.

"That the doc was coming."

"Right." Bo found the fat Perfecto he was searching for. "By way of Brooklyn."

Tonneman scratched the bridge of his nose. "What the hell was Roman doing here? Last I saw him, yesterday afternoon, he was on his way to the *Herald* in a big hurry."

Bo lit his cigar and began turning out the dead man's pockets. "Some people in this town don't think much of these newspaper fellows." He pulled out Roman's billfold, opened it. "Empty as a Protestant's heart. Dutch, shine that light around, will you?"

Tonneman made an arc with the light.

"Hold it," Bo said. "Hogan, did you look down that cellar?"

"Before you got here, Sergeant Clancy," the second patrolman replied.

Bo searched further. The dead man's blood was sticky to the touch. "Nothing else but this card case." Bo opened the silver case. "Robert Roman it is." He placed the case in a canvas evidence bag with the billfold. "What about him yesterday afternoon?"

Dutch quickly filled Bo in on the attempted theft of the photographic plates, then they rolled the battered body over. The back of Roman's coat was strewn with pieces of wood and broken glass. A close look showed Dutch that other, larger shards, glass and wood, were scattered on the ground. "Hello."

"Broken bottles," Bo said. "The drunks."

"I think not." Dutch started picking the glass from Roman's back. "Sam," he called. "You got a fair-sized sack or a box in the wagon I could use?"

Sam and Roy were still hanging on to the stretcher. "Bushel basket okay?" Roy asked.

"Just grand."

Roy set his end of the stretcher down, leaving Sam holding on to his, and went to the wagon.

Dutch turned to his cousin. "This stuff looks like it's from the photographic plates all that hubbub was about yesterday."

Bo took a long drag of his Perfecto. "What good will bits and pieces do you?"

"I haven't the palest idea."

When Roy set the basket beside him, Dutch told the patrolman, "Give me a hand." By the light of the bull's-eye lanterns, they picked the alley clean of wood and glass until Dutch was satisfied they'd gotten every fragment.

Jack Meyers watched avidly as the pieces were collected and placed in the basket. Now what was all that about? he wondered. He waited until the body and all the cops were gone before he dared come out of his cellar. They had murdered Mr. Roman. And he had seen them do it.

21

Friday,
May 31.
Midmorning.

A *dancing light flickered near the river. Fire. A moment later, the* eardrum-shattering boom of an explosion. Boom, boom, boom, more explosions, and flying pieces of timber, ashes, and thick smoke.

Leo looked toward the explosion and shook his aching head. This was New York. He was never surprised by it.

Slowly, Leo began to remember how he had got to be lying on his back in this empty lot. Those damn plug-uglies had caught him with his nose in their business, and hammered him, and when he'd flown off that wagon they'd left him for dead. He touched the back of his head. A bump as big as a baseball for sure, and tender as the skin of a tomato.

Where was his bowler? He'd have to forsake a hat for a while, for it wouldn't fit, what with the aching new addition to his head. Well, he wouldn't have to worry about that; the derby was nowhere to be seen. Damn it all, Sophie'd be in a fury when she found out he didn't have it anymore. So! Perhaps one of those plug-uglies was prancing around with Leo's new derby hat on his dome. Leo smiled. If he saw his bowler on one of that lot, he'd make profit of the sighting, for he was not beyond asking for a little payoff.

Leo Stern was not afraid. Indeed, he seemed to have been born without the trait of fear. He felt he lived a charmed life. He could do anything. Face to face he could handle himself. As for his back, Sophie might help a little. But when your time in this world was up, it was up, so why worry about it?

Now, in the distance, he could just barely hear the fire bell and the screams. Truth to say, his hearing was a little muffled from the explosions. Soon enough the horses would race along Cherry Street pulling the water wagons, and the firemen would come running. Oh, he loved a good fire.

Already workers from the docks and other buildings, workshops and warehouses, were rushing toward the blaze which appeared to be on the waterfront. That wasn't smart. Three additional little explosions had followed the first; there could be more, with all that wood in the lumberyards.

Leo wasn't so different from the rest. People liked to follow the fun. And from the sound of a vast army of feet approaching, here came more proof of the pudding. Although they'd missed the explosions, they'd come to watch the fire. He wondered how many men had been working inside. How many had been hurt.

Now the very earth seemed to shake under him as hordes of people from everywhere began to close in on the area to watch the conflagration. It was as if the whole City was here. They'd be lucky if the entire tip of Manhattan didn't break off and fall into the East River and sink, or float away, Leo thought sourly. New York was an assortment of small villages, each one jealous of its own territory. Ordinarily, he would be marked as a stranger and they'd want to know what he was doing here. But there were plenty of strangers arriving here, more by the minute.

And leading the pack was a formidable bunch of men, most in single-breasted blue frock coats with brass buttons and domed gray felt hats. The costume of the Cossacks of New York.

Leo sighed. In this mob, he would stand out as a foreigner and a Jew. He was in no mood to have any intercourse with the flat-footed minions of the law of the City. Enough lallygagging, as Sophie liked to say.

If anyone saw Leo Stern they either didn't care or didn't take notice, as he made his way from back alley to back alley behind the tenements, heading home to Clinton Street and Madam Sophie's.

22

Friday, May 31. Late morning.

With *a Persian shawl over his shoulders, Oz Cook slumped in his father's* Morris chair opposite the fireplace. The study—smoking room—had been his father's favorite in the house. Oz loved it here.

Oz let his mind float on the events of the past twenty-four hours. He was fascinated by his protégée's description of the riot in Union Square. He should have been there, but spilt milk. His mouth twisted in a sardonic smile. Spilt brandy, to be more precise.

All that aside, he took great delight in the accented lilt of Esther's excitement as she recounted the details. It returned him to this world. He'd been asking questions and jotting notes in his leather-bound notebook. "Where did you stand?" he asked now, his stylograph poised.

When she told him, he said, "You should have been farther back. For the panorama. Portraits are impossible in that circumstance."

"I know," she said ruefully.

"How fast did you shoot?"

"As fast as I could."

He laughed. "Don't chastise yourself too much if any, or even all, went wrong." Oz's lips pursed in humor as he examined her face. "That's quite a colorful eye."

"Oh, dear," she said, her hand going to cover it.

"Don't fret. Soon it will be good as—" His right foot shot out suddenly, pushing the ottoman. His legs were shaking. "Damn."

Esther jumped up.

"Could you set the footstool back in place?" Oz made no mention of his spasm and neither did she. He picked up the cigarette from the ashtray on the table beside him and drew several little puffs from it. His long thin fingers were as unsteady as his legs, but he did find comfort in his Virginia Brights.

Spring sunshine streamed through the sheer white curtains of the side-by-side windows behind Oz's desk. A soft breeze drifted under the raised sash. From the street came the occasional shouts and laughter of children.

He took a long, fulfilling puff and laid the cigarette in the tray. "Where are the plates now, Esther?"

"Robert took them to the *Herald.* I don't think he trusted me to develop them properly."

"But nevertheless you did well as my surrogate. Or we would have heard otherwise from my friend. Robert's never tardy about speaking his mind."

"Thank you," Esther said.

"We will observe your Sabbath and mine, then on Monday, we will go back to work on my book. Will that suit you?"

Before she could respond, the doorbell sounded from below. "Robert," Esther said, moving from the brown velvet wing chair crammed between the fireplace and the oak table, to the windows. She parted the curtains and looked down at the entrance to the building. But there was no one on the doorstep. Wong had already let their caller in. She returned to her chair.

"Ah," Oz said, exhibiting a weary smile. "I almost wish he hadn't come today. I'm enjoying the peace."

"Perhaps it would be better if I went out and stopped him. I could tell him you're resting."

Oz's laugh was frustrated by a cough. "That bulldog?"

A soft tap came on the door; the door opened. "A visitor," Wong said.

"Don't leave him cooling his heels. Send him up. At once."

Wong hesitated, catching Esther's eye.

She frowned, not understanding.

Wong left and returned shortly. "Detective Sergeant John Tonneman," he announced.

"Oh." Esther's curiously self-conscious exclamation alerted Oz. He turned and gave her a searching look. His protégée was up and fussing with things on his desk. She was blushing. Fascinating.

Even before Wong stepped aside, the presence of John Tonneman was palpable. It was not only his broad shoulders and towering stature. Oz had the feeling that even if he were short and narrow, John Tonneman would fill the room.

"Sir. Miss Breslau. Forgive my intrusion."

"You are not intruding, young man. We were discussing the strange events of yesterday in which, I understand from Miss Breslau, you were prominently featured." Oz extended his hand.

"It was strange, but the aftermath is stranger. I regret to say, tragic." Tonneman shook hands with Oz.

"Do have a seat." Oz pointed to the wing chair Esther had recently vacated. "My cigarettes, Wong."

Wong produced a fresh package of Virginia Brights, then emptied Oz's overflowing ashtray into a metal container. Believing his services might be required, he remained in the room, hovering near the door.

The detective seemed reluctant to sit; when he did, he perched, awkwardly, on the edge of the chair.

"What tragic event has occurred?" Oz prompted.

Esther seemed lost for a moment, then crossed behind Oswald Cook's desk and sat in the leather chair.

Oz said, "Get to it, please, Detective."

"Mr. Robert Roman. His body was discovered early this morning."

Oz turned gray as the ash of his cigarette. "Body? He's dead?"

"Oh, no," Esther cried.

"He's dead?" Oz repeated.

Tonneman was taken with the vacant expression on the Chinese servant's face. "Yes. I'm sorry to say Mr. Roman's been murdered."

Oz's hand shook so badly that Esther hurried to him and gently removed the cigarette from his rigid fingers. She placed it on the ashtray.

"Who would do such a terrible thing?" A decanter of brandy sat on a silver tray on the table. Esther poured brandy into one of the eight small glasses that surrounded the decanter.

Wong's lack of reaction made Tonneman suspicious. He said to him, "You don't seem surprised to hear that Mr. Roman was murdered."

"No, sir," Wong replied, his face blank. "But then again, I would not be surprised to hear that anyone was murdered. We cannot escape our fate. And in this City, death is quite ordinary." With a small nod he left the room.

Tonneman did not know what to make of this odd yellow man.

Oz said, "Was Robert in Five Points? He was often foolhardy when it came to searching out a story." Oz took the glass from Esther, who steadied his hand as he drank.

"Not in Five Points," Tonneman replied. "An alley off Madison Street. Do either of you know why he would have been down there?"

Esther shook her head. Oz didn't respond.

Tonneman went on. "I have to trace his steps after he left us in the carriage yesterday. Something happened on his way to the *Herald*. I'll know more when I've talked to the driver and that boy."

"What about the plates?" Esther asked suddenly.

Although he was the bearer of bad news and on the job, Tonneman felt a pleasure he was discreet enough not to show. This girl was quick. Got right to the meat of things.

"I've brought them with me. I gave them to your servant."

"Wong," Oz called.

The door opened immediately, as if the Chinese servant had been waiting just outside. He came into the room somewhat awkwardly, his arms barely circling a bushel basket.

"I found the plates near his remains," Tonneman said. "I need you to, what's the word? Make pictures . . ."

"Develop," Esther supplied. "Print."

"Thank you. These plates have been twice stolen. The next time I saw them they were connected to a murder. I would like to see what they show that someone would kill for. How many did you make?"

"Ten," said Esther.

Tonneman nodded. "Can you print them for me?"

"Easily done." Oz drained the few drops left in the brandy glass. He eyed the decanter only a few feet away on the table.

"It's not that simple," Tonneman said. "The plates are broken."

"Let me see," Oz said sharply.

Wong, still hugging the basket, now set it down next to his employer. Esther stared woefully at its contents: the dented, cracked holders, broken glass of her negatives.

"Oh, my," said Oz. He fingered several of the shards. "If there is hope, it is only slight." He picked up a plate cracked in half and hung together only by the film fronting it. He held it delicately in both hands. "This is useless!"

"Maybe there are some not broken," Tonneman said.

"Broken is not the problem. Light is. These have all been exposed." Oz's hand darted out and came up with a dented but seemingly whole lighttight holder. "Now this brings me abounding hope." The photographer smiled. "What an absorbing problem."

"Can it be done?" the detective asked. "If so, it may go a long way in helping me find out who murdered Robert Roman."

"Well." Oz took a deep breath through his nostrils. "You have presented us with quite a challenge. Robert was a dear friend."

"Can you do it, sir?"

Oz placed his forefinger to his lips as if contemplating his muse. "Present you with evidence and thus avenge our friend. That's a noble thought. Esther, my dear, if you would be so good as to pour me another brandy." He lifted his head to Tonneman, smiling. "If no light has seeped into this frame, I can supply you with one photograph. What sort of photograph will depend on the gods, and on what sort of photographer my assistant is. We'll get to work at once."

23

Friday,
May 31.
Late morning.

"*Good old girl, old Nelly old Nelly,*" *Little Jack was singsonging under his* breath.

He'd swept up the accumulated refuse and filled the empty buckets with oats, like Battling Jack told him. He'd been at the job since dawn but he wasn't tired. After a short lifetime of scratching for food, work was soothing balm. The gaslight flickered; the only other illumination in the cellar came from beyond the ramp that led to the cobblestoned alley behind the grand houses.

Which made him think of the other alley. Having money and riding in a fine carriage didn't mean a thing when you came up against a tougher man, Jack decided. You had to be tough in this world. Otherwise you was dead. Money was good, all right, but you had to be tough to keep it. And stay alive.

The boy sniffed the air. It was a good stink, this stink of horseshit and horse sweat. And it was a stink that would give him a roof over his head and coins in his pocket. Horse smells was definitely good. Better even was the smells of the leather and the hay that came with the horses.

Jack Meyers liked horses better than people. Horses didn't try to take what you had. He was happy with horses. Working in a stable was the right job for him. Meeting Battling Jack West was the best thing that had ever happened to him.

Old Nelly, she was the gentle one. When he'd walked her out to clean her stall, she'd nuzzled her soft lips into his neck. "Just like a woman, interfering with a man's work."

The stable, a small structure with a red brick front, was set in Macdougal Alley, a dead-end, run-down street frequented by some of the worst elements in the City. The crap games here more often than not led to knifings. And death.

Little Jack had toted his refuse up the ramp and emptied it out back, where the grass grew in small clumps as if afraid to relax and spread out. Maybe Battling Jack wouldn't mind if he planted a garden. It would be a shame to waste all this good dung.

After a run around to the front, the boy returned to the basement with two buckets of water from the horse trough and scrubbed the stable floor and walls with a big brush. When he finished that, he strewed hay, put Nelly back in her stall, and gave her a fresh bucket of water.

Jack went back up the ramp, whistling. Oh, yes, he liked this job.

A game of craps was going hot in front of the next-door stable, which was boarded up. A little breather wouldn't hurt; he stopped to watch.

"Dace says he makes the eight."

"Put your two cents where your mouth is."

The talk, the click of dice, and the clink of coin on the walk made him want to play, but he didn't have any money. Not yet, anyway.

Expelling a great sigh, he went on to the next chore Battling Jack had laid out for him. He swept out the first floor. At this time, only a small Brewster victoria sat in the first-floor space usually meant for it and Mr. West's brougham. Battling Jack was out answering a hire at one of them big fancy hotels on Fifth Avenue. But even with the two carriages there, Little Jack could make himself a place to sleep between them and the back wall. And as time went by, who was to say he couldn't sneak a snooze in the brougham once in a while? Though if Big Jack were to catch him, he'd probably break his ass.

For the time being, Jack Meyers would be content on the floor with his head on a sack. One day maybe he'd be able to sleep the way Battling

Jack did, in a proper bed on the second floor. The thought tickled again. Who was to say he couldn't when Battling Jack was in Brooklyn?

Jack leaned on his broom. His hands quit moving. He was thinking of the other alley again. He pictured Mr. Roman's bloody head and shuddered. No one had seen Jack Meyers—not the murderers, not the coppers—not that bloke the murderers had run off. Jack was certain of that. Since there was no money to be made from it, it was nothing to do with him anymore. He began to scrub again with a ferocity that surprised him.

When he was through with his inside sweeping, he went outside to the front and washed down Mr. West's sign. The notice, set in a long rectangular recess in the brick, was painted white on red: "*To Let,*" it said. "*Horses, Carriages, Coupes, Hansoms, Victorias. Horses Boarded.*"

This final chore done, he sat out in the almost-noon sun, having a smoke from a butt he'd found, only half listening to the noise of the craps players. He was feeling pretty good about himself. When his head began to nod, he let it. He'd had no sleep, and he'd worked hard. . . .

Jack Meyers opened one eye. Two pairs of high black Congress gaiters burnished with Bixby's Best Blacking gleamed up at him. Shit, cops. He opened the other eye and took his gaze from their shoes to their faces.

He knew them, too. The first one had given him a nickel for saving the box. And him and the other had been in the alley after the murder.

"It's a good life, this life of a stable boy. Wouldn't you say, coz?"

Bo nodded. "I'd say you're right, Dutch. We chose the wrong line of work. Should've been."

"Then we could be sitting in the sun, copping a snooze."

"Only I'd be drinking a beer. Got a beer, boy?"

"No, sir." Jack pulled his cap from his head.

"Sir, he calls me. You hear that, Dutch? I like that. Manners. But with all his fine manners the lad's a sloth. Lazing about when he should be toiling."

"I done my work," Jack protested. "I'm waiting for Mr. West to come back."

"Wouldn't you know it?" Bo said. "The boss ain't around, the help sleeps in the sun."

Tonneman squinted at the sky. He wouldn't mind sitting out here himself. "What's your name, kid?"

"Jack Meyers."

"Where are your folks?"

"Vilna."

Bo laughed. "Ask a stupid question."

Tonneman made a face at his cousin. To the boy he said, "We wanted your boss, but if we have to settle for you, lad, we'll settle for you."

"I didn't do nothing. I wasn't there."

"Where is there?" Bo asked.

Jack took a breath. Finally he had started to think. "Wherever the trouble was."

"Who says there was trouble?" Bo persisted.

"You're here, ain't you?" Jack replied.

"He's got you, Bo."

"He's a smart boy. I saw you myself," Tonneman said. "You grabbed the box. Saved the day."

"Oh." Jack was relieved. This wasn't about what he saw in the alley. He scrambled to his feet. "Yes, sir. What can I do for you?"

"You can tell me where your boss drove Mr. Roman."

"To the *Herald* newspaper on Thirty-fourth Street. Was that the fellow's name? Roman?" Jack scratched the nape of his neck where his hackles was telling him to watch his step. He'd lied when there was no need. Not smart.

"It was . . ." Bo exchanged glances with his partner. Then he glared down at Jack.

"I don't know nothing other than that," Jack said, nervously scratching his arms. "I was on back. Mr. West, he was driving." Jack looked down Macdougal Alley, yearning for the sound of dice and coin again, remembering how grand he had felt only a short time before. But the alley was silent as a graveyard. He was not the only one who knew police when he saw them. Jack watched the pigeons peck around for stray oats between the cobbles. One was seeking its breakfast in a horse pile.

"Did you see where he went? Mr. Roman?"

"Yeah. Inside the Herald Building. Ask Mr. West."

Who should roll into the alley at that moment but big Jack West himself. The carriage driver jumped down from the box, huge, yet graceful as a cat.

"Jesus, Mary, and Joseph," Bo said. "There's only one big man I know of who can move like that. Battling Jack, himself."

"And it's himself at your service, gents." Big Jack handed Sullivan's reins to Little Jack. "Cool him down, wipe him down. Don't feed him right away. Clean the carriage inside and out. Do the brasses. I want to see my face in them brasses. You got that?"

"Yes, sir." Jack Meyers set his cap back on his head and ran to tend the horse and carriage, grateful to be out from under the coppers' thumbs.

Tonneman noted the boy's enthusiasm and wondered about it. Too much. A bounce of light. Something on the boy's cap glinted in the sun.

"I saw you fight John L. Sullivan in '93," Bo said. "After he lost to Jim Corbett the year before. You nearly beat Sullivan."

"My last fight. June, it was. My Mary Jane came into the world that August. John L. was old. So was I. We were both born in '58."

"I always expected you to fight Gentleman Jim." There was awe in Bo's voice.

Tonneman eyed his cousin in amazement. Bo didn't awe easily.

"Ah, but he was younger," Battling Jack replied. "And I'm no longer a pugilist. A businessman, now." He looked them over carefully. To Tonneman he said, "I know you. Yesterday, right?"

"Right. Detective John Tonneman."

Bo put out his hand. "Detective Sergeant Bo Clancy." West gripped his hand, then released it. Bo offered his hand to Dutch. "Shake the hand that shook the hand of Battling Jack West, the man who nearly beat John L. Sullivan."

Battling Jack waved the air as if brushing away flies. "What can I do for you?"

"Robert Roman," Tonneman said. "The man the girl gave the box of photographic plates to. Where'd you take him?"

"To the *Herald*. He's a reporter."

"Did you wait for him?" Bo asked.

Little Jack led Battling Jack's stallion Sullivan down the incline to the basement.

The sound of hoof on wood stopped; Tonneman knew the boy was listening.

"No. I went back to Brooklyn. Thursdays I take Mrs. Jeffers to see her daughter."

"And the boy?"

"What about him?"

"Did he go to Brooklyn with you?"

"No, I left him in front of the *Herald*. He's a good lad. I hired him then and there. Told him to be here at sunup this morning. And he was."

"So," said Tonneman. "You left the boy yesterday at the *Herald*?"

"That's what I said. Sometime after four it was."

"And the next time you saw him was about four-thirty this morning."

West nodded and frowned. He had things to do.

"So you don't know where he was in between?"

"That's right. I'm his boss, not his father. Why? What's he done?" He raised his voice. "Boy, get your ass out here."

"We don't know that he's done anything," Tonneman said.

"But he might have seen something," Bo added.

"Jacko!"

The lad came up the incline slowly, eyes downcast. "Yes, sir."

"Where was you after I left you off in front of the *Herald*?"

"I bought a hot dog from the old man in front of the building."

"Did you see Mr. Roman come out again?"

The boy shrugged. "I wasn't watching. I found me a doorway to sleep in and came here before the sun was up."

Tonneman didn't believe him. The boy wouldn't look him in the eye. "You didn't see Roman leave?"

"No, sir. No. No."

"Look here, gentlemen," Jack West said. "He's a good lad. You saw him yourself fight that skinny thief. He saved that box. You know that, Tonneman. Mr. Roman will say the same."

"Roman can't say anything. He's dead." Tonneman stepped closer to the boy, using his height to put the fear of God into him. "Give me your cap, lad."

Little Jack Meyers, his face contorted by puzzlement and a great deal more, handed the cap over.

Tonneman examined the cap, searching for what he'd seen glinting, hoping it was a piece of glass from a photographic plate.

Whatever he'd glimpsed was gone.

24

Friday,
May 31.
Just before noon.

Sophie kohled the rims of her eyes, lightly colored her eyebrows with the brown pencil. She dusted her fair skin with rice powder, then painted her lips cherry red instead of the scarlet she wore at night. Even as she achieved the desired effect, Sophie was watching Leo's reflection in her mirror. He had returned to her bed long after the sun was up, and now lay there like a dead man.

Only dead men don't snore. His were so loud they rattled the delicate crystals hanging from the shade of her dressing table lamp, making them tinkle and chime. The chimes were not an unpleasant sound, but unfortunately they were not loud enough to cover what was coming from Leo.

She marched noisily to the door on her new curved-heel black shoes, her feather-trimmed peignoir floating behind her. She opened the heavy door wide and slammed it shut. The loud crack brought Leo fast awake.

He yawned, blinked his eyes, and stretched, a smile curling his lips. He could smell his Sophie, her heavy musk. He opened his eyes to see his mistress's arms folded across her full bosom, which overflowed her corselet.

Sophie's breasts were more than a pleasing sight. Except when her arms were folded. That was a signal that she was pissed. Leo's smile began to fade.

"How's my dear papa?" she demanded.

Her papa? How would he know? Leo frowned, then all of a sudden the previous night and early morning returned to him in one fell swoop, along with a sharp pain in his head, banishing his good humor. He touched the back of his head gingerly. The egg was still there. And tender as before. He was lucky he hadn't ended up as dead as that poor cove in the alley.

This morning after coming to his senses he'd wound his way back to Clinton Street. Exhausted and angry, he gulped a big taste of whiskey, cleaned up, and crawled into bed beside his mistress.

Leo took his watch from the night table. Shit, he'd had only two hours' sleep.

"Are you going to answer me or stare at that watch all day?"

"The actor's no worse for wear. He's oll korrect. But since he insists on living in that dump, you ought to have someone drop off groceries for him once in a while."

Sophie made a face at him.

Leo sat up. The pain stabbed again. The room spun like a top.

"Papa won't starve," Sophie said. "Elmer goes by every two, three days with a mess of food."

Leo fell back against the pink pillow.

Sophie crossed to the bed and stared down at him. "Jesus, you're bleeding. What the hell happened to you?"

"After I left your dear papa, I ran into a couple of culls and we had words. It's only with God's blessing that I got out alive."

"Listen to you, my rabbi. With God's blessing I'm starving. Why don't I let you lie there while I go to Katz's?"

"Oh, no, you won't. I'll get dressed."

"I thought that would rouse you. I'll tell Elmer to ready the victoria. When he takes Daisy to the Essex Street market they can pick up for Papa, too. And you can tell me about last night . . . Rabbi." She laughed.

He didn't see what was so funny.

• • •

Leo stepped up to the counter and laid three pennies in a neat row. That was a "before tip" for Yankee Bender, to ensure that the counterman served him an especially thick and lean corn beef sandwich. Only Rumanians, who ate *pastrama,* liked their meat fat. Leo ordered *pastrama* for Sophie.

Katz's Delicatessen had been a fixture at the bottom of Second Avenue since '88. It served a variety of Jewish meat dishes, but was not pure kosher. The same uptown swells who came down to the Bowery to sightsee in their carriages or hansoms, or on organized tours led by men with megaphones, came to Katz's afterward. Katz paid off the tour men for bringing customers. Gentiles, yet.

The restaurant room was a wood-paneled hall studded with dozens of square tables. Wagon-wheel chandeliers overhead held candles, but they weren't used anymore since the electric was brought in. The electric light came from sconces on the wall. Leo wished it was still the old way; he much preferred gaslight and candles.

Sophie watched him slather his corn beef with mustard and waited while he devoured half a sandwich and three full-sour pickles before she spoke. "Tell me what happened?" She picked at her *pastrama* daintily with her fingers.

"I was coming out of your father's building when I saw these two ditching a body in the alley."

"Why didn't you just turn around and walk the other way?"

Leo passed a hand over the back of his head and winced. "It happened too fast. Harry was driving, Terry was the bruiser."

"I don't need to know their names." Sophie took a cube of sugar from the bowl and placed it between her teeth before she sipped her glass of tea. "Is that where you lost your new hat?"

Leo said nothing, he merely looked glum.

Sophie's lip twisted in annoyance. She'd just gotten that hat for him at Callahan's. "Paid five dollars for it," she said, the cube of sugar still in place. She took another sip.

After a long draught of his Dr. Brown's Cel-Ray, Leo burped softly. "If I run into them again—especially that big one, Terry—they're going to be sorry they ever met me."

Sophie played with her silver case of Sweet Caps, moving it from hand to hand, tapping her long oval nails on its polished surface. Finally, she opened it and took out a cigarette. Leo dug in his vest pocket for matches and lit it. She tossed her head and expelled the smoke toward the ceiling, saying, "Right now you're the one who's sorry. Forget about it. Go see if Elmer and Daisy are back."

As Leo walked the long stretch to the front of the store, he heard, cutting through the myriad conversations and arguments, a sharp voice. "Take those things out to the carriage. I don't have all day."

That complaining voice sounded familiar. The swinging front door had just closed. Leo pushed it open.

Among the many carriages lined up helter-skelter, some leaving and new ones arriving, three were driving away as he stepped out. One even brushed down a cyclist who jumped up yelling and chased after it. For Leo, it was useless even to call, let alone pursue. He stepped back inside the delicatessen and to the counter where Yankee Bender was slicing salami.

"Yankel? Who was that guy that just left? Looked like a big order."

The fat-cheeked counterman squinted at Leo. "I cut meat, I don't look at people."

"He just left. With the mean voice."

Yankee Bender didn't miss a slice. "Except for what they order, I don't listen, either. Corn beef and salami I hear, voices I don't. You live longer that way."

25

Friday,
May 31.
Afternoon.

Luncheon at the Cook home was usually a pleasant and often a witty experience. Considering Robert Roman's murder, Esther didn't expect cheer and wit, but neither did she expect the wall of silence that her employer had erected.

She was still reeling from the shock of the news the policeman had brought; she had hoped Oz's conversation would bring her some comfort. Yet Oswald Cook was singularly unmoved by the tragedy.

Oz's seeming indifference to word of Robert Roman's murder threw Esther off balance, a captive of many troubling emotions. She had come to know Robert Roman well over the last few months, and while he was rather unmannered and abrupt, she felt his loss keenly. He had been part of her life at Gramercy Park.

With the remnants of the meal removed, Oz Cook put a flame to his cigarette. "Tomorrow, we will go back to work on my book. I have it in my mind to visit Ludlow Street."

"Yes, sir." While her employer had eaten heartily, Esther had barely touched the sliced chicken and pickled slaw Wong had so lovingly prepared. She felt Oz's eyes on her.

"Esther, my dear. You're not eating. Is there something wrong with the food?"

"I keep thinking of Robert hurt, dying in that alley."

Some time had passed since Esther had been to *shul*. She knew of no synagogues around Gramercy Park; to mourn, she would have to go to the Lower East Side where there were several to a block. Two, she knew, were on Madison Street. More to herself than to Oz she murmured, "He who saves a single soul saves the world entire."

"I beg your pardon?"

"I'm sorry, sir, I'm upset."

"Well you might be," he said, examining the glowing end of his cigarette.

"We must find who killed Robert."

"In good time," the photographer said. "In good time." He drew another deep breath of smoke, and didn't comment further.

26

Friday,
May 31.
Sundown.

A*s customary of a Friday night about this time, depending upon the* season, Meg Tonneman kept her eye on the dining room window. Just before the setting sun passed out of view it cast one final ray of pale gold. The light caught John's face and lit his hair like a halo. Meg's heart skipped a beat. In that instant he looked just like his father, Pete. Eighteen years gone, and she still missed him as if he'd left her only yesterday.

"Where are you now, you foolish man?" she said so only he could hear.

Meg had met Pete Tonneman, a journalist, near the end of the war. She was so happy to have fallen in love with someone not a policeman. The idea of sitting up nights, like her mother had, worrying about her man had haunted Meg since childhood.

Even though they had lived with Pete's old granddad, himself a retired cop, life had been paradise. Pete had given her but one son, her eldest, John. But the boy was her pride and joy. Pete would have been so proud of him. And after that came five lovely daughters. Then the foolish man had gone to cover a story about how dangerous it was to ride the ferry. What did he do but dive off a pier to save a life. And died a cop's death after all. He hadn't even lived to see Annie born.

"Ma," John said with a gentle prod.

The sun had all but disappeared while her thoughts lingered in the past. Meg covered her head with a cloth, lit two candles, and said the Lord's Prayer. As she prayed, her hands made circles over the flames, waving the flames to her, reaching almost to her face at the end of each wave, in anticipation of what was to come. On the third pass she brought her hands to her face for the remainder of the prayer.

"Our Father who art in heaven, hallowed be Thy name.

"Thy kingdom come; Thy will be done on earth as it is in heaven.

"Give us this day our daily bread.

"And forgive us our trespasses, as we forgive those who trespass against us.

"And lead us not into temptation, but deliver us from evil. Amen." Meg removed the napkin from her head.

"Amen," Dutch and Annie said.

Annie, her youngest, would in a year's time be married and in her own home, just like her four sisters. This would leave only John with her. He was a comfort, yet how Meg longed for him to marry and bring his bride home.

"Over the lips, past the gums, look out, Jesus, here it comes."

"John Tonneman!"

"Sorry, Ma." Dutch grinned, then poured wine into a cup as he recited the Our Father quickly, running the words together. "Amen."

"Amen," his mother and sister responded.

After taking a sip of the wine, Dutch passed it around the table. Each took a drink from the glass.

Dutch lifted the linen napkin from the bread plate and cut the bread.

They shared the bread, then ate their dinner.

Sitting in Old Peter's chair in her parlor with her swollen feet propped up on the footstool, Meg studied her immediate surroundings. The side table had been her mother's and had seen better days. Yet it looked sweet as a bride, covered in the freshly ironed embroidered cloth of Irish linen her ma had packed for her own trousseau, then for Meg's, nearly thirty years ago. Atop the linen cloth her cup of tea, her spectacles, her missal, and her rosary awaited her.

She sipped her tea and thought back on the week. With Old Peter taking his heavenly rest at last, John was now head of the family. She listened to the laughing banter from the kitchen where John was drying the dishes for Annie.

The ritual with the candles every Friday night was something that came from Old Peter's family. Meg had married his grandson and namesake in '66. She'd never known Old Peter's wife, Charity, who had died less than a year before. The old man had mourned his beloved wife for the remainder of his years.

Old Peter was the last of the old life. In five years, a new century would begin. More than ever, the world belonged to the young ones. John and her girls and their husbands. And her treasured grandchildren, now numbering seven.

"Ma? Sleeping in your chair." John clucked his tongue at her like an old hen.

"Don't sass your ma. I was just resting my eyes."

"Why aren't you at your piano?"

"I'm so comfortable."

With a mischievous smile, he lifted her propped legs and set them gently on the floor.

"You're a spoiled brat, you are." Meg walked the few steps to the "square piano," which was in fact rectangular. It sat in the middle of the parlor opposite the glass-enclosed bookcase filled with the books John had inherited from his father. After the Church and her loved ones, the piano was the center of Meg's life. She sat and ran her fingers across the ivory keys, hinting at the melody that was hers and Pete's favorite.

"Play it for me, Ma."

The song was John's favorite, too. "Why?" she asked him.

Dutch didn't answer.

Tears welled in Meg's eyes. "Lord save me from a sentimental Irishman." She played and sang, but only got halfway through the first line: " 'Believe me if all those endearing young . . .' Not tonight, if you don't mind."

"Sure." He caressed her bun of white hair.

Placing her hand over his, Meg looked up at her son. "You are a handsome devil, John Tonneman."

"Sure, Ma."

"When are you going to find a beautiful lass and give me Tonneman grandchildren?"

He raised his voice so it would carry into the kitchen. "Annie will take care of that for you in one year, nine months, exactly."

"I'll get you for that," his sister yelled from the kitchen.

Dutch laughed and rolled down his shirtsleeves.

"They won't be Tonnemans till they're yours and bear the name."

"Ma."

"Don't tell me you're going out again?" Meg asked, seeing him reach for his coat.

"Bo's coming for me. It's the job, Ma."

"The job. No time for tea?"

"I have to go, Ma."

"I wouldn't mind if it was a girl and not the evil job." Her complaint was an old story.

He hesitated an instant before saying, "The right girl hasn't come along."

Her sharp ears had not missed the hesitation. She squinted inquiringly up at her son, waiting for him to say more, but he didn't.

Instead, when a knock came at the front door, he said, "That'll be Bo."

"Don't be so sure." Meg sat up straight on the piano stool and called, "Are you of the living or of the dead?"

Dutch turned his head to hide the smile. His mother did love her rituals. Meg Clancy Tonneman believed that at any time, whoever knocked on her door could be a dead spirit. According to her, one didn't have to be mad to penetrate "the otherworld." Dutch, with all respect, thought his mother quite daft on this subject, but if her belief that something existed beyond brought her comfort and cheer, it was all right with him. He crossed from the parlor to the front hall.

"Don't open till he tells you who he is," Meg warned.

"Yes, Ma." He made it into a broad show: "Declare yourself out there. Who is it?"

"It's Moose, and you better let me in or face the consequences. I saw you lift that apple from the horse's feed bag this morning, and I want my share."

Dutch opened the door; Bo thumped in. "I'll be right with you, Bo."

"A good evening to you, Aunt Meg," Bo said.

"How's your ma?"

"Except for the rheumatism, she's grand."

"And the boys?"

"They're fine."

"Tell Nan I said hello."

"Okay."

Dutch kissed his mother good night.

Meg took her kiss and said, "All right, get on to your job. But make some time to go through Old Peter's things. Remember what you promised."

"I remember and I will, Ma. First chance I get."

"No one else, but you," his great-grandfather whispered as John held the fragile hand in his. The old man's mouth smelled of peppermint and his voice was thin as air. John had to put his ear next to the dying man's lips. "Promise me . . ." The hand clutched his. Old Peter lay in the high four-poster bed, his fine white hair almost one with the white pillowcase. "You are our memory." That was all he said, except for his last word, which rang clear as a bell. "Charity." Then he was gone.

Dutch and Bo headed for Mulberry Street, Bo talking about their investigation, Dutch quiet with his thoughts. Ma was always at him. He'd marry someday. That was natural. But right now the Detective Squad was his life. Thanks to Old Peter having been Jake Hays's right hand and "a man of great value on the Force," John had been appointed to the Force without having to cough up the regular three-hundred-dollar graft required to join the department.

Every new policeman was aware that he'd get his three hundred dollar "entrance fee" back and more so, by just putting his hand out, palm up, to local businesses.

"What do you say, give this one a week and then put it away? I mean, no one's paying us to dig deep."

Dutch nodded without really hearing. He wondered how the "fees" would work now that Moose was around. Probably just the same. On the sly, more, but same as before. Still, Moose was a good man. And like Tonneman, Moose was a Dutchman.

John Tonneman had moved quickly from uniform to the Detective Squad, where he found his niche. He also found his cross to bear. And not only from strangers. He knew one or two of his cousins were on the take. He looked at his partner. No, not Bo. He'd bet his life on Bo.

Dutch wasn't holier-than-thou, but it went against his grain to take the graft, even though the department was swimming in it. Everyone knew. It was right out there in the open. Well, he would see what Moose could do.

"I don't fancy the thought of going down to that sewer on Madison Street," Bo said. He reached into his pocket for a coin and dropped it into the tin cup a crippled old lady held out to them from her perch on a barrel in front of a boarded-up shop. Dutch followed suit.

"Thank you, your honors," the old lady cackled. She shook the coins in her cup. "Thank you."

Since joining the department, Dutch had kept his own counsel, not speaking of the graft to Bo or even Old Peter. But his great-grandfather knew. There was little about the world the old man didn't know. Old Peter had been sorely troubled by the fees and other dishonesties and done his best to get rid of them. But each time he tried, he'd hit the same old story, that without them the Force couldn't function, and he'd back off.

Old Peter was a good man, Dutch knew, but he wasn't Old Hays. Old Hays would have knocked them in the head with that stick of his, kicked them in the ass, and sent them all packing.

"You are my blood," Old Peter said one night, as the two of them sat in the parlor smoking. "Maybe it's because we're Dutchmen to the bone, and dull and plodding to boot. But we never touch what doesn't belong to us. I learned that young. I think you were simply born to it, John. And we do right by others."

"Yes, sir."

The old man had looked at his great-grandson with his sharp blue eyes, which time had failed to dim or fade. "My father would have liked you, John. John was his name, too. And he saw the Revolution come. He and my mother . . ." Tears welled in the fierce blue eyes. "My mother was a wisp of a dark-haired woman with a fearless heart. She would have loved you."

"Get a move on, coz." Bo elbowed his way into Dutch's memories. "Things to do, murderers to catch."

27

Friday,
May 31.
Sundown.

It was after seven as the sun went down. In the tiny sitting room on the top floor, Esther covered her head with a cloth, lit the two candles, and said the Hebrew blessing.

Her hands, making circles over the flames, waved the flames to her, coming almost to her face at the end of each wave, in anticipation of what was to follow. On the third pass she brought her hands to her face for the remainder of the prayer.

"Blessed art thou, O Lord our God, King of the universe, who has sanctified us by Thy commandments, and has commanded us to kindle the Sabbath-light. Amen." Esther removed the napkin from her head.

At dinner, revived by her prayers, Esther was bursting with anticipation. She was eager to develop the one unshattered plate. Perhaps they might see something in it that would give them a clue to Robert's murderer. It would be a good photograph. And it would show the right thing. Of this, Esther was positive. But she kept her hopes to herself and remained silent, as she had at that day's noon meal.

"We need to talk," Oz said.

She waited expectantly. At last.

But instead Oz said, "Would you care to help me with the text of my book?"

"I?" She was stunned. "I am not a journalist. I could never replace Robert."

"You underestimate yourself, my dear. Your spoken English is perfect, albeit accented, and the compositions I've read are quite good."

Esther blushed. Poor Robert, she thought. It was typical of this City, this country. One person goes, another quickly takes his place.

Oz immediately changed the subject and began rhapsodizing over Lillian Russell. He had seen the famed performer two weeks before at Abbey's in a production of *The Tzigane*. "It's true the company was not well prepared, and I know the critics thought the production listless, but the woman has a delightful voice and an even more delightful presence. We must invite her to be photographed, Esther. Not in the studio, though, before that tedious black drape. The park, that would be perfect for her, against a background of roses. Better still, a carpet of roses."

Esther listened with growing impatience. When Oz paused, she asked what most interested her: "Excuse me, but when will we develop the negative?"

Oz did not seem to mind that she had broken into his monologue. But he did not respond to her question. He leaned back in his chair.

"Coffee, sir?" Wong had appeared, silently as always.

"Yes. The roast beef was superb, Wong. Please consider making hash with the remainder."

Wong dipped his head and cleared away the dishes. Mr. Cook was always suggesting things for him to make. Wong prepared what he pleased.

"That's a fine Bordeaux; I hope we have sufficient on hand."

Again Wong nodded. Mr. Cook always asked that, and the wine cellar was filled to the rafters with Bordeaux and more.

"I must take you to Delmonico's some evening, Esther," he told her cheerfully. "They make the most superb venison hash."

Esther sighed. "I am not permitted to eat venison, Oz."

"Forgive me. I didn't know. Then we shall have the shrimp hash."

Esther shook her head.

"No shrimp either? Corned beef, then?"

She conceded a wan smile. Oz was acting as if Robert had never existed. She produced a handkerchief from the sleeve of her dress and patted the tender skin of her bruised and tearing eye.

"Capital. Corned beef hash it is." He called to Wong. "A taste of the Madeira would be most satisfying."

Wong nodded. Mr. Cook always said that, too.

Only after Wong provided the white dessert wine, and withdrew, did Oz Cook give his protégée a searching look. "You think ill of me, don't you? In not mourning my friend."

Esther twisted her handkerchief and studied her hands.

"I feel his loss, nonetheless," Oz continued. "Robert was of an incendiary nature. Vivid. In his own way he had the soul of an artist. I regret I did not take more photographs of him. I will miss my friend in the extreme. I envy the intensity of your race's emotions. . . ." His voice trailed off. "We will finish the book together. It will be his memorial."

"No," said Esther. "Finding his killer will be his memorial."

28

Friday,
May 31.
Night.
Just before nine.

The cop house was lit up like a birthday cake, and a steady stream of foot traffic went in and out. Some, of course, wore the blue uniform and gray helmet of the patrolman, and some the detective costume of suit and derby.

Then there were the crooks of one stripe or another, coming in, and too often, going out, having stayed their brief while and settled their account—either fine or bribe.

Add to this the crooks' mouthpieces, lawyers who won no matter what, the upstanding banker types who made the rules and broke them at their own pleasure, and the "curious cat" reporters who stuck their collective noses into everything.

The path going in and coming out of the House on Mulberry Street was well worn.

Across the street at 303 Mulberry, in the two-story shack the journalists called home, the atmosphere was sullen. One of their own had been brutally murdered. The newsmen clustered in front of their building like a belligerent honor guard, impatiently waiting for answers.

Most of the morning papers had carried word of the savage homicide, and the headlines in the afternoon press screamed the news.

The *Herald* itself had declared, "BRUTAL MURDER OF CRUSADING JOURNALIST," and lamented the loss of a talent struck down in its blossoming youth.

A delegation led by Jacob Riis and Lincoln Steffens had met with Acting Chief Peter Conlin and demanded action.

Chief Conlin gave the journalists his solemn vow that Clancy and Tonneman, two of his finest detectives, were on the job, and would bring the killer to judgment.

But Conlin's words were all lip service. Deaths like Robert Roman's were a common occurrence in Mulberry Bend and the Gas House District; they were rarely solved.

On the other hand, with Moose and the other three new Commissioners given a broad mandate to clean up the Force, one had to put one's best face front—go through the motions, that is. Which was why Conlin had selected Clancy and Tonneman as his new trouble men. Their records were clean, and Moose had approved.

Such was the climate Bo and Dutch found when they arrived at the House on Mulberry Street. Across the street, in front of the reporters' shack, the line stirred and broke, shouting.

Bo got through the door held open by Tom McGee, who had the duty, but Dutch was waylaid by a tall young man.

"Do you have any leads?" Lincoln Steffens of the *Post* demanded, his eyes blazing.

"It's too soon to say," Dutch answered. Then more formally: "We have just begun our investigation." He squeezed through the opening McGee was offering. Once Tonneman was in, the doorman slammed the door tight, commenting dryly, "Frisky, ain't they?"

"Let's go," Bo told his cousin. "They're all scavengers."

But Tonneman shook his head. "One of their own. It would be the same for us."

Inside, the House on Mulberry Street was chaos. Even with the front door barred against the Fourth Estate, the downstairs area was jammed with noisy, profane individuals all demanding to be heard and to be heard first.

Bo rolled his eyes at his partner. As they climbed the stairs Dutch asked, "What did Ned say? About fishing Roman out of the river?"

"That was it," Bo answered. "Ned offered to take him to Gouverneur, but the daft man just walked away, and him dripping wet." He shook his head.

The Acting Chief of Detectives' office was on the second floor, as was that of the Police Commission. Tonight the second floor was also hustle and bustle. Moose had called an emergency meeting of the entire board.

Only the Museum of Crime, ex-Chief Byrnes's own institution, across the hall from the Chief's office, seemed exempt from the night's frantic activity. That was because it was old news, featuring the methods of past crimes solved and unsolved: Knives and guns and poison bottles and lengths of rope, all used with murderous intent.

The Acting Chief's outer office was packed with men, some in uniform, some in plainclothes. The chief's assistant, Jim Ryan, soon spotted Bo and Dutch and sent them inside the big chamber the legendary Chief Thomas J. Byrnes had so recently vacated.

As the detectives entered, this slightly built man stood to greet them, something Chief Byrnes never would have done. Peter Conlin was of only medium height, but his erect military stance made him seem taller. Like Father Duff, Conlin had been a member of the Irish Brigade, in the 69th, during the War. And like Father Duff, he had been severely wounded. His demeanor was polished. His speech was free of the accent peculiar to the Irish-New Yorker, for he was half-brother to the actor William Florence, and had had the benefit of his example.

Conlin's eyes were ice blue, yet they seemed to hold a hot spark as he greeted his two detectives. "Take a seat, gentlemen." He gestured them to the two chairs in front of his desk. Then with a delivery and flare he could only have learned from Mr. Florence, he added gravely, "I have staked my reputation on this case."

He waited for a response.

"Yes, sir," the two young detectives said together.

"Roman was a meddlesome man. Did you know him?"

Bo shook his head.

"I met him once," Tonneman said. "Briefly."

"I want this clean," Conlin said.

"Yes, sir."

"Nothing to sully the Department's good name."

Dutch wondered what good name. It had been a rotten name of late.

Bo looked at Tonneman, a flicker of a question, then his eyes went flat.

"Do you hear me, lads?" Conlin demanded.

"Yes, sir," came the combined reply. The partners each knew that if they didn't solve this one quick and clean, they'd be walking a night beat in Five Points.

"That's it, men. Find me this killer and find him fast. Or we'll all go the way of Tommy Byrnes." Pete Conlin was never one to waste words. The short and sweet of it was that, with the new broom sweeping clean, the chief wanted to be on the right end of the broomstick.

Bo shook his head. "No offense, sir, must be hell around here, dancing to four different tunes."

"No offense taken. There may be four in the choir but only two can be heard. And neither sings a pretty song. One's running the whole shebang and the other thinks of the Detective Squad as his own personal plaything. Have you ever heard a moose and a peacock braying at each other in the night?"

Dutch and Bo traded glances, grinning.

Conlin's cold blue eyes were diverted by the various files of papers positioned neatly about his desk. He chose a file and began to read.

They were dismissed.

29

Friday,
May 31.
Night.

As Bo and Dutch headed toward the front door, footsteps thudded on the stairs behind them: "You! Paddy! A moment, if you please."

It was, wouldn't you know, Peacock himself. The man was flawlessly attired; his pointed beard was deep brown and gleamed as if polished. The Commissioner was a fine-looking man with a superior smile that Bo itched to wipe from his face. Paddy, indeed. Bo chose to take the insult on himself. "The name is Clancy, Commissioner. Detective Sergeant Clancy. My partner, Detective Sergeant Tonneman."

"You're the two who've just been assigned to the Roman murder?"

"Yes, sir," Dutch replied.

"I expect the Chief has told you I've taken a strong interest in this case."

Again it was Dutch who answered. "He has, sir."

"I merely want it said in plain language that *I* run the Detective Division. Is that clear? I want to be kept informed of your progress." The smooth smile again. "You understand me, *boyos*." Peacock didn't wait for an answer, but turned and mounted the steps to the second floor.

Bo's fists were balled and his face was florid. Dutch moved to stand between him and Peacock. "Time to go, Bo," he said softly.

"Time to twist me a peacock's neck." Bo glared after the Commissioner. "I'll give him *boyos*. Have you heard? Someone said to Moose that sooner or later a Peacock will smite a fellow when he isn't looking, particularly a Moose. But our Moose doesn't believe it. He says he boxed with Peacock and Peacock boxed like a gentleman. Jesus, Mary, and Joseph. I like Moose, but sometimes he can be that much of a fool."

The heat of the day had rapidly cooled as night took over the City. And the faint rumble of thunder promised rain and perhaps cooler days.

The heart of the City was now well lit. Even though wires had been ordered underground since 1884, the walks were overgrown with many-armed telephone poles, each arm festooned with mazes of electric, telephone, and telegraph wires. Hanging crisscrossed like giant fishnets, they cast grotesque shadows, webbing the view overhead and threatening to ensnare the birds of the air.

At least they weren't down, as they had been after some rainstorms: fire-spitting snakes, threatening havoc to life and limb.

But wires strung, above ground or below, didn't necessarily mean services rendered. Although the Financial District was lit by electricity, the dock area they were heading to was still on the gas, and barely that.

When they passed through Chatham Square, the rain began. Dutch turned on the bull's-eye lamp he'd signed out at the station house to make up for the few-and-far-between gas street lamps with their clouded globes. The bull's-eye light caught St. James Church and the odd setup of the small Hebrew cemetery next to it.

The two didn't speak as they walked. All Dutch heard from his partner was the low humming of a song about an Irishman whaling the tar out of the Protestant employer who put up the sign *No Irish Need Apply*. No doubt about it, Peacock had put Bo in a raw mood.

Not wanting to use up the battery power, Tonneman turned off the light and only turned it back on when the way ahead became too pitch black to make out.

Dutch talked while Bo seethed. Dutch reviewed what they had. The dead body. The attempted theft of the photographic plates earlier the same day. He didn't mention the broken plates. It had been a harebrained scheme to try to get a photographic image out of them. He knew that now, after what Oswald Cook had said about their exposure to light. All the plates but possibly one were useless. For the present, he chose not to say anything to his partner about the one. He needn't have worried. Bo wasn't listening.

This time when Dutch turned the lamp back on, it revealed not only the glistening, wet street ahead but the people sleeping in doorways and huddled on stoops, either because they had no other place or because the unreasonable heat had baked the hovels they called home. Few stirred as they passed.

On Madison and Gouverneur, the hall of the tenement next to the alley was even darker than the street outside. Dutch said, "Good thing I brought the bull's-eye, the light's out." He sniffed. The place smelled of rot, not gas. "Dead rats."

"Better dead than living," Bo grumbled, speaking for the first time since they'd left Mulberry Street. "I hate rats."

"Good. You can talk. I thought you forgot how."

"Don't be daft, I'm an Irishman." Bo turned and said to his partner, "You know Moose is serious about wanting to shake up the Force even more. Of course Peacock is against him. He wants the control."

Dutch shook his head. "Where do you hear these things?"

"It's out there, all you have to do is listen. You know Peacock's got Conlin in his pocket."

"I don't doubt it. And you've got a hate on Peacock you can taste."

"Ain't that the truth." Bo pulled open the front door, which sagged on its hinges and creaked a protest. The buildings here, like all tenements, had unlocked street doors. There were no bells to announce visitors, and the entrance halls were available to all sorts of vermin. Both the four-legged and the two-legged kind.

"You pick," said Dutch. "Start at the bottom and work up or viceyversy?"

"Work up," Bo said. "Then all we have to do is run down and get the hell away from here."

"Fine with me," Tonneman replied.

In a small chamber behind the stairs, they discovered a newly arrived immigrant family. The man who answered the door, fear bouncing around in his eyes, had a full beard and wore a skullcap, which identified him as an Israelite. At least five little ones were crowded in the narrow bed with the woman, and though she modestly covered herself with a threadbare blanket, it was obvious she was close to having a sixth.

They spoke no English and there were no windows. Just the bed, falling-down walls, and little else.

"Let's go," said Bo.

The round dark eyes of the immigrants were so fearful that Dutch could not leave until he reassured them, whether they grasped his words or not. Bo had little patience and was back in the hall and knocking on the next door. At a loss, Dutch finally said, "I'm sorry," to the terrified Israelites and followed his partner out.

Bo pushed open the door. Dutch followed, shining his light. This ragbin of a room smelled to high heaven. There was no evidence that anyone lived here, so the broken and cardboard-patched grimy window facing the alley did them no good. They'd find no witness to Roman's murder here.

Kicking some rags away, Bo stubbed his toe. "Son of a bitch." He bent down. "Give me some light." He cleared away the rags and let out a soft whistle. "Look at this."

"A cop's gun," said Dutch. The Smith & Wesson .32 Bo had uncovered was the official weapon of the Force.

"It is now." Bo jammed the shiny weapon into his coat pocket. "We better look and see if there's more."

When it was apparent that no more weapons were to be found in the room, Bo said, "All right, up the stairs, *boyo*, or we'll never get out of this rattrap."

They climbed the dilapidated stairs, the bull's-eye lantern lighting their way. The stairs protested loudly with every step.

"Hot," Bo complained. "How do these people stand it?"

"Hey, who you kicking?"

The lamp hadn't picked out the man dozing on the stairs. "You can't sleep here."

"Why not?" The light reflected back at them from the man's white cataract eyes.

"Shit," said Bo. "Sorry." And he pressed a coin into the blind man's hand.

The second-floor landing was, if anything, worse than the first.

Their bull's-eye provided the only light, but it merely illuminated rotting garbage and cockroaches on constant march. Each of the four doorways on the floor led to warrens of heaven knew how many rooms.

"Stick with what looks out over the alley," Bo said, his voice distorted because he was holding his nose shut. "And that have windows."

"Disagree. Someone in this tenement might have heard something, even if they couldn't see. Or might have seen someone on the street going into the alley."

His cousin released his nose and shook his head. "You being so fucking smart means we'll be here all night. Let's get at it, then. You finish here, I'll get the next floor."

Dutch set the bull's-eye so it lit not only the staircase, but the second-floor landing. He pushed open the first door. "Hello, in there. Anyone who knows anything about the killing last night in the alley? There's fifty cents reward for anyone who can tell us anything."

The silence was amazing. Dutch couldn't even hear the breathing, but he knew the room was inhabited by terror. He could smell it. Then a shadow moved so slightly that it hardly moved at all. He and Bo would have made a much faster job of it during the day. But the crime had happened at night, so that would have been a waste of time. At any rate, the silence was to be expected. Those who could understand would not tell anything for fear of retribution. All these wretches wanted was to be left alone.

Dutch ventured into the room. "Hello?"

The shadow became a cadaverous old man. "What?" he croaked, cupping his ear. "What?"

Dutch waved the man off and left the room.

From the stairs he heard his cousin curse, then continue his heavy-footed progress.

Pounding on the second door, Dutch called, "Police!" The door cracked open; he saw nothing. When he looked down he spied first the eyes, then, as the door opened wider, the tiny lad, barefoot and in a tattered nightshirt that reached barely to his middle.

The child was swarthy, dark as an Indian, skin shiny with perspiration. His black hair hung down to his shoulders. It was only because of the outgrown nightshirt that Tonneman knew he was a boy.

"Where's your father?" Tonneman asked, giving the door a soft nudge.

A voice called in Italian from within. Tonneman retrieved his lamp and peered inside. In spite of the foul air, he drew a deep breath. Kids. More than a dozen, not one over ten. Children living like rats. He'd let the Children's Aid know, but that would only get them on the Orphan Train. Telling the priest at St. Theresa's on Rutgers Street would be a better idea.

"Anyone speak English?" He squinted, attempting to see better, and in the gloom spied a small window painted over with black paint. Eye holes were scratched in the paint. Tonneman crossed the room and peered through the eye holes.

Nothing was visible, either straight ahead or down below. He was thinking more about the kids than the case. Tomorrow he'd go across Mulberry Street to the reporters' crib and tell Jacob Riis.

Dutch waved to the kids.

Timidly they waved back.

What was surprising was that Riis, with his camera and his crusade for social justice for the poor and downtrodden, hadn't found this hell-hole yet. Especially considering there'd been a murder just outside.

Dutch stepped out on the landing. He repeated the procedure he'd used on the first door on the last two doors, hammering and offering a reward for information.

With the same lack of results.

Up he went. The staircase leaned unstably into the wall. Rancid smells of cooking were imbedded in the walls. But there was another, more benevolent fragrance just ahead.

On three, he found his cousin seated on the steps, smoking a cigar. "I thought why not make good use of my last Lucifer," Bo said. He gave a mighty puff but succeeded only for a moment in driving the stink of garbage away.

Tonneman knocked on the nearest door. It was then they received their first crumb of luck.

"Are you of the living or of the dead?" a woman's voice called.

"Very much alive, missis," Dutch answered. "Not only that, we're Irish."

The door swung open wide. The woman who stood contemplating

them with outright joy was small, but flinty. Though aged and wrinkled, she stood straight as a stick. She had white hair and was wearing a neat, threadbare blue cotton dress. A knitted shawl covered her shoulders. Her face was sunken but her cheeks, what little was left of them, glowed with the vigor of a farmer's wife. In her hand was a fat candle, like those used at church. "You darlin' boys wouldn't be policemen, would you?"

"And sure, my darlin'," Bo said. "Is that a touch of the bog in your voice?"

"Who else would be answering your knock that way? And what else would you expect from a Monahan married to a Doty?"

"Well, Mrs. Doty," Dutch said, "is there anything you can tell us about the tragedy that occurred here last night?"

"You mean that poor fellow they found in the alley?"

"Yes, ma'am," Bo said.

"I didn't see nothin'." Mrs. Doty shook her white head. "Don't get old, lads. The legs go, the eyes go, everything goes. And the heat. It's killin' me, it is. Outside I'm burnin' up, inside I'm burnin' up."

"Yes, ma'am," the partners said together.

"I don't know what time it was. I never sleep, but my clock's broke." She looked at them with clear green eyes waiting to be urged.

Dutch complied. "Go on, ma'am."

"But these ruffians was makin' such a racket last night. I yelled down that I was callin' you fellows on my telephone." She chuckled. "I don't have one of them things, but I had them fooled into thinkin' I did. Bunch of idiots. A telephone here in this dump? That'll be the day."

"What exactly did you hear, missis?" Bo asked.

"A racket, didn't I just say? They was laughin' and breakin' windows."

"How many were there?" Dutch said.

"Well, I couldn't rightly see. There was two for sure."

"You got a good look at them, then?" Bo raised an eyebrow at Tonneman.

"In the dead of night? From up here?" She rubbed her eyes. "You take a look down there and see what you see." She waved them into her tiny room.

As Bo stepped up to the window, there was a quick flash of lightning followed immediately by a loud crack of thunder. He paused, then looked down into the alley. "Black as a Protestant's heart." He shook his head at Dutch.

"Thanks, missis," Dutch said. "You sleep well, now."

"Come back and see me again."

"We may just do that," Bo said, as Mrs. Doty closed her door.

The other three doors led to still more warrens where English was never spoken or heard.

On the fourth floor, which stank of burnt cabbage, everyone spoke only Russian. At least that was what they all pretended.

Dutch and Bo had been in the building more than an hour when they reached the fifth and last floor. Bo, who had completely lost his meager patience, hammered on all four doors in succession. "Anybody home? It's the Law."

"Perfect. Now no one will open up."

"So what? Except for Mrs. Doty, all we got on the way up was a lot of Dago, Yid, and Russki. How are we going to get any answers if the fuckers don't speak English?"

"Patience, coz. Everything comes to him who waits."

At that moment one of the doors swung open. Byron Brown, in full regalia for a night out on the town, stood before them. The two policemen didn't know it, but this was the same outfit the actor had worn the night before at The Allen's saloon and at the House on Mulberry Street. It was all he had at the moment that was presentable.

With no doubt in his mind about what sort of creatures stood before him, Byron struck a pose and declaimed, "And what can I do for the minions of the law?"

Bo raised furry eyebrows to his cousin. "Last night a man was killed in the alley next door. Do you know anything about it?"

Byron smoothed his mustache in an elaborate two-handed gesture. Bringing to his mind those villains he'd played, he rubbed his hands together. "And what remuneration might one expect for such information?" he asked coyly.

Bo growled. "A broken head if you don't tell us."

"Don't be that way, Bo." Tonneman spoke with embroidered kindness. "My partner doesn't mean that," he said. Dutch's sense of smell got past the cabbage-and-dead-rat stink of the hall, and inhaled the spirits that seemed to be woven into the old actor's clothing. This sparked an inspiration. "But we'd be glad to stand you a drink if you can help us out," he said.

"Or two?" Byron suggested eagerly.

"Two, it is," Tonneman said. "What do you know?"

"Alas, dear Hawkshaw, I know nothing."

Bo made a fist and leaned into Byron.

The actor flinched and added hastily, "But my daughter's friend escorted me home last night. He might be a fertile source of information."

"And who might that be?" Dutch demanded.

"The gentleman in question is one Leo Stern."

"Gentleman? Well, hardly." Bo's mouth, at last, turned up in a cheery smile. "Now ain't that interesting? Dutch, do you know who Leo Stern is? He's pimp and muscle for Marm Mandelbaum's bastard kid. The whoremonger Sophie Mandel."

"Gently, good fellow," Byron Brown, *né* Paul Skidelsky, said, a mildly hurt expression on his face. "The bastard kid whoremonger is my daughter."

30

Friday, May 31–
Saturday, June 1.
Night to morning.

The Bowery ran itself out near Seventh Street. Here, just off Cooper Square, rose a red brick tenement. The sign mounted on its front had been welcoming thirsty men for thirty-one years: "Old House at Home." No one called the tavern that, or even McSorley's Ale House. To one and all it was known simply as McSorley's, "good ale, raw onions, and no ladies."

The cadence of the place was pure Irish. Only if you listened hard could you hear the trace of German in some of the voices. During the day and early evening, McSorley's was frequented by the men who worked in the neighborhood at the tanneries, brickyards, carpenter shops, slaughterhouses, and breweries of lower Manhattan.

A free lunch of soda crackers, cheese, and raw onions was served for the price of a nickel pewter mug of ale.

In the evening, neighborhood men drifted in. A long day of work and an evening of drinking warm ale might find them nodding over their mugs late into the night until they were gently prodded to go home to their wives and families, or at the least, their lonely beds to prepare for the morrow, another day of the same.

To Byron Brown's dismay, no whiskey was served at McSorley's. But being a practical man, the actor accepted his disappointment like a gentleman and, though discontented, announced he would make do with ale.

Dutch took one of the house clay pipes and filled it with the tobacco from the bar. He had the feeling, one he'd experienced before, that he was watching himself from somewhere else.

The proprietor stood behind the bar, reading the *Pinky*.

"Hello, Bill," Tonneman offered.

"Mmm," was all he got back. Old Bill McSorley was a closed-mouthed morose fellow, not much older than Dutch himself.

Maybe if he drank his own ale he'd be in a better mood. But just like old John McSorley, his father, Bill McSorley was a teetotaler.

"Sit yourself," Bo ordered the actor, pointing to the table near the cold potbellied stove.

Byron sat with an exaggerated sigh. He dusted the sawdust from his shabby trouser legs.

When Tonneman arrived with the mugs of ale, the trio took their first drinks in silence.

"Ah," the actor sighed, "warm from the hob. I like that."

Bo yawned vigorously. "All right, Brown. What did you see in the alley?"

Outside thunder cracked. Barely a second later, lightning flashed across the saloon's windows.

"Well?" Bo insisted.

The old actor shook his head. "Never talk during a sound or light cue. Nobody will pay attention."

Bo put on his mean face. "I'm paying attention, now. You talk, now."

Byron cleared his throat. "I saw not a thing, my good benefactor. I was too far in my cups. But if there was anything to see, Leo's your man."

"Leo, again," Bo said.

"My dear daughter's business manager."

Bo snorted. "Sophie needs a business manager like she needs a hole in the head." He grinned. "Come to think of it, she might make good use of a hole in the head."

Dutch frowned at his cousin. "Bo." What good did it do to insult the man's daughter? Dutch sipped his ale and turned to Byron. "He means no harm. What do you remember from last night?"

"In truth, very little, gentlemen. Leo's the man to talk to. Mayhap he saw something after he left me."

"And *mayhap* Roman was following you?" Bo motioned for more ale. "And *mayhap* Leo beat the shit out of Roman because Roman was following you?"

Byron looked aghast. "Oh, no, Leo is not a violent man. I can assure you of that. He is an honorable man."

Dutch paid for the new round.

In spite of the blustering cop's manner, Byron was enjoying himself. There was a small charm to the glistening golden ale. Byron decided that this dusty dim place had a certain style. It was like being not in the real world, but in the set of a theatre. Which he always preferred.

Two gas lamps hanging over the bar were connected by a rod from which dangled hundreds of turkey wishbones laced with cobwebs. The webs converged on the ceiling in thick layers, giving the place a kind of panache.

Cats were everywhere, some sleeping, others having a romp over the sawdust floor.

There was a firehouse gong behind the bar. Women were forbidden entrance to McSorley's. If one came in, the bartender would ring the gong and the patrons would cry out, "No women allowed!" And it would always be that way.

Every piece of wall space was covered with newspaper clippings, paintings, photographs of actors and actresses, and other sorts of memorabilia.

"Where were you coming from?" Dutch asked Byron Brown suddenly.

"The House on Mulberry Street," Byron replied promptly. "I had a little brush with the law, though I was doing nothing to incur legal wrath. Nothing at all. I was but a bystander, merely watching. A raid at The Allen, you know. I'm innocent, I can assure you gentlemen with a clean conscience."

"So you say."

"So I do say." Byron tossed off his ale and signaled with a flourish of his hand. "Barkeep, another, please."

"No you don't," Bo snarled. "Hold up, Bill."

"Make up your mind." The taciturn McSorley was irritated.

Dutch puffed on his pipe and looked up at the portrait of Lincoln on the wall. "On your way, actor. Before my partner takes a bite out of your ass."

Byron scrutinized Bo for only a second, rose quickly, made a short bow, and scurried out the door.

Bo tramped to the bar, ate a wedge of onion from the bowl, and filled himself a corncob pipe. Teeth clamped tight on the stem, he brought two fresh ales back to their table. "So what do you think?"

"I think tomorrow we'll take ourselves over to Clinton Street and visit with Madam Sophie. And her business manager, the honorable Leo Stern."

31

Saturday, June 1. Morning.

As far as Bo was concerned, after Dutch quit on him, the night was far from over. With a few stops in between, somewhere near dawn he ended up in Black Dick's on the Bowery, just two blocks from McSorley's. Black Dick wasn't a spook, but he'd been a coal miner in Pennsylvania, and folks said he never quite got the coal dust out of his skin.

Bo wasn't surprised to see Queenie Landry, dressed in her Victoria mourning, sitting in the cop's seat at the inside end of the bar. Atop her tall stool, to make up for her lack of height, she was holding court for other morning boozers.

"Morning, Queenie," Bo said, not yet bleary-eyed. What luck, he thought.

She gave him a wink. "Morning, Bo." Seeing the detective, Queenie's loyal subjects began to get scarce.

It was just the two of them when he spoke again. "Do you know anything about that killing on Madison Street?"

"Which one? On a good night Madison Street is prime for three corpses at least." Queenie gave a gruesome chuckle.

"Did you know Robert Roman?"

Her rouged old lips pulled back. It wasn't really a smile. "Sure, all of us in the business did. He liked his women, he did. Bobby didn't have the pockets for it, though. My Mabs was what he could afford, but he preferred to do without so's he could have one of Sophie's girls."

"Anyone in particular?"

She shrugged and took a swallow of gin.

"What was Roman working on?"

"Aside from the girls, I couldn't tell you."

"You mean you won't."

"Same difference."

"I could make you tell me, Queenie."

"You could hurt me, Bo, but you couldn't make me do anything I didn't want to."

"I bet the police in Hartford, Connecticut, would like to know where the little woman who killed Ed Morgan disappeared to."

The old madam blanched under her face powder. "I don't know what you mean."

"Yes, you do. Talk to me, sweet Queenie, and I'll forget all about it."

"Till the next time you need to squeeze me, you bastard."

"Talk."

"There's a new protection racket going on. Ex-cops is running it."

"Names." A noise distracted him, as if someone had just come in. Bo turned. The front door was closing, but he saw no one. He turned back to Queenie. "I'll thank you for those names."

Fear had filled her eyes. "Go shit in your hat," she croaked hoarsely. "I ain't telling you nothing. You and Hartford be damned."

Bo scraped his shoe on the edge of the sidewalk to remove the horse manure he'd just stepped in. "Look at that."

"Stop fretting like an old woman," Dutch said. "Ma says it's good luck."

"For all the good I did on them yesterday rubbing in the Bixby's, I could have drunk the stuff."

"I don't see why not," Dutch said amiably, as the partners inched their way past a ragpicker's two-wheeled pull wagon piled with overstuffed gunnysacks of rags. The sacks were piled so high one on the other they couldn't see behind the ragpicker's wagon.

Many ragpickers ranged all over the City, digging in rubbish bins and refuse mounds outside factories or on the dumping boards along the East and Hudson Rivers. The rags they found and sold would be washed and remade into clothing or bedding or, at worst, paper.

When they got past the piled wagon Dutch brushed at his suit and finished his thought. "Last night you drank just about everything else *but* the Bixby's."

"Hell, ale won't hurt you." Bo grinned at him.

"Poor old Byron, he sure was pissed he couldn't get anything stronger."

"I could have used a drop of the sauce myself last night."

Dutch inspected his partner. Bo was clean-shaven and shiny, but Dutch knew he hadn't had any sleep. "And didn't you?"

"What?"

"Get a drop or two after I left you?"

"What are you, a detective? I stopped in a few places, had a few drinks."

As they'd approached Thirty-fourth Street and the Herald Building, they could sense an extra charge of energy. The advent of the popular newspaper had changed the area, electrified it, so to speak. Here pedestrians walked faster, even talked faster, than elsewhere in the City.

The construction of the splendid Bridge to Brooklyn had disrupted the area downtown around Park Row known as Printing House Square. While most of the newspapers, including the *Times*, the *Observer*, the *Daily News*, the *World*, and the *Examiner* stayed, making the adjustments, the previous year, James Gordon Bennett, Jr., editor of the *Herald*, had chosen to move.

Son of *the* James Gordon Bennett, who'd worked his way up from Scottish immigrant to powerful founder of the New York *Herald*, Bennett, Jr., had erected a two-story building on a plot of land on Thirty-fourth Street and moved his newspaper there. The new building occupied the entire triangle from Thirty-fourth to Thirty-sixth Streets, where Sixth Avenue met Broadway. A heroic bronze statue of Minerva prevailed over the southern facade of the Herald Building. Beneath it were two bronze figures wielding sledgehammers, with which they struck the hour on a huge bell.

The logic of calling the triangle a square was apparent only to New York residents. Wasn't Printing House Square a triangle, too?

Having done little to break the early heat spell, the thunderstorm of the previous night had given the streets an extra cleaning, which cut down the dust but barely reduced the horse droppings festering in the sun.

Here, the noise of the presses overpowered the general tumult of the City. And there was little greenery. So different, Tonneman thought, from the peaceful, verdant Gramercy area where you could hear the birds singing in the trees, and where Oswald Cook lived in such an unconventional arrangement with his Chinese servant who spoke like some English toff. And the Hebrew girl Esther.

A horde of boys, mostly newsies in ragged clothing, gathered in front of the *Herald* waiting to pick up the afternoon edition. Dutch and Bo shouldered around the waiting boys. They walked up the stairs past the presses which were roaring out that day's edition.

"On my rounds last night, who should I run into but Queenie Landry," Bo said.

"Accidentally, of course."

Bo grinned. "While you was having sweet dreams, I was working. Hell, how else am I going to be Chief of Detectives one day?"

Dutch shook his head at his cousin. "Of course, you will. Did Queenie give you anything?"

"Only that there's a protection racket going on with ex-cops running it."

"What a surprise. She tell you who's running it?"

"She told me to shit in my hat."

The newspaper's office was drab to the extreme. Desks crowded one on the other. The once-whitewashed walls were yellow from tobacco smoke. Though the light was electric, it was exceedingly dim.

Over the desks, lamps hung from long braids of chain and wire ending in metal shades, spreading fuzzy cones of light. Behind the desks sat more than fifteen reading, typing, talking men—any one of whom might have seen or spoken to Robert Roman on his final day. Back in the corner, there was even one woman.

All wore green eyeshades to reduce the glare as they clacked away on their typewriters, seeming totally oblivious to the great noise of the presses below.

The partners walked past a side room where men sat sketching at boards. The next room had its own brand of noise, different from that of the typewriters and the presses. Dutch and Bo peered in and saw that the racket came from the telegraph ticker. All of this was old hat to Dutch. He well remembered visiting his father at work at the *Post*.

The receiving operator seized a megaphone and left the ticker. Brushing past them, he called his news to the group at large. "From London. Rumor is strong Lord Roseberry will resign. Lord Salisbury says he is ready and willing to lead the government."

From the journalists there came a scattering of comments.

One man said, "At long last."

A second countered with, "It's only rumor. Let's wait for facts before we stop the presses."

Another chorus of mumbling, then they all returned to their work.

Dutch looked at the array of journalists and frowned. "Where do we start?" he asked his partner.

But Bo was already bullying his way toward the back of the long room, where an interior window revealed a man in a private office, puffing on a big cigar and talking into both of the telephones on his desk at the same time, an earpiece for each ear. All the while he was on the phones, the man was looking out his window down at Herald Square.

The Managing Editor of the *Herald* was the legendary James Gordon Bennett, Jr. Coat on, tie in place around a high white stiff collar, he no longer bore the brashness of the youth who twenty-four years earlier had sent Henry Morgan Stanley to Africa to find Dr. David Livingstone.

However, the piercing eyes had not tempered, and some thought the large straight nose had gotten larger with the years.

Like his father, Bennett, Jr., was a one-man show. He worked better in single than in double harness, and was famed for the accuracy of his reporting. If Bennett printed it, it was right.

His hair was center parted. Only the gray at the temples showed any evidence of his fifty-four years; there was no gray at all in his thick, full mustache or longish sideburns.

Bennett's desk was covered with sheets of copy. He yapped at one of the phones, then slammed the earpiece onto its hook.

Now he turned his swivel chair away from the window and cast a baleful eye on the two detectives as they threaded a path to him through the tangle of desks, telephone lines, brimming wastebaskets, and clumps of discarded paper that hadn't found their mark.

Bennett knew cops when he saw them. He'd be a poor excuse for a newspaperman if he didn't. If these two were looking for a handout, they had another think coming. He'd report them to Moose and they'd be out on their asses before they could say Jack Robinson.

Relighting his cigar, Bennett had second thoughts, however. More than likely they finally decided to come to him and ask about Robert Roman. If they were working for *him*, they would have been here three days ago. He blew a puff of smoke to greet them. They wouldn't last a day as reporters.

The detectives entered Bennett's office and waited patiently for him to hang up the second phone.

When he did, he bellowed to the newsroom without coming from behind his desk. "Foster!"

A balding reporter sprang to his feet and rushed headlong to the office for his assignment.

Bennett handed the man a slip of paper. "Small fire at Tony Pastor's. Take an artist. Make a story out of it. An *accurate* story. Go. Go. Go."

The journalist ran.

The editor's voice boomed out at Dutch and Bo as loud as he'd called for Foster, loud enough for the entire newsroom to hear, alerting every sitting reporter on his staff. Whatever it was, Bennett had no secrets from them. "And what brings you boys to the *Herald*?" he bellowed.

Dutch lifted his lapel, showing his badge.

Bennett waved it off.

"Robert Roman," Dutch said, letting his lapel fall back into place.

The editor grunted with satisfaction. He wanted this. No one killed one of his reporters, even a free-lancer, and got away with it.

"Detective Bo Clancy, sir," Bo said formally. "This is my partner, Detective John Tonneman. We're investigating Roman's death."

Bennett nodded perfunctorily, then caught himself. "Tonneman? Any relation to Pete Tonneman?"

"Yes, sir. My father."

"Good man. Good journalist. Died too young."

"My mother would agree."

"How is Meg?" Bennett didn't wait for an answer. "I knew Old Peter, too. Now there was a cop. Did you see the obit we ran on Old Peter?"

Dutch nodded. "Ma was pleased."

Bennett smiled broadly. "Be seated, gentlemen." With his cigar, the editor pointed to the sturdy chairs in front of his desk. "I'm happy to inform you that the *Herald*, along with Mr. Oswald Cook, the photographer, is offering a $5,000 reward for information leading to the capture of the killer or killers of Robert Roman."

"Good to hear," Bo said.

"What do you want to know?" Bennett asked.

"How long had he worked for you?" Dutch asked.

"Two years. Off and on. The first six months he nearly starved to death learning the trade. But Bob was coming along nicely. He had a nose for it. He could write the story, too."

"Who was he friendly with? Companions? Men? Women?"

"Companions?" Bennett snorted. "That's a joke. Bob wasn't here much. And he wasn't one to attract companions. Except . . . He hung out with Oswald Cook in his place on Gramercy."

"No women?" Bo turned and looked pointedly at the lone woman in the newsroom. "What about your secretary out there?"

"Flora Cooper? That'll be the day. Flora's not my secretary. She's my agony reporter." He added by way of explanation, "Woman's stuff."

Dutch caught Bo's look, but hell, why not? Hadn't Nellie Bly over on the *World* gone around the world in seventy-two days back in '89–'90 and written about it in the papers? Times were certainly changing. "We'd like to talk to your reporters. Maybe they heard something."

Bennett gestured with the cigar toward his newsroom. "Go right ahead. But make it fast—I've got a paper to get out and I don't want to give those rascals any excuses."

Bo stood. "Did he have a desk?"

"Yes." Bennett stood, too. "Next to Miss Cooper. You won't find anything. I've already looked." The telephone rang. The editor crammed his cigar into his mouth and answered, "Bennett. Wait a minute." To the detectives he said, "Anything else?"

"Where did he live?" Bo asked.

"I have no idea. Ask Cook if he lived with him."

"We'll do that," said Bo.

Dutch said, "It must have been a bit of a walk."

Bennett, who'd been trying to get rid of them, was now interested. "Hold on," Bennett said into the phone. Focusing on Tonneman he asked, "Why is that?"

"His shoes. The leather was new but the heels were worn down. The man was a walker. My guess is that he walked everywhere. To work. To Gramercy Park. Except that day he was really anxious to get here with his photographic plates."

"I'll call you back," Bennett said into the telephone and hung up. "What photographic plates?"

"He never told you he had them?" asked Dutch.

"No."

Bo leaned over Bennett's desk. "Did you see him at all Thursday afternoon?"

"No. Only for a brief minute in the morning. Tell me about the plates."

"Forget about them," Bo said, straightening. "They're broken."

"Agh," said Bennett and relit his stub of a cigar. "Anything else?"

Bo stared out at the newsroom.

"Yes," Dutch answered. He was still seated. "The story Roman was working on. Was that something you assigned?"

Bennett's canny eyes evaluated Dutch Tonneman. "You're your father's son, all right. Pete never worked for me, but that wasn't my fault. I tried to get him but he was happy at the *Post*. You're like him. A terrier. Never let go."

Without a word Bo left them and strode into the newsroom.

"Fifty cents," said Bennett, nodding at the desk just across from his office, "he talks to the girl first."

Dutch grinned. "You're on."

They watched as Bo walked the length of the newsroom to a desk near the entranceway and started talking to an old coot in a dust-covered black suit.

Dutch opened his palm.

Bennett paid. "I was certain he was interested in the girl."

"Oh, he is. But he's saving her for last." Dutch tucked the coin into his vest pocket. At that moment, out of nowhere, he caught himself remembering the Hebrew girl with her expressive dark eyes, her earnest manner, her tiny waist.

"I've got phone calls to make and a paper to get out," Bennett said bluntly. "I'm returning to Paris in a week and I've got things to finish before I leave." He ran his three *Herald* newspapers—New York, London, and Paris—from Paris, and traveled back and forth when it was necessary.

Dutch was tugged from his thoughts of the girl. "The story Roman was working on . . ."

"I don't know." Bennett seemed ready to continue in spite of his words. But something stopped him. Then something started him again. "Roman thought it was big enough to nag me about putting halftone pictures right on our front page. If you understood the newspaper game you'd realize how crazy that is. Nobody prints halftones on a high-speed press. It's impossible. Even if we used pictures, we wouldn't use photographs. We'd print a line-block made from an artist's drawing, like everybody else." Bennett examined the end of his cigar, then stubbed it out in a crowded metal ashtray. He picked a fresh Aphrodite from the humidor on his desk, bit the end, spat, and lit the cigar with care, distributing the flame of the match evenly about the end. When at last he was satisfied that the Aphrodite was drawing properly, he looked Dutch square in the eye. "You're Pete Tonneman's son. I'm betting you're an honest copper."

"It's a good bet. How long had Roman worked for you?"

"He never really did, actually. He didn't work here, he worked everywhere. He was a free-lancer. Which meant sometimes he was up against it for money."

Dutch nodded. "You saw him last when?"

"I saw Roman early Thursday morning. He was running out of here like a bat out of hell. I asked him where he was off to in such a goddamn hurry. 'Too dangerous,' he said. 'What the hell is there that's too dangerous for James Gordon Bennett?' I said. That's when he told me he'd stumbled on the mother lode of corruption in the City." Bennett filled the room with the rich smell of his Aphrodite.

"Did he tell you where this mother lode was?"

"Yes." Bennett eyed Dutch Tonneman for a long moment before he spoke again. Then he said, "The House on Mulberry Street."

32

Saturday,
June 1.
Morning.

"*Didn't know him well," the man in the dusty black suit was saying as he* rolled a cigarette. His hands trembled; tobacco crumbs spilled, joining the butts which overflowed the ashtray onto the plain wooden desk. "Kept to himself." The man lifted his eyeshade to get a better look at Bo. "How is the Force coming with the investigation?" He put the cigarette in his mouth, struck a match on the corner of his desk and lit it with unsteady hands, then slipped a sheet of paper into the typewriter.

Presses beneath them thundered, compelling the two to raise their voices. The floor quaked; items on desks rattled. More butts fell on the desk. Matter-of-factly, the reporter brushed them to the floor.

"We're investigating," Bo told him, amused but pissed that the old guy had turned the tables on him.

"No leads, Detective?" The journalist tapped the keys, joining the press clamor.

The telegraph-receiving operator was on his megaphone again, calling out his information. "More from London. Lord Roseberry denies all rumors of his resignation. Her Majesty, Queen Victoria . . ."

Bo moved on, going from reporter to reporter. Each one told as little as the previous. All along Bo kept his eyes on the girl at the far end of the long room, opposite Bennett's office. Inside, he could see Dutch yapping with the editor.

The old guy he'd talked to first yelled, "Copy!"

A fat kid, who wouldn't stay fat long if he kept this job, ran to the man's desk and snatched sheets of paper from the old coot's shaking hands.

The dead man's desk was already occupied by another reporter, a red-haired beanpole, his face covered with freckles. This reporter had his nose to the typewriter, trying to change a ribbon. The tip of his nose was black, and there was a matching black smudge on his chin.

"Detective Bo Clancy. I'd like to have a look at your desk."

"Why my—? Oh, sure. Roman's." He stood to let Bo sit in his chair.

"Did you take anything out of here?"

"Only some papers and a couple of pencils."

"Where's the paper?"

"In this envelope." The beanpole picked up a large, much-used envelope from the corner of his desk. "I was going to give it to Mr. Bennett."

Bo tucked the envelope under his arm.

The girl, Flora Cooper, was absorbed in her typing. Every so often she referred to a stack of letters.

Bo strolled to her desk. "Miss Cooper, is it?"

She leaned back and peered up at him from under the eyeshade that sat uneasily on her bundle of dark golden hair. A pencil stuck out from the hair above the eyeshade. Flora Cooper had green eyes a couple of degrees lighter than the shade. Cat's eyes. "And who might you be?" she asked bluntly with no female grace, her fingers pounding steadily, adding to the chorus of typewriters.

"Bo Clancy, miss. Detective Sergeant. Metropolitan Police." He touched two fingers to his derby.

"Aren't all detectives sergeants?"

"Yes, miss." He grinned; he couldn't help it. The girl had nailed him. "I wonder if I could ask you some questions about Robert Roman."

"Grab a chair," she said, still typing. "I don't fancy craning my neck at you."

The beanpole was elsewhere, so Bo appropriated his chair, glad for a chance to contain his grin. Flora Cooper was one humdinger, but he didn't think she would take kindly to his humor. She might think he was laughing at her. And she'd be right. He planted the chair before her and sat. "Mr. Bennett says you're a reporter."

"What did you think I was, a secretary?" A packet of Richmond Straight Cuts was on her desk, cigarettes half out. She snagged one and lit it, scratched a dainty ear, then leaned back in her chair, blowing perfect smoke rings into the air. Just like a man.

"Well, yes." Jesus Mary, Bo thought. A hum-humdinger.

"I'm the agony reporter."

"Agony reporter?"

"I write the notices about missing relatives and pets and lost property. Wedding stuff, too. 'The bride wore an exquisite dress of lace and seed pearls.' " In disgust she sat up straight, grabbed the pencil from her hair, and threw it at the red-topped beanpole who was approaching. The boy turned sharply and found somewhere else to go.

"You've got a temper."

"Impossible. I'm Dorothea Lovelace and I answer letters from the lovelorn. Dorothea Lovelace couldn't possibly have a temper, now could she?"

Her bitterness shocked him; Bo, the talker, the jester, could find nothing to say.

Bennett was bellowing again. "Simmons! Jennings!"

Bo could see the girl tensing up. She sucked in smoke and held it. He cleared his throat. "Robert Roman."

Flora Cooper fairly spit out the smoke. "No different from the others. Maybe worse." She took another deep drag, held it, then blew it out. The girl smoked with such great pleasure that he was mesmerized watching her.

"Did you hear him say anything the last morning he was here? Thursday?"

"You think I listen to people's conversations?"

"Yes." She looked mad as hell. "You're a reporter."

Her pretty lips stretched into what might have been a smile. "Thank you, Detective."

That was better. He was relieved. What's with you, Bo Clancy? Scared of a skirt?

She didn't say anything further but smoked her cigarette with great enjoyment, watching him.

Outside, breaking through the press noises, the two bronze men hammered the huge bronze bell in front of Minerva and announced the hour.

Flora Cooper stubbed out her cigarette in a saucer, chuckling. "Well, you're right. I don't miss much. From what I could hear of the telephone call, it was a tip that something he'd been waiting for was going to happen at the union demonstration that afternoon."

Bennett burst out of his office. "Krueger!"

A long-legged reporter threw down his green eyeshade and loped to the editor.

Bennett shoved a tear of paper into his hand. "Body pulled out of the East River. Henderson thinks it's Queenie Landry, the madam. Take an artist. Go. Go. Go."

33

Monday, June 3. Nine A.M.

Both Hebrew and Christian Sabbaths behind her, Esther rose early and had a meager breakfast of coffee and bread with honey. Then she rushed to the studio where the basket of broken photographic plates awaited her. She lifted out the one remaining good plate in its light-tight holder and took it into the darkroom.

It was still too early for Oz, who generally rose by midmorning, but seldom appeared before noon. She was eager to begin, and might have done so had he not surprised her. Although her employer looked fragile in the red glow of the table lamp, his eyes were alive with curiosity.

"Not a moment too soon, I see." He smiled at his protégée, coming to stand beside her. He picked up the scarred lighttight holder and looked at it in the dim light. "Not exactly encouraging, is it?"

Oz pressed the metal springs of the holder, releasing the plate. "Ah, not even a crack. Perhaps we can see something in this to tell us what was so important that a good man had to die." Oz's hands began to tremble. He covered the plate with a dark cloth. "Would you continue the preparations while I go out to have a cigarette?"

"Yes, sir."

After making certain that the stubborn pipes were delivering water to the sink, Esther thrust her hands into the stained gloves and mixed the developing solution in a glass container. She opened the door. "I'm ready, sir."

Oz snuffed out a cigarette and reentered the darkroom. He placed the clean enameled tin developing dish in front of the ruby-colored light, turned back the cloth cover, and examined the negative intently, avoiding the direct rays of the light.

He set the plate in the enameled dish, sensitive, creamy side up. "Now," he instructed, his fine hands trembling again, "pour the developer over the plate in one quick sweep so that the plate is covered in an even flow. Begin at the lower left corner."

Esther had learned how to do this the first month she had worked with Oz, but he was the master and she the apprentice. She followed his instructions to the letter.

A tiny bubble appeared in the developer. Oz broke it with his fingertip. Taking care to expose the plate to as little light as possible, he began rocking the dish from side to side and end to end so that the developer liquid flowed evenly over the entire plate.

They waited, their breaths held in anticipation for the magic to begin. Sky and white clothing showed first in black mourning, for the negative reversed light and dark. Then middle tones appeared, and at last details.

Oz watched with his usual joy as the images appeared. He looked down at his avid pupil. She shared his joy as no other had.

"Oh," she cried. "How wonderful."

"Now we must wait in order to add density to the negative."

After several minutes he brought the plate out of the developer and inspected it to judge its density. Satisfied with the results, he returned the plate to the developer and waited another minute just to be sure.

She was so close to him he could smell her fragrance above the chemicals; this disconcerted him. Moving, creating more space between them, he told her, "Rinse the plate for a minute in cold water."

She felt a surge of excitement, a thrill like no other she'd ever experienced as she took the negative from him.

When she was done he placed the plate, emulsion uppermost, into the hypo bath to fix; once more they watched and waited, wrapped in the suspense of the process.

The whiteness disappeared in five minutes. Oz let the plate rest another five minutes. "Now we set the plate on end in the sink with cold water running over it."

Esther knew but she did as he asked. "A half hour, yes?" Then, student to teacher, "Until we're certain the plate is clean of hypo."

He nodded, pleased.

"Very well," he said. "Let us have coffee while we wait."

When the negative was dry, they set it in a wooden frame, tightened it against the treated paper, and left it to print.

Oz knew nothing would come of it. He'd been reading negatives too many years not to.

He could see by Esther's expression that she knew, too. She was not yet a proper photographer, but she was a smart girl with a good eye. These photographs had been taken during trying circumstances without the necessary preparation. If anyone had blundered here, it was he. They'd been his pictures to take. She had done yeoman service. He was very proud of her.

"It's so overexposed, as if I aimed right into the sun. . . ."

"Not that bad."

"How can you ever forgive me?" Esther was so ashamed of her failure she was close to weeping.

"It can happen to the best of us." His voice was kind. "You cannot absorb this art and this science overnight. You will learn to judge the light and then refine that learning."

"Is there nothing we can do to bring out the picture?"

"Nothing!"

"I'm so sorry." She had failed. Oz. Herself. And worst of all, she had failed Robert Roman.

• 34 •

Monday,
June 3.
Late morning.

O*n the print one could barely make out the marchers and their placards*, but not the writing on them.

Oz shook his head. "The field of light was too narrow." He pointed to the deep shadow in the image. "You must always set up well away from the buildings, to get full sunlight."

"I was concerned about the camera. I was afraid it might be damaged."

Oz gazed at her with a half smile. "Timidity is a female trait you would be well rid of. One thing a photographer cannot be is timid."

The flash of anger in her eyes startled him. Anger threaded her reply, too. "The camera is not mine to risk as I please."

The little mouse had some spine. "Then we must rectify that. Consider it my gift to you." A smile hovered about his lips, creasing the skin either side of his dark-ringed eyes.

"I don't know what to say." Esther was clearly overwhelmed.

"Thank you will be sufficient."

"Thank you . . . Oz." This was the first time she'd called her employer by his given name.

He felt a rare stir of warmth in the region of his heart. Then, suddenly, he felt lightheaded. The room was too warm, he began to perspire.

Esther saw his distress at once. "Oz?"

He said, coolly, "Will you lend me your arm, my dear, and ring for Wong."

He leaned lightly on her. As they approached the stairs, Wong materialized and immediately assumed charge.

It was suddenly obvious to Esther that Oswald Cook was in failing health. He was perhaps twenty-five years her senior, but looked much older. His reliance on spirits and God-knew-what-else had caused him grievous injury. Oz was a kind man who armed himself against human warmth, as many of his breed did. In spite of his age and aloof ways, in the nearly six months she'd been working for him, living in his house, Esther now realized she had come to care for the man.

Unsettled by her feelings and concerned about Oz's health, Esther climbed to the fourth floor and the library. There she immersed herself in the serene dignity of the books and Mr. Whitman. Curled up in a leather chair, she found solace in *Leaves of Grass*, and slipped into a reverie which was interrupted by Wong's discreet knock on the door. He carried a cardboard box that was as tall as he was. The emblem of Messieurs Lord & Taylor on it was yellow with age. "Detective John Tonneman to see you."

Esther's eyes went to the box.

"The box is from Mr. Oz."

"Send the detective to the studio, please."

When Wong did not move, she asked, "And the box?"

"Mr. Oz would be pleased if you would wear this to the theatre this evening. You may alter it as you see fit."

"The theatre? Is he feeling so much better?"

"Mr. Oz says the theatre is his tonic."

Esther smiled. "What do you say, Wong?"

Wong dipped his head. "Shall I take it to your room?"

"No, I will." She rose and relieved him of his burden. "See to Detective Tonneman, please." The theatre, she thought on her way upstairs. She'd never been to the American theatre. Once she'd been to the Yiddish Theatre, at the Union on the Lower East Side. She'd spent a precious thirty-five cents to see the great Jacob Adler in Jacob Gordin's *The Yiddish King Lear*. It had been well worth the money. Wonderful. But so sad.

She opened the door to her cherished little sitting room and went on to the bedroom, where she set the cardboard box on the bed.

When she undid the ribbon and removed the cover and the tissue paper, she caught her breath. The evening dress of blue moiré was perhaps ten years out of fashion, but still beautiful. Esther lifted it from its nest of tissue. The dress had a low collar, a narrow waist, and a long attached peplum, which she knew immediately had to be removed. She would have to shorten the skirt as well. At the bottom of the box were a silk taffeta petticoat, and a corset and drawers of the finest silk. In a separate parcel were shoes, hose, a fan, and a little bag—also of blue moiré—containing opera glasses.

Despite the roomy bosom, Esther knew she could alter the dress to fit her. The undergarments, however, would do for two of her.

She'd discovered the small sewing room on this floor the first week she was there, but had not had an occasion to do any real sewing beyond mending. A Singer sewing machine, a large-bosomed dress form, and boxes of needles and threads and ribbons and laces were waiting for her.

As she stood in her bedroom and held the garment to her, she bobbed up and down to see her full image in the tall mirror on the bureau; she found herself humming. Oz had changed her life. Opened her to new experiences. Taught her his vocation. Now he was taking her to the theatre. She would sew this beautiful dress and look beautiful for him at the theatre tonight. The theatre.

But how could she look beautiful with this eye? Since the day of Robert Roman's murder, as it healed, it had been getting uglier. Perhaps Wong could show her some Chinese magic. It suddenly occurred to her that the detective had seen her with this ugly eye.

The detective!

Leaving the dress draped on the bed, she ran down the steps on winged feet—or so it seemed to her—catching herself at the studio door to smooth her hair, then her green calico dress, wishing it were the blue moiré so John Tonneman could see her in it.

He was peering through the lens of the Kodak camera on its tripod and didn't look up at her entrance. Instead he turned the camera toward her.

"You are very lovely through a camera lens, Miss Breslau." He brought his eyes from the camera to her. "And otherwise. Black eye and all."

She felt the blush rise from the tips of her toes. "We've developed the negative. It's not clear enough for—"

"Why not let me be the judge?"

She walked across the studio to the darkroom door. The outside red warning light wasn't lit, but still she knocked. When there was no response, she opened the door gently and turned on the inside red light.

"Come in, please."

Dutch entered. It was like a chemical laundry. Photographs hung by clothespins from the wire strung above. The not unpleasant odor of the chemicals enveloped him.

She pointed to the last photograph in the drying row. "This one."

Tonneman squinted at it. It was a photograph of marchers, perhaps in Union Square. That was all he saw. "Will you take it down, please. I'd like to study it through a magnifying glass."

"It is not dry yet. If you can come back tomorrow, you can inspect it. I know how impatient you must be, but Mr. Cook has not been well."

"Could you make it bigger for me?"

Esther hesitated before she said, "It can be enlarged. Mr. Cook will want to do it himself. This photograph might lead to Mr. Roman's killer. I believe Mr. Cook would want to be the instrument." She ushered the detective out of the darkroom.

He asked: "Perhaps you can tell me what you know about Robert Roman."

Her dark eyes were disconcerting. She always seemed to be thinking, studying him, before she spoke.

"Very few people seem to have known him well." Again he had to wait while she studied him. What was in her mind?

"Perhaps you can come to the library with me." She slipped by him out of the studio, and started up the stairs.

"The library?" he asked, following. He was confused. All he could think of was the notice two weeks before that the City was going to build a public library, where the Croton Reservoir was being demolished.

"One flight up."

As he trailed behind her, he could barely contain the impulse to place his hands around her slim waist. She led him to a genuine library, smaller than the Mercantile Library and the libraries around Astor Place. A real library, with walls of books, leather chairs, and two broad tables.

"Here's where I came to know him," she said. "Such as I did. He was not an easy man."

"I could see that." Tonneman remembered Roman's curtness when he took the box of plates from Esther.

"Robert could not abide who he had been, and dreamed of being famous."

"Who had he been?"

"A poor immigrant, like me. But unlike me, he was Italian. Roberto Giuseppe Romano." Her accent, so soft previously, grew more pronounced. "I am a Jew."

"I know." Dutch placed his hand on a plaster bust sitting on one of the tables. "This is Poe, isn't it?"

"Yes, Edgar Allan. One of Oz's favorite writers. He loves telling me never to assume, and that the answer to any problem can be as plain as the nose on my face."

Dutch nodded. Interesting, but not helping his investigation. "How did Roman and Cook become acquainted?"

"You'll have to ask Mr. Cook. I am here because of Miss Lillian Wald of the Nurses' Settlement House on Henry Street. Miss Wald told Mr. Cook about me."

"How long have you lived here?"

"Almost six months."

"Roman didn't live here?"

"No, but he came and went as he pleased." The table nearest them was laden with stacks of books. Her hand drifted to a book lying open.

"Was there . . . ?" He paused. "Forgive me, but I must ask. Was there anything between you and Robert Roman?"

"No!" Her answer was quite explosive. She examined him keenly, and decided he meant no insult. Her fingers drifted across the fine vellum pages of the book under her hand. "He read Dante to me in Italian. He was very ambitious. He should not have come to a violent end."

"No one should, Miss Breslau. But perhaps his ambition led him to his death."

"In America it is not wrong to be ambitious."

Tonneman nodded. He wanted to stay, to prolong their conversation, but it was time to go. "Thank you for your time, Miss Breslau. If you don't mind, I'll call on you again. To see the enlargement."

She hesitated just a moment after he went down the stairs, then ran after.

Wong was holding the front door open.

Tonneman, who was at the hat stand, turned and smiled at Esther as she came racing down the stairs to him.

The hat stand contained a large mirror surrounded by hooks for the hats. At the base of the mirror was a marble table, which held the telephone. Detective Tonneman's derby sat on the table next to the telephone. She said, "Now I need to ask you something. If I may?"

The detective nodded. His hands were holding his lapels so he would not open his arms to her.

But he had not counted on her smiling and looking at him with those dark moist eyes. Somewhere in John Tonneman's family history there had to have been a Frenchman or an Italian, because what he did next was prompted by neither his Irish nor his Dutch blood. He took Esther Breslau's face in his hands and kissed her on the lips.

Wong, always knowing the right thing to do, stepped outside.

Esther was stunned. Her lips parted beneath his and she felt a tremor rushing through her. He was only the second man who had ever kissed her. And she had never kissed Sholom Cohen back.

"Oh, my." She broke away first, catching her breath.

Each quickly stepped back, arms straight at their sides. Dutch bumped into the hat stand; Esther stumbled against the stair.

"Please, accept my apologies," Dutch said, beet red, mortified.

She took a deep breath, restringing her thoughts. Her heart thudded and she wanted him to touch her again. But he didn't. "Your *Shadai*," she said.

"My what? I don't understand."

"On your watch chain."

Looking puzzled, he brought the timepiece out of its pocket.

She pointed to his talisman, his good luck charm on the watch chain. "It's called a *Shadai*," she said. "The letters are Hebrew. They spell out the name of God."

"Hebrew?" Dutch was astonished. "I don't understand. It was given to my great-grandfather by his mother. It's been in my family for almost a hundred years."

"Your family is not Jewish, then?" It was her turn to be astonished. She felt a keen sense of disappointment.

"Oh, no. We're Irish. And Dutch. And English. But Catholic through and through. To the bone."

She studied this tall, fair-haired man. How could she have thought he was Jewish? The Jews were mostly a dark people, like the Italians. And dark-eyed—as she was. Yet there were Russians and other Poles who were blue-eyed and blond or had different shades of red hair.

At that moment she remembered.

"Robert said something once. He told me he lived like the baby Jesus."

Tonneman scratched his ear. "You'd think with a good Catholic education I could figure that one out." He grinned at her. "It'll come to me."

• 35 •

Monday, June 3. Evening.

"*Miss Breslau, may I present Mr. Belmont.*"

"How do you do?"

"Miss Breslau, may I present . . ."

Her head was spinning. Oz was introducing her to his friends and acquaintances as his ward.

"Keep smiling, my dear. You are causing quite a sensation." She had altered his mother's favorite dress to the latest fashion. Her talent in puffing the sleeves and raising the collar amazed him. Why was he surprised? Her sense of detail was almost as sure as his own. The gown fit his "ward" like a glove. And she had all but erased the bruise under her eye with some feminine magic.

His mother's sapphire necklace and earrings, lent to Esther for the occasion, were the perfect foil against the little mouse's lovely pale skin. No longer the mouse. With that skin, the high cheekbones and dark eyes and hair, she had the makings of a great beauty.

Her hair, dark brown with glints of gold, was luxuriously rolled and piled on her head. Holding the glass of champagne she looked elegant, to the manner born.

Oz chuckled softly. He was enjoying himself no end. The lightheadness he'd felt earlier in the day was gone.

In society, going to the theatre, though it had begun to change, was still a male pursuit. Men left their wives at home and enjoyed the play, late-night dining, and gambling with one another or with some young thing from the chorus, which led to further divertissements.

The poor, the groundlings, had nothing to do with all this. They entered the theatre by a small side door, climbed to their seats in the second balcony, and ate their sandwiches and drank their beer while watching the play.

Oz, Esther's hand tucked into the crook of his arm, presented her, ever so subtly, so all the world—aristocrat and groundling—could see his prize.

Esther had all she could do not to let her mouth drop open. Everything was so extraordinary. Entering Abbey's was like entering a palace. Or a cathedral. Esther had never done either, but she had seen pictures.

The theatre lobby was a palace of gold leaf, marble, and mahogany. All about were classical sculptures illustrating scenes from Shakespeare.

Abbey's was part of what was called the Rialto. The Rialto ran up Broadway, a crowded light-filled boulevard, the City's diamond necklace, sparkling with gems of theatres, hotels, and elegant saloons, from Twenty-third Street at Madison Square, all the way to Forty-second Street, where the electric lights came to an end in the mud of Longacre Square.

This area was studded with seedy hotels, harness makers, and brothels. But it was soon to change. The impresario, Oscar Hammerstein was building a grand music hall—The Olympia—on Broadway between Forty-fourth and Forty-fifth Streets.

People liked to say that Broadway—spacious as its name claimed and always in motion with people, omnibuses, carriages, wagons—was the greatest street in the world.

People also liked to say that the women in their bright-hued and fashionable clothes, parasols twirling, who were to be seen along Broadway and Fifth Avenue, the Ladies' Mile, were the most beautiful in the world.

As they mounted the stairs to Oz's box, a man of squarish build approached, his eyes on Esther. "Mr. Cook." Though his manner was a bit rough, his attire as always was immaculate and stylish.

"Mr. Lehman." Oz seemed highly amused. "May I present my ward, Miss Breslau."

"Your ward?" Lehman glanced from Esther to Oz, outraged.

Esther raised her chin ever so slightly. "How do you do, Mr. Lehman," she said firmly.

Realizing that Lehman had recognized Esther as an Israelite and was quite angry, Oz wondered if the man was going to accuse him of being a white slave merchant.

He steered Esther around the glaring banker and into their box, where his third cousin John Neldine Burgoyne and his two grown sons, both studying at Yale, were already seated. Oz's mother had been a Neldine.

Hands were pressed all round, then Esther was introduced. Immediately, she captivated the boys with her Polish accent. How odd, Oz thought. That accent coming from a girl in drab immigrant clothing and the dull hair and complexion of poverty, would immediately be identified as greenhorn and shunned by his high-society cousins. But coming from his elegant little mouse, it was quite another story.

Here in the theatre, the crystal chandeliers hanging from the high domed ceiling were all electrified; the light was exquisite as it fell on the glittering society. Esther caught her breath at the thought that a stranger might think her one of those women, high-born, elegant, and pampered. She blushed at the notion, yet how she longed to be one—if just for a brief moment. And brief it would be because she intended to do more with her life than stroll and shop. She would become a great photographer.

Mr. Lehman was the only Jew she had seen among this American nobility, but there had to be others. He had been so angry. As if she belonged to him.

Esther peered over the railing through the opera glasses to look at those seated below in the orchestra. It was like a fairyland of beautiful people in beautiful clothing in a beautiful setting. All were in formal dress, many more men than women. The theatre itself was carved, ornamented with gold leaf, and painted with murals of dancing nymphs. It was so unlike her one-time experience of seeing Jacob Adler at the

Union Theatre. There had been a stage and seats, but the difference was night and day, peasant and royalty, Jew and gentile. She breathed in the heady air of perfume and cigars and wondered if she could be dreaming. The lights began to dim, and as the audience fell silent and the thick maroon velvet curtain rose, she felt burning eyes upon her, compelling her to turn her head.

Somehow she'd expected Mr. Lehman again. It was not he. This time the harsh look was coming from Oz's cousin, John Neldine Burgoyne.

36

Monday, June 3. Evening.

O*z had said that this was a poor play. Not to his guest. Esther was* thrilled with *The Tzigane*, which she couldn't pronounce. Oz told her not to worry. Nobody else could pronounce it either. It had become a game in New York to see who could pronounce it properly.

The play was about Russia in 1812. The beautiful Miss Lillian Russell played Vera, a gypsy woman with long flowing black hair who spoke in a low-pitched growl, unlike Miss Russell's fine lyric soprano singing voice. And although her accent was more Hungarian than Russian, Esther was charmed by her sublime beauty and poise and immediately forgave her.

Vera was in love with Kazimir, but Kazimir's cruel uncle insisted that Vera must marry someone more suited to her station in life and decided it must be Vasili, a serf. Vera, believing that the uncle spoke for Kazimir, ran off. Good for you, thought Esther.

Years later, after Napoleon retreated from Moscow, Vera returned. She had become a lady of enormous wealth and position. When she learned that her beloved Kazimir had remained faithful to her, they were wed. The curtain came down to resounding cheers from the audience, and Miss Russell took ten bows. Esther thought it was all wonderful.

Oz's two young Burgoyne cousins whispered to him urgently. The boys were requesting permission to call upon her. At that, he whisked her away without ceremony. Ordinarily, it would have amused Oz to watch what might have happened, but to his unease he found the attentions of the young men to his "ward" offensive. And the senior Burgoyne's glares at Esther added to Oz's decision to leave.

So, with no word of explanation, he took Esther away. Outside, they were immediately caught up by the crowd of elegantly clad gentlemen waiting to get a moment with Lillian Russell. The working-class men and women also there would be happy just to get a glimpse of the great beauty.

Oz was disappointed. When he finally did get close enough to talk to the doorman, no matter how much he offered, the man adamantly refused to let him backstage to see Miss Russell.

"I'd love to take your money, mister. But if I let you in and not them, these culls would tear me apart."

Esther, jostled by the throng, was still enjoying herself. The cousins had made her laugh as they vied for her attention during intermission. She'd felt giddy and flushed with the pleasure of it all. It must be the elegant dress, she thought. And the jewels.

As she stood patiently beside Oz, watching all the fine carriages waiting for their patrons, Esther found herself staring at a big man towering above the crowd. It was the carriage man who had driven Robert the previous Thursday, the day he was killed. The man was standing politely to the side, at the ready. The crowd swelled and puffed, and billowed like a human wave, but there was a respectful circle of space around the giant. What had Robert called him?

Esther moved a few paces from where Oz stood, writing a note on his card in his spidery hand for the doorman to give to Miss Russell.

"You're Jack, aren't you?" she said, looking up, up, up, shading her eyes from the lights glancing off the marquees.

"Yes, miss. Sorry to say, I can't serve you tonight, though." The big driver beamed down at her with pleasure. "I'm here for Mr. Diamond Jim Brady. Taking him and Miss Russell to Del's, I am."

"Do you remember me, Jack? I was with Mr. Roman last week when those thieves attempted to steal my photographic plates." The crowd surged, nudging her closer.

"Yes, I remember you, miss." He smiled gently at her and shook his head. "But, I swear, you can't be the same lass."

"But I am, Jack," she responded earnestly, though she sensed he was teasing her. "Only my costume has changed. Do you know that Mr. Roman has been murdered?"

His mouth turned down, he cleared his throat. "Yes, some boys from the police came around and told me about it. A great shame and tragedy. May his soul rest in peace. Do you know his family?"

Esther shook her head. "My employer Mr. Oswald Cook might. He was Robert's best friend."

"It's a good thing we spoke, then." Battling Jack dipped into his vest pocket and came up with his card. "Give your Mr. Cook this, please. I have some of Mr. Roman's property and I would like to see it gets into the right hands."

"Property?"

"Yes. Mr. Roman lived above my stable in Macdougal Alley."

37

Monday, June 3–
Tuesday, June 4.
Night.
After midnight.

Delmonico's Restaurant took up the corners of two blocks. This was another sort of palace altogether. The building was a handsome four-storied structure, enclosed by a short iron fence, on the west side of Fifth Avenue at Twenty-sixth Street. Over every window facing front were large striped awnings, rolled up now as sunlight had long since been replaced by moonlight.

The elegant establishment was lit up with many electric lights that bounced from the beamed ceilings, to the mirrors, to the dark wood, to the jewelry on all the beautiful women. Esther thought it was as if the stars were sharing the skies with the sunshine.

Esther didn't know if Delmonico's was the finest restaurant in the City, but she couldn't envision any finer. She tried not to gape like a greenhorn as she and Oz were swept through room after room crowded with diners.

Chef Charles Ranhofer came to the table himself to greet them.

"Good to see you this evening, Mr. Cook. We have apricot-glazed pheasant tonight."

Oz shook his head. "My appetite wouldn't do you or your pheasant justice. I'll have the hash and . . ." He was referring to his favorite meal at Delmonico's: Corned Beef Hash and Champagne.

"As you wish, sir."

Oz nodded. "This is my ward, Miss Breslau. Esther, Chef Ranhofer is the finest chef in New York."

"And for Miss Breslau?" Chef Ranhofer inquired.

"I'm not very hungry," Esther said.

"I think," Oz said, "we will tempt her with the Baked Alaska."

"An excellent choice, Mr. Cook."

Ranhofer raised his hand, and a waiter appeared at his side as if by magic. Esther wasn't sure, but she thought the waiter clicked his heels.

"Baked Alaska," the chef ordered. "And champagne. Immediately."

Off went the waiter like a racehorse. Ranhofer bowed, and withdrew at a more leisurely pace. A wine steward appeared bearing a bottle of champagne in a bucket of ice chips. With great showmanship, he popped the cork.

"Oh," Esther gasped in spite of herself.

The steward poured champagne into two fluted glasses.

Oz lifted his glass.

Esther emulated her employer. Or had he become her guardian?

"To us, Esther. And the practice of photography and life."

They drank.

"It tickles my nose."

Oz smiled. It pleased him that she said the expected.

Now, Chef Ranhofer emerged from the kitchen, wherever it was, to serve the hash to Oz from a silver chafing dish.

Esther went dizzy with delight when still another waiter arrived with a mountain of whipped egg whites, all brown and crisp from the oven.

When, with difficulty, she cut into the concoction with the elegant silver spoon, she discovered a delicate sponge cake beneath the sugar-crusted toasted meringue and hard frozen cream. "Oh," she said. "It's ice cream. But how do they brown the egg white without melting the ice cream?"

Ranhofer winked. "Delmonico magic." The Baked Alaska never ceased to be a triumph at Delmonico's. It was a special favorite of all the ladies who dined there.

Many men came to their table to say hello, and Esther was introduced always as Oz's ward, Miss Breslau. She was quite thrilled with the attention she was getting, and the champagne made her want to giggle at the image of the poor Jewish immigrant Esther Breslau sitting with the gentry in Delmonico's, wearing a borrowed evening dress, sipping champagne.

The young woman looked about the gracious room with all its gleaming white tablecloths and all the couples dining this night, apparently enjoying themselves immensely.

In that moment, Esther saw the entire room as if taking an instantaneous photograph. Most of the men, like Oz, were older than the pretty young women with them. Much older. She turned to Oz, who was gazing at the contents of his glass.

Oz murmured, "What do you think of my world, Esther?" He looked up. "A far cry from Jew Town, eh?"

Esther ignored the frisson of anger she felt at that name. She'd been about to confess her happiness. And now she was stunned with the abrupt understanding that she and Oz were like all those other couples.

"I am overwhelmed," she said.

They were not quite finished eating when a stir came over the diners.

Then Lillian Russell appeared in a *ciel*-blue satin evening dress draped low across her bosom. The narrow pointed waist served to emphasize the fullness of the famed singer's bosom and hips, the exact model for the hourglass figure she herself had helped to make popular. The sleeves of the dress were short and puffed, and her blue kid gloves reached well above the elbow. The black Gypsy wig had been shed to reveal her pale blond hair.

Her companion was James Buchanan Brady, better known as Diamond Jim, a man of extreme wealth and girth, with a laugh to match his riches and size. Mr. Brady's shirt glittered. Every one of his shirt studs was a diamond. But they were poor imitations compared to the gem Miss Russell wore tucked in her stunning blond curls.

At this moment, Chef Ranhofer reappeared with a handsome man in evening clothes.

"That's young Charlie Delmonico," Oz whispered.

Miss Russell surveyed the diners, then fixed her gaze on Oz. She raised her lacy fan, and spoke to Mr. Delmonico, who promptly brought her to Oz's table. Mr. Brady sat down at a table with friends, guffawing boisterously.

Lillian Russell sailed to their table with such dignity and grace that it was once more all that Esther could do to merely keep her mouth closed. Oz leaped to his feet.

"May I present Mr. Oswald Cook?" Delmonico said.

"You may well indeed," said Miss Russell. Esther was surprised. The actress's offstage voice was lighter than the one she affected as the Gypsy. Closer in pitch to the way she sang. "I long for you to take my photograph, Mr. Cook." Lillian Russell began to laugh. "What was it you suggested? Yes, I like that. On a bed of roses. Of course."

BAKED ALASKA

Cut a thin slice of sponge cake in a circle and place it on a baking sheet, then put a slab of hard-frozen ice cream on top of the sponge cake. Trim the cake to fit the ice cream.

Coat the entire surface thickly with a stiff meringue mixed with fine sugar. Dust more sugar over the top.

Set Alaska in a very hot oven just long enough to get lightly brown.

Slip onto chilled platter and serve at once.

38

Tuesday,
June 4.
Afternoon.

"S*o, of course, Jim took the bet. And proceeded to eat one hundred oysters.* Not in fifteen minutes, but fourteen." Lillian Russell, seated grandly on the wooden bench, paused, looked at everyone, and said, "I asked him, 'Jim, how could you eat that many oysters?' He answered that the secret was in the beer. 'I swear, Lil, if I didn't have the beer to wash it down I would have died.' "

She laughed. Lillian Russell had a hearty laugh. Everyone else laughed, too. Esther thought Oz was going to burst.

"Oh, Lil." Miss Russell's friend Marie Dressler had a crusty manner and a face like a bulldog. "You're as bad as he is."

"James Brady is a lark. Everything he touches turns to gold." The actress gave Oz an impish smile. "Even me."

Oz bowed his head, then looked directly into her eyes. "Miss Russell, I would venture to say you were born golden."

"Are you flirting with me, dear Mr. Cook?"

Oz blushed. "Esther, let's see what light we have."

They were sitting in Gramercy Park, the private, serene sanctuary of the Gramercy residents, now abloom with flowers in immaculate beds.

The elegant iron gates of this private reserve could be opened only with the golden keys owned by the residents of the splendid redbrick and brownstone town houses that surrounded the square park. Through the leafy trees, one could catch here and there a snowy glimpse of a nanny watching her young charge roll a hoop.

The moment Miss Russell arrived in her elegant bicycling costume, Oz had decided to forego the bed of roses. Both ladies came wheeling their bicycles and dressed fit for *Harper's Bazaar*. So Oz decided to have tea in the park and photograph the actress there instead.

Lillian Russell stood and ran her hands over her superbly tailored and trimmed white serge dress. With swift and practiced smooths and pulls, she made a quick check of her fitted bodice and leg-of-mutton sleeves, then turned to her friend. "Marie, the hem?"

Dressler glanced at Russell's hem, which stopped at midcalf over white kid boots. "Hem's fine. Give me a minute on the hat." Dressler tilted the dainty straw hat that was decorated with thick ostrich plumes. "Now they can see that gorgeous face."

The bicycle dress worn by Miss Dressler was pale green muslin with long, full Turkish trousers and cloth gaiters to match. Even with the nipped waist, she was a broad woman.

Esther made sure the Scovill camera was secure. After she inspected the cloudless sky, she moved the tripod. Not even a faint breeze ruffled the trees. In her white shirtwaist and dark gray tweed skirt, Esther thought herself a duckling among swans. Big swans, though, she reflected mischievously, proud of how the black satin ribbon she wore emphasized her tiny waist.

When Oz snapped his fingers she picked up the tripod and, while following his hand signals, considered purchasing a red satin waist ribbon the next time she visited Lord & Taylor's.

"There," Oz said. "Why there, Esther?"

She knew. It had to do with the limitations of the camera. "Because compensating for brightness is not an exact science," she recited. "It is better to shoot in slightly overcast weather or even shade, rather than bright sunshine, to avoid overexposing the photograph. Since today is sunny, it's best to shoot in the shade."

"Bravo," said Oz, who now circled his subject, looking at and thinking of only her. From the beginning he'd been utterly enchanted by Lillian Russell, but her gold-plated bicycle was by far the *pièce de résis-*

tance. It sported mother-of-pearl handlebars. The spokes and hubs were bejeweled. The monogram *L. R.* was etched on the handlebars in diamonds and emeralds.

It was such an opulent symbol of wealth that Esther was reminded of Aaron's golden calf. How many children, she wondered, would the riches on the bike feed?

Miss Russell saw Esther's eyes on the bicycle. "Jim gave it to me," she told her. "He said he wanted the bike to sparkle as much as my eyes. How do I look, Marie?"

"What else, darling? Divine. How do I look?"

"What else, darling? Divine." Miss Russell gave an extra flick of her lovely red painted nails at each full puff sleeve, patted her hair, and said, "Mr. Cook, I am ready to be photographed."

"Esther, wheel the cycle to Miss Russell. Miss Russell, just stand holding the bike and smile." He waited for Esther to put the bike in place. "Capital." Oz looked through the lens. "First plate," he commanded. In anticipation, Esther had already lifted the plate from its slot; she handed it to him.

Lillian Russell mock-sighed. "Like a policeman, a woman's lot is not a happy one. Right, Marie?"

Dressler sang a snatch of the Arthur Sullivan melody alluded to. "You can't play that part, it's for a man."

"Ah, but you miss my point, darling. It's not the part that's important, it's the sentiment."

"Poor mistreated and lonely you," Marie Dressler said. "What a terrible life you have, what with Jim Brady to love you and shower you with jewels." Dressler crossed her eyes.

"I'd rather have my own money, my dear. Money is power. Men have known that for centuries."

Oz came out from under the hood. "What's that, Miss Russell?"

"Not a thing, Mr. Cook. And do call me Lil and I shall call you Oz. Do you think in our lifetime, Oz, that women will get the vote?"

Oz blinked. "I've never thought about it."

"I'll wager your ward and apprentice has thought about it, haven't you, Esther?"

Oz made a face. "Nonsense, Lil. Keep that pose, please. Esther's not interested in all the suffragist claptrap." He went back under the hood.

"Hold it." He squeezed the bulb and made the photograph. "Are you, Esther?" he said quite clearly.

"I beg your pardon?" Esther, flustered, handed Oz another plate.

Lillian Russell grinned at Marie Dressler. Marie laughed. Oz made another picture.

"Look what's here," Marie said. "He's a strong little fellow."

Wong was coming down the gravel path carrying a silver tea service on a large folding tray table. Balancing the table with one hand, he lowered the legs.

Lillian Russell beamed at Oz, who could only see her through the lens. "You are a thoughtful host, sir."

Oz made another photograph.

And three more.

When they stopped for tea, Miss Russell settled back on the wooden bench, while Esther folded the tripod. Making certain all the exposed plates, still in their lighttight holders, were secure, she put them and the Scovill and the tripod safely aside.

Miss Russell nibbled on a leafy watercress-and-cucumber sandwich and sipped her tea. "Mm. Quite lovely."

Marie Dressler rolled her eyes. She knew she and her friend would have to eat another, more substantial meal than this dainty fare to get through the night's performance.

To Esther, Miss Russell said, "Do you also make pictures, Esther?"

"Yes."

"She's my pupil," said Oz. "And she learns quickly."

"Marie, what was the name of that woman photographer up state?"

"Sorry, I don't recall, but we've met more than one in New York alone."

Oz frowned. "Esther, Wong. Take the equipment indoors."

Esther was hurt. He'd dismissed her like a servant.

Oz replaced the frown with a smile. "What's your next show going to be, Lil?"

Lillian Russell, an actress by instinct and a sunny creature by nature, never allowed her inner thoughts to appear on her lovely face. She looked past Oz at the tall fence enclosing Gramercy Park. "I believe someone is trying to get your attention, Esther. A very nice looking someone."

A quick glance showed Esther that John Tonneman stood near the gate to the park. She was disconcerted. But her thoughts were on Oz and how he had treated her. She did her best to smile good-bye to Miss Russell and Miss Dressler, but her heart wasn't in it. She picked up the tripod and the Scovill and followed Wong as he carried the box of plates.

When Esther reached the gate, Lillian Russell was suddenly beside her.

"If you ever need a friend, call me on the telephone or send me a note," Miss Russell said, as Wong went on ahead. The actress looked at the man standing at the gate, and smiled. Esther's heart lightened. The wonderful Lillian Russell had seen and understood. That didn't eliminate the pain of Oz's brusqueness, but it did make it easier to bear.

"Miss Lillian Russell," she said proudly, "I'd like you to meet Detective John Tonneman. Detective Tonneman, this is my friend, Lillian Russell."

Dutch turned ruddy. "Miss Russell, a great honor. Miss Breslau, is this an inconvenient time?"

"I think not, sir," Lillian Russell answered for Esther, a glint in her splendid eyes. "I think this is a *most* convenient time." And she held the gate open for Esther.

Esther passed through with an eagerness that took her quite by surprise.

39

Wednesday,
June 5.
Early morning.

The room was musty. Meg threw open the window and took the ladder from behind the door. She was positioning it in front of the window when Dutch stuck his head in the room. "Why don't you wait for me to come home to help you with the lifting?"

Annie was wrestling with the mattress, but winning. "If we wait for you," she grunted, "it won't get done till the Second Coming."

"Annie!" Meg said. She grinned at her son. "John, you'll be late. We can do this by ourselves."

"Sure, Ma," John said. He removed his mother's hands from the short ladder, climbed up, and took down the curtains.

Meg clucked about Old Peter as she collected the limp and gray curtains. "Never let me into the room with my dust mop." She added the curtains to the bed linens and took everything in her arms. The burden was so large it obscured her kerchiefed head as she made her way to the door.

"Ma!" Dutch cried. After all these years, he still couldn't accept his mother's belief that there were no obstacles she could not overcome. This included her being short.

"I've been doing laundry since before you were born. And a lot of it your dirty diapers, so mind your manners."

Annie, who had finally gotten the mattress bent double, giggled.

Dutch shook his head. Meg Clancy was a grand lady, there was no denying it.

"That dear man," Meg, still hidden by laundry, paused in the doorway, "never threw anything away. Have a look-see under the bed. Who knows, you might find a signed copy of the Declaration of Independence."

He laughed, as did Annie. It was their mother's favorite joke.

Near the bed, alongside a great burlap bag, an assortment of blankets and quilts were folded in a stack on the floor. Annie picked them up. She was taller than her mother, but not by much. With her eyes twinkling over the top quilt, she said, "So long, copper."

They left Dutch in the middle of Old Peter's room, the room the old man had moved into after Ma and Pa had married, the room he'd died in.

Dutch didn't know where to start. Every available surface, bureau, and wardrobe held boxes, tin and wood, filled with papers. Loose letters, newspapers, and journals were stacked on a night table next to a pair of wire-framed glasses. The old man's specs. Well, he wouldn't need them where he'd gone.

"Don't forget yourself. You still have to go to work," his mother called from below.

Dutch put on Old Peter's spectacles. Everything was immediately magnified. He set them back on the table, took off his jacket, laid it on the mattress, and rolled up his sleeves.

The bureau held at least five years' worth of *Harper's Weekly*. Into the burlap bag on the floor they went, revealing a standing mirror he hadn't known was there. A stack of yellowing newspapers came next.

He started at the bottom of the pile. One of the papers, *The Evening News*, was dated July 28, 1861. It told of the return of the "Fighting" 69th Regiment of light infantry to New York after having concluded its first front-line tour of duty. An issue of *The New York Times*, dated April 10, 1865, proclaimed Lee's surrender to Grant at Appomattox in Virginia.

These papers too followed *Harper's* into the burlap bag. At this moment in his life Dutch was not interested in the past. He was a young man; young men are rarely interested in the past.

Now he was rewarded for his efforts with a look at the top of the bureau, a lot the worse for the years of wear. The bureau consisted of three small drawers across the top and four large ones below. The large ones were stuffed to the brimming with ruffled jabots, cravats, and shirts of a style not worn in perhaps fifty years.

He laughed. It was that kind of day. The old man was a pack rat. Well, he'd let Ma deal with the clothes. She was good with her needle. She might be able to do something with them.

Under the bed he found more newspapers and old letters.

"John," Meg called. "Work."

"Yes, Ma," he mumbled, setting the letters aside. On his hands and knees he dug out another stack of yellowing papers, and was caught immediately by the date and the headlines. This was *The Morning Sun*, dated June 21, 1850. It told of the death the day before of Jacob Hays, New York's first and only High Constable.

Dutch sat back on his heels. "Well, we'll have a better look at these." But as he spoke the paper was disintegrating in his hands. He set it on the clean top of the bureau.

He laid his head almost flat to the dusty old carpet to see if he'd gotten everything. He hadn't; shoved almost out of sight was a black box. He would have missed it had the mattress not been folded back.

Lying prone, he got his fingers on it. The metal box was wedged under the frame. Dutch took the broom Ma had left like a sentinel near the door and poked the box. One blow batted it loose. Tips of fingers took hold, then fingers, then hand.

His mind was playing tricks on him. When he had the dusty thing out in the light, the box did a tremble, as if it were alive. Just stuff shifting, he reasoned, brushing cobwebs and dust from its lid. Some sort of design was etched into the metal. He couldn't make hide nor hair of it.

Crouching on the floor next to the box, Dutch attempted to open the lid. The hinges were stubborn. Obviously it had been an age or two since the insides of the coffer had seen the light of day.

"What?" Meg reappeared. "Sitting down on the job? Get off that floor, John, I've just brushed and ironed those trousers."

"Look what I found." He held up the box. "It's stuck fast and I don't have time to work it now." He jumped up and set the box on the bed slats.

"Leave it, then." She brushed the house moss from his shirt and pants. "Look at you, covered with beggar's velvet. Go on now. I'll put some butter on the hinges. A little elbow grease will clean it up. It can sit in the parlor if it neatens nice enough. And be part of your trousseau." She laughed. They were a laughing family.

Dutch made a face, slapped at his trousers, rolled down his sleeves, and slipped into his jacket.

"By the way, young man, I've invited Mary Corcoran and her daughter Jeannie for dinner tonight, so don't be gallivanting off to any saloon and pretending it's work. Seven o'clock, you hear me? Be on time, be clean, and be charming. Jeannie is eighteen."

He called over his shoulder as he raced down the stairs. "Ma! You're matchmaking again. Do me a favor? Stop. I'll marry when I marry." He took his derby from the rack and added, "Besides, I've met a girl."

"You have?" Meg exploded, rushing down after her son, showering joy all over him. "And when, in sweet Jesus's name, were you going to tell me?" The words kept tumbling out. "When am I going to meet her? Bring her to Sunday dinner."

"Too soon. She doesn't even know I like her like that. She may not feel the same way about me."

"That'll be the day. Well, there's no harm in having the Corcorans over anyway. I'm making a nice pork roast, and cabbage, and . . ."

She was still reciting the menu as she climbed the stairs again. For the moment, she had forgotten the box Dutch had left resting on the bare slats of Old Peter Tonneman's bed.

40

Wednesday,
June 5.
Evening.
Shortly after six P.M.

As *Dutch and Bo approached Healy's, the sun had about an hour and a* half left in the sky, and Dutch had a little less than an hour to get home for dinner. Three teeners were passing the growler among themselves, pouring the beer down their gullets fast as they could. When they spied the detective derbies they removed themselves, heading apace down Nineteenth Street.

Bo's mouth gaped happily. "We carry the wrath of God, we do."

Healy's didn't have a big store window. The bar had been a front parlor, and it showed two lighted windows on either side of the front door, like a house, which it was. Healy lived upstairs. A lad in short pants hefting a growler came out as they came in. Dutch held the door for the boy.

"Don't spill none, you hear?" Bo called to him and laughed. "Or your pa will be pissed."

Four other drinkers, each alone in his own corner, were inside. Dutch and Bo, a foot on the brass rail, stood at the bar, not bothering with the high-backed stools. In the dim and quiet of the café they downed their beers, which were drawn by Spots Healy, a lanky fellow with freckles and large ears, who refused their coin. "Not from you, boys."

When Dutch still wanted to pay, Bo said, "Put your money in your pocket, it's only beer."

Dutch looked to the front door.

"What's the matter?" his cousin teased. "Worried that Moose and his pal Jake Riis will come busting in on us?"

"Of course not," Dutch protested. But that was exactly what had been worrying him. He left the nickel on the bar and beckoned to Healy. "Do you remember when I was here on Thursday last asking about Down-to-the-Ground Conn Clooney?"

Healy nodded. But even in the poor light coming from the gas lamps on the walls, Dutch could catch the hesitation in his eyes. So could Bo.

"I ran out of here because I heard somebody yell. And this bony cull was trying to rob a girl right outside."

"So?"

"So, maybe you knew this thief. Thin as a skeleton. Do you know him? Have you heard anything?"

"Not a word. But I'll keep my ears up," Healy said.

"You do that," said Bo, grinning. "Now what about—"

Dutch's hand on his arm stopped him. Bo was always rushing headlong; Dutch preferred to bide his time. He'd get back to the arsonist Clooney when he was ready. And he hadn't missed the fact that Healy hadn't answered his first question about knowing the villain who'd attacked Esther.

Bo slapped his two meaty palms together. "Two Irish whiskeys."

He downed his drink on delivery.

Dutch relaxed onto the high stool and sipped his whiskey. Just a few minutes more, then he had to get home for dinner.

Bo grinned. "You hear Peacock's latest bitch about Moose? 'He talks, talks, talks. Can't anyone shut the man up?' So some wag says, 'Stop Moose from talking? It would kill him.' "

"It probably would," Dutch said.

"I looked through the crap from Roman's desk at the *Herald*," Bo said, getting down to business.

"And?"

"Nil. Zero . . . You know I don't think much of this photographic plate nonsense."

Dutch nodded. "I know it."

"So you chase that business on your own."

"And what are you going to do?"

"I'll talk to people. Do this and that. Follow Roman's story."

"Maybe," Dutch grinned at his cousin, "Mr. Bennett's agony reporter can help you with that."

"Now there's a thought."

They grinned at each other.

"This young girl, she steps into the confessional," Bo said without preamble. " 'What?' the priest howls, hearing what she has to confess. 'I said I'm a prostitute,' she tells him. The good Father crosses himself. 'Thank God,' he says. 'I thought you said *Protestant*.' "

Healy laughed and topped off their double shot glasses. "That's a good one."

Dutch didn't comment. He'd been listening to Bo's jokes since they were boys, and most of them he'd heard more than once or twice.

Bo raised his glass. "Here's to Ireland and Parnell."

"When did you start getting political?"

"Ever since that bastard Peacock put his mealymouthed Protestant face into mine."

"So you don't like him because he's a Protestant?"

"No, I don't like him because he's a son of a bitch and a Protestant who thinks his shit don't stink. I'd love to find out his mitts are dirty."

Dutch chuckled and swung a dismissive hand, nearly knocking their drinks over.

"Careful, my lad, that's sacrilegious," Bo said.

Dutch pulled a face.

"I deceive you not. We just need the soda bread. Healy, some soda bread."

"Give me a minute." Healy went through a door that apparently led to the kitchen. He returned in less than the minute he asked for.

The bartender set down a round loaf on a wood board, a sharp knife next to it. Again he made sure their glasses were filled. Bo fingered the bread. "Stale, but 'twill do." He sliced a chunk, shoved it in his mouth, chewed, and washed it down with whiskey. "There, whiskey and soda bread, Irish Communion. I've received the Body and the Blood."

"You'll burn in hell for talk like that." Dutch was half-serious. After all, he was Meg's son.

"I may burn, but not for talk like that." Bo drank again, savoring the taste. Content for the moment, he set the glass down and burst into song, his favorite, "No Irish Need Apply." " 'Well, some may think it a misfortune to be christened Pat or Dan. But to me it is an honor to be born an Irishman. . . ,' " he bellowed.

"I'll drink to that," Dutch said, and drained his glass.

Bo joined him, and they slammed their shot glasses to the bar. Once again, Healy refilled them.

"Where was I?" Bo asked.

"To Ireland and Parnell."

"Forget Parnell. He's dead, and a Protestant to boot."

"Aye," Dutch replied. "And which is his greater flaw, do you think?"

Bo laughed. "To William of Orange, may he burn forever."

"Have a drink with us, Healy," Dutch said.

The bartender screwed up his face. "You know I don't touch the stuff, Detective."

"Detective? I thought you called me Dutch."

"Sorry, Dutch."

"Could it be that you're a little formal with me because you're holding something back?"

Healy raised his right hand. "I swear by my sainted mother—"

"Don't swear. You'll end up burning with Bo. And don't put your mother's soul in jeopardy by linking her with your lies."

"I don't lie. I didn't lie. I never lie."

"Healy?" Bo's voice was ripe with whiskey and menace. "It was about Down-to-the-Ground Clooney, wasn't it?"

Reluctantly, the bartender bobbed his head. "You told me he was locked up, but I saw him just today." The front door to Healy's had a squeak to it. Dutch heard the squeak as Healy's eyes grew wide. "Speak of the devil."

"Don't make a fuss," Bo warned. He and Dutch stayed perfectly still while they listened to the newcomer's shoes tread the old oak floorboards. Dutch noted the faint odor of goose grease mixing with the sweaty beer smell of Healy's Café.

Dutch picked up his glass. On the pretext of drinking, he held his hand up to his face while he sauntered toward the front door, positioning himself between the door and the newcomer. It was the snaky Mr. Clooney, for a fact. Who the devil had let him out?

Bo eased himself to the end of the bar in order to cover the kitchen and the back door. Dutch started for Clooney.

Clooney, that fire-burning, wild look blazing in his eyes, finally recognized the two detectives. He leaped, crashing through the glass and wood of the nearest window.

"Hellfire!" Healy cried.

Before Dutch could move or even think, Bo had followed Clooney out the broken window. In less time than it had taken Healy to find the soda bread, Clooney came flying back into the saloon through the same window.

The burn marks on the arsonist's forehead and cheeks were raw with imprints from Bo's fists.

"How'd you get out, Clooney?" Dutch demanded.

"Bail."

Bo pushed him across the room. "Bail? You? Talk, miserable spalpeen."

Clooney rested against the bar. "You hear about the girl goes into the confessional—"

"Shut up."

"Yes, sir."

"No jokes. Facts. Who bailed you out?"

"A friend."

"Who paid for the Vander Smith Lumberyard fire on Cherry Street?"

"No one. My own idea. Nice blaze, wasn't it?" he asked Dutch proudly.

"Another yard burned the next day. Brevoort's. When did you get out?"

"Today. On my honor."

"On my honor?" Bo guffawed. "On my honor? You're a liar. And a blackguard. When I find out the truth, I'm going to have you for breakfast."

Clooney turned imploring eyes to Dutch. "Make him lay off me, Detective." The arsonist seemed close to tears.

"What do you say, Bo? If he tells us what we want to know . . . ?"

Bo glared at Clooney, then shifted his look to Dutch. "By God, I'll feed his liver to the—"

In a second, Clooney had snatched the bread knife from the bar and leaped on top of Bo, the knife poised to stab the detective in the back.

Bo grabbed Clooney's wiry arm and caught it in descent. Even so, the point had broken skin before Bo finally wrenched it aside. Roaring, Bo lifted Clooney high and bounced him on the bar, scattering and breaking glasses, splashing whiskey. The arsonist rolled to the floor, grabbed sawdust in both hands, and threw it at the detectives.

Dutch could hear the noise of feet and the squeaking of the front door as Healy's emptied of customers.

When he rubbed his eyes clear, he saw Clooney biting Bo's ear and trying to gouge Bo's eyes with his thumbs. Bo thrust Clooney out in front of him, then brought him back to smash Clooney's face with his knee. Blood flowed as from a fountain. Bo grabbed Clooney by his coat and flung him into the wall, sending a chair flying in the process. Clooney slid down, leaving a swath of red, and lay there, panting.

But he was down for less than half a minute. He staggered to his feet and feinted left, then went right toward the chair. Bo was waiting. Double-fisted, he hammered Clooney to the floor again. Clooney could hardly breathe at all. Crying, blood and snot dripping, he tried to crawl away. Bo kicked him in the ribs.

Clooney's face was one large bruise leaking blood onto his clothes and the floor. When Clooney's hands moved to protect his face, Bo kicked him in the ribs, kidneys, and legs. When the hands moved down, Bo stomped Clooney's head.

Dutch touched Bo's shoulder.

Bo wheeled, eyes blazing, fists cocked.

"You're killing him," Dutch said.

"Good."

But Bo stopped. Dutch's shot glass was still intact on the bar, and there was a remnant of liquor in it. Bo drank it down, then glared at Clooney. "Well?"

"It's protection," the arsonist croaked, from the floor. "You don't pay, your business gets burned to the ground." Clooney's damaged body shook with his sobs. "This is high up. And these boys are rough. These boys would steal the nails from Jesus's cross."

"Talk, you miserable son of a bitch," Bo said.

"If they hear I told, they'll kill me in a minute."

Dutch said drily, "If you don't, my partner will kill you right now."

41

Wednesday, June 5.
Night.
After ten P.M.—
Thursday, June 6.
Early morning.

What with taking Clooney down to the House on Mulberry Street and booking him and all, Dutch never did make it home for dinner. He and Bo had repaired to a blind pig down the block from Police Headquarters on Mulberry Street, putting away an abundance of ale and sausage.

The arsons were solved—at least on the lowest level. But in spite of their threats, Clooney never told them anything else. They did not learn who ran the protection racket, or who got Clooney out of jail. Well, that was work for another day. If Clooney would just stay put. Bad enough they had had Pete Conlin on them to solve the Roman murder case yesterday. Now they had to deal with this arson, because Dutch had nailed Clooney in the first place. They had to find out who paid Clooney. On the Roman killing they had nothing. And the Roman killing was the case Chief Conlin was hot about.

It was well after ten when Dutch got home. Grand Street was peaceful except for the howling of cats in heat. There were always those, it seemed. He circled the house, went in through the back door, and turned on the electric light. His mother's kitchen was neat as a pin, but smelled richly of pork roast and cabbage. Half an apple pie rested on the kitchen table under a linen cloth. On the cloth was a note: "Don't wake your ma. She made a fine dinner for you and missed you sorely."

"Oh, shit," he muttered. He hadn't been that anxious to get home and meet the Corcoran girl, but he had had the best intentions. Then Clooney came along. . . . Liar, he told himself. You knew you weren't coming home when you walked into Healy's.

A soft glow was coming from the parlor where he knew Ma had left a turned-down kerosene lamp for him.

He opened the icebox. On a platter, sliced, was what was left of the roast. He made himself a sandwich between two thick slices of bread spread with German mustard, followed that with a large slab of pie, and washed it all down with a bottle of milk.

Dutch found himself thinking about Esther Breslau. He had never met anyone like Esther; her dark eyes haunted him. So pretty, so wise. But she certainly wasn't the nice Catholic girl his mother wanted for him.

It was time he married. What amazed Dutch was that he had set his cap for Esther Breslau. But he had to convince her. And Ma. Oh, wouldn't he need a sight more booze than he'd had tonight to handle that job.

In the parlor, the clock that had belonged to his great-grandparents chimed eleven. Dutch cleaned up after himself, set his plates in the sink and let the water run over them, then went into the parlor and turned up the lamp. The light shimmered, filling the shadows. It found a receptive glow in the beautiful silver box he'd found beneath his great-grandfather's bed, decorated like a king's treasure chest. Well, if all Irishmen were kings, it rightfully belonged in this house.

Dutch ran his fingers over the design; the silver was warm to the touch. Meg had polished it, and now it fair took his breath away; it was hard to believe that this was the black box he'd discovered only that morning. But he knew it was.

He held the back of the silver chest fast, then tugged at the clasp. It gave, coming open easy as the butter his mother had obviously applied to it. The hinges were well greased, too.

There was an inscription on the inside lid.

German? "No, idiot," he whispered. "Dutch."

He recognized *Tonneman* and *Pieter*, which he knew was the Dutch spelling of Peter. And the date 1665.

Pieter Tonneman. His ancestor? The thought was staggering.

Deliberately, by the kerosene light, John Tonneman began to remove the contents of the silver box. A brass five-pointed constable's star. A vellum scroll wrapped in white silk. As he unrolled the scroll, the top split in various places with tiny spider-web cracks. The scroll proclaimed with many flourishes and odd spellings that John Tonneman, Doctor of Physick and Surgery, was hereby appointed Coroner of New-York. The document was dated 1775, and signed by Whitehead Hicks, Mayor of the City of New-York, by the grace of His Majesty King George III.

One hundred and twenty years. Old Peter's father, and his father before him, had been Coronors of the City. Dutch had heard about it in dabs and pieces when the old man got to talking.

Old Peter had outlived his peers, his sisters—there'd been two—and his wife, Charity. His children and his grandchildren. For family he'd had the rollicking Clancys.

Dutch sat in his da's old wing chair holding the silver box in his hands. He recalled Old Peter's sister vaguely, Auntie Lee, a tiny lady with snowy hair, in constant motion like a bird. She was someone special. She'd been a doctor, and had never married. Auntie Lee had died when Dutch was seven or eight.

He dug into the box once more, removing items one after another. They overflowed the side table, so he brought everything, including the box, to the dining room. Catching the ball at the end of the light string under his chin, he gave it a tug. The electric light came on. He set his prize on the dining room table.

Dutch was about to pick up an ancient magnifying glass when he thought to move Ma's cherished cut crystal bowl to the other end of the table and out of harm's way.

Using the magnifying glass he examined a silver coin. An old English shilling by the look of it, from 16-something; the rest of the numbers had rubbed away. The profile, however, was clear. Some English king or other.

He found a short-stemmed clay pipe—not unlike the ones in McSorley's—held the bowl in his palm for a moment. Someone long ago had loved this pipe. He laid it down almost reluctantly.

He unrolled another sheet of parchment. This one did not crack. The words were surrounded by intricate designs from which most of the colors had faded. The letters were like the Hebrew signs he'd seen on the stores in Jew Town. That didn't make any sense. He set the parchment aside.

Dutch now removed a flat, book-shaped object wrapped in heavy blue silk. When he lifted it, the silk slipped, exposing the book. There were strings hanging from the end of the silk. Fringes. That was like . . . No, couldn't be. He'd had too much to drink and couldn't think straight. Or was he dreaming this?

He draped the silk on the back of the nearest chair. He knew the book had to be a Bible even though it was not in English. The text was in Hebrew. A Hebrew Bible? Why were these things in Old Peter's box? What meaning had they possessed for the old man?

Dutch left everything, went into the kitchen, and put his head under the faucet. As he dried his head with the dishtowel, he decided he should go to bed and sleep it off.

But the silver box was a magnet, drawing him back. Near the bottom of the chest he found more papers. A recipe for making soap. A musket ball. A packet of old daguerreotypes. He untied the white ribbon binding them and leafed through them carefully. Portions of some pictures flecked away. He recognized no one until Auntie Lee, with dark hair, along with two young women and a tall young man.

Then he saw the photograph of Old Peter. Younger, though not really young. And his Charity, white-haired, was holding a little girl in her lap, a lad of about eight beside her. The boy was Dutch's father. There was no mistaking the set of the jaw, the tilt of the head.

Dutch set the photographs aside. At the bottom of the box was a thick leather-bound volume. Printed on the volume's spine was *The Tonneman Family: A History*.

Overtaken by a powerful yawn, Dutch opened his eyes wide and shook his head. Tired or not, he was intrigued. He slipped the book under his arm, turned out the light, and returned to the wing chair in the parlor.

John Tonneman opened the book in his lap and turned the pages. Again he saw: *The Tonneman Family: A History, as recorded by John Peter Tonneman, Physician, in the year 1810. Printed by Benjamin Mendoza and Sons, Printers, Princeton, New Jersey*. Dutch began to read. He didn't stop until faint streaks of light came through the parlor windows and sounds of people stirring on Grand Street disturbed the dawn.

Only then did he close the book and lean his head on the antimacassar. It was as if everything in his life had fallen into place. But what a place. It explained a great deal. Not enough, though. There was so much still he didn't understand.

Although he'd gotten along, he'd always felt like the outsider among the Clancys. Even with Bo. And in spite of Ma. It was complicated, too complicated for him to absorb right now.

He closed his eyes. The words he heard were as if the two people talking were standing right next to him, even though one of them was him.

"*Your* Shadai."

"My *what? I don't understand.*"

"*On your watch chain. It's called a* Shadai. *The letters are Hebrew. They spell out the name of God.*"

"*Hebrew? I don't understand. It was given to my great-grandfather by his mother. It's been in my family for almost a hundred years.*"

"*Your family is not Jewish, then?*"

"*Oh, no. We're Irish. And Dutch. And English. But Catholic through and through. To the bone.*"

Dutch opened his eyes. Without a conscious thought on his part, his fingers were on his watch chain. He was Catholic. To the bone.

He held his lucky charm up to the light of the kerosene lamp. Why had he never recognized them as Hebrew letters? It was there for him to see.

Shadai. The Hebrew word for God.

42

Thursday,
June 6.
Early morning.

"Morning, Bo." *The Desk Sergeant was just ending his shift. He picked* up his threadbare pillow from his chair.

"Sergeant Dulaney."

"For a night man, you've been putting in a lot of mornings."

"You know how it is when you've got a case," Bo said. "I thought I'd roust Conn Clooney and see what I can get out of him while he still has sand in his eyes, and no coffee in his gut."

Dulaney sucked his lower lip. "You're going to have to go some to roust Conn Clooney."

"Why's that?"

"The poor bastard hung himself in his cell last night."

Sunlight poured through the studio's wall of tall windows. But the light only seemed to make Esther feel she had failed.

If only she had made notes . . . But Robert had rushed her, and she had trusted the camera and her skills to record what was happening in Union Square. Esther resolved never again to go out without a small notebook in which she would write the pertinent facts, the subject, the date, time of day, lens openings, a brief description of the subject, and a description of the light.

She stepped into the hallway. Only as she closed the studio door behind her did she become aware of the cadence of male voices from above. Oz and someone else. Not Wong. He was in fact coming up the stairs toward her that very moment, carrying a tray.

"Good morning, Miss Esther," Wong said, passing her. "There is breakfast in the dining room."

"Does Mr. Cook have a visitor?"

"He asked that I inform you he will be occupied all morning, and requests your presence at luncheon."

Esther watched Wong's back, thinking almost resentfully, I'm always present at luncheon. With a toss of her head, she continued down the stairs. In the dining room she helped herself to the scrambled eggs from the silver chafing dish and took two slices of buttered toast from the rack. Wong no longer put bacon and sausage out for her, as he had in the early days until she explained that her religion forbade the eating of pork. She added fruit to her plate and poured coffee into the fragile bone china cup.

She ate her breakfast at leisure while reading that day's edition of *The New York Times* which she'd selected from the stack of newspapers on the sideboard. Esther had been breakfasting in this fashion for almost half a year now, and how she cherished it. Each time it was as if for the first time. Esther, the poor little Jewish girl from Zakliczyn, dining at the rich man's table.

As she skimmed through the newspaper, she sighed. No mention of Robert Roman. The world had already forgotten him.

Her humor was ragged today. She felt out of sorts, guilty that she had failed to discover anything that might help find who had killed her friend. At sixes and sevens, she pushed aside the *Times* and picked through the *Herald*.

What she saw there surprised and reassured her. A boxed-in notice stated: "In cooperation with Mr. Oswald Cook, of Gramercy Park, the *Herald* is offering a $5,000 reward for information leading to the capture of the killer or killers of Robert Roman."

Esther was glad that Oz had done this, but she was piqued that he had not seen fit to inform her.

Just below the reward notice she saw an article discussing Robert's murder, and berating the police for their inability to bring the murderer to justice. Satisfaction replaced pique. But her momentary pleasure was dampened by her realization that the article was scolding John Tonneman and another detective, Fingal Clancy. "Poor Detective Tonneman," she murmured. He had seemed to her a very dedicated man.

The *Herald* reminded her that the murder had happened on Madison Street, in an alley overlooked by a tenement. The *Herald* wondered why the police couldn't find any witnesses or answers. Apparently no one had seen or heard a thing. Esther sat back in her chair and touched the tips of her fingers to her forehead. "Perhaps," she mused, "it's because they are asking their questions in English."

She became so excited she jarred her cup, sending a wave of coffee onto saucer and white linen tablecloth. Satisfied that none had soiled her shirtwaist, she hurried to her room for her straw hat, and slipped over her wrist the tiny black purse that matched her skirt.

You're being impetuous.

The words were in her head. And she couldn't make out whether she heard them in Oz's voice, her father's, or Detective John Tonneman's.

Think, before you act.

Giddy with excitement, she tried to calm herself by sitting in the slipper chair beside her bed and slowing her breath. Her eyes fell on the slim volume of Mr. John Keats's poems, open on her bedside table. She had left it open because she wanted to reread a poem that had struck her fancy: "*La Belle Dame sans Merci.*"

Something about it nagged at her mind. Very slowly it came to her. Not the poem itself: the title. Robert had told her that day at Union Square that the group of toughs who were trying to disrupt the march worked for a company called the La Belle Association.

In the library she found the City Directory. It listed the La Belle Association on Worth Street. A telephone number was given along with the address. She jotted down the number and the address in her small notebook.

She went back to the studio, where she removed a photograph of Robert Roman from the files and picked up one of the small Detective cameras. This camera was disguised as a leather-bound book. It held six

$1\frac{3}{4}$-by-$2\frac{3}{8}$-inch plates. She placed the photograph in her purse along with a pencil and a small notepad, and hid the camera in a covered wicker basket. She would describe her experiment to Oz later.

Downstairs, Esther stopped at the telephone and pondered the instrument. Then she picked it up, placed the receiver to her ear, and asked the operator to ring the number for the La Belle Association.

"Good morning," a gruff voice answered. "This is the La Belle Association."

"I have a job for you," Esther said, imitating Miss Lillian Wald's firm tones as best she could.

"Oh, yeah? What kind of job?"

"It is highly confidential," Esther said. "I can only discuss that with the owner of your company."

"Well, he ain't here now."

"I'll call back, then. What name should I ask for?"

"Alexander Williams. Who is this?"

Esther hung up the earpiece, just a little shaken at her audacity. She'd harbored thoughts of going to this place once she found out where it was. Now, she wasn't so sure.

To Wong she said a brief, "I'll be back in time for luncheon." She fastened her hat with a large pearl hatpin, inspecting her image in the mirrored hat stand. On the table before her were a man's fine boater and an ebony walking stick. She gave them only a fleeting glance and wondered who it was that Oz would change his routine for.

This morning, Gramercy Park was radiant. Zinnias in the little garden in front of the house were abloom, their petals still damp with morning dew. Too soon, even the lesser heat of today would dry them, perhaps even scorch them. She went past the park on her way to the Eighteenth Street stop of the Third Avenue El.

The elevated railway trains were both a boon for and a blight on the City of New York. Their advent allowed for the development of the City beyond Forty-second Street, and they were the largest and finest transit system in the world. But the noise they created was hideous, and the grit was unrelieved. Furthermore, the struts and posts and the rails themselves created permanent darkness, blocking out all sunlight on the street below.

Still, it was the fastest way to travel in the City, and Esther knew it. She could take the South Ferry train to Chatham Square and walk from there.

At the top of the stairs she paid her ten cents, and got her ticket. A sizable number of people were waiting for the train. She walked out to the high platform and joined the others, all looking uptown in expectation. The many tracks crisscrossing each other made wonderful patterns as far as her eye could see. What an interesting photograph that would make. She slipped the Detective camera out of the basket.

In a mischievous mood, Esther held the camera up and pretended to read *A Tale of Two Cities*. She aimed and pressed the catch on the cover of the case. This moved a small flap of leather at one end, uncovering the lens, allowing her to make her photograph. She returned her "novel" to the basket, then recorded what she had done in her small notebook.

A whistle was followed by a shriek, then a sudden cool breeze signaled the imminent arrival of the train. Puffs of dark smoke stained the sky. As the platform filled with those who had preferred to sit in the waiting room, Esther gloried in the fact that among the bright hats and parasols, no one could tell she was not a born American.

Even though the El was a tower of screeches and hisses, it was what Oz called just another part of the discordant orchestra that was New York. Esther loved the steam train; the places one could go, the sights one could see. Why, she could look right into offices and homes as if she were an invisible flying creature.

As the crowd gathered around her, Esther felt a sudden prickle of fear. A hand grazed her back. Someone screamed. Esther uttered a small "no" as she tottered on the edge of the platform for a moment, the basket gripped tightly in her hand. She was falling directly into the path of the train as it pulled into the station. Dear God, she thought.

Someone clutched her arm, wrenching her shoulder, and just as suddenly as she'd been falling, she was safe on the platform.

Esther let herself be propelled by the crowd into the car.

A voice in her ear said, "You'll have to learn to be more careful, little lady."

PART THREE

The Solution

43

Thursday,
June 6.
Early morning.

Thoroughly unnerved, Esther sat huddled in her cushioned seat, her feet firmly on the braided floor mat, as if she never intended to move them again. She did not dare to raise her eyes. Who had pushed her? Who had saved her? Was either nearby still watching, waiting? One to attempt harm again. The other to rescue again? She was thinking like a crazy woman.

But then she composed herself. Had it been an accident? Or was somebody trying to kill her? Ridiculous. Esther grinned so foolishly the woman opposite her changed seats.

Would it be wiser to go back home to Gramercy Park? Home and Oz seemed so safe.

She sat up straight and took a deep, even breath. Nonsense. She had set out for Madison Street. Madison Street it would be.

Chatham Square was an immensely busy intersection of lines: the El overhead and the trolley cars below, horse wagons, pushcarts, and people.

Just south of the square was a place she had discovered soon after her arrival in New York: A small Jewish cemetery, almost hidden behind an iron gate, on which hung a sign saying, "Congregation Shearith Israel."

The gravestones were ancient, the names strange. It was Lillian Wald who had told Esther the history of this congregation, that there had been a small Sephardic community in New York since the seventeenth century, descendants of those who had survived the Inquisition in Spain. Now when she visited the cemetery she felt her connection to things past as if it were a long lifeline to her future.

Turning away from the silent burial ground and the noise of Chatham Square, Esther wondered if perhaps Worth Street was the more logical first destination.

She paused, then decided that the scene of the murder was a more promising prospect. She went a few paces toward Madison Street, turned right around, and headed for Worth Street and the La Belle Association.

The address on Worth Street was just off Chatham Square. It proved to be a three-story brick building with a flat roof. The building was painted black and the heavy shutters on its first two floors were closed, giving it the forbidding appearance of a fortress. A sign over the front door proclaimed this to be the La Belle Association.

The black structure sat on a corner lot; a narrow side street ran alongside. Esther could see the back of a cart at the end of the side street.

The area was filled with warehouses; delivery wagons cluttered the lanes and men shouted to one another. Goods were unloaded from or loaded into the wagons as horses waited patiently in their harnesses. People were going about their business on each corner.

Esther knocked sharply on the front door with the brass horseshoe knocker. Getting no response, she tried the door. It was locked. She circled round the corner, edging past the cart. A high fence blocked the way to the rear entrance.

Sunlight glared down at her on Worth Street from the dirty panes on the third floor. The building was ominously silent. She was first disappointed, then relieved. What would she have done, or said, if someone had answered her knock? Or if the door had been unlocked? Esther stepped away from the La Belle Association, brought out her Detective camera, and made a picture.

With only a small feeling of accomplishment she resumed her original journey to Madison Street.

She did not see the man peering at her from behind the grimy panes of the third-story window.

Her walk to Madison Street took her past empty lots, wooden buildings, and brick tenements. Now there were fewer synagogues, even a church or two. The people living here were for the most part Jews and Italians, with only a few Irish who had not moved farther uptown with their more fortunate kinsmen and friends.

She passed a knife sharpener who smiled broadly at her, never stopping his honing of a large knife. A wagon loaded with barrels of pickles tempted her nose and tongue, but she didn't stop. She was on a mission. She hurried past the umbrella-shaded pushcarts, which held merchandise of every variety—from gloves to shirtwaists to *sheitels* to potatoes and carrots and tin pots. Children played on the sidewalks and in the gutters, heedless of the traffic and the dirt. Everything was so alive, she thought, though she knew how lucky she was. The filthy conditions would cause many here to die from tuberculosis and the other diseases that killed the poor.

She walked past Market Street, then Pike. At Pike she paused. The Pike Street Synagogue was nearby. She had read about Rabbi Chaim Weinschel in the *Forwartz*. A rabbi knew everything about a neighborhood.

When she arrived at the modest building at No. 12 Pike Street, she saw a group of small boys in dark clothes, religious fringe hanging from under their coats, their heads covered with *jarmulkas*, sitting around a table on the sidewalk. Their noses were buried in their books. The rabbi, a striking gray-haired man with pale skin, a short beard, and a sharp nose, hovered over them. He held a yardstick with which he tapped on the sidewalk in rhythm. He was shading his eyes from the bright sunlight, singing the words with great resonance quite loudly, precisely, and with emotion while the boys dutifully attempted to echo his intonation and diction.

From inside the building came the sound of hammering and the pungent odor of paint.

She stopped near the makeshift school table and waited.

The rabbi glanced her way but continued the lesson.

At the first pause after an amen she spoke rapidly. "Excuse me, Rabbi, may I ask for a few private minutes of your time?"

The rabbi's eyes widened. Was it because he was shocked that someone dressed as she was spoke Yiddish? Perhaps it was her bruised eye, which now showed tinges of yellowish green in spite of her careful application of powder. Or was it because of her effrontery? A woman speaking to a man, a rabbi, who was praying.

The rabbi, a half-smile on his lips, took a deep breath and said, in Yiddish, "Of course, madam." He tapped the yardstick. "With feeling. You are speaking to God, not the candy man. Isaac, you lead."

It was simple to determine which one was Isaac. His pale face flushed with pride, and the other boys looked at him with something like envy.

"Madam?"

"Miss. Esther Breslau. You are Rabbi Chaim Weinschel, yes?"

"Herman, not Chaim."

"You have a beautiful voice."

"Thank you. Anyone who praises God has beauty in his voice. Come tomorrow night to services."

Not responding to his invitation, Esther took Robert Roman's photograph from her bag and plunged into the story of his death. "This man was murdered last week on Madison Street. In an alley next to the corner building on Gouverneur Street. Away from the river."

"I know it."

Esther showed the rabbi the photograph. "Do you know him?"

"No."

"Are you acquainted with any of the families who live there?"

"One, the Grabinskys, a Russian family. They are destitute. Young children and the father who has a bad heart and can't work." He turned his eyes to the boys. "Tuvya, you're lagging behind." Back to Esther, he said, "I visit them, bring them food. I took young Isaac with me when I was there two days ago."

"Did they say anything about the night of the murder?"

Suddenly there was a silence behind them. The boys were listening avidly. "What?" asked the rabbi. "So soon finished, Isaac? Boys?"

Isaac began again. The boys followed suit, but amidst smirks and knowing looks.

"I can't give you much more time, Miss Breslau."

Esther brought out the dime she'd been holding ever since she'd turned the corner on Madison Street. "Would you permit me to offer some money for the poor?"

"What?" The rabbi's smile broadened. "You would bribe a man of God?"

"For the poor."

"I accept with great appreciation, Miss Breslau, but I must ask you to be quick. I have duties."

"Of course. I don't mean to interfere with your work. Did the Grabinskys possibly see or hear anything that night?"

"Not that they said. They have all they can do to keep the wolves from their door."

"Perhaps I can ask them . . ."

"I must warn you it is not a place for a lady."

"Ah," she said, with an odd pride, "I have seen the worst."

"Ah," the rabbi echoed, almost singing the sound. "Then take your dime back, Miss Breslau, and give it to Haya Grabinsky. And take them some food from me, I beg you."

"I can afford another ten cents. Keep the dime, Rabbi. I thank you for your time."

The rabbi turned his back on her, their exchange concluded, or so Esther thought. "Boys! Lessons!" the rabbi thundered. He started for the synagogue.

Esther smiled at the boys, who were staring at her. Rabbi Weinschel looked back, pointed at his students with the yardstick, and entered the *shul*. Seizing her opportunity, Esther pulled out the book camera and made a picture of the boys. As she did so, she realized she was a better photographer than detective. The camera was meant to be for the case. For evidence. Not for boys reciting their lessons.

She had almost forgotten why she'd come here in the first place. Annoyed at herself, she put the camera away.

The rabbi was back on the street in minutes, a bulging sack in his hand. "Isaac, help the lady. Take her to the Grabinskys."

"Yes, Rabbi," the pale boy said, a glint of excitement in his dark eyes.

Esther measured the young scholar. He wore short pants and his knees and shins were full of scabs, which told her he was a regular boy as well as a scholar. She wanted to make his photograph, too, but did not give in to the urge.

She showed him Robert's photograph; the boy shook his head. Together, they began walking, Isaac leading the way.

As they approached Madison Street, Isaac said, "Mendy knows about it."

"Who is Mendy?"

"Mendy Grabinsky. He told me. *Di Alte* told him."

Esther's heart thumped powerfully in her breast. "Told him what? Which *Alte*?"

"She's not Jewish. An old Irish lady in Mendy's building. *Di Alte* saw what happened."

44

Thursday,
June 6.
Morning.

There was no mistaking the building; it leaned over the alley almost unsteadily. In the alley, amid garbage and debris, a drunk lay on the ground cradling his bottle.

The entrance was even worse than where she had lived on Ludlow Street. She took a breath. A mistake. All the old fetid odors were here to torment her.

Three scrawny dark-haired children, two boys and a tiny girl, played a jumping game on the filthy sidewalk. All three stopped to stare at her, then surrounded her, clinging to her dress, fingers darting at her basket and the sack of food.

"Stop!" Isaac commanded, raising the sack high.

While the children stood and gaped, Esther gave in to temptation and brought out her Detective camera. Quickly she made a picture of the children, then put the camera away, ashamed that she could see a good photograph when children were starving.

"This nice lady has brought you food." Isaac gave the sack to the tallest, the older boy, who was scuffing around in some adult's ancient, ill-fitting shoes.

"Mendy?" Esther asked. "Are you Mendy?"

The boy hugged the sack to him, his expression cautious.

"Tell her about *di Alte,*" Isaac said.

Mendy clutched the sack while the two smaller children hid behind him. Suddenly Mendy turned and ran into the tenement, followed by his siblings. Only then did Esther notice that the two youngest wore no shoes.

Isaac beckoned. She followed with some trepidation.

"No climbing," the boy said, leading her into the shadows behind the stairwell. The hall was dark and the smells putrid. Indeed, Ludlow Street had been heaven compared to this.

Only one candle lit the room behind the stairs. The space was a hovel. Urine and body odors filled the chamber. A bearded man held a crying infant while two other babes crawled on the grimy floor.

"Excuse me," Esther said. "Food from Rabbi Weinschel."

Mendy brandished the sack like a hunter with fresh game.

The man exchanged infant for sack with his son.

A small sound made Esther look harder into the shadows, and as her eyes acclimated to the darkness, she saw a pregnant woman lying on a mattress. "God in heaven," she whispered angrily. The man was too sick to work, but not too sick to make babies. Who would feed all these children? What would become of them? Would the mother survive? Esther had to leave quickly or she would tear her hair and cry. *Is this what we come to America for?*

"She wants to talk to *di Alte,*" Mendy told his father.

The father didn't answer at once, nor did he look Esther in the eyes.

"Please," she pleaded in Yiddish, displaying Robert's photograph. "It's very important."

"Take her upstairs," the father said to his son.

"Thank you." Esther pressed several coins from her purse into his hand.

The man nodded but did not acknowledge the gift.

In the hall she said to Isaac, "Thank you, I can manage the rest myself."

Even in just the shadow of light from the street she could see disappointment in his expression. She gave him two cents. Detective work was turning out to be an expensive pastime. Holding his pennies,

Isaac ran off. She wondered if he would go straight back to the synagogue. Then, resolutely, she followed Mendy up the stairs.

On the third floor, a white-haired old lady came to the door. "Oh, Mendy," she exclaimed in a plummy Irish accent, "you're such a good lad."

The tiny woman wore an ancient but tidy yellow cotton dress. Her wrinkled face showed great strength, as if neither old age nor God himself could slow her down. Holding a thick candle in front of her, she looked past the boy and beamed at Esther. "And who is this grand lady, may I ask?"

"She wants to see you, Mrs. Doty," Mendy declared in perfect English. Then, without another word he scooted down the dark staircase, disappearing into the shadows.

"He's a good boy for a Jew," the old lady said.

"I'm a Jew," Esther said.

"I meant no harm," the woman replied, not at all put off. "Live and learn. You don't look like them, miss. Come in, sit yourself down and have a cup of tea. Tell me why you came to see me."

Mrs. Doty's room was crammed with dilapidated furniture, but it was as clean as could be in such circumstances. Esther sat in a rickety chair next to a table on which a knitted tea cozy covered a teapot.

The old lady said, "You see a woman in a pitiful state. The husband dead and gone, taken by the drink. Six children, only four living, and not one of those boys stayed, but went west as soon as they was able. That's an elegant hat you're wearing, dear."

She served strong tea in cracked cups, talking six to the dozen. The heat of the sun beating on the roof of the building cooked the room. There was a window but little air.

Nevertheless, Esther bided her time, sipping the bitter tea, and listening. Finally the old woman gave her a sharp look. "What would you want?"

"A friend of mine was killed in the alley under your window last week." Esther showed her Robert's photograph. "I wondered if you saw or heard anything."

The old woman fingered the photograph. "Nice looking. Sad." She peered at Esther. "You're not drinking your tea, dear."

"I was letting it cool some," Esther said. "Did you see anything?"

"The boy," she said. "I told the police about him. He was riding on the back of the wagon. I saw him after they threw the bundle out. I didn't know it was human. How could I know? The boy went out of my sight, then. Maybe the cellar. But after the police left I saw him again."

Esther felt a rush of emotion. A witness to Robert's murder. But if Mrs. Doty had told the police, why was there no mention of it? Why hadn't Detective Tonneman . . . ? "How old was this boy?"

"I couldn't tell. Bigger than Mendy. Thirteen or fourteen perhaps. He wore a cap. I told the police about him. Two nice Irish lads, they were." Mrs. Doty frowned and scratched her head. "At least, I *think* I told them."

Musing on what she'd just heard, Esther hurriedly made her way down from this world of darkness to the one of light.

Much to her amazement, a hackney coach was pulling in to the curb as she stepped out of the tenement on Madison Street. This was an unexpected and happy occurrence. Madison Street was certainly not where the carriage trade was to be found.

She called out, "Driver!"

The cabby tipped his topper.

"I need you to take me to Gramercy Park."

"With pleasure, madam, as soon as I discharge my passenger." He raised his voice. "Madison Street, sir." When there was no response, the driver, a lanky fellow, leaned down and deftly unlatched the carriage door with a jiggle of his whip handle. The door swung open. "Sir?"

Esther peered inside. "There's no one there."

"Blast it. Pardon, madam. That's the third time this week I've been hoaxed." He breathed an exasperated sigh. "Get in, if you please, madam. Where can I take you?"

"Gramercy Park. And I'll make up your loss. I'll give you a dollar."

Hearing that, the driver leaped to the sidewalk, pulled down the step, and held her hand in support as she climbed in. "Thank you, madam. It will be my pleasure to serve you."

Esther relaxed against the back of the leather seat as they pulled away from Madison Street. She was ashamed of her feelings, but she was so relieved to have left the dreadful tenement and its miserable tenants. Except for Mrs. Doty, she thought. The old woman seemed to have salvaged some sort of dignity.

As they drove past Henry Street, Esther received a terrible shock. A face showed at the window, eyes ogling her. A man was clinging to the side of the carriage.

"*Gott in Himmel!*" Esther's hand went to her mouth.

"Pray, dear lady, do not scream," the face implored, clearly hoping to forestall any outcry. "I am but a harmless lout, a humble player. I hid out here because I had not the funds to pay the stalwart Apollo who drives this chariot. I would have dismounted at my destination, but my boot caught on some blasted piece of metal."

Esther had all she could do not to burst out laughing. It was such a relief to have to deal with this silliness after all the horrors she had witnessed in that obscene gray building on Madison Street. "You could have eased your foot out of the boot," she said, wanting to prolong this delicious moment.

"And lose my boot?" The creases framing the noble nose came closer together. " 'Tis a worthy suggestion. One I had not considered." The stowaway's majestic face went through countless expressions as he concentrated. Finally he smiled. "I'm free," he exulted and disappeared.

Esther worried that the old man had tumbled to the street. "Sir?"

"Have no fear, dear lady," he exclaimed, reappearing at the window, showing her his not-so-shiny black boot. He dropped the boot into the carriage and unlatched the door. But the cabby above chose this moment to make a turn. The carriage door opened taking the stranger with it, just as a large open wagon bearing a mountain of beer casks thundered toward them.

Before Esther could call a warning to the driver, the carriage shifted again and the door slammed, the stranger flattened against it for dear life.

"Ah," the man exclaimed elongating the sound, "now I know the true meaning of being between Scylla and Charybdis." He shook his mane of dyed blond hair. "May I come in?" he inquired politely. Without waiting for her answer, he opened the door and swung in with the grace and athleticism of a far younger man. Now he stroked his mustache, first one side, then the other. "Though I must admit, being annihilated by all that beer would have been a most tasty end." He fastened the door and fell into the seat opposite her.

"You could have been killed," Esther told him. "Are you all right?"

"Never better. You should have seen my *Monte Cristo*. I out-O'Neilled O'Neill."

"I beg your pardon?"

"You have never heard of the great James O'Neill? Good. Forget O'Neill and know the greater Byron Brown, the most magnificent Monte Cristo of them all." Even in his cramped position he managed to stand and bow. This time he sat beside her. "Where are you bound, fair damsel?" When she hesitated, the stranger waved an eloquent hand and said, "If you could drop me at my daughter Sophie's establishment at 79 Clinton Street, I should be eternally grateful."

45

Thursday,
June 6.
Morning.

" '*Ten lovely ladies. Beautiful costumes. Visit the chambers of delight. Fine* whiskey. Good beer. Madam Sophie's. 79 Clinton Street.' "

"What's that?" Leo Stern lifted his nose from the *Police Gazette*.

"My advertisement," Sophie replied. "Beginning this week you can read about me in the *Herald*."

"Why not just say, 'To get laid, bring dough, come to Sophie's'?"

"Leo, you have no sense of style. Your version might be more honest, but it wouldn't attract the type I want to frequent my establishment. I want everyone to know and say that Sophie runs a classy house."

"They do already. You're a classy woman, my Sophie. What say we grab a hack, drop your ad at Herald Square, then go on to the Central Park? I'll row you around the lake a few times, then buy you lunch."

She set her ad aside, took a thick ledger book from a drawer, and donned spectacles, which Leo, perversely, found alluring. "That sounds inviting."

Leo put the *Gazette* down, got up, and kissed the back of her neck where soft tendrils of blonde hair rested.

Absently, her hand reached up for him. "I have a little more work to do, then I'm yours."

"How about now, darling?" he murmured.

She shrugged him off. "Not now, Leo."

Leo, his ardor undiminished, returned to his chair and put a fresh cigar in his mouth. He opened a new deck of Black Eagles and laid out a solitaire game. While he pondered the layout, he struck a match on his gold front teeth and heated up the cigar. Puffing and playing, he wasn't actually thinking about the cards. His thoughts were on the dead man in the alley and the culls who'd done him in and tried to do the same to Leo.

And on the $5,000 reward offered by the *Herald* and a man named Oswald Cook, for information leading to the capture of the killer or killers.

The day after he'd seen those blokes in the alley, Leo had read about the dead man. Robert Roman, newspaperman, killed while doing his job, searching out the truth, Lincoln Steffens had said in the *Post*. That was all Steffens seemed to know. That was all anybody seemed to know in the whole Frog and Toe, according to the other papers. Leo had put the question to the coveys and cats on the stroll. Not even the Clinton Street Frog, who was on Sophie's payroll, could tell him anything.

Leo knew he probably knew more than most. The murder had happened after midnight. There'd been three of them in that wagon. From the smell of it a bakery wagon, but that was a maybe.

The driver was called Harry. The other, the big strong son of a bitch Leo had fought with, was Terry. Leo had put out the word on the street about them too. Nothing yet.

"I'm ready," Sophie announced. She was wearing a white pleated shirtwaist and skirt. She had pinned a fashionable red straw hat to her rolled hair, and carried a red parasol. Leo jumped up and snagged his snappy boater from where it was hooked on the finial of the highboy.

"Where's your derby?"

"You know damn well where it is. I lost it last Friday when I picked up your father and got mixed up with those . . ."

But Sophie wasn't listening. She was sailing down the stairs.

Leo planted his straw hat at a rakish angle and hurried after.

"We'll be back before two, Daisy," Sophie said.

"Yes, ma'am." The little black woman bobbed and opened the front door just as someone outside rang the bell, producing the opening notes of the Mendelssohn serenade.

Standing on the stoop of Sophie's whorehouse, his hand still on the red tasseled pull, was Bo, the biggest and broadest of all the copper Clancys.

46

Thursday,
June 6.
Morning.

A*t just that moment a hackney coach clattered to a halt outside No. 79* Clinton. The driver leaned down. "Are you sure this is where you want to go, madam?"

The carriage door opened and out darted Sophie's father, Byron Brown.

"Hey, you, stop!" the carriage driver thundered and leaped to the sidewalk. He grabbed Byron by the collar. "You deadbeat, you owe me forty cents."

"Let go of that man," Bo yelled.

"Let go of that man," Sophie and Leo echoed.

Leo was the first to move. He didn't throw any punches, merely got between Byron and the irate cabby.

"I don't want any trouble," the hack man said, releasing his grip on Byron's collar, softening his truculence at the sight of the frog in the derby hat. He watched Bo and Leo warily.

"Give him a dollar, Leo," Sophie said.

Leo handed the driver a dollar. "Get on."

Esther, fascinated with the entire display, brought out her Detective camera and made a picture.

"A moment, please." Byron Brown pulled wide the coach's door. "Daughter. Leo. May I present my pretty little savior? Miss Esther Breslau."

"Please," Esther protested, from within the carriage. "You're quite welcome, but just allow me to be on my way."

A frown appeared on Bo's face. "Miss Breslau?" He stepped toward the hackney.

"Driver, I'd like to leave now," Esther said firmly.

The cabby climbed back to his post. But by this time Bo was standing at the carriage door and tipping his hat. "Miss Breslau, I'm Detective Clancy, and I . . ."

Esther relaxed now that this hulk of a man had been identified as friendly. "Oh, yes, you're Detective Fingal Clancy who works for Detective Tonneman."

"Fingal?" Leo piped. Always curious, Leo had followed close on Bo's heels. A smile distorted his face. His gold teeth gleamed.

"Shut your gob," Bo ordered Leo. To Esther he said, "I work *with* Detective Tonneman, not for him." He grinned. "You're the girl. A pleasure to meet you, lass. I'm Dutch's cousin. Marry him and the Clancys will be your relatives and protectors forever."

Marry? Esther blushed, and although not given to blathering, she blathered. "I need to find Detective Tonneman. Two things he has to know. One, Robert Roman rented a room above the coach driver's stable. Battling Jack. And two, this morning I learned from a Mrs. Doty who lives upstairs from that alley on Madison Street that there was a boy who witnessed the murder."

"Miss, please, don't talk anymore. Allow me to see you home." Bo stepped in agilely and sat beside her. He turned to shout, "You, Leo, don't go anywhere. I want to talk to you. You, too, Sophie." To the driver, he commanded, "Let's go."

On the sidewalk in front of 79 Clinton Street, Leo Stern rubbed at his gold teeth with his forefinger. His grin was wider than before.

47

Thursday,
June 6.
Midday to afternoon.

At No. 5 Gramercy Park, luncheon came and went without Esther. This had never happened before and Oz was distressed.

"Miss Esther didn't say where she was going?" he asked Wong for the dozenth time.

"No, sir."

"You told her I wanted her here for lunch?" At least an eighth asking of this question.

"Yes, Mr. Oz."

Oz snuffed out his cigarette and lit a new one immediately. "I cannot imagine—this is so unlike her." He turned to his guest. "Edward, my deepest apologies. I very much wanted you to meet her."

His visitor, a middle-aged portly gentleman with a bald dome and fuzzy gray side whiskers, said, "There is time."

"Not much. I wanted you to understand why . . ."

"There is no need."

A sudden thought struck Oz. "Wong, was she carrying anything?"

"The covered wicker basket from the studio."

"Ah." For the first time since he'd noted Esther's absence, Oz was his usual composed self. "She's taken one of the smaller cameras. She has a palpable talent, Edward. She's become a fine photographer."

His guest, the attorney Edward Ten Eyck, cleared his throat. He said sternly, "These New Women run all over the City by themselves as if they were men, without a thought of danger, or propriety. They value their so-called independence. We must keep them in check, if only for their own protection." Ten Eyck had an eighteen-year-old daughter who was studying at Vassar College, determined to be a medical doctor. The notion sent shivers up Ten Eyck's spine, as it would any proper father's.

Ten Eyck had a point, Oz thought later. After lunch, he'd determined that Esther had taken one of the Detective cameras, the one disguised as *A Tale of Two Cities*. It held only six plates. She had left very early. So the chit had gone out to make photographs on her own. The question was where had she gone? And for what purpose? She had taken Robert's death badly.

He wondered now if Esther had been in love with Robert. What was that? Jealousy? Oz was certainly unused to that strange emotion. Most of his life he'd been a man who preferred the company of other men. Except for his mother—she was gone now—and Lillian Wald, who had convinced him to hire Esther Breslau, even though he'd had a young man in mind at the time.

Robert and Esther were both immigrants. Oz hadn't taken any notice, but young people today seemed to talk an entirely different language, whether immigrant or native-born. And middle age had crept up on Oz on quiet feet.

If Esther were delayed, wouldn't she have called on the telephone? Short of having Wong get the brougham or hiring a hackney to go searching for her on the streets, what could he do? Call the police? "Don't be an old woman, Oz," he said aloud.

He went into the darkroom and began the process of developing the photographs he'd taken of Lillian Russell two days earlier. Esther's welfare nagged at his thoughts. He'd spent the bulk of the morning with Ten Eyck seeing to it. So engrossed was Oz in his worries that he did not hear the doorbell ring at three o'clock, or know that his latest visitor was Detective John Tonneman.

"Miss Esther went out this morning and hasn't returned."

Tonneman pulled out his watch. "It's five minutes after three. Did Miss Breslau say when she'd return?"

Wong was uncomfortable. Not a normal state for him. Against all his discipline a deep crease appeared between his eyebrows. "For luncheon."

"Luncheon? It's almost time for tea." Dutch handed Wong his bowler. "Where's Mr. Cook? I'd like to talk to him."

"I never disturb Mr. Oz in his darkroom."

"I'll wait."

With a minute tilt of his head, Wong led Tonneman into the parlor. Then he withdrew.

The detective seated himself in one of the brocade-covered wing chairs. It was quite comfortable. He'd gotten no sleep the night before and the thoughts that scrambled in his mind had left him exhausted.

Reading the Tonneman family history was like reading about strange creatures from a different world. One night's reading had made him doubt his very existence. Like something from his mother's tales about the fairies, the Shees who lived in the wind. Could he be some sort of changeling child the Shees had left somewhere? A Hebrew cuckoo's egg left to hatch in an Irish songbird's nest? Now that he was sitting here, he couldn't help wondering: Had he come to Esther Breslau for information? Or salvation?

"It occurs to me you might be thirsty." Wong stepped back into the room. "Would you care for lemonade, Detective?"

"Yes, I would." Tonneman touched the Chinaman's arm. "Where is she? You know, don't you?"

Wong stepped back out of Tonneman's long reach. He didn't leave to fetch the lemonade, but neither did he respond to Tonneman's question. Still, it seemed he wanted to say something.

"Out with it, man."

Wong's impassive face seemed to open, as if he'd made up his mind.

"We have no idea where Miss Esther is. She was expected home for lunch. She hasn't telephoned. I am not an excitable person. But since Mr. Roman's death . . ." Wong let that thought trail off. "I am concerned about her."

"Get me that lemonade. I'll call Mulberry Street and put out the word to keep an eye open for her."

They walked down the stairs to the entrance hall together. Dutch, who couldn't keep the Tonnemans of the past out of his mind, was struck by the family portraits on Oswald Cook's stairway walls glaring down their aristocratic noses at him. No doubting who *they* were, that was a fact. Bloody Englishmen. But who was he? Certainly an intruder in this house, this elegant world. Who the hell was he? Dutch Tonneman, a fecking bloody Irish Catholic Israelite.

All the time tapping his fingers on his derby which was sitting next to the phone, he called Mulberry Street. After he'd placed the call to Headquarters, he retreated to the comfort of the chair in the parlor where Wong's cold lemonade now awaited him. A gentle breeze shivered the curtains. And the cold drink felt good on his parched throat. He heard the high sheer voices of children from the sidewalk where he'd seen primly dressed rich little English-American girls playing at hopscotch.

The soft clop of hooves on the Belgian block of the streets around the park lulled him. He drifted into sleep.

He was struggling up a mountain. He could hear the birdsong from the woods around him, the melodious flow of a stream. He could smell the pines. He could see the light above him.

"John, come back!" the voice called to him. Again and again. Meg's voice.

John felt the weight of the pack on his back, its corners digging into his shoulders. He shifted it, feeling the now familiar carved surface, its silky warmth. As Meg's voice faded, he saw the clearing, breathed in the fragrant boxwood only a few feet above him. A hand reached down to help him, clutching his, easily lifting him, bringing him into the clearing, and he felt a great rush of joy. And then sorrow.

Why had he accepted this so easily? Why hadn't he fought? For Christ's sake, he was a good Catholic. How could he turn his back on his mother? On Jesus?

. . .

The voices awakened him, but his senses were still flooded with the emotions of the dream. He'd never known how it was to feel good and bad at the same time, but he was feeling it now.

The moisture on the lemonade glass dripped onto the silver coaster. Tonneman rose and walked to the window, parted the lace curtains, and looked down at the street. A hackney coach had stopped in front of No. 5.

Out of the carriage stepped his cousin and partner, Bo Clancy. Bo held a supporting hand to the other passenger inside the coach: Esther Breslau.

• 48 •

Thursday,
June 6.
Midafternoon.

Dutch and Wong arrived at the front door at the same time. Embarrassed, Dutch released the doorknob and allowed the Chinese butler to do his job.

"Miss Esther." Wong's composure wavered, then righted itself. "We missed you at lunch."

"Is he very upset? It couldn't be helped." Esther gave Tonneman a worried little smile. Sooty smudges soiled her white shirtwaist and the tips of her gloves. The skin around her left eye had a yellow tinge.

"Mr. Oz is in the darkroom," Wong said. "Have you eaten?"

Bo, who had no patience with civilians and their chatter, plunged right in. "Please, Miss Breslau, tell Detective Tonneman what you told me."

"Wong, please inform Mr. Oz that I'm home. And I have not had lunch. If you could bring some lemonade. For the gentlemen as well. Detective Tonneman, forgive me, I neglected to tell you this the last time we met, but when I was at the theatre Monday night I saw the coach driver, Jack West, and he told me that Robert Roman rented a room above his stable in Macdougal Alley."

Dutch nodded. That was what Robert Roman had meant when he

said he lived like the baby Jesus. The stable. This was important, but he hesitated to interrupt. Esther's accent had thickened, whether from exhaustion or the passion of telling. The music of it pleased his ears.

Bo was not so influenced. "Tell him the rest, miss."

"Did Mrs. Doty, the woman who lives upstairs from that alley on Madison Street, tell you about the boy she saw that night?"

Tonneman lost his restraint. "Is that where you were today? In that hellhole on Madison Street? Alone? That was wrong of you, not to consider the distress of those who care for you. You can never do this again."

Esther was staring at John Tonneman, as was Bo.

"You have no right—" Esther began.

Raising his right hand to signal his partner to desist, Bo broke in, "The old lady didn't mention a boy, did she, Dutch?"

Dutch recovered his self-control. "No."

Esther said, "She's old. Old people forget. She told me that there was a boy who saw Robert's murder."

"Did she tell you what he looked like?" Bo asked.

"She said he was wearing a cap."

Dutch took his derby from where he'd left it on the mirror table. "Thank you very much. We appreciate all you've told us."

"Please," Esther said. "Could I go with you? I can speak several languages. I could be helpful to you."

Bo cast his eyes upward.

"Of course not," Dutch told her, curtly. "This is police business."

"Is there anything else you have to tell us?" Bo was fidgeting, anxious to leave.

"There is something. . . . I don't know if it's important. On Union Square that day, Robert mentioned contractors who were beating people trying to break up the rally. He said they were from the La Belle Association. This morning I found the La Belle Association listed in the City Directory on Worth Street. It's just off Chatham Square. That's why I went by—"

"You went by, Miss Breslau? You went by? Alone?" Dutch was appalled.

"Easy, *boyo*," Bo said through his teeth, frowning at Dutch. "Did you talk with anyone there, Miss Breslau?"

"No. There was no one, but I made a photograph of the building." She took the Detective camera from her basket.

"I'd like to see that photograph when it's developed," Dutch said.

"Let's pay them a call and see who's the boss." Bo was already on his way.

"Oh," Esther said, "I can tell you that. The La Belle Association is owned by a man named Alexander Williams."

The two detectives looked at each other. "Clubber," they said together, grinning.

As they walked swiftly toward Washington Square, Bo kept shaking his head. "I don't believe it. We bust our asses doing all the right things, asking all the right questions, and this little Israelite girl comes up with three important pieces of information all neatly tied together."

"True," Dutch agreed.

Bo slapped Dutch on the back. "Watch yourself, coz. You're getting too interested. I thought at first she might be right for you. But it all comes down to one thing. She's a Jew."

"Jesus was a Jew."

Bo punched Dutch on the arm. "Blasphemous clown." After a moment he said, "The word is that Peacock held back his vote for Conlin's confirmation as Chief until Conlin agreed to cooperate with any ploy Peacock made against Moose."

"That makes sense," said Dutch. "Both Peacock and Conlin are Democrats. Moose is a lonely Republican around cops, you and me included."

"You know what that bastard Peacock wants, don't you? He's hoping for a Democratic victory so he can be the one and only Commissioner."

"On that day," Dutch declared, "we learn to ride horses and go West, young man." He cleared his throat. "You think the boy who saw the killing might be the one who works for Battling Jack?"

"Nothing ventured, nothing gained."

When they arrived at Macdougal Alley, Jack Meyers was industriously sweeping down the area around the stable. The boy was puffing on a cigarette.

"Hello, Jack," Tonneman said, soft and easy. "We want to talk to you."

"About what you saw on Madison Street." Bo closed in on the boy, his voice booming, his face red. He loomed over the youth like the wrath of God.

Jack Meyers began to tremble. He was afraid that the big Irishman was going to fall on him and crush him. "I didn't see nothing on Madison Street. I wasn't even there."

"Jesus, Mary, and Joseph," Bo ranted, pulling the cigarette from the boy's mouth. "Do I have to put up with this? Tell me the truth, lad, or I'll have to explain why your body is a bloody pulp."

"What do you want from me?" Jack fingered his lip. "I have a good job. Leave me alone."

Dutch patted Jack on the shoulder. "Easy, lad. I won't let him hurt you. We have a witness who places you on Madison Street that night."

The boy nodded his head. He did not look at Bo. "Yes, sir."

Dutch pressed. "Why were you there? What did you see?"

Jack Meyers took a deep breath. Snot ran from his nose. He was trying not to cry. Maybe he had to talk to the police, but he didn't have to snivel in front of them. He was still a man. "Thursday, I saw Mr. Roman dragged from the Herald Building by two men. One was the thin bloke I fought with for the box, the other was a *shtarker*." Jack jerked his thumb toward Bo; he still would not look at him. "Big as him. The skinny guy they called Harry. The big one, Terry. Mr. Roman had the box. They pushed him into a bakery wagon and I followed. I can run real good. I followed them to St. Mark's Place, across the road from a church. That's when a new man got in the wagon with Mr. Roman. Bigger than Terry. And him." Again, Jack indicated Bo. "Harry drove. The new man, he had his hat pulled low, so all I could see was his big mustache. They all got inside the wagon with Mr. Roman. It sounded like they was beating him up."

"Why didn't you look for a cop?" Bo snarled.

Jack started talking faster, as if that would make the huge copper leave him alone. "They stayed there till dark and then drove down to Madison Street. I hitched a ride on back. In the alley Terry broke a lot of glass things. Harry helped him. Then they threw Mr. Roman out of the wagon. That's when Harry spotted the other guy."

Dutch and Bo exchanged looks. "What other guy?" Dutch asked.

"They wanted to kill him because of what he saw. Terry, the

shtarker, and the new guy was fighting on the top of the wagon when it drove away. An old woman yelled at them, but they didn't pay her no mind. That's all I saw." Jack touched his torn lip tenderly. "I swear on my mother's grave."

Bo grabbed the boy by his shirt and lifted him off the ground. The boy held tightly to his broom. "What did these people look like?" Bo demanded.

Jack shook his head. "Except for Harry, I don't know. It was dark. Ask *him*." Jack nodded at Tonneman. "He saw Harry better than I did."

"If you think of anything else, you'll tell us, won't you, Jack?" Dutch said it kindly.

"Yes, sir, Detective Tonneman."

"Oh, yes, he's the law-and-order kid, he is," Bo sneered, setting the boy back on his feet. The broom clattered to the cobblestone.

Dutch glared at Bo. Sometimes he went too far. "There's a room over the stable, right, lad?"

"Yes, sir. Two. I sleep in one."

"Was that Mr. Roman's room?"

"I don't know, sir. Battling Jack sleeps in the other when he's here."

"Let's get a look at yours," Bo said.

A narrow steep staircase led to the room over the stable. The room was as small as a cell. In one corner stood a cot. In another corner, half a dozen horse blankets were draped over a long sawhorse. In a third lay a heap, covered by still another blanket.

The only decoration was a color chromo over the cot. The print was of the Statue of Liberty. At the bottom was the legend: *God Bless America*. In the picture, the statue in New York Harbor was a beautiful pure copper color. In reality, Frédéric Bartholdi's statue on Liberty Island, which had been unveiled in '86, was already beginning to streak with green.

"Was this Roman's?" Dutch asked, pointing to the chromo.

"No, that's mine," the boy said proudly.

"What's this?" Bo lifted the edge of the blanket on the heap and threw it back.

Jack shrugged. "Belongs to someone who used to stay here. Battling Jack keeps saying he has to do something with it."

Bo picked through the meager pile of belongings. A Gladstone bag was the most promising; Bo opened it and looked through the two compartments of the bag. "Have you been into this, boy?"

"I never touched it," Jack protested. "I swear."

"I know," said Bo. "On your mother's grave. Get out."

The boy was gone in the blink of an eye.

"Find anything?" Dutch asked.

"Yes," Bo replied. "Gold." He brought out a fistful of papers and a small black notebook. "Maybe now we'll find out why our journalist was killed." He handed the papers to Dutch and leafed through the notebook.

"Listen to this." Bo read from the notebook. " 'Begin with description of legitimate business, then go to the Lab and all its tentacles, reaching from the pulpit to Wall Street to the House on Mulberry Street.' "

49

Thursday,
June 6.
Afternoon.

Leo Stern strode angrily up to the blind Negro beggar who stood on the corner of Clinton Street muttering his litany: "A penny will do, have you a penny for a hungry blind man down on his luck?" The beggar cocked his head. Leo was mad.

"Coley, why the hell didn't you warn me about that cop?"

"And get my head busted?" the blind man protested. "He came right at me, pointed two fingers in my eyes, and asked me if I wanted to be *really* blind? While I was saying no sir, no sir, no sir, he was halfway to your door."

Leaving Coley in disgust, Leo charged up to his other sentry. He asked Sally, the woman selling stale bread, the same question.

Sal merely shrugged her hump and nibbled with her toothless gums on a crumb from one of the large wreaths of day-old bread.

"A shrug ain't going to do it, Sal," Leo raged. "Did he tumble to you, too, or were you on the nod? You're doping again, ain't you?"

"Hey, Leo? Ain't that your derby you said was stole?" Sally pointed to a bicycle going by. On it, head half hidden by Leo's too-large derby with its bright wine-colored band, was the bone-thin fellow who had driven the bakery wagon when he fought with that bastard on Madison Street.

All other concerns forgotten, Leo started running. His shoes slapped the pavement loud enough to warn his unwitting quarry. One look over his shoulder was enough. Harry started pedaling as if his life depended on it. Since it was not hard to read the fury on Leo's face, it probably did.

As fast as Leo ran, Harry pedaled faster, skidding around wagons and carriages, past startled horses. When a boy on an ordinary—a bicycle with one large wheel in front and one small wheel behind—nearly ran into him, Leo grabbed the bike and snatched him off.

"Hey!" the boy hollered. "Let go! It's mine!"

"Sorry, pal. Go into 79 Clinton and tell Sophie that Leo says to give you two dollars."

"I want my bike," the boy wailed. "You think I'm stupid?" He was running after Leo now.

"I don't have time to argue." Leo picked up speed scattering pigeons and pedestrians crossing the street as he fought to control the machine. Harry was still in sight. On his stolen ordinary, Leo wobbled up Clinton Street toward Division, his eye on his derby ahead.

But just as Leo was starting to gain on Harry, the sound of a whistle came shrieking out of Fourth Street and a policeman on a bike of his own, just as wobbly as Leo, cut Leo off.

"Where's your bicycle badge, chum?"

"I don't have one," Leo said, trying to keep his eye on his derby and fish in his coat for his money at the same time. Catching the lout could mean a chance at the reward. $5,000.

"Don't have a permit, can't ride a bike," the wheel-patrolman droned.

"What the hell kind of copper are you?"

The cop looked chagrined. "Not my idea. I usually ride horse patrol. Commissioner Andrews has a bug up his ass about a bicycle squad he wants to form. I'm it for the time being." He grinned at Leo. "And you're my first collar."

Leo brought out a dollar. "For a buck can somebody else be your first collar?"

The cop looked around, then snagged the bill. "Get lost, sheeny."

"Yes, sir. What's your name?"

"Bill Tierney. What's it to you?"

"Nothing." Leo took off, teetering. Sheeny, was it? He'd remember that bog trotter. One day he would get his back. Yes, he would.

His quarry was nowhere in view. Leo roundly cursed Bill Tierney as he rode up and down the side streets. Then, with the most cockeyed luck, he caught sight of the back end of the derby thief as he wheeled his cycle into a gray stone building on St. Mark's Place, just across from a church.

50

Thursday,
June 6.
Late afternoon.

Over Bo's protests, Dutch snagged a passing hackney. The partners rode to St. Mark's Place while Dutch attempted to read the notes in Robert Roman's notebook. They appeared to be in some kind of personal shorthand. Deciphering them would be a time-consuming job.

"We should have asked the Hebrew kid what time he saw everything in that alley," said Bo.

"I doubt if he owns a watch," Dutch mumbled, reading.

"He does if he stole it." When that got no reaction from his partner, Bo dug at an old reliable vein. "There's talk of war in the House on Mulberry Street."

"Between?"

"Who else? Moose and Peacock."

"Tell me something I don't know. . . . Hello," Dutch exclaimed.

"What?"

Dutch's index finger was traveling the page as he read pieces. " '. . . rat in lunch pail.' This is about what happened to cops who tried to stop graft in the force."

"What else is new?" Bo asked, his eyes on the streets and not on Dutch.

"Here's one about a captain who told his men to arrest prostitutes. Not only didn't they listen, they shunned him. Dead rats again. Cheese, too. In his desk. Took it to the Chief, who said maybe *he* was doing something wrong."

"Which Chief?"

"Doesn't say."

Dutch looked for a date; there was none. "Has to be Byrnes."

Several small scraps of paper slipped from between larger ones. Dutch caught them before they hit the carriage floor.

"What's that?" Bo asked absently. Paperwork was not his strong point.

"List of businesses, looks like. No date. Paying out money to what you said before, the Lab. The Allen's in here. Jesus. So is Delmonico's."

"Important?"

"Could be, if this turns out to be the graft list. We've got to find out who or what the Lab is. A laboratory makes the most sense, cover-up for a collection depot. Who would suspect?"

"If your mind wasn't so full of that girl, you'd have figured it out by now." Bo was laughing at him.

"What the hell—"

"Lab is La Belle, stupid."

Dutch laughed. "Back to the murder and my turn to be smart, coz. Didn't that old bum of an actor say—? That's it. What if the other guy that kid saw is Leo Stern?"

"I'm thinking the same," said Bo. "Leo Stern brought what's-his-name—Byron—home to Madison Street that night. Our Leo might just be that other guy."

Nodding, Dutch returned to his reading. Roman had written about the capitalists oppressing the working class and how workers of the world had to rise up and cast off their chains. Lots of bosses might want to break his head for this writing. Murder him, even. But even if what Roman had written was incendiary, it didn't point a finger directly at anyone as his killer.

"Well, cut off my legs and call me a midget. Driver, stop at the end of the street."

"What?" At Bo's exclamation, Dutch closed the notebook and stowed it under his belt at the small of his back.

"That gray stone building across from St. Mark's Church."

"What about it?"

"Stern is standing on the corner pretending he's not watching it."

The two detectives left the hackney coach and walked back to where an ice-cream vendor was selling his wares just shy of the church. A small group had formed about the Italian's cart, but he served the detectives first. No one protested. Except the vendor, when Dutch attempted to pay. Dutch and Bo in their derbies and suits looked like what they were, clear as day, and the vendor was no fool. While the partners ate ice cream from twists of hard paper, they sized up the situation.

"What do you think our Leo's waiting for?" Bo asked.

"Someone to come out or go in."

"What are we waiting for?"

"Same thing. And for Leo to make a move."

"Who do you think is in there?"

"I hope one or more of the three guys who were in that alley." Seeing no sign of one of the City's fancy new trash baskets, Dutch dropped the empty paper twist into the street.

"How do you know this is their place?"

"I don't, but our Leo is up to something not kosher." Dutch laughed. "You can bet on it." He placed his hand on Bo's arm. "The door's opening. Jackpot. See the thin one with the derby on his ears? That's Harry, the one who tried to steal the box of photographic plates in the first place. I tangled with a big bastard wearing a bandanna that same time. This looks like him. Terry."

"Let's take them," Bo said, chomping at the bit. "We'd be off the hook with the Chief. The case would be solved."

"Maybe. But I'd kind of like to follow them and see if they lead us to the third one, the cull with the big mustache."

"Uh-oh, Leo's making his move," Bo said eagerly.

"Jesus, I hate amateurs," Dutch said.

Brandishing a Colt .32, Leo crossed to the stone building and yelled, "Hold it, assholes. I'm taking you to the cops. You just made me 5,000 simoleons. *And* I want my hat back."

Eyes wide, Harry snatched the derby from his head and sailed it at Leo. When Leo's Colt tracked Harry, Terry flew at Leo, knocking him down. Leo dropped his gun. Terry grabbed it and began beating Leo about the head with it.

"Amateurs is right," Bo said. The two partners drew their Smith & Wessons and separated. They ran across the street at different angles, attempting to flank the three men in front of the building.

Seeing the scuffle, the ice-cream vendor ran, rattling his cart uptown. Other people hurried for the safety of the church.

"Halt in the name of the law," Dutch ordered.

Spinning Leo's gun, Terry started to raise the weapon toward Dutch.

"Do it and I'll shove that heater up your ass," yelled Bo.

The Colt kept coming up.

But Bo was quicker than Dutch. He fired first hitting Terry in the throat. A fountain of blood spewed from the thug's carotid artery.

Leo scrambled to his feet, tottering around dizzily.

"I give up," Harry screamed. "I give up."

A huge woman, shawl wrapped around her head, market basket on her arm, came out of the gray stone building.

"Thanks, Bo."

"Don't mention it, coz. See the woman?"

"That's no woman. Hey, you, stop where you are."

The woman kept walking toward Ninth Street in long strides, passing Leo, who, stared right in her face. The woman swung a powerful arm, swatted Leo, and started to run. Leo, falling, grabbed the woman's skirt, then her legs. They both fell. The woman bounced off Leo and hit the sidewalk, hard.

Bo hurried to Terry, who lay sprawled on the sidewalk, bleeding like a stuck pig, and kicked Leo's weapon aside. He checked Terry's wrist for a pulse, all the time keeping his .32 on Harry. Satisfied that Terry was dead, Bo shoved Harry against the gray stone and searched him for weapons.

In the meantime, Dutch had given his attention to Leo and the woman. He leaned over and pulled the shawl from the woman's face. And hooted. "There are so many big mustaches in this town I didn't think of the obvious one. Hey, Bo, you have to see this."

Bo prodded Harry over to Dutch and peered at the fallen woman.

"Do you want to say it or should I?" Dutch asked.

"Be my guest," Bo said.

Dutch grinned. "Alexander Clubber Williams, I arrest you for the murder of Robert Roman."

"Don't forget about me, boys," Leo shouted, even as he reeled about. "I get that reward. If I hadn't stopped him, he would have got away. I earned the $5,000."

Dutch, in a generous mood, said, "I'll put in a word for you to Bennett and Cook."

"Not so fast," Bo objected. "We could have caught him without your help. Why should you get 5,000 for a one-day chore when all we get is 1,200 a year for doing this kind of work every day?"

"I'll tell you what," Leo said. "When I get the 5,000, I'll give you each a thousand."

"Make that 2,500 all told," Bo said.

"Wait a minute," said Dutch.

Bo grinned at his partner. "And you go over to Grand Street and give it to Father Patrick Duff for St. Agnes Church."

51

Sunday, June 9. Morning to afternoon.

It was barely light when Meg climbed the first four stone steps, joy in her gait.

Six o'clock Mass was her private time. Annie, that lie-a-bed, went later, if the girl went at all. What was happening to these children? Meg had given up on Dutch for the time being. Young men always strayed, but they always came back.

After her family, there were two things that Meg loved: Holy Mother Church and Holy Mother Ireland. America was all right. More money and always food to eat. But although she'd been brought here as a tot, Meg treasured the Ireland of her mother's stories. And no matter how good America was, it wasn't the old country. It wasn't Ireland.

The flowers in the small garden in front of St. Agnes Church were still wet from the rain during the night, as were the statue of the Madonna on the left and the statue of St. Agnes on the right.

And even at this hour the pigeons were everywhere. New York was afflicted with pigeons, had been since the first white man got off the first boat. Meg forgave the pigeons; they were dumb creatures, and God's creatures at that. No, it wasn't the birds she minded. It was the mess they left. On the sacred statues, on her own front steps, on her clean windowsills.

She climbed the next four steps, overlooking their droppings, for this was the entrance to the House of God.

The sun was shining through the stained-glass windows. The windows, the vaulted ceiling, the cross, the statues of Jesus and the saints, always filled her soul with joy and contentment. Even rainy days didn't dampen her spirits. Last night's rain had served to ease the heat wave they'd been having, and that was God's gift.

She knelt at the entrance. At the holy water she dipped her fingers and made the sign of the cross. The Mass had already begun. Meg blushed at her tardiness and prayed to be forgiven. Father Duff wouldn't fault her, but Meg rebuked herself. She liked to be there at the beginning. Hurrying to her row, she knelt again, crossed herself quickly, and gave her full attention to the beauty of the Mass and to God.

In certain social circles, Sunday afternoon in New York had settled into an almost frantic round of elegantly dressed people calling on one another. It was a custom Oz loathed, and since the death of his mother he had taken particular care to remove himself from its fervor. The rite created a breeding ground for gossip, something else Oz abominated.

Now he rarely received calls at 5 Gramercy Park on Sunday afternoons. He was well aware that in his circle he had the reputation of curmudgeon, albeit a charming one. And curmudgeons were forgiven if their social credentials were impeccable and if they were Old Money. Both of which were true about Oswald Cook.

That he had a rare talent and a respectable reputation as a photographer was not at all important. Only one's standing in society was. A man's position was everything in this City.

So it was that this balmy Sunday afternoon Oz sat alone reading in his study, his feet up on an ottoman, a Virginia Bright in his hand. He was reading *The Atlantic Monthly*, the presumed oracle of the upper classes. Nearby, a snifter of cognac, and the crystal decanter, half filled. Hazy yellow sunshine streaked the room.

He inhaled the cognac's bouquet, then drank. For this brief moment, Oz was at peace with his world.

But Esther Breslau invaded his thoughts, troubled his harmony.

She had quite recovered from Thursday's adventure, but he had not. In his extreme relief that Esther was safe, Oz had reprimanded her in front of the two detectives, and she had been humiliated.

On Friday, though they were both elated by the capture and arrest of three men for Robert's murder the day before, Esther had responded to him only in monosyllables. They had worked side by side developing and printing the remainder of the Lillian Russell photographs in near silence. Dark smudges remained under her eyes. Oz knew that something had changed between them. He'd lost her esteem. He was astounded by how devastated this left him.

For Oswald Cook, such a circumstance was an entirely new experience. Was she considering leaving him? Where would she go? Off with that brutish detective? That oaf of an Irishman acting the swain out there on a bench in the park at this very moment?

Oz was determined that this would not happen. He would save her from herself. He took a sip of cognac.

His tortured meditation was interrupted by Wong. The Chinaman bore cards on his silver tray, which meant guests had arrived. Oz had not heard the doorbell. He growled at his manservant, but Wong didn't flinch.

There were two cards. One read: *Mrs. John Neldine Burgoyne*, the other, *Mrs. Harrison Stokes*. His cousin Jane and her daughter, Louisa, both of whom he'd last seen at his mother's funeral a full two years earlier.

They considered him an eccentric, unfit for their society, yet here they were with their ridiculous calling cards, presenting themselves in his parlor only days after he'd seen John Burgoyne and his two sons at the theatre.

"Tell them to go away," Oz ordered Wong. But then he changed his mind. They were up to something, these two female schemers, and Oz was convinced that it revolved around Esther Breslau. He'd seen the beginning of it in John Neldine Burgoyne's eyes at the theatre, watching his sons and heirs as they fell under his Esther's subtle magic.

Oz set the magazine aside, swiveled his feet off the ottoman, and stood, taking a moment to stab out his cigarette. It tickled his fancy, this turn of events.

"Lemonade for the ladies, Wong," Oz said quite cheerfully. "And some of those sugar wafers." He rubbed his hands together. He was going to enjoy this. On his way downstairs he stepped into the studio and gathered his Lillian Russell prints. He hoped his callers would find "the new woman" in her cycling costume and boots shocking. He could just envision his proper middle-aged cousin in Lillian Russell's bloomers, pedaling her bicycle around the Central Park.

"Oh, my God," he cackled. "Cousin Jane in bloomers."

He was still laughing when he entered the parlor. The ladies, Jane in a tea-rose pink dress embroidered with multicolored beads, and Louisa, in a pure white cotton frock, stood with their backs to him, gazing up above the mantel at the painting of his mother in a white dress.

Clarissa Neldine Cook, his mother, had been a very beautiful woman. When they turned to his greeting, Oz was startled by Louisa's resemblance to her. Louisa's eyes were the same startling blue as his mother's. As his own.

"Jane, my dear, how pleasant." He kissed her powdery cheek. "And Louisa, so nice of you to call."

"Oswald," Jane began.

"Do make yourselves comfortable. I've asked Wong to serve lemonade."

Mother and daughter settled themselves on the damask sofa.

"Perhaps you'd like to see my latest enterprise," he said, handing the photographs to Jane.

"Oswald." Jane looked at the photographs, then gasped. "Really, Oswald."

"What is it, Mother?" Louisa took the photographs from her mother and leafed through them. "Oh, my."

Wong appeared. He set the tray bearing a pitcher of lemonade, a plate of cookies, three glasses—though he knew Oz would not use his—and three pressed linen tea napkins on the coffee table in front of the sofa. Quiet as a mouse he left the room.

"Shocking," Jane said. "Give me those foul things, Louisa."

Louisa did not relinquish the photographs. Her mother beckoned with her finger. "Louisa."

"I'm a married woman, Mother." Louisa stared down at Lillian

Russell in her bicycle costume. "Besides, everyone's doing it now; it's all the rage." She smiled at Oz. "Miss Russell is very beautiful."

Oz grinned. Louisa was of better stuff than he'd supposed. "She is indeed. Lil keeps her fine figure by pedaling in the Central Park."

"Oswald! Really!" Jane fanned herself with a lace-covered fan.

"I would like it, I think," Louisa said.

"Louisa! What would Harrison—?"

"Oh, Mother, don't be old-fashioned. It's 1895. Harrison has offered to buy me a bicycle—not like this one, of course."

"So gauche," her mother interjected.

Louisa was blushing prettily, and for a brief moment matched the young image of Clarissa peering down at them from her perch over the mantel. To cover her blushes, Louisa poured the lemonade.

"My dear Louisa," Oz said, smiling broadly, "you have the Neldine daring and determination, and, if I may say so, the beauty as well." He nodded to his mother's painting.

Jane sat straighter on the sofa, if that was possible. She'd been a wonderful horsewoman in her youth, and had kept her perfect posture even into middle age. "Yes, indeed she does, Oswald dear. And that is precisely why I wish to talk with you." Jane paused. When Oz didn't respond, she pursed her lips and continued. "That little Hebrew girl you're living with." She took a dainty sip of the lemonade.

Oz's smile froze on his face. "Cousin, this is none of your affair."

"We are not talking about *my* affair." Jane's eyes had turned to steel. "We are talking about *your* affair. What you do with some harlot in a back street, out of sight, is none of our business, but your liaison with this Jewess concerns the entire family; it reflects directly on my boys and on Louisa. They have Neldine blood. They are your only living heirs."

"Mother, I think—"

"Be still, Louisa. Our cousin's behavior bears directly on our position in society."

Oz rose. He felt a band of fire across his chest. If he were not a civil man, he would have struck Jane Burgoyne. He rang for Wong. "Put down your glass, Jane," he bade his cousin.

"You do understand that what I'm saying is for your own good and that of our family?" She set the glass on the coffee table and wiped her fingers with the yellow tea napkin.

"You have helped me arrive at a decision, Jane, and I thank you for that."

"There, you see, Oswald, dear. I told John you're a man of good sense." Jane dabbed at her lips with the napkin before putting it down. "I understand she's a pretty little thing, your Jewess."

Wong stepped into the room. "Yes, Mr. Oz."

"My cousins are leaving."

"Oh, my," Louisa murmured, then seemed surprised that she'd spoken.

"I don't understand. . . ," Jane said.

"Come, Mother." Louisa stood and offered her mother her arm.

Face pale under her sheer powder, Jane stood, too.

"I think it's safe to conclude we are no longer welcome in Cousin Oz's home." Louisa looked at Oz. Was there understanding in those blue Neldine eyes? "I'm sorry, cousin, if we have offended you."

"Louisa, Jane, I had intended to make Miss Breslau my heir, but I've quite changed my mind."

Jane's sigh of relief had a sound to it. "Very wise. To show there are no ill feelings, Oswald, why don't you join us at our cottage in Newport for the Fourth of July?"

Oz ushered them out, holding tight to Jane Burgoyne's bony elbow. "I'm afraid that will be out of the question. I shall be very busy. You see, I'm going to marry my little Jewess."

52

Sunday,
June 9.
Afternoon.

G*ramercy Park was lush, moist, and summer-fragrant. The sky was* clear of clouds and as blue as the eyes of the man who sat beside Esther on the bench.

Along the paths, people strolled, children played, birds foraged for worms or insects, flowers nodded in the soft breeze.

He'd arrived at the house only a short time before in an odd state as if he were unwell. He'd asked to see her privately. She had gotten her hat and the golden key to the Gramercy Park gate, and gone with him into the park, where they had strolled in silence, and where they now sat on the bench in silence. Several times he had turned to her, but said nothing.

She had thought that this was an attempt to apologize for shouting at her. But he spoke not a word.

Finally, Esther broke the heavy silence between them. "Is there more news about Robert's murder, Detective Tonneman? Do you know why he was killed?"

"No," Dutch replied. "But there is something I must tell you."

She waited. But he said no more. Instead, he removed the *Shadai* from his watch chain and held it out to her. "Tell me again what this means."

"It is a name of God. Just as *Adonai* is."

"Wait. You're confusing me. *Shadai* is God. *Adonai* is God. Are Hebrews heathens who have more than one God?"

She answered stiffly. "Do you mean like the Father, the Son and the Holy Ghost?"

Dutch half grinned, uncertain how to proceed, baffled. "I . . . No. I'm sorry if I've offended you."

He seemed so lost, this powerful man beside her, that she relented. "*Shadai* means the Almighty. It is spoken in place of the name of God, which we are not allowed to speak. *Adonai* is another permitted substitute. It means My Lord."

"The God of the Hebrews."

"The God of the world." She took the amulet from his palm, her fingers glancing his.

"I told you that this belonged to my great-grandfather, Peter Tonneman. He died two weeks ago."

"I am sorry for your loss." She examined the *Shadai* in her hand. It was very beautiful.

"He was one hundred and six."

"Methuselah." She smiled. "Was your great-grandfather a wise man, too?"

"Yes." Dutch took her hand and closed her fingers around the *Shadai*. "He was a Hebrew man."

She could feel his pulse beating. The heat of him. Or was the heat coming from the *Shadai*? Could she be imagining it? "But you said you were Catholic. Were you ashamed to admit to being Jewish?"

"I didn't know. In my memory, he never spoke of it."

"Then how . . . ?"

"Among his effects was a silver box filled with objects that were strange to me. A Hebrew Bible. A silk scarf such as the ones I've seen Israelite men wearing. Other things."

"I would like to see them."

"My mother would be very happy if you came to dinner. Would Friday night suit you? I'll come for you."

"Friday night begins the Sabbath. I light the candles at sundown and pray."

Astonishment filled his face. "My mother lights candles every Friday at sundown. It's been a tradition in my family for as long as I can remember."

"Do you pray?"

"Yes. Ma always bakes a fish. Say you'll come. The whole family will be there."

She sat there, obviously torn. "The whole family?"

"I have five sisters. Four are married; the last, Annie, is betrothed."

"Do they know about their great-grandfather?"

"No. I've told no one, not even Ma."

Esther shook her head. "I don't think Friday would be . . ."

"Saturday, then. It will be only Ma and me. Annie has dinner with her intended's family on Saturday."

"After sundown?"

"Then you'll come, Miss Breslau?"

"I would be honored, Mr. Tonneman."

53

Sunday,
June 9.
Early evening.

They'd had a light supper of steamed chicken served over rice with a strange but piquant sauce that Wong promised Esther contained no pork or other offensive ingredients.

"The two of us together. And alone, as always." Oz was in excellent spirits.

Esther smiled at him. "You have forgiven me for being tardy, then?"

"I can never be angry with you. I was in fear for your safety. A woman cannot go wandering about this City without caution, or better, a male companion at her side. It is much too dangerous. There are too many people who would think nothing about harming you."

Wong started to clear away the dishes.

"Champagne, Wong," Oz said, without taking his eyes from Esther. "By any chance did you make any photographs while you were doing your detective work?" he asked.

"Just five. Champagne? What is the occasion?"

"The capture of Robert's murderers seems like a good enough reason. Have you printed the photographs?"

"Not yet." She'd put off printing them because she couldn't bear looking at the faces of those children. Still, she had been intrigued by the woman called Sophie, her bearing and demeanor, and her companion, the man with the gold teeth. Idly, she wondered if she could ask Sophie to pose for her.

"Well, let us take a look at them after supper, shall we?"

"Yes." She had kept at bay the conversation with John Tonneman and what he had told her about himself. As if by setting it aside, like a hard peach, it would ripen and turn sweet.

Hesitantly, she asked Oz, "Did you have time to enlarge that photograph for Detective Tonneman?"

"No."

His reply was so curt she did not pursue the subject.

For dessert, Wong served tiny strawberries with rich clotted cream. He opened the wine and poured it into two handsome fluted glasses. Then he left them alone.

"To a long successful life, my dear Esther." Oz raised his glass, unmindful of the tremor in his hand. Or at least pretending not to notice. He touched his glass to hers.

"To life," she echoed, taking a sip of champagne. Now that she was accustomed to it, the tickle of the bubbles in her nose and mouth was enjoyable.

"What did he want of you this afternoon?" Oz watched her keenly.

"You mean John Tonneman?" Strawberries and cream, champagne, while those wretched people on Madison Street starved.

"If that's his name."

"He's invited me to dinner with his mother Saturday evening next."

"You've not accepted?"

"But I have. Why wouldn't I?"

"He's in love with you."

She shook her head. "Perhaps." He is, she thought suddenly. He is.

Oz drained his glass. "Do you love him?"

"I don't know."

"My dear, it's utterly impossible and can't work. The Irish like their ale and they beat their women."

"Oh, no, he's not like that at all." Did Oz say that about her people, too? Or perhaps he'd say something about all the children the Hebrews had.

Oz filled her half-empty glass to the top. "No, I've quite made up my mind. You will marry me."

Esther gaped at Oz in shock. Had she heard correctly?

"My money will provide for you after I'm gone, and you will always have a place to live and people to care for you." Oz's long speech seemed to exhaust him. When he was done, he sat back in his chair and closed his eyes.

"Marry you?" She could barely speak. "Oz?" She could still feel the imprint of Tonneman's *Shadai* in the palm of her hand.

"Yes. You can have Mother's room. You will never want for anything as long as I live. And I will never . . . force my attentions on you. After I'm gone . . ."

"No. Stop!" She stood, tipping over her glass. Champagne spilled over the linen cloth.

Oz ignored the spreading liquid. "I'm no fool, Esther. The state of my health is precarious. I see the signs. As my wife, you will be protected from my covetous, avaricious relatives. And you will be able to complete my work. Answer yes, please."

"I—"

He stopped her. "No decision yet. Think about it."

54

Saturday,
June 15.
Evening.

*The Tonneman house was one of several like four-storied brick-and-*mortar houses on Grand Street. All had been built by the same architect in 1830. The differences, one from the other, lay mostly in the shutters and the stoops. These few homes were all that was left of what had once been a thriving middle-class residential area.

This small section of Grand Street, between Sheriff and Willet, although somewhat run-down, still held private homes. But as the older people died, heirs quickly sold out and moved farther uptown, close enough to one of the Els on Second, Third, or Sixth Avenues to use the services, but not so close the noise of the trains battered their ears.

The house had been Old Peter's. The surrounding homes had been owned at their outset by various members of the Jacob Hays family.

Meg had come to the house as a bride in 1866, only months after Charity Tonneman's death. The young bride had been astounded by the luxury of the parquet floors, the mahogany banisters and paneling, the patterned plaster ceilings, the beautiful fabrics on the walls, the elegant furniture, and the Persian carpets.

Much had changed since '66. The house now had running water

and electricity. Flower boxes adorned the first-floor front windows, and the six steps leading to the front door had a wrought-iron railing that was well kept and painted every year.

But the house, underneath the new whitewash that Dutch and his cousins and friends had laid on in March, had an air of weariness about it.

What Esther saw when they drove up was a modest brick house on a quiet street. Lights glowed through lace curtains in the lower windows. John Tonneman had said very little on the ride over. Only, "You'll like Ma. She's excited at meeting you."

For this dinner Esther had made a special trip to the Ladies' Mile. At Stewart's, she'd bought a simple pale blue-and-white striped cotton dress with a high collar, black patent leather shoes with a small heel, and a small ribboned hat that matched the dress.

And John Tonneman, she'd noticed at once when he'd arrived to escort her, had trimmed his hair. His skin glowed as if shaving had polished it, and he smelled of soap and starch.

He led her in the front door and into the parlor. "I'll tell Ma we're here."

The spicy, rich fragrance of sugar, cinnamon, and apples mingled with the dense odor of cabbage, and gave the old house a warm homey feeling.

The small parlor was spotless, and though neat, seemed crowded with furniture—a sofa, chairs, side tables—everything covered with embroidered cloths. Footstools of various heights were set in front of chairs and the sofa. A glass-enclosed bookcase and a "square piano" took up what little floor space remained. In a corner, an old grandfather clock clicked its way toward the hour.

A few feet from the clock, a large arched doorway led to a dining room where Esther could see a table set with linen and crystal.

She sat on a stiff-backed chair in the parlor letting her eyes roam the room. There was so much to look at. She twisted her head to see behind her.

High on the wall was a cross. She did not, could not, look at it. Her gaze went instead to the left and a chromo of Jesus in a red robe, a nimbus behind his head. At his breast hung a heart emanating rays of light. To the right, resting in a niche, was a plaster statue of the Virgin Mary.

Esther's eyes went unwillingly to the crucified Jesus bleeding from nails hammered into his flesh, on his head his crown of thorns.

What was she doing in a house like this?

55

Saturday,
June 15.
Evening.

She got to her feet again with no other thought than to leave, run away, as she had done once before. In Poland, she had never had second thoughts. But here . . .

As if to prompt her, the clock near the entrance to the dining room began to chime. Eight o'clock. Esther stopped, uncertain. She could hear Tonneman's voice and another, a woman's.

She could see the dining room table, the crystal bowl of flowers, and something else. Something reflected in the bowl. She took a step into the dining room. A gleaming silver box sat on the sideboard.

Stay, it pleaded, stay.

Esther knew this was madness, but she did not run.

A stout little woman, wearing a black dress with a floral apron over it, entered. Her skin was fair and she had a stubby nose. Her white hair was pulled into a tight bun. Behind her was John Tonneman.

"Ma, this is Esther." John was carrying a big platter of roast lamb and potatoes. "Esther, the grand Margaret Tonneman of the lace-curtain Tonnemans." He said the introduction affectionately as he set the large plate on the table.

Meg handed her son her burden, a heaping bowl of fried clams, then dried her hands on the floral apron and stepped forward, her hand outstretched. "Don't be listening to him. Call me Meg. I am that happy to make your acquaintance. This rascal has been keeping you a deep dark secret."

"Ma."

"Come, let's eat before it gets cold," Meg said. "No, you come here next to me, Esther, and John can be on my other side." She sat down, looked around. "The bread and butter, they're on the kitchen table."

"I'll get them, Ma." Dutch left the room in such a hurry, Esther wondered if he was eager to leave them to get acquainted without his presence.

Esther was seated facing the silver box. Beyond the box was a wall on which yet another crucifix hung.

"Well, now," Meg said, "how long have you and my John known each other?"

"Not long. He's very nice."

"He's a fine young man."

Esther's hands were cold in her lap. Never had she been at a loss for words; she was now. So she was relieved when John Tonneman returned.

"Here we are," he said, looking from Meg to Esther and back to Meg again. He set the bread and butter on the tablecloth.

"John, will you say the grace?"

He sat and said, "Lord, we thank you for what we are about to eat. Amen."

"Amen," Esther said.

"That was short," Meg said.

"I'm hungry," her son answered. At that moment Esther realized he was as nervous as she was.

"Give Esther some clams, John."

"No, thank you," Esther said hastily. "I don't eat clams."

"Well, that's a shame. These are wonderful. But I know myself sometimes they don't agree with me, neither."

"Ma, you're talking Esther's ear off." Dutch sliced the bread.

Meg attacked the clams with gusto. "Where are you from, Esther? Who are your people?" She turned to her son. "John, you're not eating."

"I'm slicing."

Esther watched, fascinated, as the clams in the big brown bowl disappeared. "Poland. A little town called Zakliczyn."

"Poland is a good Catholic country," Meg said.

Esther raised startled eyes to Dutch, who looked embarrassed. He hadn't told his mother she was Jewish. She squirmed in her chair. This was all wrong.

Meg went right on as if she hadn't noticed the increased tension in the room. "You live in Gramercy Park, John says."

"Yes, I—"

"Is St. Anthony's your parish then?"

"Ma, listen." John stopped slicing and set down the knife. He saw Esther's face, saw she was getting to her feet. He shook his head at her, mouthed "please," but she refused to meet his eyes.

"Excuse me, Mrs. Tonneman," Esther said. "I am not Catholic."

"You're not Catholic?" Meg repeated.

"Ma." Dutch came and stood beside Esther. "Ma, Esther is an Israelite."

Meg's face blotched in horror, white to pink to white again. She pushed her chair away from the table. "You killed our Lord," she said.

Esther felt a sharp pain in her breast. She ducked around Tonneman's arm and was out the door, on the street, running. Running.

56

Saturday,
June 15.
Late evening.

Esther returned to Gramercy Park by hired carriage. She slipped into the house, she believed, unseen and unheard, thinking to find solitary refuge in the studio.

Wong's arrival with a pot of tea disabused her of that. It was not in Wong's nature to comment on her life, but he understood more of this world than she did. He departed as unobtrusively as he had come, leaving the door slightly ajar so that the soft light from the hall crept into the studio.

The confusion in her mind overwhelmed Esther. She'd somehow, by luck, by desire, escaped the poverty and thus the design of life for a poor young immigrant girl.

Had she not met Miss Wald, and then Oz, she most likely would have met the brother of one of her coworkers and married him, for love or nothing, and had too many children.

No, she would never . . . What, then? Had she met Miss Wald but not Oz, she might have become a disciple of Miss Wald and remained a spinster.

Esther sat in the dark, her stockinged feet curled up under her, her new shoes where she'd thrown them on the far side of the room. She cried bitter tears of shame and frustration.

The light from the hall caught on the white teapot and two cups. As she dried her eyes with her handkerchief, she thought that she would like to take a picture of them. Ah, that was a good sign.

Still, she felt as if she were choking. She untied the high neck of her dress and removed the little ribboned concoction of a hat. How naive she had been.

How could she have let this happen? Had it been a ruse—his tale of the silver box—to get her to his house? No. She'd seen the box. What he'd told her about the contents of the box rang true. He couldn't have made it up.

But not to tell his mother that she was Jewish . . . Esther bit her lip. Meg Tonneman had said what so many gentiles said, Christ-killer, conveniently ignoring that Jesus was a Jew himself.

So, once again, she had run. But he had not followed. What was the use? They would never marry, never have children together. It was never meant to be. All because she would not wear a *sheitel*. So now she would pay the price for rebelling. God always got his due.

On the other hand, she could marry Oz. He would ask nothing of her. His sin was drink and opium, not women. She could remain loyal to her God, and she and Oz could be very happy making beautiful photographs together. She could hide in his name, in his house. Wong would be there as always. Oz's money and name would protect her. And she'd always have a home.

But it wasn't Oz she loved.

She said it aloud. "God forgive me, I love John Tonneman."

The pain of the admission and the thwarted emotion swelled in her chest like a balloon, choking her. Her body felt bound, like the feet of Chinese women.

She reached up and pulled the pins from her hair. By its own weight, her hair tumbled past her shoulders. It was when she placed the hairpins on the table that she saw the two cups again. Two cups?

Almost at the same moment, a figure was silhouetted in the doorway against the light from the hall.

John Tonneman. "Esther," he said.

She started crying again and turned away, but not before she saw he was carrying the silver box. "Go away, please," she said.

He came into the room and set the box on the floor in front of her. "You shouldn't have run out onto the street like that."

"I had reason to."

"I was a coward." He knelt beside her reaching for her hand. "I should have told Ma."

"If you had, she wouldn't have had me in her house."

"It's my house, too. And it was Old Peter's house before that. And he was a Hebrew."

"Something your mother either doesn't know or refuses to acknowledge."

He got to his feet and searched for a light. The lamp on the worktable came on, bathing the room in sepia. Esther didn't object. But she found it odd that the bust of Edgar Allan Poe from the library was sitting on the table. And her camera, the Kodak that Oz had given her.

Tonneman hated her tears, but they gave him a small thrill of promise. Down on his knees again, he opened the box. He had her attention now.

After removing the magnifying glass, the coin, the clay pipe, and the constable's star, he came to the blue-silk-wrapped Bible. He gave it to her. The cool silk slipped in her hand, revealing the long fringes. A moan came from her throat. "This is a *tallis*," she whispered. "A prayer shawl."

"The Bible," he said. "It's a Hebrew Bible."

She folded the *tallis* carefully in her lap, then opened the Bible. It was very old. The Hebrew inscription was so faded she could barely make it out. " 'This Bible was given to Abraham Pereira by his father Victor on the occasion of his bar mitzvah.' Who is Abraham Pereira to you?"

"I don't know. I believe he's one of my ancestors." John touched her hand. "What is *bar mitzvah*?"

"A young man's confirmation. His coming of age. A sacred ceremony held in a synagogue on Saturday morning. When a Jewish boy becomes thirteen, it is time for him to be received as an adult member of our community. But first he has to complete a prescribed course of instruction in Judaism." She managed a small smile, and he allowed himself to hope.

As John watched Esther turn the pages slowly, he caught a glimpse of a yellowed paper tucked between two pages. "What's that?"

Pieces crumbled and flaked from the paper as she opened it. "A letter," she said. "In Dutch, I think. I'm afraid to handle it further." She put it back where they had found it between the Bible pages.

From the box, John Tonneman removed a rolled-up parchment and a thick leather-bound book. He set the book down and unrolled the parchment.

They stared at the document. It was a work of art. The Hebrew writing on it was ornamented with intricate designs, the colors now long faded but still carrying a suggestion of their original beauty.

"What do you suppose this is?" he asked, but he could tell by her expression that she already knew.

"It's a *Ketubah*. A formal Hebrew marriage contract. A *Ketubah* sets out the mutual obligations between a husband and a wife. This is the marriage contract of Benjamin Mendoza and Racqel Pereira."

"Dr. John Tonneman, Old Peter's father, wrote a history of the Tonneman family." John showed Esther the book. "According to him, Racqel Pereira Mendoza became the second wife of the Dutch Sheriff of New Amsterdam, Pieter Tonneman in 1665. I am descended from them."

"Then Benjamin Mendoza must have died. Otherwise, Racqel could not have married Pieter."

"Yes. There have been Racqels in my family all the way back." Dutch opened the thick book. "Look at this family tree. These are my people. It's amazing," he said, awe in his voice, "Meg Clancy's boy is a Hebrew."

PART FOUR

The Print

57

Saturday,
June 15.
Late evening.

They sat together on the sofa for a long time, her head on his shoulder, his arm around her, his hand stroking her hair.

The silver box had yielded one more detail. On its inside lid was an inscription in Dutch with the names *Pieter and Racqel Tonneman, Conraet and Antje Ten Eyck,* and the date *30 August 1665.*

"You see, this makes it right," Dutch whispered.

"Because of your ancestors?" She smiled at his foolishness. "John, you must be born of a Jewish mother to be considered Jewish. And if you converted, your mother would never accept it."

Dutch was silent. Meg had been adamant. He had never seen her so. "No son of mine will marry outside the Church," she'd told him. "Over my dead body." Was he going to have to choose between Meg and Esther? He had never considered converting. He was Catholic. And that was the end of it.

As if she'd read his thoughts, Esther said, "And I could never be a Catholic. If you choose me over her, you will hate me in the end."

"And if I choose her over you, I will hate myself. Where will I be? Who will I be?"

"If I am not for myself, who is?"

"What?"

"Merely a saying. What a long way we have come these past two weeks since I took those photographs in Union Square." She sighed. "I have enlarged the photograph for you." She was in and out of the darkroom quickly. As he studied the enlargement, she said, "There is nothing to see."

He agreed. The image was blurred. Marchers carrying placards, the writing on the placards unclear. He set the photograph aside. "Bo and I are looking deeper into the La Belle Association." He put his arm around her. "Clubber had your name and this address in his pocket."

Esther's body jerked suddenly.

"I don't think he had a chance to act on it, but I want you to be careful when you go out. Don't go anywhere alone. . . ." He realized he had lost her attention. She wasn't concerned about Clubber. Something else . . .

Esther's eyes were on the worktable. She'd been wondering about the Poe bust and her camera. Now she removed herself from his embrace and crossed to the table.

Anchored by Mr. Poe was a large envelope with her name inscribed on it in Oz's spidery hand. She opened it. Inside were five photographs and a fold of paper.

The photos were: Crossed railroad tracks, the La Belle Association building, Jewish boys studying, Madame Sophie in the doorway of her house, and three scrawny dark-haired children—two boys and a tiny girl. The tallest, the older boy, wore his oversized ill-fitting shoes; the two little ones were barefoot. While the sight of those children clutched her heart, Esther couldn't help admiring how splendid the pictures were. The contrast of light and shadow was absolutely perfect. These were the pictures she had taken with the Detective camera a week ago Thursday.

She unfolded the paper and read what it said aloud.

My dear Esther:

Never assume. Correct? After printing the five photographs you took last week and seeing how excellent they were, I decided to inspect the Kodak camera I gave you to see if perhaps the poor quality of the one plate we had to work with was the camera's fault and not yours. I'm afraid, my dear, that I couldn't help you there.

But I discovered something more important. And I remind you of my edict to never assume. I also remind you of Mr. Poe's story, "The Purloined Letter," where the most important item was in clear view. Though I was tempted to print the plate, I thought you deserved the pleasure. I am so exhilarated by my discovery that I've decided to go out and have a little fun. Until the dawn.

Oz

"I've read 'The Purloined Letter.' The letter was in a book in plain sight," Tonneman said.

Esther found herself poised like a cat closing in on a mouse. "I am a fool!" she exclaimed.

"Why?"

"Oz gave me this camera after Robert was murdered. The camera of my failure. I was so upset with myself that I haven't touched it since." She placed her hands on the Kodak, savoring the moment. "I don't know how I could have been so stupid. . . ."

Letting her hand slide to the holder slot, Esther removed the light-tight frame that was sitting patiently right where she'd left it two weeks before.

Inside the frame was a plate. Buried under its skin might be a photograph that would explain everything.

58

Saturday,
June 15.
Night.

Oz sat opposite Leo Stern at Leo's table in Sophie's main parlor. Sophie was saying good night at the door to a satisfied customer. Most of the girls were upstairs; three sat on the couch chatting amongst themselves. The two clients in the room were asleep in their chairs.

"I want to thank you again for your bank draft, Mr. Cook," Leo told Oz. "The messenger brought it over on Friday. I appreciate that. Mr. Bennett's share of the reward is going to take longer. He's in Paris."

Oz, who'd already had one session with the opium pipe, laughed delicately. "And I appreciate your stalwart action. Word has come to me that you were quite the hero."

Leo preened. "Well, the cops were there, too. I just helped. Not saying I couldn't have nabbed the villains myself."

"Of course you could have, dear fellow. You've missed your calling." Here Oz drifted off, envisioning himself traipsing through fields with a lovely young boy. Even more delightful, the boy had Esther's face. When he came back to reality and saw Leo staring at him, he said, " 'All that we see or seem is but a dream within a dream.' "

"Absolutely," Leo said heartily, still reflecting on his own heroism.

"The best part of it was nailing Clubber Williams. He caught me in the Tenderloin once and hammered me good. This was nice vengeance."

"You believe in vengeance, Mr. Stern?"

"Of course I do. It's in the Bible."

"That's the Old Testament."

"It's all I read."

"Ah, how interesting. That a fellow such as yourself should read the Bible at all."

"Funny you should say that, Mr. Cook. I've often thought how different my life would have been if I had done as my father wished. He wanted me to be a rabbi. Can you believe that? Leo Stern, a rabbi."

But Oz wasn't listening. He was lost again in his fantasy world. He was holding the young boy close in his arms. "Esther," he sighed, and slipped languidly to the whorehouse floor.

59

Saturday, June 15–
Sunday, June 16.
Night to morning.

The night grew steadily longer and more desolate by the hour as Meg listened in vain for John's return.

In her mind she went over and over what had happened that night. What she had said, what the girl Esther had said, what John had said.

He had never before brought any girl home to dinner. Why hadn't he told Meg this one was an Israelite?

Anguish coursed through her. "You must think *I* killed Him, too?" John had shouted at her. Then he had snatched Old Peter's silver box and gone off after the girl. What was she to do?

Meg struggled from her bed and heated some milk, adding a dash of whiskey to the cup for what ailed her. Though she doubted the whiskey would help with this particular affliction. She sat herself in Old Peter's chair and sipped her milk slowly. She was getting old, arthritis in the hands, and sometimes in the mind, too, blocking the memories.

But the memories were clear tonight. She saw herself again as a rebellious young girl, earning her own money, cleaning up after rich people as a chambermaid.

The Church had been too confining for her, then. She had wanted Jesus to help her to go on the stage. It was such a long time ago. An exciting time to be young, with a war on and the City full of exciting people.

She had married for love into a family of heathens—some Presbyterians, some Hebrews as Old Peter's people had been.

And Meg's ma had said to her pretty much what she had said to Esther. "They killed our Lord."

Why had she said that hateful thing to the girl? Jesus forgave. Why couldn't she?

It had been so many years now. Pete had been a good man, but no churchgoer. His father John, another Presbyterian, had raised no objections, either. And after she came back to the Church, Pete had done as Meg and her mother and Father Duff had wished; her children had all been confirmed. Hebrew blood, yes, but Catholic souls. All belonging to Jesus.

She sat up abruptly, the cup listing in her hand. The Tonnemans had tried to fool her. Auntie Lee, the medical doctor, had talked to her about cleanliness and infections and tried to persuade Meg to allow them to circumcise her boy. She had foiled them, then.

But she had lost him, now.

She'd regretted her behavior tonight almost immediately, but it was too late. The girl had run off, and John right after her.

In a few hours it would be time for Mass. She would get dressed. She could talk to Father Duff before early Mass. No. She needed the Mass to sustain her first. And afterward, Father Duff would tell her what to do.

60

Sunday,
June 16.
Just before dawn.

Esther had gone through the developing process with the tenth plate, John Tonneman in his shirtsleeves beside her in the rosy light of the darkroom.

When the images began to appear, the dark areas light, the light areas dark, she let loose a sigh of relief.

"Is it all right?" he asked.

"Yes. It will be a photograph. I didn't falter with this one." She couldn't keep the pride from her voice.

She placed the negative under the cold running water.

"How long must we wait?" Tonneman's desire to see the photograph, to know once and for all what Robert Roman's killers had worked so hard to destroy, was making him a little crazy.

"Only another half hour to clean the negative," she replied, "so it can print." She removed her gloves. "Would you like some cold tea?" She smiled at him. The anguish she'd felt earlier had settled like a dull ache in her breast. In the studio, she poured tepid tea into the cups, then, spying her hairpins beside the pot, Esther realized that she had taken her hair down and loosened her dress. Flustered, she began to roll her hair and pin it.

"Don't," he said, staying her hand.

"I wouldn't want Oz to find us like this." She slowly completed the ritual of her hair, coloring even more when she saw how intently John was watching her.

"I don't think Mr. Cook would be shocked simply because your hair was down."

"He asked me to marry him."

"Marry him?" Tonneman was astonished, then angry. "He's a sick old man. What would he want with—"

"A Hebrew immigrant girl?"

"That's not what I was going to say."

"What, then?"

"You can't marry him, Esther. Before I allow you to marry Oswald Cook, I'll become a Hebrew."

She smiled, understanding that he had spoken in haste. "But I wouldn't want you that way, John Tonneman." After a silence she went on. "Oz offers me security. And he hasn't asked me to convert to his religion."

"He can't give you children," Tonneman persisted, doggedly, his own impulsive words about becoming a Hebrew resounding in his ears.

"You have no call to say that."

"He is addicted to opium, Esther."

"How do you know?"

"It's my business to know. Where he was at the time of the murder was his alibi. And he was smoking opium that night."

"You thought Oz might have . . ." She left the thought unfinished. She could not say the words.

"Jealousy brings out the worst in men. And women."

"Jealousy?" Esther stared at Tonneman with new eyes. He looked so superior. What had she ever seen in him? "No, you're wrong about jealousy."

Softening, he took her hand, not allowing her to pull away. "Perhaps this time."

When he held her as he did now, Esther had the answer to all of her questions. She loved him and him alone. Still, she pulled away. "I think you'd better go now. You can come back later and see the photograph when it is a finished print."

"It can't be much longer. I'd like to stay."

"Please."

"It's already Sunday," he said. He knew Meg was up and getting ready for Mass. He just might miss her. Bo had been right, had understood Meg Clancy better than her own son. But Bo was pure Irish, pure Catholic, on both sides.

"What will you do with these precious things?" Esther returned everything carefully to the silver box.

"Leave them in your care, if I may." As he put on his coat he thought with horror that Meg might destroy them if she knew what they were.

"It's a great trust."

"Who better would I trust with them?" He bent and kissed her. "They're our children's legacy."

61

Sunday,
June 16.
Morning.

Just as he'd hoped, Meg had already gone to church. Dutch cleaned up and shaved, had milk and a sweet bun, then returned to Gramercy Park.

He found the front door ajar. He raced inside. "Wong?" No answer. "Esther?" He took the stairs two at a time. But when he got to the darkroom the red light was on, so he could not enter. He tapped at the door. "Esther, I'm back. Are you all right?"

"Of course I am."

He was relieved to hear her voice, even if her tone was short.

"I'm almost finished." Esther had printed the photograph. She had not heard the telephone ring nor Wong go out.

In the studio Dutch settled himself in a roomy armchair and napped, only awakening when Esther emerged from the darkroom. "Is it a good one?"

"Yes. Quite good, if I may say so." Esther showed Dutch the print.

He looked at it with utter shock. "Jesus, do you know who these men are?"

She squirmed at his expletive. "This one I know. That's your Clubber Williams."

"How do you know that?"

"Robert wanted me to make his picture. He said something about the man being off the Force, and wondered why he was there."

"So you took this on purpose?"

"No, I wanted to but I didn't see him after Robert pointed him out. I was aiming at a police wagon driving right into the crowd. People fell to the ground, hurt. I had only one plate left. See, this Clubber is off to the side talking to that well-dressed man with the pointed beard. Do you know him?"

"I know him well," Dutch said grimly. "Wait till Bo sees this."

At St. Agnes, Dutch saw that Meg was in her usual pew. She often stayed one Mass to the next. After blessing himself Dutch didn't go to his seat; he stood in the back.

What he expected here, he didn't know. But whatever it was didn't happen. There was no direct communication from God telling him what to do.

Walking only a short way down the aisle he found a bleary-eyed Bo slumped among others of the Clancy clan. "Come on."

"Leave me be, Dutch. The smell of incense is good for my hangover. And Father Duff always gives me a lovely sound to sleep by."

"We've got a problem, coz."

Bo nodded sleepily and they started for the door. Bo's mother, Dutch's Aunt Nan, sent them both an irritated look.

On the street, Dutch showed Bo Esther's photograph.

Bo laughed. "Looky, looky, looky, the Peacock and the Clubber. What evil pact is one devil making with the other, do you suppose?"

"It's about the protection business, I bet," Dutch replied, "and hiring culls like Clooney to burn places down if the marks don't pay. I guess we take this to Chief Conlin."

"I guess we don't. Conlin is Peacock's boy."

"Then what?"

"Let's go to Mulberry Street, and see Moose."

Before they even reached the House on Mulberry Street, they heard the shrill "Hi-yi-yi." Moose leaned halfway out his second-floor window yelling to Jake Riis, who stood with the other newspaper reporters across the street. The call was something Moose had picked up out West. "Are you with me tonight, Jake?"

"Yes, sir, I am," came Riis's reply.

"Well, good, then." Moose pulled back, then came out the window again. "Boys! Tonneman, Clancy! Well done on catching Clubber and his gang for Roman's murder. Get on up here and let me shake your hands."

Dutch and Bo exchanged looks and hurried inside.

"Moose is our man all right," Bo muttered, "but that Peacock is a wily fellow. He always taunts Moose till Moose is about to explode, then, wouldn't you know, he says something nice. I heard Lincoln Steffens asked him why he does it. And Peacock he says, 'Oh, just for ducks. Just to see the big bomb splutter.' "

"This is stinking political shit, Bo, and we're going to get our asses caught in—"

"Correct. I'm just wondering myself if Moose can handle him."

Moose's straw English boater on the hat rack a few feet from his desk was tilted at a rakish angle. The morning sun filtering through the narrow window gleamed off his spectacles, giving him an odd, glint-eyed look.

Every so often the usually proper Moose gave in to his eccentric tastes. Today his shirt was pink, and the black silk cummerbund wrapped about his black trousers had a tassel tail that hung almost to his knees.

"Delighted to shake your hands." And he did, pumping each in turn, sincerely, but like the politician he was. "A fine job. Yes, a fine job." Each word was accompanied by a grand gesture, both arms waving to and fro. Moose's boater reacted to its owner's gestures as though it was the wind, tilting even more to the man's passionate gusts of expression.

Congratulations given and accepted, Moose went back to his carved mahagony desk. Neither detective moved.

The usual soft tick of the short grandfather clock to Moose's right seemed to grow louder. The Commissioner rubbed the side of his nose. He looked from one to the other of the detectives with his strange eyes, then drew the upholstered footstool from underneath his desk, set it the correct distance, propped his feet on it, and sprawled in his wicker-backed chair. "Talk to me, boys. What is it?"

Without a word, Dutch took the photograph from the envelope Esther had supplied and placed it in Moose's hand.

Moose adjusted his spectacles. "Now, that is intriguing. When?"

"May thirtieth. The Union Square riot."

"You know how I feel about the demoralizing gangrene eating away at this police force?"

"Yes, sir," Bo said dryly. "Heard the speech."

Moose granted Bo one of his big buck-toothed smiles. "This is a grand picture, boys. One for my album. But as far as the law is concerned, it doesn't prove a thing."

"That can't be true. Take a look at this," Bo said. "Show him, Dutch."

Dutch brought out Robert Roman's notes and handed them to Moose. "The La Belle Association is a front for a huge bribery and protection racket."

Moose glanced at the sheet with the numbers on it, and pulled open a drawer in his desk. He brought out a thin handbook. "Guidebook to New York." He opened the guide to a folded-back page. "*Cost to be a captain on the New York Police Force: ten thousand dollars*." His eyes went to the opposite page. "*Brothel Contributions: Over eight million dollars. Saloon Contributions: One million, eight. Gambling House* . . ." He looked up and shook his head. "It's in the guidebooks, for heaven's sake."

"Jesus, Mary, and Joseph," Bo exploded. "If the picture's worthless, why did Clubber kill Roman?"

Moose looked thoughtful for a moment. "Because Clubber and his associates didn't know what the photograph caught them doing and they weren't about to take any chances."

"What are you going to do?" Dutch asked the Commissioner.

"What I've been doing. Watch him and wait to see if he makes a mistake." Moose plucked a large red bandanna with white steer skulls on it from the desk and polished his spectacles.

"With Clubber locked up," Dutch said, "Peacock is too smart to make any mistakes. Our only hope is that Clubber talks. And he won't."

"Peacock, eh? That's what you call him? What do you call me?"

"Moose," Dutch replied.

Moose's teeth and glasses glinted in the sunlight. "I like it."

"We'll be going now, sir."

"Don't be upset, boys. I don't wish to jeopardize your fine careers. All we have is this photograph, which I shall treasure. But it doesn't prove horse poop. With what you've given me, we have the La Belle Association to tie to Clubber's tail, but since we have him for murder already, it really doesn't matter. Except to expose the corruption." He stood up and offered his hand, first to Bo, then to Dutch. "Thank you, boys."

"What about Peacock?" Dutch said, shaking Moose's hand.

"Ah, Peacock," Moose said thoughtfully. "That's an entirely different story. Except for the photograph of him and Clubber, we have nothing. We could no more make a case against the man than we could nail currant jelly to a wall. I'm afraid there's nothing in this whole wide world we can prove against Commissioner Peacock . . . for now. Peacock isn't much of a man. I could carve a man with more backbone out of a chocolate eclair."

"Yes, sir," Bo said. Pithy sayings were all good and well. But they wouldn't put a crook behind bars, that was for sure.

"But don't forget Mr. Roman's report. Or these graft sheets. You'd better keep them for your continued investigation."

Dutch and Bo grinned at Moose.

He grinned right back. "Capital," he said.

62

Sunday,
June 16.
Late morning.

The first thing Oz was aware of was the smell of vanilla. Then the sound of singing. "I gave my love an apple without a core, I gave my love a dwelling without a . . ."

His nanny used to sing that to him. "Beatie," he mumbled, blinking his eyes.

All he could see through blurred eyes was a field of snow white. "What next?" he asked, barely able to form and sound the words. "A choir of angels? If I've achieved heaven, there's been a ridiculous miscalculation."

"Don't try to speak, Mr. Cook." The woman who uttered this was the largest Oz had ever seen. It was her broad backside in nurse-white that he'd mistaken for a snow-white field.

He closed his eyes. They fluttered back open. His hands felt for purchase and he attempted to sit up.

"That wouldn't be wise." A firm hand pressed on his shoulder. It hadn't been necessary; he'd already felt the searing pain across his chest.

"Where am I?"

"Home."

"Who are you?"

"Nurse Jean Dietrick. Miss Wald sent me to care for you."

Since each move induced further pain, Oz lay like a stone. "Esther," he said.

63

Sunday, June 16. Morning to early afternoon.

Esther was confused, to say the least. She needed counsel. But where to turn? A rabbi would tell her to shun the two gentiles and marry a solid Jewish *mensch*.

No, she didn't need spiritual advice, she needed another woman to talk to.

Had she faced these problems two weeks earlier, that woman would have been her teacher and benefactor, Miss Lillian Wald. But even though she was Jewish, or perhaps because she was, Esther knew Miss Wald was not worldly enough for this problem.

Lillian Russell lived in a lavish suite at the Waldorf Hotel on Fifth Avenue and Thirty-third Street.

A thin lady in a blue uniform with starched white collar and cuffs opened the door and led Esther through room after room. Somewhere ahead, Esther could hear Lillian Russell's splendid voice, but its rich tones were hardly melodious this morning. "Marie, you get bigger by the day—"

Esther must have passed a dozen steamer trunks, most open, bursting with elegant dresses of silk and satin in all the colors of the rainbow.

They finally arrived in a huge sitting room. Miss Russell was seated upon a grand divan that Esther imagined must have come from the court of a French king. She was wearing her bicycle costume and talking on the telephone. At her feet were newspapers and magazines. At her elbow, coffee and sweet cakes.

This suite, and all that was in it, must cost a pretty penny, more than even Oz had. Some said that Diamond Jim paid for the whole kit and caboodle of Miss Russell's worldly goods. But others said that Miss Russell invested in the stock market and paid for everything herself.

The sitting room was pale blue, and a blur of clothing hung from every available protrusion. In Miss Russell's lap was a long silky thing. When Esther approached the divan, it yapped at her.

"Quiet, Albert, she won't hurt you." Miss Russell hung up the telephone and patted the Pekingese, who yawned and licked its flat nose, staring at Esther greedily. "Sit, Esther, there's coffee. Would you care for some sweet cake? You'll have to change your clothes." She turned to the maid. "What do you think, Maureen?"

The maid nodded. "I can do it." Maureen took a garment hanging in yet another open trunk and left the room.

"Thank you for seeing me, Miss Russell."

"To you, Esther, I am not Miss Russell." She patted the divan. "Here, sit next to me. Tell me about my photographs."

"Oz is still working on them. Thank you, Lillian."

"Why don't you call me Nelly? My real name is Helen Louise Leonard, Nelly for short. Even after all these years of being the other, Nelly's the name I answer to quickest. As soon as your costume is ready, I'll demonstrate how to warm up your muscles."

"Miss Russell—"

"Nelly."

"Nelly, you're not asking me to bicycle with you?"

"But of course, I'm not asking you." Russell grinned, showing small pearly teeth. "I'm *telling* you. You will take my Marie Lazybones's place today as we tour the Central Park."

Esther was bewildered. "But I don't know how to cycle."

Her hostess gave a triumphant laugh. "You will, soon enough."

Then she added with a wink, "And you'll tell me all about your troubles as we ride."

An hour later they entered the Central Park at Fifty-ninth Street and kept to walking paths along the East Side. "Start by sitting solidly on the seat, my dear," Miss Russell instructed. "Good. Now push off with the ball of the foot. That's it! Pedal, pedal, don't look down. Follow me!" Miss Russell pedaled twenty feet ahead and back, while Esther slowly became a wheelman.

When she could lift her concentration from keeping her precarious balance, Esther saw that Oz wasn't the only one who wanted to take Miss Russell's picture. People stood beside the path holding cameras.

They pedaled past the lake where swans glided peacefully amidst rowboats. A voice called, "Hey, Lil!"

The actress blew a kiss to the lake.

"As far as money and position, Oz is a catch. But, my dear Esther, you must ask yourself, is this what you want? Most likely your young detective will never be rich. And he will want children. Once you decide whether they will be Catholic children or Hebrew children, all roads are open."

"What would you do, Nelly? I will always be a Jew. But I like my new life too much." Esther shuddered. "The idea of barely existing in Jew Town, working for pennies in a sweatshop . . ."

On a second circle round, they swept past Sheep's Meadow, Lillian Russell leading, Esther still rocking on her borrowed cycle, not quite steady.

"Well, you can have it all," Lillian Russell said, with a smile.

"How?"

"Simple. Marry Oz Cook. When he kicks the bucket, you'll be the wealthy Widow Cook. *Then* you can marry your detective and live happily ever after."

Lillian Russell's driver delivered Esther to No. 5 Gramercy Park, still dressed in her new bicycle costume.

Wong was showing Dr. Van Rooten out as she entered.

"Miss Esther," Wong called.

The physician stared at her as if her dress were offensive to him.

"Is Oz ill?" Esther asked Wong without preamble, in no way concerned with what the physician thought.

"He's had a seizure. A bad one. There's a nurse watching him now. He's been asking for you." There was nothing judgmental in Wong's voice, but Esther instantly condemned herself. She'd been gadding about in the Central Park while Oz was suffering.

From the second floor, she called, "Is he very bad?"

"Don't tire him," the doctor admonished. "I'll be back later in the evening. Please! Come down at once, young woman, so I can talk to you face to face. I will not shout."

Torn, but obedient, Esther ran back down the stairs.

"Thank you. His heart is extremely weak. There is no way of knowing . . . anything, so keep him from upset or excitement."

After the door closed behind the doctor, Wong whispered, "Mr. Tonneman came some time ago. He's waiting for you." Wong relieved her of her bundle of clothing. If he had noticed her bicycle costume, he gave no sign of it.

"Where?"

"In the parlor. I looked in on him a while ago. He's sleeping in the wing chair."

"I'll see Oz first."

She ran back up the stairs to the third floor full of dread. Oz was very ill, but he'd been very ill before and had recovered. Yet she was afraid. For the past six months Oswald Cook had been her entire life—a father, a teacher, a friend.

Tapping lightly, she pushed open the door. The nurse rose, finger to her lips. "He's just drifted off to sleep."

"Is that you, Esther?" Oz's voice was so faint she could barely hear it. "Where have you been?"

The nurse threw up her hands and stood aside.

Oz's skin had no color at all, and his eyes were ringed in black. He made hardly a dent under the bedclothes.

"I was cycling with Lillian Russell." She sat on the bed and took his frail hand in hers.

"That bodes ill for us poor men. Each of you alone . . ." His voice grew weaker. "But the two of you togeth . . ."

"Oh, Oz. Sleep and we'll talk later."

"You haven't given me your answer." His voice was weak, but his hand was as strong as a death grip. Why did she think that phrase?

"You know, I care deeply for you. You have changed my life entirely and have given me a vocation. I will always be grateful."

"Gratitude is not love." But Oz smiled when he said that.

She bent and kissed his cheek. "Get well and we'll discuss it."

He released her hand with a contented sigh. His eyes closed.

On the landing Esther paused, catching a glimpse of herself in the hall mirror as the new woman in her bicycle bloomers. Yes, she thought, she liked what she saw. After all, it was 1895. Esther started down the stairs.

Who said she had to choose *either* man?

A Footnote

The City of New York in 1895 was already grasping at the twentieth century while its feet were still solidly planted in the nineteenth. The physical changes and scientific advances of the years since the end of the Civil War were formidable.

In 1895, the population of the City of New York reached 1,600,000, and it was pushing farther and farther uptown, following the paths of the El. Already in the planning stages was the New York subway system, which would extend the possibility of urban living to the outermost corner of Manhattan Island.

The nineteenth century was a great time for words. The English spoken then was expanding at a furious pace, adding the essence of the immigrant languages, becoming more and more American. Someone from 1895 would have no trouble understanding, or making himself understood, in New York today.

On May 6, 1895, Teddy Roosevelt took office as one of four Police Commissioners of the City of New York. We chose to call him Moose, and not mention him by name to keep him, by the force of his personality, from taking over our story, which he most certainly would have.

The other three Commissioners elected Roosevelt president of the police commission, and thenceforth he behaved as if he were the only Commissioner. As Commissioner, the most important part of Roosevelt's mission was to restructure the Detective Bureau and have it answer to Police Headquarters. In that way, he would eliminate the power of crooked precinct police commanders and purge the corrupt Detective Bureau. Only then would the citizens come to trust them and let them do their job. This cleanup actually took place at the end of May in 1896. We moved it back a year for the sake of our story.

The four Commissioners were: Avery D. Andrews, Colonel Frederick Dent Grant (the son of Ulysses S. Grant), Andrew D. Parker (whom we've christened Peacock), and Theodore Roosevelt.

Roosevelt and Parker were at odds as long as both were Commissioners. Lincoln Steffens wrote in *The Evening Post* that they "were foreordained to disagree, and they did."

By April of '96, the two men's enmity for each other was an open phenomenon. New Yorkers were being entertained by their public battle. But Roosevelt was a strange if honorable man. Even when he knew Parker was going to be "in an evil house uptown," Roosevelt refused to pounce on him there, saying that he didn't fight that way.

Although Roosevelt attempted to oust Parker from the board, a trial showed he had no provable grounds with which to force Parker's departure.

William McKinley was inaugurated President of the United States on March 4, 1897. His destiny would affect Roosevelt's.

On March 17, Mayor William Strong formally dismissed Commissioner Parker for neglect of duty, but because Governor Levi P. Morton did not approve the dismissal, Parker stayed on.

On April 6, Teddy Roosevelt was nominated as President McKinley's Assistant Secretary of the Navy. Roosevelt's last day as Commissioner of the New York Metropolitan Police Department was April 17, 1897. Parker was still there when he left, and remained Commissioner until the end of 1897. Nothing is known about Parker after his stint as Commissioner, so we had no compunction about hanging villainy on him.

In 1901 William McKinley was assassinated by anarchist Leon Czolgosz, in Buffalo, New York. That's how Moose, the Vice President, became our twenty-sixth President.

Thomas Byrnes, New York's Chief of Detectives when Roosevelt became Commissioner, was a tough customer, totally corrupt. Byrnes kept the Wall Street area clean of criminals by declaring the Fulton Street Dead Line, beyond which criminals could not pass and stay whole. In 1891, it was Byrnes who made the use of identifying photographs of criminals part of police procedure.

On May 18, 1895, Roosevelt told Henry Cabot Lodge, "I think I shall move against Byrnes at once." Nine days later Byrnes was asked to resign. One of the most powerful men in the City, Byrnes finally handed in his resignation on May 28 and retired on a full pension. He was replaced by Acting Chief Peter Conlin.

Not until 1896 would Commissioner Avery D. Andrews come up with the "bicycle squad," which consisted of twenty-four patrolmen careening on wheels. After a long absence, in the spring of 1972, New York once again had a bicycle squad.

As for Clubber Williams, he was such a proven reprobate we figured a few more crimes wouldn't soil his already tarnished reputation. The payoffs, blackmail, and graft he collected were legendary, allowing him to live like a high potentate. He let evil thrive, and got paid for it. The real Clubber died in his bed in 1918, a shameless sinner.

In the 1890's Jewish street gangs—pickpockets and petty thieves—often worked for Jewish fences. "Mother" or "Marm" Frederika Mandelbaum, a 250-pound Rumanian woman, and her husband Wolfe, their son, and two daughters ran a shop out of a three-story building at 79 Clinton Street, on the corner of Rivington. The shop pretended to be a haberdashery, but actually received stolen goods and was a center for young Jewish thieves. In a clapboarded annex, which extended down Clinton Street, was her storehouse of illegal swag.

The first police record of Marm is 1862. From then to about 1884 she ran between five and ten million dollars' worth of goods.

Sophie and Leo are our inventions completely.

Jack West is patterned on Mae West's father, a boxer, who was indeed known as Battling Jack. When Mae was born in 1893, Jack gave up his fighting career and got into the livery business. When the automobile became the more prevalent vehicle of transportation, Jack opened a detective agency. We like to think Battling Jack's escapade with Dutch Tonneman was the seed of his later profession.

It took John L. Sullivan, wearing gloves, to popularize boxing in America, which up until then was fought with bare knuckles. During the years before Sullivan neither the British Crown nor the American government approved of prizefighting.

Sullivan fought James J. Corbett with gloves in New Orleans in 1892. The fight was illegal. Corbett knocked Sullivan out in the twenty-first round and became the first heavyweight champion of the world. The purse was $25,000. There was a $10,000 side bet between the two boxers.

In 1896, New York became the first state to permit boxing.

We don't know if Jack West ever fought John L. Sullivan. We hope he did. And if he did, we know he gave Sullivan a hell of a fight.

Marty's father, Joseph Meyers, was born in 1880, in Vilna, Lithuania. In 1895, when Joseph Meyers was fifteen, Czar Nicholas II wanted him for the Russian army. His mother smuggled Joseph to the United States. There he lived alone, often on the streets, speaking broken English, Yiddish, and Lithuanian. It is our conceit that he met Battling Jack and worked for him. Since in real life Joseph was nicknamed Jack, we called him Little Jack.

In 1893 an upper-middle-class nurse named Lillian Wald founded the Visiting Nurse Service, charging only what people could pay, a nickel or a quarter per visit. She called it Public Health Nursing. By the turn of the century Wald's service was also educating people on health and child care. Babies were still being delivered at home.

Along with nurse Mary Brewster, Wald got the financial support of some wealthy friends and established a small settlement house on Rivington Street. From there, they moved to a temporary location on Jefferson Street in 1893. It was here, at the Nurses' Settlement House, that Miss Wald introduced our heroine to Oswald Cook.

Two years later Lillian Wald moved her Nurses' Settlement from a nearby tenement to a small brick house at 265 Henry Street, which remained her home for forty years. Because a child told her that the boys' sports team was mocked for being from the "noices," Wald changed the name of the Settlement to the Henry Street Settlement.

Research is like gold lying on the ground waiting to be picked up. From Neal Gabler's book *Winchell* (Knopf, 1994), we learned that during 1895, Chaim (Herman) Weinschel was rabbi and cantor of the Pike

Street Synagogue at 12 Pike Street. It amused us to have Walter Winchell's grandfather make a cameo appearance in our story.

The art of photography was in its heyday. By 1895, roll film had been a fact for five years, but professional photographers and devoted amateurs continued to use the dry glass plates well into the twentieth century because of the high quality of definition they gave a print. Photography was also a very hospitable profession for the New Woman, as the independent woman was dubbed at that time.

By 1895, it was understood that the Croton Reservoir, which was situated on the blocks between Fortieth and Forty-second Streets, flanked by Fifth and Sixth Avenues, having outlived its usefulness, would be demolished.

On May 23, 1895, the Tilden Trust (Gov. Samuel J. Tilden), in association with the Lenox and Astor Libraries, combined their collections of books and opened them to the public. A small but generous group of New Yorkers made a compact with the City to create a library for these books that offered free and open admission if the City provided them with a site.

Because the reservoir could not be removed until water mains were installed through to Thirty-eighth Street, it did not begin to come down until 1897.

In 1912, on the Croton Reservoir site, the magnificent New York Public Library finally had its grand opening.

AM, MM
New York

Glossary

Adonai My Lord (A name for God in place of the unspeakable name of JHVH in the Hebrew scriptures. Jehovah, another substitute, is an erroneous rendering of JHVH.)

Beggar's velvet House moss, dust balls

Billy Noodle An unsubstantial chap, thoroughly convinced that all the ladies fancy him

Bingo-boy A drunken man

Blind pig Illegal saloon

Bloke Man, fellow

Bog trotter Offensive name for Irishman

Boyo Irish form of boy

Cat Whore

Chinkie Offensive name for a Chinese person

Cove or covey Man

Cull Man

Dace Two cents

The Dead Line During the 1890's, Chief of Detectives Thomas Byrnes, in order to keep the Financial District free of crime, set a boundary at the Wall Street District (the Fulton Street Line) that known criminals were not permitted to pass. It was known as the Dead Line, the Line, and the *cordon sanitaire*.

Di alte heym Yiddish for the old home

Di Alte Yiddish for the old one

Feck Irish for vulgarism fuck

Forwartz The *Jewish Daily Forward*

Frog Policeman

Frog and Toe New York City

Gelter Money, from Yiddish *gelt*

Gob Mouth

Gott in Himmel Yiddish for God in heaven

Goy (Goyim) Yiddish for gentile(s)

Growler Bucket of beer

Hamfatter The original form of ham, an overacting actor. From *The Hamfat Man*, a black minstrel song, about an awkward man.

Hawkshaw Hawkshaw was a detective in the play *The Ticket-of-Leave Man* (1863) by Tom Taylor. The word doesn't actually enter the language as a synonym for detective until 1900, but Byron, who has played the part, would use it sooner.

Hoosegow Jail

Huey *The Police Gazette*

Jarmulka Earlier form of yarmulke (Polish), skullcap

Jewish butter Goose grease

Landsleiter Yiddish for a person from the same town

Mab A prostitute

Mamzer Yiddish for bastard. A mischief-maker

Mensch Yiddish for man, a stand-up human being

Mick Offensive term for Irishman

Mitts Hands

Moll buzzer A pickpocket who specializes in women

Monicker Name

Moose Commissioner Theodore Roosevelt

Oll korrect O.K. Initials of a comical folk phonetic spelling *oll korrect*, representing all correct. Associated with Martin Van Buren's nickname, Old Kinderhook, from his birthplace, Kinderhook, N.Y., and used by Democratic followers during his election campaign in 1840.

On the stroll Being a streetwalker

Paddy Offensive name for Irishman

Pastrama Pastrami

Peacock Commissioner Andrew Parker

The Pinky *The Police Gazette* (because of its pink pages)

Shadai The Almighty (A name for God in place of the unspeakable name of JHVH in the Hebrew scriptures)

Shee In Irish folklore, a fairy. Plural: Shees. (Also spelled Sidh; plural: Sidhe, pronounced Shee.)

Sheeny Offensive name for Jew

Sheitel A wig worn by Orthodox Jewish women, in accordance with the rabbinical precept that proscribes a woman from leaving her hair uncovered before any man other than her husband.

Shtarker Yiddish for strong man

Shul Yiddish for synagogue. From the word for school

Spalpeen Irish for rascal

Spook Offensive name for African American

Yid Offensive name for Jew